FIRST

DOCTOR WHO – THE NEW ADVENTURES

Also available:

TIMEWYRM: GENESYS by John Peel
TIMEWYRM: EXODUS by Terrance Dicks
TIMEWYRM: APOCALYPSE by Nigel Robinson
TIMEWYRM: REVELATION by Paul Cornell

CAT'S CRADLE: TIME'S CRUCIBLE by Marc Platt
CAT'S CRADLE: WARHEAD by Andrew Cartmel
CAT'S CRADLE: WITCH MARK by Andrew Hunt

NIGHTSHADE by Mark Gatiss
LOVE AND WAR by Paul Cornell
TRANSIT by Ben Aaronovitch
THE HIGHEST SCIENCE by Gareth Roberts
THE PIT by Neil Penswick
DECEIT by Peter Darvill-Evans
LUCIFER RISING by Jim Mortimore and Andy Lane
WHITE DARKNESS by David A. McIntee
SHADOWMIND by Christopher Bulis
BIRTHRIGHT by Nigel Robinson
ICEBERG by David Banks

BLOOD HEAT by Jim Mortimore
THE DIMENSION RIDERS by Daniel Blythe
THE LEFT-HANDED HUMMINGBIRD by Kate Orman
CONUNDRUM by Steve Lyons
NO FUTURE by Paul Cornell
TRAGEDY DAY by Gareth Roberts
LEGACY by Gary Russell
THEATRE OF WAR by Justin Richards
ALL-CONSUMING FIRE by Andy Lane
BLOOD HARVEST by Terrance Dicks
STRANGE ENGLAND by Simon Messingham

FIRST FRONTIER

David A. McIntee

First published in Great Britain in 1994 by
Doctor Who Books
an imprint of Virgin Publishing Ltd
332 Ladbroke Grove
London W10 5AH

Copyright © David A. McIntee 1994

'Doctor Who' series copyright © British Broadcasting
Corporation 1994

Cover illustration by Tony Masero

ISBN 0 426 20421 2

Phototypeset by Intype, London
Printed and bound in Great Britain by Cox & Wyman Ltd,
Reading, Berks

This book is sold subject to the condition that it shall
not, by way of trade or otherwise, be lent, resold, hired
out or otherwise circulated without the publisher's prior
written consent in any form of binding or cover other
than that in which it is published and without a similar
condition including this condition being imposed on the
subsequent purchaser.

Author's Notes

Yes, I'm sorry, but I'm at it again. Before I get on with acknowledgements for this book, I'd like to add another for *White Darkness* – namely thanks to Phil Bevan for his illustrations to the Prelude in *DWM* 201. This was all done long after the book was finished, hence I obviously couldn't mention him then.

This time, thanks are due to Peter and Rebecca, obviously for commissioning this book and being so helpful during the writing process (free drinks at the Conservatory in particular); Gary Clubb for the odd one-liner; and Gary Russell, but I can't say why without spoiling the major plot twist. And, last but not least, Tony Masero for the splendid cover.

This has been another research-heavy book, and I wouldn't want to leave you without a few pointers as to the non-fiction sources. The organizations referred to all did or do exist, though the IPU was disbanded in 1947 – that's dramatic licence. All the locations also really exist, with the exception, for reasons which will become obvious, of Corman AFB, though it is a combination of different elements attributed to different bases in UFO myth. The main sources of research for this facet, and the occasional UFO report which has been fictionalized here, were: *Aliens From Space* by Donald Keyhoe; *Above Top Secret* by Timothy Good; the reports of Robert Lazar which appeared in *Alien Liaison*, edited by Timothy Good; *Farewell Good Brothers*, an Oscar-winning short documentary about 1950s contactees; and finally Finnish TV's *UFOs*, which was shown on BBC2 over Christmas 1993.

The characters are fictional, except for Shadow.

Finally, I've been warned to mention my mum and dad, who complained when I didn't do so last time.

If you're wondering what to expect here, well: last time I did a doom-laden historical, next time – chance'd be a fine thing – I plan a doom-laden historical, so for now let's just have some fun, eh?

Cue the white circle.

I knew myself, at the first breath of this new life, to be more wicked, tenfold more wicked, sold a slave to original evil.
The Strange Case of Dr Jekyll And Mr Hyde

Heat scalded every cell. The searing molten fire of liquid rock overwhelmed every sensation, a red-tinged whiteness the only vision possible.

Shuddering tremors racked the body, painfully threatening to shake the very cells apart, molecule by molecule.

The only thought that existed in the blinded mind was to be free of the fire, free of the pain, and free of the searing brightness.

Two minds flowed, fusing briefly of necessity, sensing an opening, an opportunity between what was and what could be. Mutual strengths interlocked, seeking remembered calmness.

If time still existed at all, there could be little of it left, but the speed of thought was fast enough to take advantage. The minds' eyes, operating as one, saw past and present, and focused, blotting out the liquid fire.

Deep within the heart of linked minds something burst free, flashing outwards in the blink of an eye. The heat flared beyond the limits of imagination, searing the mind with a flash. The senses revelled in their freedom, far from their erstwhile prison.

And then there was merciful blackness.

FIRST FRONTIER

Prologue

May Day, 1957

Occulting the diamond-scattered sea of stars beyond, the dark night-side of the planet wheeled slowly amidst the sluggish backwaters of the galaxy. Through the cloud-cover, tiny pin-points of light were barely perceptible from low orbit, marking the locations of several cities on the surface far below.

Although its origin was too tiny to be seen by the naked eye, one small spark abruptly swelled into a blazing torch as it tore its way out of the atmosphere. With the light stretching out into a trailing pillar of flame, a cylinder of gleaming steel, already scorched in places by its own exhaust, broke free of the restrictive blanket of gases around the planet. The flame flickered and died as the rocket coasted out into the vacuum, sharp moonlight picking out the scarlet 'CCCP' that was the only matt area on the polished surface.

At a preprogrammed altitude, explosive bolts fired around the nose-cone, splintering it to allow a smooth metal sphere with four trailing antennae to float gently out of its metal womb and into its own orbit.

In a cavernous bunker deep within the northerly Nykortny Cosmodrome, warning lights flickered crazily along the serried ranks of battleship-grey consoles and telemetry stations. Dozens of technicians in the olive drab shirts of the *Raketnye Voiska Strategicheskogo Naznacheniya* branch of the army struggled to douse the warning lights and restore control.

Heavy doors at one end of the room burst open and a

group of uniformed men bedecked with medals strode in. One of them, with a granite face, briefly glanced at the world map dominating the far wall of the room, on which a skewed orbital track was being projected. 'What has gone wrong?' he demanded gruffly.

A nervous scientist in his shirt-sleeves looked up from studying a console. 'The satellite has gone out of control. It has deviated from its projected path and will not respond to our instructions – not even the abort signal. Also,' he went on reluctantly, 'it appears to be transmitting some kind of signal which we cannot understand.'

'Meaning?' the officer prompted.

'It registers on our receivers but is not a radio signal. In fact it doesn't appear to follow any sort of logical binary sequence. Here, I'll let you hear it,' the scientist finished, leaning across to twist a dial on one panel. Immediately the room was filled with a strange and atonal electronic warbling.

'Western?' the officer queried in a low voice.

'Unlikely. The transmission is directed away from Earth and, as you can tell from the orbit plot, the satellite is also spinning away from the planet.'

The granite-faced man nodded, looking around at the staff with a calculating air. 'This operation is at an end,' he declared finally. 'The Praesidium will consider what action to take. Meanwhile, make sure that no word of these events leak out. When we next launch a satellite, it will be designated Sputnik One, not Two. This failure must be erased from the records.'

A seepage of amber desert twilight speared across concrete, staining it darkly with bloodied shadows. Blackness flickered as a girl, perhaps in her late teens or early twenties, slipped through the narrow doorway that admitted the light. Her badge-encrusted bomber jacket rustled faintly as she looked around in the dim light, a small silver can in one hand and a metallic baseball bat in the other. 'No ground station and no guards, Professor,' she whispered in a faint west-London accent.

'There'll be some somewhere, and I wish you'd remember to call me Doctor,' her companion replied exasperatedly. He was a small man in checked trousers and a chocolate-brown jacket. Barely sparing a glance for the empty hallway they were passing through, he stalked over to the far wall, running an extendable electronic probe over the prefabricated sections. 'I thought as much,' he announced with a satisfied nod. 'There's some sort of hidden chamber here. Blow me a nice hole in this wall, Ace.'

'Right.' The girl grinned eagerly, twisting the cap of the can she held, and laying it at the foot of the wall. 'Down!' she called, hurling herself to the floor. The man who had reminded her that he was the Doctor did likewise, an instant before a hollow boom heralded the blast that left a smoking hole in the grey wall. Lights flickered distantly on the other side of the breach.

Beyond the shattered edges of the wall was a sloping corridor that led down to a room filled with machinery and electronics. Lights flashed brightly over the ebon surfaces of tall cabinets ranged around the walls, while thick pipes and cables rose in a column in the centre of the room and spread out along the walls at the same level as a catwalk, some twenty feet up. Two doorways stood open on either side, with another two above, giving access to or from the catwalk. The Doctor stepped smartly up to the column of pipes and cables as Ace turned on her heels, sniffing at the air and looking around suspiciously.

'Aha. Ace,' the Doctor commented, 'there's a console here that seems to be the main – ' A harsh rattle cut off his words, and his left leg was smashed out from under him, spots of blood spraying across the floor as steel shutters slammed down around the doors. His face a mask of agony, he clutched at his leg as Ace scuttled behind a computer bank, searching for the gunman. 'Professor!' she called.

Her anguished cry brought only a muffled groan in response, and another burst of gunfire from the beige-uniformed guards who were barely in view at the ends of the catwalk.

There were at least three guards, and Ace could hear more approaching. Tugging another can from a bulging pocket, she triggered it and hurled it upward towards the guards' position. The explosion bloomed like a rose and pitched the bloodied guards to the floor below.

Another couple of guards appeared through a ground-level doorway as it opened again, and poured a stream of fire into the Doctor as he tried to rise. His body jerked spasmodically and collapsed once again. With a howl, Ace threw herself towards one of the guns that had fallen with the guards from the catwalk. It was a Thompson sub-machine-gun, but the method of operation was simple enough. She unleashed a volley of fire into the guards, who were knocked to the floor under the impacts.

Ace took a deep shuddering breath, too stunned to attempt anything else. Nevertheless, it was only an instant before she took her first step towards the Doctor's body and its satellite blood pools.

That first step was as far as she got. A harsh drumming so strong as to be beyond pain pounded into her back, shattering ribs as she pitched face-first to the floor, and all sensation faded.

Boots crunched shards of metal and concrete as the guards circled the room, ignoring the metallic scents of blood and acrid cordite fumes that clouded the area. With a snap, a powerful spotlight came on in an alcove, illuminating a tall blue British Police Box with frosted windows and a light on top.

'Well?' a rich voice asked, coming from a figure standing expectantly in the shadows of the nearest catwalk doorway. A ghostly reflection tinted his almost invisible eyes as he looked down at the bloodstained scene.

In answer, one of the guards walked over to the bodies. He knelt by Ace, feeling for a pulse at her neckline below the blonde roots of her otherwise dark hair. Pulling her aside, he listened at the left side of the Doctor's chest. He looked back up at the figure in the shadows and drew a hand across his throat in a curt gesture.

A faint chuckle drifted from the corner as the man consulted his gold watch. 'Precisely twenty-eight seconds. That's excellent. Have this room cleared ready for installation of Shok'Arl's telemetry equipment when it arrives.' He turned away towards an inner door, then paused for a moment, a glimmer of light outlining his sardonic smile. His arm shot out, pointing at the blue box. 'Now destroy that object,' he hissed as he vanished back into the shadows.

Chapter 1

October 4th, 1957

When the shop door opened, a wave of cooled air rolled lazily out of the store, leaving a roomful of dry heat ahead of the customer who was entering. At the sound of the door, a balding man who wasn't quite gone to fat yet looked up from the boxes of nails he was counting. His gaze met a stocky man, deeply lined and going grey, wearing faded denims and workshirt. 'Oh, it's you, Joe,' the storekeeper acknowledged. 'Looking for anything in particular today?'

'The stuff from Exeter's, if it's in yet, Larry.' Though Joe's smile was easy and time-worn, the faint guttural accent always seemed to the storekeeper to hold a faint edge of implied threat. He shrugged the thought away and bent to look in the storage area under the far end of the counter. 'Plenty of stuff got delivered today,' Larry called as he shuffled the boxes and cartons around, 'but I'm not sure if – ' He broke off, examining a box and its attached delivery note. 'No, here it is. Capacitors, valves... Hell, I don't know half of this stuff – but it's your order all right.' He slid the box across the counter as Joe took out his wallet and began peeling banknotes from it.

'That'll be thirty-two fifty,' Larry announced.

'Here you go,' Joe smiled, handing over the money and lifting his package.

'So,' Larry shrugged, 'what are you doing with all this stuff anyway? Building a rocket-ship?'

'Something like that,' Joe agreed, leaving with the box tucked under his arm, the door letting in another hot breeze. Larry frowned to himself, wondering once again what the old Pole could be doing with all the electronic stuff he'd been buying over the past few months. On impulse, and almost subconsciously, he stepped over to the window, from where he could see Joe nod amiably to Sheriff Brady as he passed by in his squad car. Shaking his head, Larry stepped back from the window, as the sheriff's car also vanished from sight.

The tag reading 'S Brady' gleamed on the sheriff's barrel-chest as he got out of the Sheriff's Department Ford Thunderbird outside the County Sheriff's Office. He had already forgotten acknowledging Joe's nod outside Larry's hardware store, his thoughts occupied by wondering whether anything of importance had happened over lunch. Somehow, he doubted it; nothing ever happened in Alamagordo these days. It was a situation which left him wondering whether he should be disappointed by the boredom or relieved that people were, by and large, behaving themselves.

The sheriff's office was set slightly back from the road, a few light trees screening the redbrick construction that was so different from the adobe style of most of the other local buildings. Brady skipped up the steps with a lightness that belied his size and build, pushing through into the air-conditioned front area.

The fan-cooled room was devoid of either complainants or suspects, so Brady simply nodded to the long-faced Muldoon, who had a newspaper spread across the front desk beside a mug of black coffee. 'Any business?' Brady asked.

Muldoon looked up from the paper, the upward tilt of his eyes giving an even more hangdog look than usual. 'Nothing much. The Johnsons reckon a coyote's hiding out in their shelter, and that's it.'

Brady grimaced. 'Coyote, shit. Ten'll get you twenty it's the dog the widow Brown reporting missing on Monday.'

'I'll pass on that bet. What was the problem this morning?'

'The usual,' Brady sighed, recalling this most recent of a series of visits to a local farm. 'Just the Hunt kid seeing shadows on the sandpit again. Okay,' he muttered wearily, 'I guess I'll go see about the so-called coyote.' He paused before turning to the door. 'Anything in the paper?'

'Another cupcake says he had a ride in a flying saucer.'

Brady simply grunted as he made for the door. 'No such thing,' he rumbled. 'They're either Russkies or our boys, and there's no such thing as people from outer space.' Sparing only the briefest of final glances for the two-tone photograph of the contactee in question, he left, leaving Muldoon to contemplate the wide-eyed and thin-faced features that stared out from the page.

Wide eyes, narrowed against the desert sun, gazed up at the cloudless sky, as if searching for something. Robert Agar himself, of course, didn't really think of himself as having either particularly wide eyes or a particularly thin face but people rarely see themselves in quite the same way that others do. He might, however, have agreed with Brady's assessment of him as a 'cupcake', since Agar himself was beginning to doubt the stability of his own mind.

Unlike Brady or Muldoon, he didn't have to consult the copy of the *Socorro Sun* in his glove compartment to find out about aliens. He had met them.

Fanning himself gently with his hat, he leaned against the warm metal of the car and searched the blue expanse above, ignoring the sulphur-and-sawdust surface of the desert all around. The being he had told the man from the paper about had said that he and his people would meet him again today; that fact, above all else, he recalled from the previous meeting. He had wanted to bring some friends along, but they had advised against it. Agar recalled the voice of the one who had seemed to be their leader. It was a soothing and reasonable voice, which had told him that one-to-one contact was best for now, as they did not wish to frighten their brothers on Earth unduly.

He wasn't sure that he understood what they meant by

that, but it had seemed such a reasonable point of view that he couldn't really disagree with them. He had to admit, however, that 'brothers on Earth' was an odd turn of phrase.

He wasn't about to let a trick of semantics dissuade him from seeing his unusual friends again, however, and he smiled contentedly at the prospect. Somehow he felt at ease with them, unlike his fellow humans who always made him feel so small, like an insect crawling on the planet's face.

The forms of Agar and his car were no bigger than an ant as they glowed faintly within the spherical hologram viewer, the image clearly taken from some point far above. The holosphere was one of many such devices suspended in the centre of a round room like bubbles trapped in amber. The spheres illuminated the room softly with the glow of dozens of images, sensor read-outs and communications messages. Shadowy figures flitted around them, dancing through the air in the microgravity. The reflections of that light gave a chilling depth to the inky black eyes that peered out at them from bulbous, mushroom-coloured heads. Although the electronics were all but silent, a faint susurration of whispery voices emanated from the shadows all around.

Presently, one pair of midnight eyes glanced at Agar's image, and flickered over the glyphs that floated at the edges of the image. The watcher added its voice to the soft chorus, activating its communication line: 'Ph'Sor specimen #337. Execute collection as per Precept 1765-3.'

'As you command, Captain,' a voice acknowledged. Satisfied, the captain moved to consult another of the spheres which dotted the darkness.

Agar somehow felt the presence of the craft before it appeared, his ears popping under the pressure and his hair swirling as if from a static charge. Apprehensive in spite of his excitement and curiosity, he looked up, tilting his head far enough back to make his neck ache. A few tens of metres above, the sky shimmered and rippled as if it was a pool of blue ink into which someone had tossed a pebble. As the laws of optical physics reasserted themselves, the light ceased swirling as a large silver disc swam into steady focus.

With the exception of the three equidistant hemispheres sited around the circular exhaust on the lowermost surface, the disc was completely smooth and featureless, sunlight seeming to wash from its polished surface like water from a duck's back. 'Stay where you are,' a melodic voice chimed. It was clearly an order, but its tone was not unkind. 'Do not be afraid. We mean no harm to you.'

Agar already knew this from his previous meeting, and strove not to feel fear. He couldn't help being a little shaky, however, and quite nervous. His legs too shaky to take him anywhere, he watched as the craft descended. Three landing legs extended themselves from the underside, though there had been no sign either of them, or of any hatch-covers or mechanisms. Silently, and without disturbing any dust, the disc settled onto the ground.

For a moment nothing happened, then an invisible seam parted in the form of a door and a ramp lowered itself. No one emerged, but the implicit invitation was plain. Taking a calming breath, Agar walked up the ramp, having to bow his head slightly as he passed through the low door. On the other side, he found himself in a smooth-walled chamber six feet across. As he had done before, Agar squinted at the wall, trying to either spot the seams or identify the strange metal it was made from. It certainly wasn't steel, brass or any alloy he was even remotely familiar with. Abruptly, an inner door slid open and a man beckoned to him.

The man was lean and clean-shaven, with straight shoulder-length blond hair. He wore a pale blue overall of some smooth material, though, try as he might, Agar could see no sign of any zippers or buttons. The smooth chin was slightly narrow, and the man's large and slightly canted eyes were a strange shade of violet that reminded Agar of his service in Korea five years earlier. 'Welcome, brother,' the man greeted him, his voice cultured yet toneless. 'We are glad you returned.'

'How could I stay away?' Agar asked, momentarily wondering why he hadn't.

'This way,' the man said, gesturing through the inner door with a smile that looked genuine but flat, as if he had never smiled before and wasn't sure how it was done. He led Agar into a larger chamber, twenty feet across and eight high. The centre of the room was dominated by two hemispheres, each two feet high, one growing up from the floor while the other bulged downwards from the ceiling. A thick, four-foot crystalline column, pulsating with blue light, joined the two domes. At the edges of the room, a series of partitions divided the surrounding area into alcove workstations. Several other men and women, all as exotic as the first, were calmly at work in the alcoves, not even sparing a glance for Agar.

Nervously, Agar stepped towards the nearest alcove, trying to spot some kind of recognizable instrumentation. It was a wasted effort as the panels were all covered in some kind of touch-sensitive spots. There were circular dials, but with no needles, pointers or incrementations. Cautiously, he reached out towards one, but the man's long-fingered hand blocked his path. 'Do not touch the consoles.'

'How can you tell what those meters are reading?' Agar asked curiously.

The man looked at him steadily for a moment, his eyes distant and unfocused, before answering. 'The degree of illumination indicates the status level,' he stated, turning away before a puzzled Agar could ask for clarification.

Agar followed hastily as the man led him over to a glassy sphere which glowed with an inner fire. As Agar stood in front of it, the fuzzy glow gave way to a perfect three-dimensional image of a gladius-shaped vessel basking in the unfiltered sunlight of a high orbit. Though the image was only as large as Agar's hand, something about it gave him the impression of tremendous size and power. 'Is that how you came here?' he asked.

'It is our ... mothership. It transported us from our planet.'

'Which planet is that? Mars? Venus?'

There was another odd pause before the man nodded. 'Your astronomers would term it Venus.'

Agar's breath caught in his throat. So Venus was inhabited by men and women as well! He tried to swallow his excitement and think of a rational question. 'What is it like there? I mean ...' he racked his brain for the right words. 'What's the climate like? Do you live like us? How do you keep the peace?'

This time, the pause was longer. For a worrying instant, Agar was afraid he wasn't going to get an answer at all. 'We have no crime,' the man – the Venusian, Agar reminded himself – replied finally. 'No wars. Our life is ... different. Because we have no diseases, our life expectancy is many times that of yours.' He made an adjustment to a control and the view changed to that of artistically curved domes and spires under a vibrant golden sky. 'This is how we live.'

Agar looked on in fascination. If he could only tell the world, he thought. The papers would lap this up ... 'Why do you come here?'

'Observation.'

'To observe us, you mean?'

'No. For you to observe us.'

Somewhat shocked, Agar looked at him blankly. 'I don't understand.'

'We are all brothers in this solar system. Your people must know not to feel ... lonely. You may tell them of us.' The alien paused again. 'You must tell them of us,' he added.

A chill touched Agar's spine as he wondered if the alien had read his mind. 'One last thing. Do you have names?'

The alien man smiled faintly, and a little more naturally. 'You may call me ... Xeno.' He led Agar to the doorway. 'Tell your people – do not be afraid.'

No one was around in the garish desert countryside when

a red Plymouth convertible with white trim and, naturally, plenty of chrome, pulled to a halt at the side of the road, wearing its cloud of tan dust like an Arab woman wears a yashmak.

Almost immediately, the short man in the passenger seat got out and looked around approvingly from under the sagging brim of a limp fedora that matched the cream-coloured field of his rumpled linen suit, unbroken but for a jade Aztec brooch on his lapel. He had had to give special instructions to Groenewegen's Millinery on Neo-Sydney to get the white hat made, but it was worth it in climates like this. Ahead of him, a hazy sea of gleaming gypsum crystals glittered with the searing whiteness of an Alpine snowscape under the cloudless azure sky. The grey-blue tint that the haze gave to the surrounding mountains reinforced the impression of coolness, despite the afternoon heat. A faint breeze wafted across the sparkling sands with a scent of stone and dry spices. 'The old home universe again,' the Doctor commented.

Ace stood on the driver's seat and leaned the heels of her hands atop the windscreen, her 26th-century combat suit partially hidden by the long black duster coat she occasionally wore. Mirrored sunglasses and a wide-brimmed black hat which kept half her face in shadow completed the ensemble. 'For how long?' she said suspiciously, surveying the gleaming wilderness. 'Are you sure this is the real Earth and not the Twilight Zone?'

'Of course it is,' the Doctor answered crossly. He bent to scoop up a handful of the glittering crystals, proffering them to her. 'White Sands.'

Benny slid out of the back seat, a battered brown fedora jammed atop her dark hair not quite managing to clash with her plain jeans and reddish checked workshirt. 'You're probably right – nobody would create a climate like this deliberately. What is this anyway? The waste-tip from a salt mine?' Ace nodded in sympathy.

'Hardly. Walk this way,' the Doctor said mysteriously, and hopped away from the car in a peculiar manner. When he saw that the women were strolling normally after him, he harrumphed loudly and wandered off towards a low rise just to the left.

Benny followed, and Ace strolled after her, admiring the scenery but not particularly inspired. Soon they topped the rise and the Doctor stopped to allow them to catch up. When they reached him they drew to a halt, looking curiously on the scene below. 'Well, I'm impressed,' the Doctor prompted.

Spread out below the other side of the rise was a sprawling mass of differently shaded surfaces that made up roads, parade grounds, launching pads – some with metallic spires still in position – and low bunkers half-buried in the soil. Toy-sized people and vehicles moved along the greyish lines of the roads. A couple of miles beyond that were the stretched-out runways and hangars of an airfield. 'That,' the Doctor said, pointing off towards the airfield, 'is Holloman Air Force Base.' He spread his arms wide like a tour guide from hell. 'Welcome to White Sands Proving Grounds.'

One of the minuscule vehicles crawling through the complex network of roads at the heart of the Proving Grounds was a jeep moving at a stately five miles per hour. Caked in dust, it finally pulled off the narrow roadway and into a space between two blast walls at the back of a long, slope-walled concrete bunker. Two men in tan uniforms hopped out; the driver's sergeant's stripes wrinkling as he moved, while the passenger's peaked cap betrayed his officer status even before his colonel's pips caught the sunlight. While the sergeant held the heavy door open, Colonel John C. Finney ducked into the cool shade of the launch control bunker. Even under the strong desert sun, the lights were on, since the narrow windows were heavily tinted against the glare.

In the sunken area in the middle of the bunker, a row of circular radar screens and bulky predictor calculating machines crouched against the back wall. A clique of shirt-sleeved technicians patrolled the machines watchfully, taking note of every reading. On the far wall, a platform ran below the thick windows with a field telephone beside each one. Next to the door was an array of radio equipment, while a number of men were marking plottings on a plexiglass partition that separated the machines from the observation platform. A couple of interior doors led off from the main room, but were closed. 'Duty Officer,' Finney called.

'Sir?' Lieutenant Wood stepped smartly over.

'What's the status of the launch crew?'

'They checked in just before you arrived, sir,' the young lieutenant reported. 'Fuelling is complete and they're now engaged in the final preflight.'

'Good,' Finney nodded. His slate-grey eyes flickered towards a technician who was talking softly on one of the field telephones while ticking off items on a clipboard. His craggy face shifted in a smile. 'The test is on schedule.'

Gently twirling the question-mark-handled umbrella he was using as a parasol, the Doctor strode on ahead, whistling some jaunty tune, as Ace and Benny hurried to keep up.

'You don't intend to just walk into a Cold War base, surely?' Ace called out to him. 'They'd probably shoot us, just in case.'

'You've been watching too many cheap TV shows, Ace.'

'Sod that!' She halted immediately, Benny drawing up beside her. She'd learned to live the permanent threat of death, since space travel in her experience was inherently dangerous, but on Earth in the Fifties?

After a moment, the Doctor realized he was forging on alone, and turned back to them. 'Don't you have any curiosity about the history of this little planet of yours?' Ace ignored that: she'd proved just such an interest many times before, and she knew he was only trying to wind her up. 'Or in how man took the first tentative steps that would eventually lead to Spacefleet and beyond?' he went on. His tone was imploring as he returned to the two women, but Ace could see him realize that he wasn't really getting through to her. 'Look,' he added, 'how long have we travelled together?' He snapped up a hand in a silencing gesture before she could answer. 'Exactly, and I've never got us killed, not even once.'

'The lunar surface?' Ace put in with considerable patience.

'Well . . . All right, just the once,' he admitted as Benny looked on blankly, 'but never since. So come on. It'll be all right – I have friends in low places.' With that, he turned away and continued on towards the base.

Ace and Benny exchanged weary looks. Ace knew they would probably have to give in, since when the Doctor was in this sort of mood there was no point in arguing. He was set on seeing the base and that was that. Still, she recalled with a faint rush of hope, he had claimed to have brought the TARDIS here to show Benny this place. Perhaps, she thought, that could be turned into an advantage. She ran to catch up. 'I thought you said there was something you wanted to show Benny.'

'Yes, of course. As an archaeologist, the earliest orbital vehicles produced by humanity should be of interest to her.' He looked at Benny for confirmation. The look on her face was all he needed. '1957 seemed like a suitable time,' he finished.

'In that case,' Benny put in, 'wouldn't a more panoramic view be in order?' She pointed in the direction of several tiny figures swarming around a rocket on a launch pad. 'There seems to be some activity going on down there, so a nice high vantage point would be better to watch a launch from, wouldn't it?' Ace breathed a silent sigh of relief.

'Well, I suppose that's one way of looking at it.' He peered around at the surrounding low hills, then pointed to a shaded rock outcrop with his umbrella. 'How about there?'

'Perfect,' Ace agreed quickly.

'All right.' He started off towards the outcrop with as much visible zeal as he had displayed in his intention to visit the Proving Grounds. 'These are important times, Benny,' he began, without pausing for breath. 'Mankind is just preparing to enter the big wide world that is the universe, and it's from places like this that he'll take his first steps over the frontier that is Earth's atmosphere...'

'Wait a minute,' Benny began slowly. 'When we landed last night, you said this was the beginning of October, right?' Humming noncommittally in answer, the Doctor looked back at her owlishly. 'So,' she went on, 'why didn't you just take us to the launch of Sputnik?'

'Ah, that,' the Doctor murmured, shifting uncomfortably, or even – thought Ace – guiltily. 'There are at least two of me there already, and if I go as well, it'd treble the risk of me bumping into himself.' He paused as if to check on the logic of what he had just said. 'You've no idea how embarrassing that can be,' he added finally.

Without lowering the binoculars he had trained on the launch pad, Colonel Finney slashed his free arm down in a chopping motion towards Lieutenant Wood. The younger man immediately lifted the bakelite phone beside him and barked the order to fire.

Half a mile from the blast-proof bunker the men were stationed in, a plume of smoke billowed from a sunken launch pad, and a blaze of white-hot flame speared into the sky, forcing the sixty-foot Atlas missile out of its cradle into the blue yonder.

Behind Finney, three airmen sat hunched over the green radar screens and telemetry read-outs. 'Bird is airborne,' one called out. 'Burn is good.'

'Plotted and on track,' someone reported from the plexiglass partition.

'T plus five, board is green.'

Finney grinned behind the binoculars, following the missile's progress through the sky with interest. If the programme went well, he knew, they would be able to toss warheads at the Soviets – or anyone else – without ever leaving home soil. No one need ever go through an experience like Chosin again. He shuddered involuntarily at the memories the name inspired, and wondered if he would ever be able to face flying again. It was a shame, he felt, that the project was so highly classified, as he would have been proud to be seen as one of the people who had made such an achievement possible.

'Primary burn complete. Solid burn within projected tolerances.'

'Gyros stable at eight-five.'

'Altitude now Angels nine-nine and climbing.'

'Status of recorders,' Finney demanded.

'All film cameras functioning normally,' Wood announced. 'Minor distortion to closed-circuit television.'

'Oh?' Finney craned his head around to a point where he could see one of the small monochrome screens that displayed a fuzzy image of the missile. He nodded to himself. 'It'll pass. Get it fixed for the next test, though.' He returned to watching the missile through the binoculars. His father and older brother wouldn't call this real soldiery, he knew, but this was his command, so he didn't care about their opinions. More accurately, he reflected, he did care but wasn't going to let the fact affect his actions.

The steel skin of the Atlas was so hot that the stencilled markings on its side were beginning to bubble and split. This was an irrelevant occurrence which the designers had anticipated, but there are always events which can never be anticipated or prepared for. One such event was outside interference from an unknown quarter.

Growing larger with increasing proximity by the moment, the missile was already a pen-sized rod in the glowing holosphere, inhuman eyes concentrating on it as luminescent glyphs and grid marking scrolled around it.

'Intercept vector plotted and laid in, Commander.'

'Prepare to redirect graviton field.'

Finney's blood froze in his veins as the mirror-like disc appeared in the missile's path. A bright flash seared his eyes, the green and purple spots it left on his retinas fading to show the disc heading towards the base in a dive. Beyond, the missile was tumbling like a twig in a breeze, smoke streaming not just from the exhaust but also from a point just behind the nose-cone.

By the time the low rumble of the blast reached the bunker, the bloom of fire that marked the missile's passing had already faded, to leave only a trailing pall of smoke which drifted across the desert sands like a ghostly shadow.

Leaping from the raised platform, and grimacing as his left leg hit the floor, Finney snatched the phone from the startled Wood. 'This is Finney – orange alert! Scramble the Ranger team, I'm coming over.' Beckoning to the sergeant who had driven him to the bunker, Finney hurried to the door.

The Doctor had leapt from his rocky perch and was halfway down the slope before Ace and Benny even heard the explosion. Momentarily stunned, they suddenly realized what was happening and dashed after him.

In a dispersal area beside a runway at Holloman, two pilots clambered hastily into the cockpits of their F-86 Sabres. While their harried ground crews disconnected fuel pipes and snapped ammunition-loading panels closed, the two pilots ran through hurried preflight checks. By the time they had finished, the ground crews were scattering out of the way across the baking concrete.

As the deep roar of the engines began to counterpoint the rising whine of the turbofans, they taxied out onto the runway. As soon as they reached its end, they hurtled down the long concrete strip, banking to follow the course of the mysterious disc the moment their wheels left the ground.

Finney took the steel steps two at a time to get up to the top of the control tower at Holloman. Favouring his left leg as he burst in, he made straight for the nearest radar screen. 'Status?'

'Ranger team is catching up with the bogey, heading

north,' the young operator reported. 'They're pushing their fuel expenditure to the limit, though.'

'That doesn't matter,' Finney snapped, unable to conceal let alone control his irritation. 'I want this stopped.'

Xeno, the alien whom Agar had spoken to, held onto the low command stool as the ground flashed past in the holosphere. 'How long until we can re-engage the graviton drive?'

'Seventeen seconds. Gravimetric interference from the Earth's magnetosphere in this area is slowing our rate of recharge.'

'The humans will be within firing range by now. New course one-eight-zero mark three-one-five. Implement one second before resumption of graviton drive.'

'As you command.'

Captain Bruce Stephens kept a firm hand on the throttle while scanning for the disc. The faint pitching of the aircraft was reassuring to him, reminding him that he was given the gift of being able to defy gravity by the F-86H. A quick glance over his shoulder gave him a view of his wingman's F-86F just beyond his port wingtip.

'Ranger leader, this is control. Bogey is at four-zero-zero m.p.h., vector two-eight-seven for intercept.'

'Roger control. Ranger leader out.' Banking to port, Stephens had a brief blurry view of the rippling desert below before he straightened the aircraft onto a course parallel to the Zuni mountains in the direction of the Rio Grande and Acoma. The western curve of Route 54 vanished behind and below him as he thumbed the arming switch for the gun-camera and four 20mm cannons. Changing frequencies, he called on his wingman to arm his own gun-camera and six 30-calibre machine-guns.

Stephens knew it wasn't just the lower pressure of the altitude that made his blood sing as he flew. True, being up here like a bird did bestow a certain feeling of freedom, but the fact that being a fighter-jock was a quick route to promotion was the most important facet for him.

Some distance ahead, something flashed briefly and glinted in the afternoon sunlight. He was sure there was only one thing it could be. Switching the radio to a broad-band setting, he thumbed the mike. If truth be told, he was half-hoping that communication would do no good – he had long wanted to know how the nose-mounted cannons would perform in real combat. 'Unidentified aircraft, you are in violation of military airspace. Identify yourself and prepare to be escorted back to our airfield for questioning.' He left the set on receive after that, a faint static buzz issuing from the helmet speakers.

He blinked curiously – was it his imagination, or was the gleaming disc getting larger? The hell with it, he told himself. This is a fine airplane, not a one-shot missile. 'Unidentified aircraft, identify yourself immediately or be fired upon.'

There was no reaction, save that the disc continued to grow in the windscreen. Well, Stephens thought, they were over an unpopulated area where no harm could come to women or kids. Wondering absently if the disc had a red star painted on its side, he pressed the trigger.

Abruptly, the disc flared. For the briefest of instants, Stephens thought it had exploded under the cannonfire, but the truth became obvious when an unseen hand – which Stephens' rapidly numbing mind barely recognized as an exceptionally powerful slipstream – batted the Sabre across the sky. Hauling on the stick while the desert floor did insane cartwheels above his head, Stephens fought both to stay conscious under the pressure that was tightening around his head, and to steady the aircraft before it went into a flat spin.

After a few moments, during which his eyeballs threatened to escape their sockets, Stephens finally managed to right the aircraft. A glance at the instrument panel showed all the dials spinning as crazily as the sky had done a few seconds ago. Turning his head delicately so that it wouldn't fall off, he saw a few streamers of smoke trailing earthwards beyond his starboard wing, and no other sign of his wingman. But, he asked himself, where was the disc? Craning his head in all directions, he couldn't see it, and his ragged breath steadied slightly. Dogfights weren't supposed to be like this, he screamed silently to himself. Remembering the radio, he reset its frequency and called Holloman.

'Control from Ranger leader...' He wondered if that was really his own voice echoing through the helmet speakers. It never used to sound as quavery as that, did it?.

A vacuum had opened up under Finney's breastbone, and threatened to allow everything beyond to burst free and escape. Only when the voice screeched over the radio could he finally tear his eyes away from the sickly green radar display, which had just showed the events in the sky with frightening simplicity.

The green pixels of the disc's sudden acceleration, followed by its signal's merging with that of the downed F-86F, had engraved themselves into Finney's mind as effectively and lastingly as an epitaph is carved into a tombstone. He hadn't needed to see what had happened to the disc, certain that it had just shot up into the sky and disappeared. At least, that's what they usually did.

He glanced around at the rest of the tower crew, their eyes reflecting enough of those tombstones for an entire graveyard. 'Tell him to come on home,' Finney ordered. 'We'll have someone waiting to meet him.' Pausing until the crew had shakily – but nevertheless efficiently – returned to their work, Finney lifted a phone from one wall and dialled a single digit. 'OSI? Finney here, at the tower. We have a Code Blue, is Kreer available? Good. Get him up here on the double.' He hung up the phone and turned back to survey the room.

A few moments later, the tinny click of the door handle opposite drew Finney's attention. As it opened, he was relieved to see that his orders had been promptly acted upon.

Two men, in formal air force blues rather than the usual tropical uniform, stepped silently into the cluttered control room. The first was a chiselled-featured blond man with pale eyes and wavy hair. He set his briefcase atop the nearest radar console as the second, dark-haired man entered. This man had a fuller face, but his thin lips formed a surprisingly charming smile as his dark eyes surveyed the assembled men. 'Please excuse us, gentlemen,' he began affably, 'but I must make certain demands on your time.' He held up a wallet to display an ID card which was stamped with the letters AFOSI. 'I am Major Kreer of the Air Force Office of Special Investigations,' he began. 'This is my aide, Captain Stoker.' The blond man nodded.

'We will debrief you about this incident,' Kreer explained, his voice displaying a certain amount of relish. 'I must first warn you that this incident will be classified at Majestic level, and that any breach of security surrounding it is a federal offence under the regulations of JANAP 146.'

Finney left quietly as Kreer began his spiel. Something about those two made the hair rise on the back of his neck, and it wasn't just the fact that they were representatives of the air force's closest thing to a secret police force. For a moment, he thought he might be allowing himself to be prejudiced by the way they had all but ignored him. He dismissed the idea, but then looked back as another thought occurred. Even though these discs had been seen many times of late, the rest of the men were still unnerved by them. Why were those two so calm about the whole thing, he wondered.

Chapter 2

The Doctor vaulted over the car door with surprising agility, dropping into his seat as Ace and Benny got in more normally. The smell of the leather upholstery, after it had basked in the sun for a while, was strange to Benny, but she refrained from saying anything when neither of the others mentioned it. It must just be one of those things the history books don't say, she thought. Although the Plymouth didn't give as smooth a ride as an air-car, she had to admit it did have a certain style. It occurred to her that if she could have returned one of these cars to her own time she'd be financially set for life.

Ace gunned the engine and swung back onto the road. 'The Proving Grounds, I presume?' she suggested.

The Doctor remained silent for a moment. 'No,' he answered finally. 'They certainly wouldn't let us walk in now. Bad news travels faster than anything else I can think of, so by the time we get into Alamagordo, we should be able to pick up more details from Rumour Control.' He pointed ahead of them with his ubiquitous umbrella. 'Home, James.'

Ace nodded and set the car in motion. 'At least we're travelling in a bit of style this time,' she commented, unconsciously echoing Benny's own appreciation.

'I suppose we are,' the Doctor answered thoughtfully, his face clouding. 'Just don't ever – and I mean ever – tell me where you got this car.'

A quarter of a mile upslope, a man with short-cropped hair of pale gold watched the car leave, not through binoculars but through a small rectangular plate. Even though his tan uniform had hidden him sufficiently, he nevertheless stepped back into the shadow of a large boulder before tapping the small but solid bulge at the right-hand side of his neck. 'Targets have left en route for Alamagordo. Alteration to previous data; there are three targets: the Doctor, the human female known as Ace, and a second human female.'

The anonymous watcher was only a flyspeck against the expanse of desert, which was in itself merely a tiny patch on the rough surface of the Earth. There were no discs above him, and so he did not appear in any of the holospheres that surrounded the dwarfish captain who was listening to his report. The captain ignored the other small grey beings who were working at the surrounding circle of holospheres, concentrating instead on the report issuing from the speaker fixed above his command seat. 'Noted and logged,' the captain snapped when the watcher had finished giving his description of the other woman who accompanied the Doctor and Ace. 'Return to Stoker's unit at once.'

'As you command.'

'Surgeon-Major,' the captain said, switching to the intercom.

'Your command, Captain?' the voice answered.

'Extend full pressurization and life-support to all sections of the ship. When complete, notify the Triumvirate that they may take full command of the mission.'

'As you command.'

Kreer pocketed the small crystal that was in his hand as he left the control tower. 'You should have let me administer the full neural inhibiter,' Stoker opined, following him out.

'That would not have been sufficiently selective,' Kreer said dismissively. 'Such total amnesia would have been suspicious. As it is, anyone who asks will simply assume that the staff are following regulations not to talk.'

'What about the surviving pilot?'

'His mind will be too disrupted to be properly responsive, but I believe we can quiet him too. A few words with the medical staff are in order.'

Ace halted the car in the driveway of a sprawling one-storey building about half a mile outside of town. Long wings stretched to either side, though no lights shone in any windows. Just outside the front double-doors, a pole was topped with a sign reading 'Starlight Motel'. The word 'MOTEL' was repeated in three-foot-high letters above the entrance, the letters formed of light bulbs, none of which were working. A windblown and dusty star hung crookedly below. The dining area had the word 'SODA' in faded paintwork above boarded-up windows. 'At least it's not as bad as Rura Pontins. I've been meaning to ask,' Ace said to the Doctor, 'just how you come to have all these homes dotted around?'

'Oh, they're not homes,' the Doctor replied in a relaxed tone. 'It's just a matter of remembering to pop back after we leave here, and rent this place for ourselves before we arrive – retrospectively, as it were.' He got out of the car.

'You can't do that,' Benny protested, disembarking and following him to the door. 'It's just – '

'Paradoxical? Unethical? A two-fingered salute to Time Lord law? Basically there isn't much choice in the matter when you're as unsure about the next destination as I usually am.' Tilting aside a plant pot that resided next to the door, the Doctor retrieved a set of keys and an envelope from under it, brandishing them triumphantly. Inside the envelope was a short letter. 'It's from the estate agent,' he explained, 'or perhaps I should say realtor, since this is America. "Dear Doctor, here are the keys to the building you have arranged to lease. Each is labelled for your convenience, and I hope you and your friends enjoy your stay in New Mexico." ' He slipped the letter into a pocket and swiftly found the front door key. Opening the door, he motioned to Ace and Benny to enter.

'I don't suppose it says how long we're going to have stayed?' Benny asked dryly.

'I'm afraid not. I probably asked them not to mention it.'

Joseph Wiesniewski balanced the electrical goods from the store in the crook of one arm, while he retrieved the latest issue of *QST* magazine from his mailbox.

Pushing open his front door, he dropped the magazine onto the telephone table and carried his recent purchases down into the cellar. There, opposite the washer/drier his wife had bought a couple of years ago – despite his insistence that it was a noisy piece of junk – were ranged a series of plain grey and green metal boxes, with dials and knobs set into them. Pinned onto a board on the wall above were sheets covered in names and frequencies. Joe sat down to examine his new purchases, running mentally through the procedures he would use to wire them into his set-up. It wouldn't be a difficult job, at least not for someone with his experience of signalling during the Second World War.

Whistling an old folk tune, he went back upstairs to fetch the magazine, which was the favourite of his various radio-ham club magazines.

In his sitting room, tinted in warm colours by the setting sun, Brady groaned as the already fuzzy rendition of *I Love Lucy* on the TV screen degenerated completely into a haze of snow. 'Aw jeez, what now?" he groaned.

'TV on the fritz again?' Jeanette asked, popping her head round the partition from the kitchen.

'Yeah,' her husband nodded, glowering at the flickering screen. 'It was bad enough when Joe first put up that aerial of his, but now . . .'

'I'll speak to his wife tomorrow,' she promised, returning to the kitchen.

Brady nodded glumly. He wondered if the local kids would be causing trouble at Joe's place again that night. It wouldn't be the first time over the past few months; ever since he put the aerial up, in fact. Perhaps, he thought, I should have a quiet word with him in the morning.

Outside, in the slightly darkening sky, something shimmered briefly, a pulsing glow flitting across the sky.

The captain stood deferentially as Councillors Tzashan and Sr'Shol of the Triumvirate entered the command area amidst the circle of holospheres that separated it from the rest of the bridge. The two new arrivals were taller than he was, but would still be small for a human. Their dead-looking skin was masked with shadows as they entered.

'At ease,' Tzashan – the slightly taller of the pair – nodded.

'Thank you, Second Councillor. Surgeon-Major Ksal has completed his report: there are no complications arising from your suspension in stasis for the journey.'

'Has the Doctor made any move yet?'

'Negative,' the captain replied calmly, confirming the fact on a read-out. 'He witnessed the destruction of the missile, however, so we can expect him to do so.'

'What is the status of the compatability trials?'

'The Ph'Sor,' he said, indicating a display of Xeno and his crew, 'are conducting disinformation exercises by day with humans who are, or could be, influential. By night, my S'Raph pilots,' he gestured at the smaller beings manning the sensor stations all around, 'are sampling suitable physical specimens. Surgeon-Major Ksal reports that full compatibility will be achieved soon.'

Since the three kitchen fridges were all unstocked, it had seemed reasonable that the time travellers should eat out. Benny jumped at the chance; it wasn't often that she got to have a night out on the town on Earth, and she wasn't about to pass up a chance to paint it red.

Unfortunately, Ace was unwilling to drive all the way back to the TARDIS to fetch suitable eveningwear, protesting that even an army of only three still marched on its stomach. Although the Doctor had tried to mollify her by pointing out that they were merely going to a local diner, not the Savoy, Benny was still somewhat morose about going out in jeans and workshirt. 'Anyway,' she asked as they cruised along the streets at dusk, 'why not the Savoy?'

'Apart from the fact that there isn't one in New Mexico, you mean?' the Doctor asked teasingly. 'Cafeterias, diners and the like are all good sources of local news. So, if we're going to find out what happened here today, one of those would be a good place to start.'

'I see.' Benny gave his back a sour look. 'Here endeth the lesson for today?'

'Experience counts.'

'Batmobile at eleven o'clock,' Ace announced. Benny and the Doctor looked across to see a Sheriff's Department car parked outside a window marked 'George's Rib Room'. The place looked inviting enough, Benny thought, if nothing particularly special despite its carefully engraved window decoration.

'Perfect!' the Doctor crowed. 'Let's see what we can hear from the horse's mouth.'

'Right.' Ace threw the car into a U-turn, and parked just behind the police car. 'Looks like they've got a couple of tables to spare.'

Jack Siegel relaxed, the weariness dropping from his shoulders as his hat dropped from his hand onto the nearest hook.

He considered his hat to be as much his badge of office as the sheriff's star was Brady's, and consequently always felt much more off-duty once he took it off. His gaze flicked briefly to his father's portrait, recalling how the old man had always said that a farmer, like a policeman, was never really off-duty. 'Sorry, dad,' he muttered, before going into the kitchen.

The rest of the family had already eaten, and he could faintly hear the half-coherent sounds of the TV in the sitting room, but someone had left a plate of steaming stew at his place on the table in anticipation of his return. He thought it most likely that they'd heard him out at the stable.

Deciding that the deep plate was unlikely to allow any gravy to spill, and therefore willing to risk his wife's wrath, Jack lifted it up, along with a towel, and moved carefully through to join the others in the lounge. The rest of the family were gathered around the TV set; Donna throwing him a disapproving look from her chair, while his brother Rick and his wife reclined on the settee. The kids were scattered across the carpet in front of the TV like windblown tumbleweeds. 'What's on the boob-tube?'

'OSS,' Donna replied. 'You know you shouldn't have that plate in here,' she added half-scoldingly.

'I know,' he agreed with an inward smile. Her disapproving look made her seem more sultry somehow, but he had never dared to tell her so. He suspected that she knew anyway, and played up to it, but he didn't really want to spoil the game. 'It's a deep plate and I got a towel, OK?' he grinned.

'Aw, rats,' Jack's eldest offspring, Jack Junior, groaned.

'What's up, Jay?' both parents asked together. Jack needed no answer, however, as he could see for himself the snowy fuzz that had blanketed the TV screen and blotted out Ron Randell's wartime exploits. 'Gone on the fritz, huh?' Jack grimaced and set the plate down on the coffee table. 'I'll go out and check the antenna. There might be a bird sitting on it or something,' he suggested. Certainly, he knew, there had been no strong winds to blow it down.

Outside, the sun was sinking in the west, turning the rocky desert to a shadowy vision of hell while the sky turned pink and purple when Jack re-emerged from the house. He circled the building a few yards out from the walls, trying to get a good view of the TV antenna, and finally found such a spot at the base of the chimney. Squinting up at it, he judged it to look the same as always. Shrugging, he moved to go back inside, but suddenly froze. His eyes were glued to a patch of pastel sky to the west. There, high above the foothills beyond the farm, two pearlescent ovals drifted silently, pulsing with inner light.

As Jack went back inside, the two ovoids sank behind

the hills with the sun, casting a pale luminescence on the rocks.

Benny, Ace and the Doctor took a table next to a Sheriff's Department deputy. The deputy was a Hispanic, and was talking to a man in a business suit who almost had 'travelling salesman' tattooed on his forehead. All three time travellers pretended to be more interested in the decor, which mixed Spanish and Mexican styles with those of the Zuni and Navajo peoples, than in their neighbours at the next table. Benny looked around to see if there was a waiter or waitress in the vicinity, and was rewarded with the sight of a dusky, almond-eyed woman heading towards their table from behind the long bar.

'Hi,' the woman began cheerily. 'I'm Sara; how can I be of help to you?'

Benny noticed that the Doctor didn't bother looking at the menu. 'Huevos rancheros e chorizos, por favor,' he said, with a disarming smile.

'I'll have the same,' Ace shrugged.

Benny scanned the menu before her, but little of it made any sense. 'Do you have any soup?' she asked, falling back on the old travellers' stand-by.

'Sure, there's posole.'

'I'll have that, then,' Benny confirmed, giving Sara a winning smile.

'I won't be long,' Sara promised, leaving for the kitchen door behind the bar. With no other distractions around, Benny let her attention stray towards the deputy at his table, while ostensibly studying the menu.

The deputy was shaking his head as the salesman's voice started to show strain at what Benny strongly suspected was the effort of trying to get through to him without actually shouting across the diner. 'I tell you, I saw it as clear as day; a disc like . . .' He lifted the saucer out from under his coffee cup, and waved it under the deputy's nose. 'Like two of these joined at the edges, but all made of silver. Two jets were chasing it out of Holloman.'

'You been paying too much attention to those freakos in the paper, Frank.'

'Jesus, come on – it's me. I'm not talking about these nuts with their "space brothers" crap! Are you trying to tell me you haven't seen one of these things in the last couple of months? They've been all over the place.'

'Look, Frank, I was over at Holloman yesterday, taking over the week's supply of saucer reports. Wouldn't they have said something if these things really existed?'

'Not if they don't want to announce to the voters and taxpayers that foreign aircraft of some kind are buzzing our bases, and that our planes can't stop them.'

'That's true, I suppose...' the deputy answered in a slightly mollified tone which made Benny grimace as if there was something distasteful in the air. Obviously, she thought, this pair preferred to worry about Russians more than anything else. She looked up as Sara returned with two large platters, which she deposited in front of the Doctor and Ace. Each was heaped with scrambled eggs on a tortilla, and covered with chilli and melted cheese. Spicy red sausages were at either side, but, before she could speculate on their origin, Sara reappeared with her posole.

'Thanks,' Benny murmured, and stirred the soup with a spoon. It appeared to have something like popcorn floating in it, and it smelled strongly of garlic and chilli.

'Lime hominy and pork,' the Doctor announced, and Benny realized he must have seen her wrinkle her nose a little at the scent.

'Sounds more like a cocktail.' Tentatively, she tasted a drop. It wasn't too bad, but the tanginess would take some getting used to. Ace, meanwhile, was wolfing straight into her platter with obvious relish while the Doctor, as usual, seemed content to simply pick at his food for the sake of appearances as he watched the other patrons. The deputy rose, paying his bill at the bar, and Benny sipped the soup thoughtfully.

* * *

Rick and his wife Mary were putting their two children to bed, as Donna was tucking in Jay, when they first heard the sound. A strange scratching and scraping, accompanied by what sounded like soft footfalls, was filtering down through the bedroom ceilings.

Jack came up at once, as Donna's startled call joined Rick's puzzled one. Bounding up the stairs gracefully, he halted on seeing the three worried faces waiting for him on the landing. Mary's head was tilted as if trying to determine the direction the sound was coming from, while Rick fingered a shotgun nervously. 'What is it?' Jack asked.

'There's someone on the roof,' Rick whispered.

'You're kidding, right?'

'We all heard him,' Donna told him.

'Them,' Mary corrected her. 'I think there are two or three of them out there.'

'Okay,' Jack said slowly, the looks in his family's eyes convincing him that they weren't joking. 'Hang on to that twelve-gauge, Rick, and I'll get the 30-06. Then we'll go take a look. He slipped back down the stairs, making for the gun rack in the hall. As he lifted the Winchester free, a frenzied barking and whinnying erupted outside. 'What the hell...?' he grumbled, snatching the rifle from the rack.

Rick and the women descended, bringing the children. The youngest was eight, so none of them were crying, but they all looked hunted, their eyes darting about. 'What's wrong with Jerry and Dino?' Jay asked.

'Same as what's bothering us and spooking the horses, I expect. Come on, Rick,' he urged, slipping ammunition into the rifle as he walked to the door. As Rick opened it, Jack turned to the others. 'Keep the door locked – just in case.' With that, he followed Rick outside.

There was no sign of anyone around as they stepped off the porch and away from the house. For the second time that night, Jack stepped away, trying to get a good view of the roof. As they walked, they came into sight of Jerry and Dino, the two German Shepherds, in their fenced-off little enclosure. The dogs began to bark more furiously, tails wagging in relief; or so Jack guessed. The horses in the stable whinnied fearfully and stamped their hooves, though there was no sign of whatever was causing their agitation.

An abrupt sound of movement drew their attention as soon as their backs were turned to the house to investigate the stable. Spinning back round, Jack saw a small shadowy figure flit around the corner of the house and vanish into the encroaching darkness. 'Did you get a look at him?' he asked Rick. 'Looked like a kid.'

'One weird kid, then. I just caught a glimpse, but it moved way too weird for a kid.' They had already reached the corner of the house. Rounding it, they looked westwards. A faint glow lit the foothills eerily and Jack had to fight to suppress a shudder.

Without warning, something dropped from the sky, slamming into the two men and knocking them into a sprawling heap. Jack rolled with his own momentum, and rose to a kneeling position in an instant. Vanishing ahead was a stalky figure, less like a young vandal than some kind of monkey. Unsure as to whether it was the same one they had seen a moment ago, or another of the same type of creature, Jack fired at it as it dashed for the water tower. Rick also fired a blast from the twelve-gauge, but there came no cry of pain or thud of a falling body.

'Here's an idea,' Rick suggested. 'We go back to the house and lock ourselves in. That definitely wasn't no kid.'

'You're damn right it wasn't, but I want a good look at whatever it was.' Cautiously, Jack edged towards the water tower, the ghost stories of their old Navajo cook coming back to haunt his mind.

'Anything from anyone?' Benny asked.

'Not really.' The Doctor shook his head. 'Half these people seem to think the disc was a secret American craft out of control, and the other half reckon it was a Russian spy-plane of some kind.'

'The exception,' Ace added, pointing to a thin-faced, wide-eyed man in the corner, 'being that guy; his story being that they're space brothers come to save us from ourselves. How about you?'

'The deputy thinks it's Russian.' She looked over at the bar. Now and again she would ask herself if trying to visit every bar in the history of the universe and acquire one of their beer glasses was a frivolous hobby for an archaeologist. Her answer to herself was invariably 'no'. 'I won't be long,' she informed her friends, getting up from the table.

It was Sara who approached Benny's bar stool. 'What'll it be?'

'A Spine-Spinner?' she asked hopefully.

'This isn't Las Vegas,' Sara answered in a not unkind tone.

'Warnog? Zombie?'

Sara shook her head.

'Vodka Martini? Shaken, not stirred,' she added, a little self-consciously.

'Coming right up.' Sara took a glass from under the counter and started filling it from the relevant bottles. 'You're obviously not from around here. The other girl sounds English – '

'She is.'

'And the man sounds like he's from Scotland – '

'Probably.'

'But your accent, I can't place.'

'I'm from . . .' Benny paused. Clearly she couldn't tell the truth, so she tried to think of somewhere suitably colonial that couldn't be seen as a hostile power in the Cold War era. 'Australia,' she finished finally, fervently hoping that Sara had never heard a genuine Australian accent.

'Really? So what brings you to New Mexico?'

'I'm an archaeologist.'

'No kidding?' Sara brightened considerably. 'Taking a look at the Carlsbad caverns?'

'I have seen them, yes.' In about half a millennium, she added silently.

'There's an old pueblo much nearer here, you know. Some people think it may be Anasazi. It was discovered only very recently.'

'There is? Where?' Perhaps this trip wouldn't be a total loss, she thought.

'Just off Route 54. You can't miss it – there's a turning off to a farm just outside of town, and the pueblo is in the hills beyond that.'

'Thank you,' Benny said, with feeling. 'Oh, there is one other thing – about your beer glasses...'

When it came, it was with the speed of a jet. Emerging from the lee of the water tower, a spindly grey form with night-black eyes that looked straight through the men hurtled spiderlike across the intervening ground, its stick-thin limbs propelling it with unnatural agility.

Yelling in horror for the women to stay indoors, Jack and Rick each loosed a shot at the creature before bolting for the safety of the house. Mary had already slammed the door, leaving them to crash helplessly into it, carried on by their own momentum.

Pounding on the door, they glanced fearfully back, to see only empty ground between them and the water tank. From behind the door came the metallic scraping of the bolt being drawn. Relieved, Jack took half a step back, to let Rick through the opening door.

As soon as his shoulder jutted beyond the eave of the porch, something snatched it in a steely grip. A pair of thin but incredibly strong arms had swung down from the awning and sunk long talons into his shoulders. Jack barely had time to look up into the empty black eyes staring out from the bulbous head above before, with a terrified howl, he was pulled up out of sight.

Rick stuffed a pair of cartridges into the shotgun as Jack's cry echoed on. Before he could use them, he was knocked off his feet and blown through the door by an invisible hand that left him out cold.

With a continuing high-pitched whine, the unseen force then slammed into Mary, hurling her aside.
The whine continued for a very short time.

Chapter 3

Major Marion Davison climbed the tower steps eagerly, her notebook and pen held tightly in one hand. As she was in charge of press and public relations for the whole southern sector of Air Defence Command, she had been avoiding her office for the past few hours, knowing only too well that the phone would have been ringing all day with calls from news agencies and local stations, all wanting to know the official position on what they would undoubtedly refer to as the 'flying saucer'.

Davison would have liked to think that she could have told them something about it. This wasn't going to happen, though; the AFOSI representatives had already given her the bones of a dismissal story to be written. They were claiming that a weather balloon, launched as part of the preflight activity, had somehow come down and become entangled with the missile. Everyone on the base knew differently, of course, but none of them were willing to risk the steep penalties that would follow any such revelation.

Theoretically, Davison knew, she could just go ahead and write the cover story. She could issue it to the locals without bothering to check the background to it. That wasn't her style, however. She had been intrigued by the disc or discs, ever since she first saw it – or one – several months earlier.

Davison had joined the air force in the hope of becoming a pilot, and flying like a bird. Women were only permitted to be transport pilots, of course, but she felt that was enough. The injuries she'd received in training had put paid to that ambition, however. Instead, her grades and former position on her high-school newspaper had convinced her superiors to assign her to military journalism, and her natural curiosity had agreed with the sentiment. Therefore, although her job didn't always require the precise truth to be told, she liked to ferret out the facts just for the record, and for personal satisfaction.

Searching for facts on a military base wasn't exactly encouraged, of course, and she did get the occasional suspicious look while on duty. For that reason, she was most at home digging through reports and researches rather than actually interviewing people. She wondered fleetingly how the tower crew would react to her today, and paused for breath outside the door. Though only in her early twenties and leanly built, she felt the way that Alfred Hitchcock might if he'd had to run a marathon. She filed a thought to apply for quarters nearer the centre of the base.

Next to the door, above the fire extinguisher and safety notices, was a sign reading 'Loose lips sink ships.' She shook her head wearily – didn't they know the war was over? Or were they just preparing for the next one? Never mind, she told herself, just don't say it aloud.

Of course, there were certain advantages to her position. She was the one person who might be positively expected to ask questions about the day's events, even if she was nervous about it. She didn't want to shirk her duty, did she? Opening the door, she stepped through.

A guard was inside, but the officer of the day waved him away. Lieutenant Vincente was the OD on duty, and he gave Davison a querying look. 'Hi Marion, come to see where the real work happens?'

'Sort of,' Davison replied after the obligatory chuckle at the standard joke. 'I thought I'd pick your brains for a few quotes about the afternoon's excitement.'

Vincente frowned. 'What excitement?'

'Well, the flying disc,' Davison prompted with a determined seriousness.

'Flying disc?' Vincente looked askance at her. 'What are you talking about?'

'Wait a minute.' Davison's voice threatened to break into a laugh. Surely, she thought, Vincente was trying to pull a fast one on her. 'You've been on duty since sixteen hundred, right?'

'Yeah.'

'So you must have been here fifteen minutes later, when the missile blew up and the two Sabres were sent up after the flying disc that...' She trailed off as Vincente looked blankly at her.

'Someone must be fooling with you, Marion; there's been no scramble today.'

For a moment, Davison considered asking one of the others in the tower, but a quick glance confirmed that they looked as surprised and baffled as Vincente. Davison hadn't particularly expected to be told anything as such, considering the security classification, but there should at least have been a 'no comment'. 'I guess you're right,' she said slowly, and backed towards the door. 'Somebody must be jerking me around. Sorry to bother you.'

'Any time,' Vincente replied in a bemused tone.

Leaving the tower, Davison paused outside. How could the crew have failed to notice what had happened? They certainly weren't good enough actors for this to be a simple clamming-up. This, she was sure, was something worth looking into.

A pair of jets hurtled overhead as the Doctor, Ace, and Benny all left the Rib Room. 'More aerial activity, obviously,' the Doctor said with a nod. 'The morning papers should be full of all sorts of amusing stories. We can pick some up on our way to this pueblo of yours, Benny.' His head snapped round as Ace shuddered involuntarily, before looking round with a searching expression. 'Something wrong?'

'I just had that feeling – you know, somebody walking over your grave.'

'Interesting,' he murmured inscrutably.

'Aren't we going to be poking our noses into that flying saucer?'

'Probably, but there are so many things zipping around Earth's atmosphere at this point in time that we could be stuck here forever trying to find out which one we'd seen.'

'What's that supposed to mean?' Benny asked.

'Well, people in this era were always seeing UFOs, and usually considering them alien spaceships, but,' he added pointedly, 'even in the unexplained cases, you have historians from the future; ball lightning; a rather odd bunch of Sidhe who inhabit the upper dimensions of Earth's timeline ... the list is endless. Either way, it's all a recorded part of Earth history, and exactly the sort of thing you'd expect to see in this time period.'

Benny wasn't born yesterday, however – or tomorrow, for that matter – and grinned slowly. 'That's why you really brought us here, isn't it? So you could see for yourself what these things looked like.'

'Curiosity is a virtue in the traveller,' he answered cheerily. 'Otherwise what'd be the point in going anywhere?'

Far above, high in the desert air, two luminescent discs banked off towards Holloman and the Proving Grounds.

The last copy of Finney's final report of the day's events fell into his out-tray, and was quickly crowned with a heavy paperweight. Finney studied the paperweight thoughtfully; it consisted of a model Dakota mounted on a metal support which had double knuckle-like metal hinges, the whole assembly being glued into a perspex block. Any of the mechanics on the base would have been able to identify the hinged metal as a throttle-cable support, the model indicating that it was from a Dakota, but to Finney it was much more. It was the reason he was now in a desk job, for one thing, as well as being the reason why he now had to stretch out his stiff leg to ease its ache.

Etched into the perspex block, as indelibly as it was etched into the core of Finney's being, was the date 'Dec. 7th, 1950'. Occasionally, someone would ask why that date was inscribed on it, but only a few field surgeons and some personnel staff knew the answer. Finney, of course, couldn't forget. It was the date on which the cable support had been removed from his thigh after being blown almost clean through it by a cannon-shell in the skies over the Chosin Reservoir.

Leaning back in his chair, and absently trying to rub away the ache in his thigh, he reflected that he should have been more careful going up the tower steps that afternoon.

He opened his eyes and immediately wished he hadn't, since the circular lampshade hanging above was a stinging reminder of both the test failure and the subsequent death of the fighter pilot. Worst of all, this was the third successive Atlas test failure. He could already hear his superiors at the Pentagon calling for his head. He felt that they would most likely invalid him out of the service, as they had barely held back from doing before. 'And probably using you as the excuse,' he whispered to the paperweight.

Pulling himself together, he wondered what deductions Kreer had made after his investigations. He glared across at the chair opposite, as if he could materialize his special scientific adviser by sheer force of willpower. 'What's the point in having a scientific adviser who's never around to advise?' he grumbled to himself. The telephone rang then, the noise jarring him into alertness. 'Yes,' he snapped when he had lifted the receiver.

'Lieutenant Vincente, at the tower. We have a Code Blue.'

'The disc's back?'

'Two of them, sir. They're buzzing the military reservation south of us.'

'Has Kreer been notified?'

'We've put the word out for him, if that's what you mean.'

'Red alert! Ready a flight of Sabres; half the duty squadron, but don't scramble them yet. I won't risk any more men for an empty stretch of bombed-out desert. I expect those dozen planes to be waiting on the runway by the time I reach you.' Not waiting for an acknowledgement, Finney slammed the phone down and rushed out, the alert sirens ringing in his ears.

While Ace was off exploring the length and breadth of the locked-up motel, Benny relaxed on a couch in the communal lounge while the Doctor tried to tune in a radio set that was on the sideboard. 'What happened to the previous owners of this place?' she asked finally.

'The husband was killed in Korea, and the wife went back to her parents.'

'Did you leave that in the note as well?' She had now travelled with the Doctor long enough to know that his explanations were often facetious – though not often the ones she might have preferred to be that way.

'Not exactly. I rendered certain medical assistance at Chosin and Panmunjom. With varying degrees of success,' he added, as a shadow passed across his face.

Benny nodded understandingly. 'That's why you prefer not to delve into medical matters unless it's absolutely vital, isn't it?'

'Is it?'

'May I ask how all this came about, then?'

'You may ask,' he said dryly.

'Thanks, but no thanks; my head feels like M. C. Escher's waste bin most of the time anyway. You said we're "probably" going to investigate that disc?'

'Yes.' He straightened as a burst of rock and roll came from the radio, then turned the volume down.

'Why do I get the feeling that it's the reason why we're really here? And, please, don't go on about the different types of flying objects.' Do I get that feeling because he always has an ulterior motive, she added mentally.

The Doctor stood silently for a moment, then leaned thoughtfully against the sideboard. 'The TARDIS is an old model, you know, dating back to the time when Time Lord engineers were a little more ... innovative,' he went on, with a ghost of a smile. 'They were always trying new circuit combinations and new functions, with no idea how they'd work – if at all – but always striving to add new refinements.' He smiled faintly, looking into empty space; though not, Benny suspected, empty time. 'She's a very sensitive old girl, you see, and now and again she picks up things I'd miss. Somehow I got the feeling that she was trying to bring us to this time and place, and I want – I have to see why.'

'So the TARDIS is as curious as you?'

'Well,' he shrugged, 'we are symbiotically linked, so there's bound to be a certain amount of growing together in terms of mental processes.'

'Oh,' Benny answered, and sipped the beer she'd filled her latest glass with. She felt it best not to mention that the best known parallel for this sort of behaviour among humans was between married couples. A surreal image of the Doctor and the TARDIS in front of a church altar flashed before her eyes, and she had to bite her lip to keep her face straight. When she looked up again, he had vanished.

A few moments later, Ace came in. 'Where did you put the rest of that?' she asked, pointing at the drink in Benny's hand.

'In the smallest fridge.'

'Right.' Ace nodded, and departed after the Doctor.

Watching the Sabres taxiing into position out on the runway, Finney felt a guilty pang of relief that he was safely ensconced in the control tower. 'Bearing to target?'

'Bearing one-seven-zero, altitude Angels-two-zero, thirty miles downrange,' Vincente replied. 'They're still together, sir; shall I launch a surface-to-air?'

'After what happened to the Atlas? Missiles are hardly going to be useful against them. Scramble the fighters – this time they can watch each other's backs. If the bogeys should split up, six aircraft are to engage each one.'

'Yes sir.'

Kreer padded silently across the dispersal area between the engineering workshops and the tower, watching impassively as the first pair of F-86s powered along the runway and screamed into the night air. Pausing in mid-step, Kreer looked back up at the diminishing navigation lights of the fighters. 'How can he hope to conduct an aerial combat in the dark?' he murmured to himself. His eyes widened with a snarl as a thought struck him. 'Oh no . . .' Breaking into an enraged run, he resumed his course for the tower.

If I'm too late, he thought, I'll disembowel Finney with – He forced the feelings down. It wasn't time for that yet.

Having found a glass and a selection of beers, Ace made to return to the lounge and rejoin Benny.

Almost despite herself, however, she looked out at the low bulge in the ground beyond the kitchen window. The earthwork marked the location of a half-built fall-out shelter which extended from the main building. Wryly, Ace wondered just how much difference its walls would make to the occupants. She personally had no objection to being protected by good defences, be it a deflector shield, woven kevlar fibres, or bonded polycarbide armour; but she felt that – given the choice – she would probably have forsaken the fall-out shelter. After all, she wondered blackly, who wants to survive the first blast just long enough to die of multiple cancers over the following few weeks? She turned away from the window, sneering inwardly at her preoccupation with death and destruction, which seemed to have become an occupational hazard.

It was all academic in any case, Ace reminded herself. Certainly there had been no nuclear exchange before she had left Earth in 1986, and her visits since had shown no sign of any such devastation either.

She paused, her hand on the fridge door, and looked out with the feeling that she had overlooked something. Peering out, she stepped closer to the window, now realizing what it was that had so nearly escaped her attention.

Standing silently at the far end of the incomplete shelter, head cocked to watch the sky with an unreadable air, the Doctor stood like a pale ghost watching over an ancient longbarrow under the drifting moon. Curious, Ace went to the door and out into the chill night air, wishing she had brought her duster out from her room. 'Stargazing?' she suggested.

'Statistically, the hours from eleven p.m. to one a.m. are the ones in which you're most likely to see unidentified flying objects.'

'Really?' She shrugged. 'You're not even wearing an anorak.'

'Does it make a difference?' he asked, turning slightly towards her. She noted that his eyes were still tilted upwards nonetheless.

'Absolutely, they're standard equipment for trainspotters, UFO-spotters, fans of – '

'Even in a desert?'

'Well, there *was* a worried-looking brass monkey at the front door a minute ago, asking if we had a soldering iron handy.'

'No clouds or moisture to keep in the day's heat,' the Doctor went on absently. 'I never did like deserts much; not since I was in the Gobi, anyway.'

'What are you really watching for?' she asked in a more serious, and – though she would neither admit to, nor recognize it herself – authoritative tone. To her surprise, he looked round at her.

'Whatever I might see.' He glanced skywards again with a concerned expression. 'By the pricking of my thumbs . . .'

'Something wicked this way comes?' Ace couldn't help but look up suspiciously. 'I know what you mean. I keep getting this feeling, like I can smell something nasty and can't figure out what it is.'

'That's more or less it. I often get that feeling when there are Daleks around.'

'Do you think there are?' Ace asked in a businesslike tone. Though concerned about the effect they had on local populations, she half-hoped there were some Daleks in the vicinity. She understood Daleks.

'No, not at all. I've felt it in many other situations,' he explained. 'On Segonax, for example.'

Reminded of the nightmarish events at the Psychic Circus on Segonax, Ace grimaced, most assuredly unreassured, and went back into the kitchen.

Kreer burst into the tower control room, eyes blazing. 'Do not use the new phased-frequency radar array!' he thundered.

'And why shouldn't I?' Finney demanded in an offended tone from the window. 'Or have you suddenly been placed in command?' he asked pointedly.

'Sorry, sir,' Kreer corrected himself smoothly, the hesitation barely noticeable. 'The new array hasn't been properly tested yet – '

'Then it'll be tested now. Vincente, keep the pilots updated with the vectors from the new array.' Finney turned away as Kreer looked at his back with burning eyes.

The Doctor turned, head cocked in a listening position, as a rising whine pierced the air. Looking up impassively, he barely had time to blink as two bright circular forms flashed overhead, rapidly vanishing into the night. A few seconds later, a number of dully metallic jet fighters hurtled past in hot pursuit with an angry roar.

Tapping his fingers on the handle of his umbrella for a moment, the Doctor stepped around the mound of the half-built shelter and returned to the motel.

In the distance, something flashed bright among the stars.

Xeno, commanding the skiff *Laz'Ar*, kept a close eye on the holosphere's computer-enhanced images of the pursuing fighters. 'Match their leader's velocity,' he told his pilot, 'but do not allow them to close.'

'As you command,' the woman acknowledged, her cheekbones looking cadaverous under the blue lighting.

'If we increase power output by a further five per cent, we will be cloaked.'

'Maintain current output until all operational parameters and manoeuvring capabilities of the Earth aircraft have been transmitted to *R'Shal*.'

'As you –' She broke off as a low-pitched alarm hummed sonorously. 'Alert! Six further aircraft in sensor range; three bearing zero-one-five mark zero-two-four, the remainder bearing three-two-zero mark three-three-five! All units on intercept course.'

'Flag notation to telemetry of aircraft performance; individual actions indicate two-dimensional thinking, but group strategy shows evidence of limited three-dimensional consideration.'

'Confirmed,' the crewman at the communications console announced. 'Limits of design tolerances and performance now noted and logged. All data uplinked to tactical database aboard *R'Shal*.'

'Send to skiff *Kron*: new course; one-one-zero mark zero-nine-zero. Engage graviton drive at will.'

'Sending.'

'Humans in firing range,' the helm reported. 'Flight leaders are arming weapons; now firing. Multiple projectile impacts on outer hull – no damage.' The atmosphere in the ship remained completely calm, with neither sound nor motion to indicate that the vessel was either in motion or under attack.

'Engage graviton drive.'

The two glowing discs dulled like doused fires, their clean-lined edges swimming as the moonlight was bent around them by the gravitational fields produced by their drive systems.

They swam back into focus without warning, swooping down erratically over the desertscape.

Deep blue emergency lights pulsed in the interior of the *Laz'Ar* as the ship juddered like an aircraft passing through turbulence. 'Report!' Xeno snapped.

'Phased magnetic radiation of some kind is causing untelemetred gravimetric interference in the drive field.'

'Reduce power to standard! Disengage graviton drive!'

All too aware that the same problem would be affecting the *Kron*, Xeno called up an image of the other skiff in the holosphere. Its glow sparking randomly, it hurtled downwards. 'Contact with *Kron* lost,' Xeno was informed.

Finally, the *Kron* flared up once and vanished. 'Notify the captain on *R'Shal* that one skiff has been lost. Helm; current course, best speed until we're out of the interference field.'

His full, hard face eerily lit by the green glow from the radar screen, Kreer scowled as the traces unmarked by transponder codes vanished. 'They've gone, Colonel,' he informed Finney.

'I think one of them might have gone down,' Vincente reported from his screen. 'The other definitely got away, though.'

Finney looked down at Vincente's screen, mulling over that possibility. His attention so distracted, he failed to notice Kreer give Vincente's back an unpleasant, predatory look. 'Try and work out where,' he ordered. When he turned round, Kreer had disappeared.

Shadow watched with cool dispassion as the greasers, jocks, and other arcanely named youths cavorted in the night air, unconsciously evoking memories of the ritual dances performed by local tribes long before the forefathers of these people had arrived in the region.

She sat comfortably in a dim corner across the road from the youths, serenely watching the display. Why the youths played with such abandon before even getting their prey in sight, she didn't understand, but she was unconcerned. Her partner in the hunt seemed to know why they behaved as they did, and his satisfaction at the way the proceedings were going was echoed in herself. One of the immature hunters was making some sort of staccato call in the direction of a tall metal pole at their prey's lair, but the sounds were unmusical and meaningless to her.

There seemed to be some brief argument between two of the youths, as one wearing a dark brown leather jacket gestured impatiently towards the house beyond, and the plaid-jacketed boy with him pulled away, shaking his head. Shoving him aside, to the amusement of the others – and to that of Shadow's partner, she felt – the leather-clad youth lit a rag which was stuffed into a bottle. Drawing his arm back, he hurled it through the window of the house.

A flash of flame and heat burst out, which the other youths appeared to take as a signal of some kind, hurling further bottles with gleeful cries.

Throughout the house, bursts of flame flared up and licked hungrily around the walls. Their appearance was as sudden and as damning as the appearance of any summoned demon of ancient myth. The jeers and laughter of the atavistic youths overran the clear air more chillingly than the buzzing of a locust swarm.

Abruptly, a clawed scream struck up from the interior of the blazing lair, rising above the roar of the flames and crash of brittle glass to cut off most of the laughter. Silhouetted by the increasingly furnace-like glow behind, a figure appeared at the door, clutching at the doorpost as wisps of smoke curled from his clothes and hair.

Several of the youths fled immediately, while a couple of others stood indecisively to look for guidance. With a malicious laugh, the leather-clad one stooped to pick up a rock. The boy with whom he had argued earlier lunged for him, trying to knock the stone from his grip, but he was quickly felled by a blow to the temple. Without any further sound, he folded up and slumped in the middle of the road. Standing there, possibly scenting the crisp blood as Shadow did – *that* she could understand – he hurled the rock at the backlit figure, knocking him sprawling back into the inferno with a pained moan. With the rock he also hurled jeering cries which, though Shadow didn't understand the words, were in a clearly venomous tone.

As if fate had been awaiting this, the roof of the hallway suddenly fell in, fire pouring down onto the recumbent figure like molten gold.

The anguished moans stopped.

In the distance, a scream of sirens grew quickly louder. The leather-clad youth, now looking more like a startled bird, bolted off down the street, leaving only a burning house and a body in the road.

As soon as he had gone, neighbours began to appear in their doorways, pointing to the metal pole and up at the sky.

Shadow didn't stay to watch their reaction. She could feel her partner's amusement as clearly as she could scent the tang of blood and charred flesh in her nostrils. The heat from the fire reminded her uncomfortably of the heat of flames that had so nearly consumed her once before, but the other presence in her mind was unaffected, the calmness quieting her nerves. If she could read, she might have noticed the name Joseph Wiesniewski written on a charred-edged fragment of a *QST* magazine cover that blew past her in the light breeze.

Instead, she turned and slipped silently down the street.

Chapter 4

The walls of the circular chamber were smooth, with inlaid panels that may have been either decorative or functional, if Jack Siegel had been in any fit state to look. Instead, however, his glazed eyes faced the phosphorescent ceiling unblinkingly.

Lying, like the rest of his family, naked on a clammy plastic bench, he was completely unresponsive to the large coal-black eyes of the diminutive surgeon-major checking an instrument set in the headrest. Several other fragile three-foot high beings busied themselves at the benches of the others, taking samples of skin, blood and hair.

When a tone sounded from the headrest, Surgeon-Major Ksal disconnected a slim transparent tube from a piston-like arrangement on the underside of the headrest. With a faint sucking sound, a slim needle withdrew itself back into the piston. Holding the cylinder in whiplike fingers, Ksal carefully slotted it into a panel in the wall. Immediately, traceries of light rippled along its ebon surface, scrolling into strange forms. Ksal watched them impassively, then turned to his assistants. 'These humans are suitable. Conduct full processing, then give them the neural inhibitor.' He turned back the panel. 'Surgeon-Major Ksal to the bridge.'

'Bridge,' the captain's voice acknowledged. 'Report.'

'The humans are being processed now. They should be ready for transfer back to Earth by dawn.'

'Noted and logged.'

On the bridge, the captain looked up from the holosphere

showing Ksal and nodded towards Tzashan, who loomed over him to see the display. 'I shall order the use of one of my S'Raph pilots,' the captain announced. 'They can switch to emergency manoeuvring on low power, if the phased radar array begins operating again and disables the skiffs' graviton drives. A S'Raph can withstand pressures that would kill a Ph'Sor crew.'

'The human subjects must not be harmed. They are not designed to withstand such acceleration and changes in inertia as you are,' Tzashan admonished. 'However, matters are in hand. The radar array will be disabled within the hour.'

A dark figure shuffled carefully through the crawlspace under the ground floor of the control tower, pressing tentatively upwards every few feet. After a few moments, a small access panel popped open and a hand slipped through to feel around for a set of cables that ran above it. Pulling himself up, the intruder found himself in the workings of an electronic cabinet of some kind. Working swiftly, even though there was no light at all to see by, he cut through several of the cables.

Pulling a small box from a pocket, the intruder quickly connected it to the severed cables and flicked a small switch on it. A tiny LED blinked softly, and the intruder slid back down through the panel, resisting the urge to laugh aloud.

He set the dial on an identical box, and pocketed it. 'For when the interference will be useful,' he murmured to himself.

Night, as is the way of things on most worlds, gave way to dawn, the sun painting the desertscape with broad strokes of burnished gold. Molten sunlight gave the sky a yellow hue, the farmhouse and its associated outbuildings silhouetted against a sheet of gold as a new but dusty Plymouth convertible bumped along the road that bordered the open ground before the house.

'Stop the car,' the Doctor snapped suddenly. Ace did so,

looking round to see him staring across at the farmhouse. 'Look,' he told the women, pointing with his umbrella. Benny followed the direction and was shocked to see two men lying slumped in front of an open door. 'There's a gate,' the Doctor added. 'Take us in.'

Ace guided the car through the wide wooden gate and down the track that led to the porch. Benny and the Doctor leapt out almost before she'd stopped the vehicle. The Doctor dropped to his knees to check the nearest man's pulse. 'This one's alive, at least.' He rolled the unconscious man over, looking, Benny was sure, for signs of injury.

Meanwhile, Ace had checked the second body. 'This one's alive as well, but I don't see any wounds.'

Benny stepped around them and pushed open the front door, which was ajar. The sight made her feel faintly sick. 'There are more in here – women and kids.'

'Wake them up,' the Doctor told her, gently slapping the face of his patient. 'It's half past cockcrow and there's work to be done.'

The dark oval that had such a grip on Jack's mind slowly resolved itself into the shade of the unlit bulb over the porch. Putting a trembling hand to the back of his neck, where an itch was persistently gnawing at him, he blinked away the fuzziness of sleep with a groan.

Although the dusty porch of his own house was totally familiar, he didn't recognize the short man who was peering into his bleary eyes from under the sagging brim of a white fedora. Two women were busy gently waking the rest of the family. 'If you were sleep-walking, it must have been quite a nightmare,' the man opined in a noticeable Scottish accent. He gestured towards the battered front door and some spent cartridge cases by way of explanation.

'You wouldn't know,' Jack muttered through a raw throat.

'Don't be too sure; I once had one where all my old foes chased me round a soap opera. You must have had a very busy night,' he went on without changing his cheerful tone.

Fighting against an onrush of bafflement, Jack stood, clutching at the doorpost as the world swam woozily. 'I wish I knew,' he groaned.

'I doubt that. Don't worry; the effect will soon wear off.'

'What effect?'

'Well, it's difficult to be sure, but at an educated guess I'd say you've all been hit with multiple blasts from a phased energy weapon on a heavy stun setting.'

'What the hell is a phased . . .?' Jack staggered into the house and collapsed into his favourite chair, his head pounding. The strange little man followed, the two women leading the others slowly into the lounge.

'Nothing to worry about: just something that hasn't been invented yet. You know, your nightmare could be a result of concussion,' the stranger theorized. 'Let's have a look.' Before Jack could gather his wits enough to protest, the man had pulled his head forward. A gentle pressure prompted a dull yet stinging pain in the side of his skull. 'Nothing serious. Odd, though: that wasn't where you put your hand when you woke up.'

'I've got a crick in my neck, that's all. Are you a doctor?'

'No, I'm *the* Doctor.'

Jack could have sworn he heard the capital letter. 'Who are you people?' he finally blurted. 'What are you doing on my farm?'

'My friend Benny over there,' the Doctor pointed at the woman with the jeans and brown hat, 'is an archaeologist. The young lady in the coat is Ace. We were on our way to visit an old pueblo when we saw you lying out there, so we came to help.'

Jack nodded understandingly. 'Mighty kind of you. Not many people would do that these days. Are you all archaeologists?'

'No we're . . .' the Doctor paused, as he moved over to check the rest of the family. 'Troubleshooters, if you like.'

'Troubleshooters?'

'Well, everywhere I go, I seem to find trouble,' the Doctor explained with a grin.

'And I shoot it,' Ace added, with a lopsided smile of her own.

Finney looked about the tabletop-flat environment as he went into the central radar room in the main building under the control tower. There were far more radar displays here, with desks around the edges of the room. The centre of the floorspace was taken up with a large tabletop relief map of the surrounding hundred square miles. A long wall of plexiglass, like a larger brother of the one in the launch control bunker, partitioned the radar consoles from the tabletop map.

Vincente was at the plexiglass wall, marking off distances with a pair of dividers. Finney absently thought that Vincente looked as if he hadn't slept since last night. With a guilty start, the colonel realized that it was probably true, and that Vincente had been working down here since his duty shift finished at midnight. Approaching, he motioned to Vincente to remain at ease.

'What have you got, Carl?' he asked, indicating the ink-marked transparent surface.

'I've been using the radar tapes from last night; running them through a test cycle. I think we can say for sure that one of the discs definitely came down east of here. Whether it soft-landed, or was totally blown away, I can't tell.'

'How specific can you be as to the location?'

'Not very – once it dropped below a hundred feet it was gone; the signal was none too clear for a while before that.' He put down the dividers and picked up a pointer, moving to the tabletop map. 'The best I can say for certain is that it came down in these foothills,' Vincente explained, pointing to the western edge of the bulge that marked the Sacramento Mountains.

'That's a certainty, what would be your best guess?' If nothing else, Finney valued the fact that his men were thinking individuals with ideas of their own. Another item on which he disagreed with the other military members of his family.

'That's a tough one,' Vincente smiled, 'but if pushed...' He moved the tip of the pointer in a circular motion over an area of ground between the two small settlements of High Rolls and Cloudcroft. 'Somewhere in here.'

Finney looked at the area in silence for a moment, wondering how reliable he could treat the guess. 'About twenty miles from here... All right, even if you're off a little we can still search outwards from High Rolls park –'

'An excellent idea,' Kreer's voice agreed from the doorway. The major walked around the table, his hands clasped in front of him, pursing his lips as he studied the map. 'Of course, if anyone saw it, they will have to be brought in for debriefing.'

'We'll give them the usual talk,' Finney acknowledged. 'If you're so keen to be involved with this operation, you can go and order a pair of Dragonflies to those co-ordinates. By the time we get a quarantine team together they might be able to direct us to the site-ref.'

'Consider it done,' Kreer said smoothly, turning away. He turned back. 'There is one other thing,' he began, with a honeyed tone of reluctance. 'Under regulations AFM 190-4, all physical recoveries pertaining to Unidentified Aerial Phenomena are to be forwarded to the S-Four area at Corman AFB as soon as possible. Such transfers are to be supervised by the ranking AFOSI representative.'

'I'm well aware of your section's claim on any skyfalls for Project Moondust,' Finney said testily. If truth be told, not only did he dislike Kreer but he would have given anything for a look at the disc that could run rings around his missiles so well. 'Let's just find out if the damn thing actually still exists first,' he recommended.

'Of course,' Kreer smiled, leaving the room.

Finney was anything but a stickler for discipline, though he was aware of the need for it, but something about Kreer's informality made him want to clap the AFOSI officer in irons.

* * *

'You saw two discs,' the Doctor was saying, 'and then what?'

'I don't remember.' Jack shrugged. He frowned in concentration, trying to recall what had happened and why he had been lying outside. Something rose up from the back of his mind, urging him that some things were best left forgotten. His mouth felt dry, and he seemed to have a sour taste in it.

'Is something wrong?'

'Just a rotten taste in my mouth.'

'Hmm, you should have remembered to bru– ' The Doctor looked at him sideways. 'Like lemonade with salt in it instead of sugar, by any chance?'

Jack thought for a moment. It did seem to have a bitter, lemon-ish tang. 'You could put it that way, I suppose.'

'I should have known,' the Doctor said, half to himself. He looked over at the others as if weighing something up. 'Rick, isn't it?' the Doctor asked the third man in the room. Rick nodded. 'The children will probably be tired and frightened, so I suggest you put them to bed. Once they're settled, take Donna and Mary into the kitchen and get something to eat.'

'Go ahead, Rick,' Jack nodded. He was puzzled and apprehensive, but the authority in the Doctor's tone was unmistakable.

'Ace, Benny, this might be important.' Ace remained by the door, to make sure they weren't disturbed, but Benny approached, glancing through the window as a helicopter clattered past somewhere in the middle-distance.

Jack began to wonder just what he had let himself in for by leaving himself alone in the room with these strangers. Nervously he looked around for his rifle, but Ace had carefully replaced it in the empty slot in the gun rack. 'All right,' the Doctor said in a friendly tone, 'turn your head to the side.' Jack did so, and noticed out of the corner of his eye that the Doctor was craning round to look at the back of his head.

A prod at the base of his neck produced an insistent itch.

The Doctor reappeared before him. 'Pull your shirt up,' he commanded.

Without really knowing why, Jack pulled the hem of his shirt up to his chest. To his surprise and astonishment, a red weal with a pinhead-sized spot of dried blood at the centre was plainly in evidence, about an inch about his navel. 'Tissue sampling,' the Doctor murmured. Nodding grimly to himself, he put his hands to Jack's temples. 'Listen to me,' he ordered. 'Concentrate, and listen to me.'

Suddenly powerless to do anything else, Jack met the Doctor's gaze, and found himself falling into infinity.

'It is night,' the Doctor told him. 'Your wife and brother think there is someone on the roof...'

To Jack's surprise, it was true.

Ace had seen the Doctor's hypnotic ability a number of times, and had to admit that it was a useful technique. Nevertheless, it still made her feel somewhat uncomfortable to see him use it on someone. She wouldn't dream of using violence to uncover a story from an innocent bystander, but she couldn't help feeling that there was something more honest about the more physical means of doing things than this raping of the soul, which could have dangerous and invisible side-effects.

Repressing a shudder, she watched from the doorway as the Doctor removed his hands from Jack's temples. 'Tell us as it happens.'

Jack's head lolled on his shoulders as if his neck was broken, occasionally raising itself jerkily as if on strings. His teeth were gritted and his lips drawn back from the gums with fear. 'Open the door,' he gasped hoarsely, looking over his shoulder sightlessly.

'Thank God,' he groaned, sagging in the chair with relief. 'Move it Rick – ' With a wide-eyed stare of horror, he looked down at his shoulder, then quickly up at a point above his face. 'Holy Christ,' he moaned, his fingers twitching spasmodically. 'Let me go!'

'What is it?' the Doctor hissed. 'What has a hold of you?'

'Some sort of shape ... Rick? Mary, where are ...'

'Describe the shape.'

'Small, grey ... I don't want to see! There's a door. Lights inside ... metal.' He snorted and gagged. 'What is that smell? Cleaning flui ... ammonia. More shapes pushing me ... I don't want to go to ... to ... It's a table. I'm on a table; my clothes, where? I can't move.' His voice began to rise. 'Something above me ... Oh shit, no! Needle, with machinery at the far end. It's longer than my hand! Digging into my stomach!' he screeched.

'Who? Who is doing this?'

'I can't! I mustn't see!'

'You must!'

'Not like us,' Jack gasped, through gritted teeth. 'Dead skin, but their eyes ... No! Mustn't see their black eyes,' he gasped painfully. 'Oh jeez, the eyes are pure black, and I ain't hypnotized any more, Doc,' he finished, drawing in shuddery breaths.

Aghast, Ace let out a breath she hadn't realized she'd been holding. The Doctor, his features a mask of concern, touched his finger to Jack's forehead. 'It's over. It's all over,' he murmured reassuringly. 'Now it's time to sleep. Sleep, Jack Siegel, sleep ...' Jack's face relaxed slowly and his head fell back onto the pillow. The Doctor stood up. 'He should sleep normally now.'

Ace felt a weight lifted from her shoulders now that Jack was sleeping normally. Benny looked a little uneasy but unimpressed. 'Hallucinations,' she suggested. 'An attack of night terrors?'

'I don't think so,' the Doctor disagreed. 'I think he just told us about a very real event that happened to him last night. I believe he was abducted by aliens who took tissue samples from him. The marks are still there.'

'What do we do now?' Ace asked, cutting straight to the quick.

'If they're only coming down at night, there's not a lot we can do at the moment.' He started towards the door. 'For now, we go and visit Benny's pueblo. Tonight we'll offer our services at Holloman, and see if we catch the culprits. Get the car started, Ace. I'll go and fill the others in on what's happened. Well, mostly, anyway . . .'

Chapter 5

The Plymouth convertible rumbled solidly along the dirt road, its huge silver grille remaining obstinately gleaming and chromed as vortices of dust trailed away from the impressive rear fins.

The wind curling around the gently curved windscreen gave the time travellers a much-needed respite from the dry heat. While Ace guided the car along the bumpy road into the foothills, the Doctor squinted suspiciously up at the sky. Benny reclined along the back seat, trying to keep her hat on her head where it belonged.

The countryside that they passed was something of a camouflage pattern, with a surprisingly large amount of green scattered around in the form of shrubs and bushes, though the beige of the desert remained predominant. Benny had half expected to feel like she was in a brick furnace, but there was a fresh smell to the air that was almost spicy. It almost took her mind off the parched earth, in fact.

'What the smeg is that?' Ace suddenly said, bringing Benny out of her reverie. She looked around and saw a faint haze in the air to the left. Though not exactly a column of smoke, it was nevertheless too localized and opaque to be a simple heat haze.

'Looks like the after-effects of a smoke column,' the Doctor answered, voicing Benny's suspicion.

'Could be. I assume you'll want to take a look.'

'Of course,' the Doctor answered, as if the question was totally ridiculous. 'It may be a crash of some kind; something may need help.'

'Right. You mean someone, don't you?'

'Do I?' He shrugged. 'Probably.'

The foothills rose and fell ahead of the car as Ace drove off the road and onto the gritty desert floor. The car bumped, and some metallic spangs started coming from somewhere underneath as small stones were bounced up by the wheels. 'They're not going to like this one little bit,' Ace muttered, wincing with each spanging noise.

'I told you, Ace; I don't want to know,' the Doctor reminded her.

The rough hills stared back silently.

Jagged mountains surrounded Corman AFB with outflung arms, leaving only a narrow gap through which a runway stretched out across the edge of a dry lake that gleamed whitely under the Nevada sun. Unlike the small town that was formed of Holloman's scattered buildings, the flat-topped complexes of Corman were all grafted onto the mountainsides at ground level; spy-planes, therefore, saw what they thought were natural outcrops.

Three long hangars stood out at the lake; white-roofed, they blended in with it from the air. A large tower-mounted parabolic dish, not unlike a small radio-telescope, stood incongruously at the north end of the complex.

A thickset bulldog of a man, Major-General Hugh Nyby sat with his back to the window overlooking the dish. The rest of the room, like the rest of the base, was painted a pastel blue. Tossing envelopes into his out-tray, he sorted through the day's influx of mail until he found the dispatch which he had been waiting for. His dark and slab-like hands opened the envelope with surprising precision to gain access to the photostat sheets within.

He had tried to tell himself that his interest in the officer whose records he had requested from Washington was merely a part of his general random sampling of loyalties. Senator Joe McCarthy had paved the way, and it was up to those like himself to heed the senator's warnings in order to protect the American way of life, he felt.

He wasn't sure what he had been expecting to find, but perhaps he had suspected there might be some inconsistency with the records in the base's files. It took only the briefest of glances, however, to see that this was not the case. The records gave a perfectly ordinary account of the service history of a mid-ranking officer. Wishing they had eased his discomfort, Nyby tossed the sheets aside.

The general knew, of course, what had sparked his concerns. Thirty years of service had granted him an instinct for spotting the waffle of military bureaucracy, though it also left him with an unwashed feeling every time he felt it necessary to challenge that bureaucracy. More specifically, as the commander of a research base he had seen enough oddly worded orders for black-budget programmes to know when something wasn't quite proper.

The orders that Major Kreer had presented upon his arrival at Corman back in May had had a vagueness about them that made Nyby's teeth itch. That had been bad enough, but when the equipment for Projects Snowbird and Moondust had begun to arrive, his base had started becoming ever more strange to him. And for when Snowbird itself had turned up...

If only Snowbird wasn't so important to the Pentagon, he thought, an investigation would quickly clear up the problem with Kreer – or prove his innocence and loyalty.

Kreer, and his staff...

Ace trotted on ahead of the Doctor and Benny with the first-aid case, kicking up little puffs of dust as she moved up the steep track from the car. Adrenalin preventing any sense of fatigue despite the heat of the day, she topped the rise and looked down towards the source of the faint cloud of haze.

She stopped in her tracks.

The Doctor and Benny arrived a few seconds later, Benny pausing to fan herself with her hat, and joined Ace in surveying the area before them.

Spread out below the soft sandstone cliff, a bone-dry

arroyo meandered across the desert, a few small shrubs growing in its basin. Bisecting the arroyo, a churned furrow of desert soil several yards wide speared towards the low cliff like an arrow, a scattering of different tones of dust and earth surrounding it like the foam of a ship's wake.

At the base of the cliff under their feet, shimmering in the murky and acrid haze rising from its smouldering hull, the source of the disturbance lay.

Tilted at almost forty-five degrees, half of it buried under a pile of dirt and smashed sandstone, a scarred and blackened disc of metal about thirty feet across was embedded in the desert floor. A miasma of tiny glittering pieces of wreckage surrounded it like a halo.

For a moment none of them could speak, until the Doctor pointed grimly downwards. 'Whoever or whatever they are,' he said in a businesslike tone, 'they may still need help.'

'They may just be about to get it – in spades,' Benny warned, pointing out a rising trail of dust from a distant road. Whatever the vehicles were, they were ignoring the turning in the road and making straight across country towards the disc.

'The helicopter we heard must have vectored them onto it,' Ace suggested.

'Never mind them,' the Doctor urged. 'Come on.' He began scrambling cautiously down a narrow mule-track that lined the face of the bluff.

Ace and Benny followed, sending small rocks tumbling down with trails of dust. The mule-track doubled back on itself a couple of times, and reached the ground some distance to one side of the disc, thus sparing them the worst of the rising heat. Ace and Benny still had to fan themselves with their hats, though the Doctor seemed characteristically unaffected.

A strange and acrid metallic scent choked the air as they approached the disc, and they could see that small fires were still burning in places among the blackened juniper bushes and buffalo grass. Fortunately the air was still, and the fires were dying rather than spreading.

The disc itself rippled and wavered in the heat, and hollow groans and popping sounds emanated from it. The Doctor stopped, taking a few steps back, and Benny soon discovered why. As she got within a few yards of the disc, the heat became so intense that she felt so sluggish she doubted she would be able to remain standing upright. Nausea washing over her in waves like those of the heat haze, she withdrew to where Ace stood with the Doctor. 'What the hell is it?' she gasped, the air thick yet seemingly drained of oxygen.

'Some sort of scout-ship by the look of it.'

'Amazing. You've been talking to Holmes and Watson again, haven't you? I'm not blind; I meant what species flies things like that?'

'Impossible to tell,' he said, ignoring her irritated sarcasm. 'That's a very generic design structure. If I could get a closer look ...'

'Why is it still so hot?' Ace broke in. 'If it came down last night, it should have cooled by now.'

'Its drive system may be still running. Since it obviously can't move, the energy is being radiated off as heat.' The Doctor gave the disc a quizzical look. 'It's obviously just a short-range scout, though. It can't be long before its fuel runs out.'

'Any danger of explosion?'

'I shouldn't think so. It must have been a lot hotter last night, so I would imagine it would have gone critical then if it was going to at all. Wouldn't you?'

'If you say so.'

The distant rumble of traffic had now grown louder and dust was beginning to fill the air to a great extent than the pot-pourri scent of grasses or the stench of burning. The trio started jogging away from the disc, but it was too late and the vehicles were upon them.

A jeep full of air police cut across their path, drawing to a halt in front of them. Even as the air police were setting foot on the ground, two trucks had passed by and drawn up before the disc. A boxy M59 APC rumbled past, churning up scorched earth as it took up position near the disc. Benny glared in open hostility at the air police as they approached. 'Are we under arrest?' she demanded.

'Not yet,' a voice announced behind them, and they turned to find a lieutenant approaching them from the M59. The name on his chest read 'E. Wood'. 'You will have to be debriefed on what you've witnessed here.' He looked at her suspiciously. 'You're not American?'

'Does it show?'

'Colonel Finney will want to question you. Sergeant, take these three back to Holloman, and keep them under guard until the colonel or Major Kreer can see them.'

In a drab ante-room decorated with aircraft-recognition charts and security posters, the Doctor checked his pocket-watch as several figures passed by on the other side of the frosted windows, then gave the wall-mounted payphone a thoughtful glance. Ace leaned at the side of the closed door, looking daggers at the backs of the two guards stationed outside and empathizing with Benny as the archaeologist paced irritably around the magazine-laden table. A movement drew Ace's attention, and she turned to see the Doctor move decisively towards the phone. 'Who are you thinking of calling?'

'Hmm?' He looked up from sorting through a variety of currencies. He seemed to have money for every occasion, from wooden groats to the occasional twenty-narg note. 'I thought it would be useful if we could get a friend to give us some references.'

'Wonderful idea,' Ace commented. 'This is a military base, with security. They're not going to let you just phone out.'

'We're allowed one phone call by law, or so I believe. Besides, I have a few tricks.' He transferred a few suitable coins to his hand and dumped the rest back into his pocket. 'So much for security,' he commented, tapping the padlock over the phone. Brandishing his alternative self's sonic screwdriver, recovered from a world in which Homo

Reptilicus had destroyed humanity, he triggered it at the lock. It dropped away from the phone, and the Doctor lifted the handset.

As he dialled, Benny threw Ace a questioning look. Ace could only wish she was able to answer.

The Doctor smiled relievedly, proving to Ace that the call had been answered. 'Ah, Allen; glad I caught you at home. It's the Doctor here – you remember, I helped out with all that trouble over at Santa Mira last year...?' There was a pause as he evidently listened to some response. 'Yes, well, I've had a face-lift or three...'

Stoker crouched amid the men sitting on the narrow benches of the three-ton truck, which had just passed through the set of windowed gatehouses that guarded the entrance to Holloman. Each of them had violet eyes peering out from under the helmet rims which hid their fringes of blond hair. 'You,' he began, speaking to the men on one side, 'will go to the nuclear storage bunker at the south end of the complex. The requisition papers you have been given will allow you to remove two warheads for transport. Load them onto this vehicle and then return to the administration block, where the rest of us will be waiting.'

'As you command,' they chorused. The truck slowed to a halt and the men on the other side opened the tailgate and climbed out.

Stoker jumped down after them and the truck moved away. They were left standing outside a simple prefabricated office structure of a dusty sandstone colour. 'The witnesses to the crash will be debriefed in the main briefing room. You all have your neural suppressors?'

The men nodded.

'Set them on maximum. The witnesses must have no memories that may provide incriminating evidence of our activities on this planet. A sustained treatment of three seconds will be sufficient to wipe the past day's memories. If they resist, use disruptors – on light stun only.'

* * *

John C. Finney was more tired than he could ever remember. It had been a long night with several airspace violation alerts and now, when he needed sleep more than anything, the local authorities were on to him constantly, demanding to know what had crashed near High Rolls. At the moment, he couldn't care less if the entire Red Army came marching down the street, so long as they brought a bed with them.

Sergeant Montoya popped his head round the door as Finney finally managed to spare some time for a strong coffee. 'Excuse me, sir,' he began deferentially.

'What is it, Sergeant?'

'The locals from the High Rolls area are all in the main drill hall, but we've got three non-American civilians who were at the crash site itself. They're under guard in the visitors' waiting room. Shall I bring them in?'

Before Finney could react, the telephone rang. 'Finney, Project Javelin.' His lined face visibly paled. 'Yes sir, that is correct...' His eyes widened. 'Yes sir, I understand.' He put the phone down, forgetting that the sergeant was even there.

'Shall I send the civilians in?' Montoya reminded him after a moment.

'No,' Finney said grimly. 'I'll go out to them. I want to get away from this damn phone for a while,' he added with feeling.

A number of farmers lounged in folding chairs around the beige briefing room, looking uncomfortable and concerned. Jack Siegel didn't appreciate the nervousness that had been inflicted on his family so soon after they had been subjected to the previous night's terror. He knew that the air force boys were only doing their job, but keeping them locked up here wasn't right.

He had been letting his anger simmer and stew until it reached the point when, as Stoker opened the door, it boiled over. Shoving him aside, Siegel burst from the room, determined to find the base commander. Several other men were outside, all with strange weapons in their hands.

Something flitted into Jack's mind from the previous night. They held the same weapons as . . . as whatever it was had held. Screeching with anger and fear, he thrust them aside before they could aim properly, and ran for the main door.

He burst free just as the stun beam hit him.

He might have been consoled to know that several puzzled air policemen witnessed this, and ran to see what the commotion was.

The time-travellers looked up as alarm bells started ringing on the other side of the olive drab wall. An officer rushed up to the two guards at the door, and pushed them on ahead of him. 'Curious,' the Doctor commented.

'They must have something more important to deal with,' Ace pondered aloud. 'I think I'll take a little look around.'

'There'll be people around,' the Doctor warned.

'They seem to be occupied. I've been on enough military bases to know how to keep out of sight.' She smiled crookedly. 'Or to act as if I own the place.' She slipped out of the door.

'Very funny,' the Doctor muttered.

Everyone seemed to be running towards the prefabricated building outside, so Ace felt it was logical to blend in with the crowd. She was nearly run over by a truck which screeched to a halt in front of the door. Two large crates were just visible in the back of it.

Several bodies were sprawled in the dust and, as Ace watched, a harsh whine accompanied the collapse of the remaining men. Beyond the prone bodies, more whines came from within the doors. Dropping behind a jeep in the row of parked vehicles before the doors, Ace checked the charge remaining in her blaster. She couldn't let these shootings go without at least some attempt to stop the criminals. The shot men were owed that at least.

She noticed a body lying in the floor of the jeep, and stretched out a hand to feel for a pulse. There was one, though it was weak. 'Set on stun again.'

The Doctor looked around with a calculating expression as Finney entered the waiting area with a faint limp, while Montoya took up station outside. 'Where are the guards?' Finney demanded.

'I don't know, sir. I left them here with strict orders...'

'An officer took them away when the alarms started ringing,' the Doctor interrupted helpfully.

'Someone'll answer for that,' Finney growled. 'Thank you, Mister...'

'Doctor. Doctor John Smith.'

'Yeah, right,' Finney snorted. John Smith indeed... It was such a cliché.

'I've been thinking of changing it,' the Doctor went on breezily. 'Have we met before?' he asked, looking Finney up and down. 'I'm sure we have.'

'Not that I'm aware of,' Finney answered, diplomatically keeping to himself the thought that he would certainly have remembered this strange little man.

'I could have sworn... Perhaps I just mistook me for someone else. I'm sure it'll come back to me.' The Doctor smiled winningly.

'Right,' Finney drawled uneasily. 'Where is the third one, the other woman?'

'Search me,' Benny told him.

'Why have you shut us in here, Colonel...?' the Doctor asked.

'Colonel Finney, in charge of Project Javelin. We believe you may have stumbled across some... wreckage that relates to our work. As you are, shall we say, visitors to our country, we're naturally concerned about your views on this matter.'

'Well, as I said, I'm the Doctor; this is my friend Benny – '

'Professor Summerfield to you.'

'And that wreckage certainly has nothing to do with your Atlas missile tests.'

Finney hastily suppressed an instinctive urge to step backwards. 'How could you know about Project Javelin?'

'Well, we saw the test yesterday, and what happened to it.'

'So I've been told. It's been an unusual week – our test is disrupted by something unknown, which later crashes; and, as if that wasn't enough, I've been ordered by the Pentagon, at the behest of the CIA, to release you and let you go about your business!' He knew it was wrong, but somehow couldn't keep the distaste out of his voice when he thought of the intelligence services poking their noses into his base.

'Do you dislike taking orders so much that getting some angers you like that?' Benny asked pointedly.

Finney turned on her coldly. 'Didn't you see all of yesterday's show? After downing the Atlas, our unknown friend then downed an F-86; sent it into a flat spin. We'll be damned lucky if we can find enough pieces of the pilot to hold a decent funeral. There was a survivor, but he's under sedation ready for a Section 8 discharge from the service on psychological grounds, due to shock. And now I have to let three CIA spooks come in and take over the investigation.'

'Sorry,' Benny said quietly.

'We truly are sorry about the death of your pilot,' the Doctor told Finney. 'And you're right, we didn't see that.' Finney nodded, a little mollified, as the Doctor continued: 'But the reason Allen suggested that you let us go is because he knows we can help you. My assistant and I helped him out last year in California, when a town was almost taken over by . . . illegal aliens.'

'Helped him out? But you are CIA?'

'It's not unknown,' the Doctor said dryly, with a heavenward glance. 'I have Majestic clearance, but really I'm a freelance. I'll help anyone who needs it.'

Finney was almost convinced, but was nowhere near happy with the situation. 'How could you help us?'

'By identifying the origin of that disc, for a start.'

'I doubt even the CIA could manage that,' Finney said slyly. 'There is a possibility that it may originate from another world.'

'You accept that?' the Doctor asked, throwing him a sidelong look.

Something about his manner seemed vaguely familiar, and Finney wondered if perhaps they really had met at some point. Ignoring the idea, he nodded. 'Our special scientific adviser theorized that months ago, when these things started invading our airspace.'

'Scientific adviser?' the Doctor asked, eyes wide. 'He's not a tall, white-haired –'

'Major Kreer of the AFOSI is neither particularly tall nor white-haired.'

'Thank goodness for that,' the Doctor muttered, baffling Finney. 'Did you say Kreer?'

'Yes. Do you know him?'

'Never heard of him. Is there any chance we could discuss this with him?'

'I'm afraid not. He is ... indisposed.' He could hardly admit to these two that he didn't know where his own adviser was.

'In that case, why don't we go and carry on outside, and your Major Kreer can investigate from the inside.'

That was an odd choice of words, Finney thought. He wondered if he could really trust the CIA to do what was best for his base. 'I've a better idea. You can go and get something to eat in the mess. This evening, when the disc is cool, you can accompany some of my staff to it. The escort will be for your own security, of course, in the interests of co-operation.' That way we can keep an eye on you, he thought, while still exploiting any good you might do.

Cautiously peering around the bonnet, Ace saw several men climb into the truck and slam the tailgate closed. Two of them jogged forward to the cab, the leader a baby-faced blond with a chill look. Ace stepped out around the

73

front of the jeep, blaster levelled squarely at the nearest man. 'Hold it, you,' she called.

The two men halted and looked around with surprised expressions. Immediately upon seeing Ace, they raised their weapons. Ace hurled herself back behind the jeep as a strange distortion caused the muzzles to waver with a whine. It was certainly no flash of combustible materials. The sudden realization took hold of her with a start; those were disruptor discharges.

Focusing her surprise into more useful anger, she swung herself around the front of the jeep and squeezed off a couple of shots as the men bolted for the cab. Her first shot caught one in the back, blasting him away from the cab. The second shot blew the wing mirror off as the baby-faced one vanished inside. The rearmost men at the back of the truck leaned out, and the whine of disruptor-fire overlaid the truck's throaty roar as it pulled away from the building.

Ace loosed off more shots at the rear of the truck, the blazing energy bolts sending sprays of sparks from the tailgate. Rapidly obscured by a rising cloud of dust, the truck roared off into the distance. Not interesting in wasting her power-pack's energy by firing blind, but equally unwilling to countenance the idea of letting them get away, Ace looked around for some way to get another chance to deal with them.

The jeep she had sheltered behind had a blown-out tyre, but an idling motorcycle lay beside its stunned rider a few yards away. Ace grinned wolfishly and holstered her blaster. The Doctor wasn't going to stop her riding one of these things like he had back in Perivale.

Lifting the dusty machine from its side, she swung a leg over and twisted the throttle with relish. 'Steve McQueen eat your heart out,' she muttered, gunning the engine. Kicking up a spreading cloud of dust, Ace hurtled off in pursuit.

It was a matter of moments to catch up with the truck, which began weaving from side to side before crashing through one of the flimsy plasterboard gatehouses.

Between the roar of the engines and the rush of blood in her ears, Ace never heard the Doctor and Benny's yells as they ran out into the dusty road behind her.

She had occasionally borrowed Midge's bike when she was just a teenager, more to spite her mother than anything else, and had subsequently ridden similar hoverskimmers on various planets. Neither Perivale tarmac nor future air, however, had prepared her for the uneven road she now hurtled down. The plexiglass windshield did little to keep the dust and grit out of her face, and she rode with her eyes screwed up against the grainy onslaught. She clenched her teeth as her stomach was left behind on several bumps and sharp turns once her quarry had turned onto a churned desert track.

The truck continued to weave, throwing up more dust in her face. Ace was finding it difficult enough to keep the machine going in a straight line, and she too was soon weaving unintentionally across the road. This was fortuitous, as the now all too familiar disruptor whine squealed out ineffectually.

Somewhat shakily, and as reluctant to crash the bike as to stop and let her quarry escape, Ace drew her blaster. She leaned it on the right handgrip, to have a chance of being able to work on keeping the bike steady. She took an experimental pot-shot at the weaving truck, which blew a scorched hole in its tarpaulin cover.

A volley of disruptor shots swept across her path, creating little vortices in the blown dust.

Ahead, in the driver's seat of the truck, a sergeant floored the accelerator. A curved silver surface gleamed in a hollow a short distance ahead. 'Did any of the base personnel see you, sir?' he asked Stoker.

'Only the ones inside the briefing room. They've been given memory wipes as well.' The two guards he had posted at the ship were alert, he noted with a sense of pride. He could see them take up firing stances among the rocks that masked the ship.

The truck shook again as a flash lit up the rear-view

mirror, and a cry from behind rapidly faded. Glancing out of the door window, Stoker saw one of his men roll to a halt in the dirt, almost run over by the motorcycle. Gritting his teeth, Stoker felt a part of himself die with his man.

Forcing himself to pay attention to the road in front, he saw the guards fire on his pursuer mere instants before the truck skidded to a halt in a cloud of dust.

Kicking the door open, Stoker kept glancing back towards the motorcycle as the dust cleared. To his satisfaction, its position was marked by another cloud of dust, its twisted wheels barely visible lying on the ground. Dashing to the rear of the truck, Stoker opened the tailgate even as two of his men clambered out, carrying one of the crates between them.

Ushering his men to take the crates into the disc, Stoker watched for any sign of movement from his erstwhile pursuer. Vaguely relieved that there was none, he climbed in after his men, and the silver wall of the hull flowed closed.

Chapter 6

Benny kept a hand clamped down on her hat as the Doctor, thin-lipped and grim, drove manically along the desert track, the Plymouth's bodywork dented and scratched by stones kicked up by the wheels. Squinting against the baleful glare of the low sun, Benny could feel her heart beat faster in its desperation to know what had happened to Ace. She tried to tell herself that it would be best to know, and promised herself that heads would roll if Ace was... Well, she didn't even want to think of that.

Up ahead, a throbbing hum presaged the lift-off of a silver disc, which shimmered and vanished as it rose and banked westwards.

Amidst the dust stirred by the disc, a twisted mass of metal lay beside a motionless figure slumped in the dust. The Doctor stopped the car and leapt out. Benny followed anxiously.

In the middle of a patch of churned ground, Ace lay sprawled a few feet from the overturned motorcycle, a large bruise forming on her cheek and blood oozing from several small cuts. The Doctor pulled the curved part of the handle away from the stem of his umbrella and removed the sphere that punctuated its question-mark shape. Undoing a small cap on the red globe, he waved it under Ace's nose. Benny's nerves calmed themselves as Ace coughed, waving away the phial as she struggled to rise. She winced as she touched her temple gingerly, almost immediately falling back to her knees and retching loudly. 'Shades!' she muttered thickly. 'I hate disruptor stuns.' She stood a little more steadily, spitting out a mouthful of dirt as she looked towards the abandoned truck. 'They got away, obviously.'

'Didn't they teach you about plans and tactics in the military?' Benny sighed, lifting the first-aid kit from the car.

'You must be joking! Spacefleet weren't *that* concerned about the mere Irregular Auxies.'

'That figures,' Benny agreed wryly. She sprayed some antiseptic on Ace's cuts and then waited as Ace attached healing patches to them, using the car's wing mirror for accuracy. The truth was, though Benny was reluctant to admit it to herself except on occasions like this, that the Doctor and Ace were the only family she knew now. She had already lost both her parents to raw hostility, and was beginning to realize of late that she couldn't face losing either of them the same way. With ordinary people that wouldn't have made much difference, but considering the way Ace grabbed trouble by the throat it probably wouldn't be long before she gave herself an ulcer. If her heart didn't give up before that, strained by its innumerable leaps into her throat, she added mentally. 'Come on,' she said to her – almost – adopted kid sister, 'the Doctor seems to have found something interesting.'

Together they strolled – or at least Benny strolled, while Ace limped – to join the Doctor at the damaged truck. The Time Lord was waving his pocket radiation probe around the floor, and it crackled like hot fat on a stove. 'So they were nukes then?' Ace thought aloud.

'Yes,' the Doctor agreed with a frown of distaste. 'Probably simple medium-yield warheads and not hydrogen bombs, but bad enough.' He jumped down from the truck. 'The question is, what do they want them for?'

'Blackmail?' Benny suggested.

'Blowing up Fort Knox,' Ace put in.

'It can hardly be anything so obvious, simple or mundane. Look at it this way,' he added, pointing at Ace. 'You were shot with a disruptor on medium stun, and you,' he turned to Benny, 'saw the ship that took off. With technology that far above current terrestrial developments, they could empty Fort Knox, destroy the White House, conquer any and every country they chose. But for some reason they feel they need inferior human technology...'

'Fuel for their ships?' Ace hazarded.

'They'd have brought a supply with them, surely?' Benny pointed out.

'Yes,' the Doctor agreed absently. 'Something doesn't add up here.' He snapped the radiation probe closed with a sigh, and jammed it back in his pocket. 'There's something not quite right about any of this.'

'What now?' Ace asked. Several jeeps were heading towards them and a helicopter buzzed overhead.

'Colonel Finney has offered us a place to wait, and an escort to the crash site,' the Doctor answered, 'and I think we should accept. Not only do I need a closer look at the disc if I'm to find out what we're up against, but...'

'But?'

'But it's also a valuable piece of equipment which, with any luck, they'll want back.'

Chapter 7

'Take us to Corman,' Kreer ordered smoothly as Stoker secured the two casings for flight.

'As you command, sir,' Xeno responded from the central station of the circular flight deck. In the main holosphere, the desert fell away, blurring as the skiff accelerated.

'You were almost late,' Kreer chided as Stoker came to stand beside him. Kreer seethed inwardly at Stoker. What was the point of planning the operation to the second if you were unpunctual? 'Was there any difficulty?' Kreer asked irritably.

Stoker shrugged. 'The girl who accompanies the Doctor was there. She tried to stop us.'

'So he is here. I knew it! I told you he'd show up when his favourite planet came under threat. You destroyed her, of course?' Kreer went on warningly.

'Possibly. We couldn't stop to check. She was certainly out of the action, though.'

'I suppose that will have to do,' Kreer mused with displeasure.

'We are approaching Corman, sir,' Xeno announced.

'Reduce power. Take us in.'

The artificial mountain root that was Corman AFB echoed to warning bells that sent airmen scurrying out into the circular area enclosed by foothills. No aircraft was approaching through the narrow gap that allowed the end of the runway in from the dry lake. Instead, a silver disc lowered itself onto the helipad opposite the parabolic dish.

Even as the electric hum that surrounded it began to fade, the metal of its hatchway flowed back into the hull and Kreer and Stoker hopped out. An overall-clad groundcrew approached the skiff with low trolleys. 'I'll arm the warheads tonight,' Kreer announced. 'Meanwhile, your men can store them in hangar 18 along with Snowbird here.' He patted the hull of the skiff as he finished.

'Your strategy is well prepared,' Stoker acknowledged.

'Of course,' Kreer said with proud dismissiveness, as if he had been praised by a child for completing the simplest task that seemed magical to a youngster. 'Let's just say that isn't the first time I've hijacked something. Although at least this time I have a more suitable band of followers,' he added in satisfaction, indicating a group of men – in Air Force uniforms and dark blue berets – who were forming up before the ship.

From a nearby concrete root, a small tractor was towing a large Sikorsky S-58 transport helicopter. 'We'll need the other skiff recovered before the authorities can examine it too closely. Finney has it under guard already, but the drive is still operating so it will not be cool enough to approach for a couple of hours yet. Take Dr Marlowe in the helicopter – it's slower, but you can't show up in another identical ship. You should arrive about midnight.'

'It would make good sense to fly it out before dawn.'

'You'd have to dismantle it first,' Kreer said.

'Leave that to me. If you keep the runway clear for morning, I'll have the skiff split into its separate sections and flown here in a transport.'

'Excellent, Captain Stoker,' Kreer agreed with a faintly mocking smile. 'By the way,' he drew out a manila envelope from an inside pocket, 'Personnel asked for this to be passed on to you.' He handed it to Stoker.

'Thank you,' Stoker acknowledged with a baffled frown. 'I'm sure it's nothing important.' He walked off towards the helicopter.

'Oh, but it is,' Kreer murmured to himself. 'Divide and conquer,' he reminded himself.

Ace whistled a faint tune as she toyed with the unappetizing food in the memento-decorated officer's mess at Holloman. 'We could pop back to the TARDIS and pick up some stuff from my room,' she suggested between mouthfuls.

'Whoever has been abducting those people has brought enough dangerous anachronisms to this area,' the Doctor said beside her. 'We don't want to compound the problem, do we?'

Ace didn't mind; she was used to this reaction from him by now. Being prepared was something else she understood, though. 'Who could it be?'

'Akkers?' Benny suggested.

'Tennis-playing blancmanges?'

'How should I know?' the Doctor grumbled. 'I thought you said one fell from the truck.'

'One did. I don't know where the body went. As for how should you know . . .' Ace shrugged. 'You always do.'

His dark skin and temperament giving him the carefully cultivated image of a human thundercloud, Nyby liked to tour his mountain-encircled base once in a while, in the firm conviction that fear of such unexpected inspections would encourage his men to stay on their toes.

He liked to find them hard at work when on duty, or asleep when not. He was willing to tolerate the fact that the men played healthy, exciting, American sports like baseball and football when off-duty, though he accepted it only as a poor second best to resting or preparing for their next shift. Sleep was fine as far as he was concerned, as it meant they would stay alert when on duty.

He felt honoured that his men now knew him well enough to break up conversations when he approached. He had nothing against talk *per se*, of course, provided it wasn't about sensitive subjects. Cosy family chats were, after all, a cornerstone of his beloved society, and he liked his men to feel that they were all part of one big happy family. Three was a crowd, however, and he didn't like seeing crowds even that small, unless it was as part of a platoon or work squad. He could never be certain what such a group might be talking about, or planning, or even ... conspiring. He knew that Communists were organized in cells, and that was just another name for groups, wasn't it? That sort of thing was un-American, and to be guarded against.

Nyby therefore was on guard constantly. He watched for gatherings of men and discussions in private. He had decreed long ago that the base was one big family who held no secrets from each other – except official ones of his own – and that there should, therefore, be no private discussions, which were the preserve of secretive Communist cells.

There were those men under Nyby's command who said that the general was a paranoid schizophrenic with a Napoleon complex, who had been brain-damaged by the head-wound he got in England during the second world war. There were also those men under his command who hadn't suffered unfortunate 'training accidents' before being put on permanent punishment detail.

When Nyby arrived at the entrance to S-Four, a huge concrete door set into the rise on which the large dish was mounted, he was shocked – if unsurprised – to see Major Kreer and Captain Stoker in muted conversation with Dr Marlowe; Nyby having been stuck with the bespectacled scientist as head of Project Snowbird.

Before Nyby came close enough to hear their words, Kreer waved the other away towards the S-58 as he moved over. Nyby added another black mark to Kreer's roster for when the project was over. 'General,' Kreer greeted him.

'Busy, Major?'

'Some new equipment has arrived. I'm having it stored safely.'

'I'm glad to hear that,' Nyby said, looking into the dim hangar beyond with a sense of unease. The Pentagon had sent some strange things along to his base along with Kreer, and Nyby sometimes wondered if there weren't some suspect characters among the top brass as well. In particular, he didn't like being given the responsibility of looking after *it*. Or perhaps he should say him, though it was difficult to tell. Kreer was the focus of all these irregularities, however, and so Nyby invariably focused his ire on him. 'Was this authorized?'

'Of course,' Kreer answered smugly. 'I have complete discretion to procure equipment. The papers are all signed and sealed.' Nyby didn't doubt that for a minute, but Kreer's posting orders were all in order as well and he didn't think much of them either.

'That's fine, I'm sure. It's just that I sometimes wonder if you and *it* have America's interests at heart the way I do.'

'How can you doubt that?' Kreer tutted softly. 'Didn't President Eisenhower himself give you the orders when he came to welcome EBE-1 to America?'

'Yes, of course,' Nyby rumbled happily, remembering with pride. Nyby himself meeting the legendary Ike. He had been... It was odd, but he couldn't quite recall exactly what had happened.

'Excellent,' Kreer said in an approving tone that made Nyby furrow his brow in thought.

Leaving Marlowe in the rear compartment, Stoker pulled himself into the empty co-pilot's seat as the ground fell away beneath the helicopter.

The pilot was listening to Chuck Berry over a commercial radio frequency. Stoker considered ordering him to switch it off, but decided against it. Nyby would have censured the pilot for listening to subversive music, Stoker thought, probably believing that only the likes of Sinatra and Crosby were worthy American entertainers. He doubted that it would make any difference if Nyby knew that this type of music was considered subversive in the Communist bloc as well.

Stoker suspected that too many restrictions would harm

morale. He let the pilot have his fun, since he sensed the small pleasure afforded would make him more relaxed and happier, and therefore more efficient. Discipline had its place, but the carrot was as important as the stick it was tied to.

Settled in, Stoker drew out the envelope which Kreer had given him before departure. Inside was a four-by-six monochrome photograph of a group of smiling men in uniform. Stoker recognized only one of them.

Impossible though it seemed, it was himself.

He stared at the picture, wishing that one of the frozen grey faces could begin speaking and tell him what he was doing among them several months before he first came to the planet Earth.

Chapter 8

Ace had been looking forward to repaying some of the bumps she had already received, and had been grimly eager when the Doctor announced that he had a plan of action. Unfortunately, this had consisted solely of letting the Hispanic Sergeant Montoya drive them that evening to the bluff where the disc had crashed.

The Doctor, Ace and Bernice walked through the twilit activity with equally false calm. Small groups of overalled soldiers were trotting around the perimeter and roughly pounding fence-posts into the ground, while another team followed in their wake with huge rolls of barbed wire. Under the lee of the weathered bluff, men were erecting a marquee-sized camouflage tarpaulin over the disc. Drably painted trucks and jeeps were spaced at irregular intervals, some of whose engines were still idling to provide start-up power for the several generators that were connected to arc lamps set up under the tarpaulin.

The crunch of footsteps and the metallic rattle of equipment was an unending accompaniment to the time-travellers' passage through the crash site. Occasionally Ace or Benny would have to cover their mouth and nose with a handkerchief to protect against the dust that was filling the air.

Abruptly, as they rounded the front of the M59 that was serving as a field command post, the Doctor waved them to a halt. He silently pointed out a bus with blacked-out windows, which was disgorging men and women in civilian dress. The newcomers were invariably doing almost comical double-takes at their first sight of the disc.

A pair of officers were greeting them as they emerged, gesturing towards the disc now and again. 'Scientists,' the Doctor whispered. 'Let's go and see how wrong they get things, shall we?'

Marion Davison stepped off the bus and froze, as shocked as if she had just seen Eisenhower kiss Nikita Khrushchev. The sounds of hurried activity all around were blocked out by her own private silence, which seemed to emanate from the disc.

Captain Vincente waved her aside with a disgruntled expression that reminded Davison that there were others waiting to disembark behind her. She stepped away from the bus, her line of sight a leash that tied her to the gleaming disc which was swimming with liquid gold reflections from the arc lamps.

The disc was incredible, projecting from the shattered earth like a frozen bead of quicksilver. Davison had never seen its like, and was sure that no one else had either. She wasn't old enough to remember Orson Welles' *War of the Worlds* radio broadcast of some twenty-odd years earlier, but had heard a rerun as part of a documentary on the panic it had caused. She had listened to that as an excited twelve-year-old, blissfully unaware of the chaos that the show had created in some towns. She had heard the documentary that followed with a great deal of shock, scarcely believing how anyone could have given any credence to such a fanciful broadcast.

Yet here she was, she told herself, facing a genuine alien artifact, and possibly one even more fanciful than those of Wells and Welles. The sight of the disc made her think twice about her idea of announcing its discovery to the press. If one Victorian drama could cause such panic then the revelation of the existence of a truly alien craft was one she quite frankly wasn't willing to take the responsibility for.

Her opposite numbers in the civilian press wouldn't see it that way, of course. They would advise a more courageous course of 'publish and be damned', doubtless complaining about Government cover-ups. She wondered if this was how Finney and Kreer would come to their decisions, or whether they really did have ulterior motives. She shrugged the thought away; Finney wasn't a bad man, she thought, and would probably share her view. Kreer though...

As soon as Montoya looked away, the trio melted into the darkness. Slipping behind a pile of crates, they conveniently paused to rest just within earshot of several civilians. 'It couldn't be Russian,' one of them was saying, and Benny rolled her eyes at his lack of imagination.

'Absolutely impossible,' a German-accented voice replied. 'The metal is so tough we can't cut through it, even with oxy-acetylene, diamond or borazon. Going by the hatch rim, though, it must be incredibly thin and flexible.'

'Hatch rim?' Benny mouthed silently, her interest piqued.

'It might have blown out on impact,' the Doctor murmured in a low voice. 'Or was opened from the inside...'

'If we can find that, we can get in for a look,' Benny suggested.

'Right. You carry on in this direction, and I'll go back the way we came. If we circumnavigate the disc we're bound to come across the hatch at some point.'

'I'll stay here and listen out for anything this bunch come up with,' Ace added. Nodding silently, the Doctor and Benny slipped off into the night and left Ace sitting on the crates.

The pattern of approaching lights attracted Ace's attention a moment before the sound of the rotor blades reached her. Looking up, she saw a dark mass blotting out the stars as it overflew the crash site and neared the ground a couple of hundred yards away. Checking that no one was looking her way, she slipped off in the direction of the landing helicopter.

* * *

Stoker hopped from the helicopter with practised ease and started off towards the activity under the arc lamps. He had neither eaten nor slept in over forty-eight hours, but showed no signs of weariness. He was concerned, however, about the photograph. He knew he hadn't been on Earth at the time it was taken, but that wasn't what was bothering him.

He had wondered where he had been when the picture was taken, and had been trying to remember just that. It was a natural progression; little incidents tended to provoke memories of one kind or another, though most were things of which one took no notice. He had been forced to take notice, however, when he realized that he could not recall where he had been six months ago – not even which planet he had been on.

It had probably just been somewhere very boring, he told himself in an effort to dispel his unease, and not like Earth. Then again, he thought, he wasn't particularly excited by landing on Earth either. He tried to recall how he felt immediately before coming to Earth, and stopped in his tracks. He couldn't even remember that. It was all very odd, he thought, but nothing that concentration couldn't help. One thing he did remember was that there were people waiting at the disc, so he collected his thoughts in a more professional manner and moved onwards.

The here and the now were all that mattered.

Following the edge of the hull, the Doctor touched it tentatively. Although the disc had now cooled off, the surface still felt warmer than metal should, even accounting for re-entry and the afternoon heat. Pausing briefly, he leaned in closer to the surface and squinted at it. It was silvery enough, but had the glossy sheen of a thin crystalline or ceramic layer. 'Pure terullian.' He continued on his way lest the attention he was giving the hull should become suspicious.

In a matter of moments he came to the gaping hatch. There was no sign of strain on the metal around it, simply a smooth round opening in the hull. Peering closely at the edge, the Doctor couldn't find any sign of a rim or slot for a retracted hatch. His attention was suddenly drawn, however, to a scarlet ridge about the size of his hand which bulged from the hull like clotted blood above a deep cut. It was a circle, inside which were three short horizontal lines, one above the other. A slightly longer line stretched up from the centre, and was topped with an upward-pointing chevron. 'Oh no,' he muttered grimly.

'Well?' Benny asked, appearing out of the darkness.

'It's a scout-ship. Wait here.' He stepped into the hatchway.

Davison was so taken with the unearthly beauty of the flimsy yet strong material of the disc's construction that she had all but forgotten her notebook, preferring to run her hands over the smooth onyx surfaces that surrounded a crystal column as thick as a tree-trunk. 'Whoever built this were artisans, not monsters,' she said to herself, ignoring the half-dozen or so scientists in the chamber.

'They might even have been both, you know,' a stranger's voice answered, causing her to start violently, not having realized that she had spoken aloud. Turning to the hatchway, Davison saw a short man in a pale suit half a size too big for him, who came over to join her. 'It's all pretty standard engineering, of course,' the strange little man added in a sharp Scottish accent.

'Yes. Though how they flew it without controls...' Davison found herself wondering. 'Mental power, perhaps. I remember a film once, where –'

'Of course there are controls,' the little man said crossly, tapping the nearest onyx panel. 'You can't see them because the power's dead, so there's no energy being routed through the optical processors to configure the crystal membranes formed into this software-defined console.'

Davison was not the sort of woman to relish pulling rank, but this man's casuality bordered on the treasonous, even by her liberal standards. And as for the gibberish he was speaking... 'Is that your considered opinion?' she demanded pointedly, hoping she had the right tone of command.

'The rank and file getting nervous about outside interference, eh?' The stranger smiled engagingly, and Davison returned the expression half-heartedly.

This man was certainly sure of himself, Davison thought, but he was an outsider. A spy? Davison doubted it somehow, though such a thing would be refreshingly normal, feeling that a spy would at least try to blend in with the crowd a little more. A thought struck her, reminding her of Finney's announcement that afternoon. 'Are you the guy called the Doctor?'

'Among other things, I suppose. And you are Major...?'

'Marion Davison. So you're the spook in our midst?'

'Why does everyone here assume that?' the Doctor asked exasperatedly.

'You're either that or the worst agent on the GRU's books. Who else would have known about Kreer? I imagine the CIA sends delegates to the monthly IPU conferences that he attends.'

'Colonel Finney mentioned that he was your scientific adviser.' The Doctor trailed off, looking around. 'In which case why isn't he here? To him, this ship should be like Tutankhamun's tomb was to Howard Carter.'

'He divides his time between Holloman and Corman AFB in Nevada. He's in charge of Project Snowbird up there.'

'What's Snowbird?'

'How the hell should I know?' Davison's suspicions began to resurface. 'Classified information,' she added dryly.

'Yes, it doesn't matter. How very interesting, though.'

'What is?' Davison asked cautiously.

'I was just wondering what product of a mere level five civilization could possibly interest one of your scientists more than the arrival of an alien craft made of pure terullian and run on a gravity drive powered by a catalytic matter-antimatter intermix.'

Davison looked blankly at him, not following a single word of it. To one side, the scientists were shaking their heads in pitying gestures. 'Too much sun,' one of them whispered a little too loudly.

It seemed to Davison, however, that the Doctor knew something about the ship – he was just too matter-of-fact about the whole thing to be making it up. But, she told herself, surely that was impossible. 'This has obviously been an unmanned ship. That makes it less important in strategic – '

'Nonsense and you know it!'

'Have you ever heard of a manned missile?'

'There was a manned version of the V1, and the Japanese "Baka" – '

'Then what happened to the crew of this one?' Davison asked, a chill creeping up her spine as the shadowy areas at the edge of her vision seemed to draw closer.

'We're standing on them,' the Doctor told her. Davison looked down in horror, and saw a bipedal-shaped ashy scorch-mark on the deck plates. Several other burnt patches were nearby. 'It's funny though; they have transmat technology, so why didn't they just beam out?'

By now the scientists had gone back out to report to their superiors, with the exception of the German-accented one. 'This "transmat"; it is, I imagine, an audio-vibratory physio-molecular transport device of some kind?'

'You mean – ' Davison suggested.

'Yes, Major, it's something we ourselves have been working on for quite some time.'

'Need to know basis, Doctor Von Scott,' Davison interrupted hurriedly. The scientist nodded with a resigned expression and followed his colleagues out.

'One of them must have opened the hatch first,' the Doctor went on. 'Probably accidentally; thrown onto the control by the impact.'

'Doctor Marlowe thinks it was blown off by a rapid pressure change. Men are looking for the cover right now.'

'They won't find anything. The hull is software-definable as well, you see; it forms a hatchway as and when one is needed.' The Doctor smiled. 'How would you like to be seconded to Allen Dulles' operations for a while?'

Davison couldn't help feeling that she didn't really have that much of a choice of answers. She reviewed her thoughts about the Doctor, deciding that he couldn't be a spy, but certainly could be an escapee from an asylum. She was about to dismiss him and have him arrested when another thought struck her. Finney was certainly aware that this man worked for the CIA, so there shouldn't really be any doubts about him. There had been a recent report, however, that the CIA were experimenting with psychological warfare techniques culled from the Chinese via former POWs returned from Korea. Is this man using me as a guinea-pig in some sort of test, she wondered. Perhaps the whole crash was rigged to see whether the *War of the Worlds* scenario would repeat itself among service personnel ... Now this was a story worth exposing, Davison decided, determining that she wasn't going to fail this test – no matter how strange it got. 'I'd be delighted,' she smiled. Give the CIA enough rope, she thought ...

Benny ran her hand over the bas-relief symbol on the hull. It was vaguely familiar somehow. She was damned if she was going to stay outside this relic from her past, however, and entered as soon as the last scientist had gone. The Doctor was talking to a slim, bespectacled woman who seemed to have an air of charming naïvety. The corner of her left jawbone was pink with burnt tissue, as was her left hand, though her uniform hid any other mark.

The symbol was repeated here and there on panels, accompanied by some kind of written language. 'We're having some people sent out to try and decipher that,' the woman was saying.

'Benny,' the Doctor said, seeing her enter. 'What do you think?'

She lifted her hand from the symbol. The Doctor stood aside in a manner that told her he knew the answer and was a proud teacher waiting for a favourite pupil to show her worth. She didn't like it much. 'It looks like the glyph of the old Tzun Confederacy, but they never reached Earth.'

'Something else the history books got wrong, it seems. This is a Tzun scout-ship all right, or a skiff in their naval terminology. The hull's made of high-grade terullian and the interior furnishings fit their physiology to a T.' He gave the surroundings another long look. 'What do you know about the Tzun?' he asked suddenly.

She shrugged, but not too much, since she was in her element. 'Not as much as I should, since S'Arl has been in Draconian space since the last Dalek war. The Confederacy lasted a good twenty-five thousand years, until they were destroyed by the Veltrochni around the 2170s and S'Arl was rendered uninhabitable.'

'S'Arl?' Davison asked.

'Their home,' the Doctor said with a nod. 'Sixth planet of Hadar – that's Beta Centaurus to your astronomers, about a hundred and twenty parsecs away. What bothers me is that, even according to the Matrix records on Gallifrey, the closest they ever came to Earth was the establishment of mining colonies on three planets of the Reticulum system, which is still a good fifty-odd light years away.'

'And these Velto – whatever it was; they're aliens too?' Davison asked incredulously. 'The future now,' she muttered. 'What are they going to try next?'

'Obviously,' the Doctor went on, apparently oblivious to the comment. 'Veltroch is the second planet of Fomalhaut.' He tapped at a panel under one of the panels on the central circular console. 'The Tzun tried to establish a colony there in 2172,' he went on. 'The first thing they did was try to clear a bridgehead in what they thought was uninhabited jungle.'

'Unfortunately for them,' Benny said, relishing the

chance to give a history talk, 'the jungle was a hatching ground. The Veltrochni are egg-laying mammals, like the duck-billed platypus, except that they're arboreal – '

'They're what?'

'They live in trees,' the Doctor said indistinctly, his head burrowed inside the console. 'Like sloths.'

'The whole region was flattened,' Benny resumed, 'and the eggs destroyed. The Veltrochni clans are a very close-knit race, though, and family is everything to them. The natural course of action for them was to hit back. In two years they had turned S'Arl into a radioactive cinder and destroyed the entire Tzun starfleet, along with as many colonies as they could find.'

'They destroyed the whole species?' Davison asked in a mortified tone.

'A few Ph'Sor Tzun colonies survived because they had been absorbed into the territorial areas of other powers, such as the Terran Federation, but none of them are capable of spaceflight any longer,' the Doctor finished, emerging with a small crystalline cube in his hand, which pulsed softly. 'That's all in the future. This beacon could bring a flotilla of Stormblades on top of us right now.' Benny was momentarily alarmed, but relaxed as he drew out the sonic screwdriver and triggered it. The cube stopped glowing, and the Doctor dropped it absently into a pocket. 'I doubt they'd be so rash, however. They're nothing if not strategists.'

'You've met them before?' Benny asked.

'Twelve hundred years ago, at Mimosa II.'

'They're conquerors, then?' Ace put in, greeting them as they exited the skiff.

'Far worse,' the Doctor said in a sour voice. 'Warrior races are ten a penny. Every civilization goes through a warlike phase – it's an outgrowth of the "survival of the fittest" ethos. Most races either see the error of their ways, or else they wipe out either themselves or each other. The Tzun never did; they just got more intelligent and more dangerous. As well as being among the most skilled warriors in history, they're also . . .' He tailed off, looking lost.

'Sneaky bastards?' Ace supplied.

'Not quite the phrase I'd have used, but . . .'

'In what way?' Benny asked.

'In every way,' the Doctor replied unhelpfully. As his pause lasted Benny realized he was no longer looking at her and Ace, or even at Davison. Turning, she saw one of the scientists talking with an Aryan-looking man. Something nagged at Benny's mind until she realized that the scientist was standing almost dully, his shoulders slumped and hands hanging limply by his sides. After a moment the two walked off around the other side of the disc, the scientist moving with a somnambulant gait. 'Especially when helped,' the Doctor added.

Benny wasn't sure if he was finishing his earlier sentence or adding to another, unspoken, one. Somehow, neither possibility failed to send a shiver up her spine.

Stoker was too engrossed in his conversation with Dr Marlowe to notice the Doctor and the others sidle up nearby, skulking around the far side of a slim crane as if trying to decide how best to lift the disc with it. 'All power's dead in the disc,' Marlowe was saying, 'but we've found an odd gear mechanism under the central core that may be some kind of emergency manual connecting point for interlocking segments making up the disc – exactly like the one on Snowbird.'

'That could be,' Stoker said tightly, trying to remember to keep a certain amount of wonder in his voice. 'If it fits together in an iris form,' he suggested with a faint spread of his hand in the direction of the disc.

'An iris!' Marlowe exclaimed. 'I should have considered that for a circular aeroform – especially if it spins in flight. If they'd only let me dismantle Snowbird for a full examination, this would be much easier . . .'

'The flight trials are more important.'

'Yes, I suppose so.' He looked up at the jib hanging from the crane arm. 'If we could separate the segments, it'd be easier to ship out quietly. We could fly it out of Holloman in a Guppy tonight and reassemble it at S-Four over at Corman.' His lined face took on a smirk that told Stoker he was already mentally examining every part of the craft at S-Four.

That was a bridge Stoker was willing to cross when he came to it. For the moment, he was glad of Marlowe's attitude, since it meant that he would stay with the disc every waking hour and so not need to be guarded and kept out of the way. 'Go ahead. I'll take full responsibility under AFOSI authorization. You separate the segments and have them loaded onto the trucks while I call Holloman to have a Guppy made ready for our arrival – I don't want to leave this thing sitting on the runway for even one moment if I can help it.'

Leaving the scientist to enter the ship, Stoker surveyed the activity for a few seconds, then walked off towards the M59.

'You're a Major, Davison,' the Doctor said thoughtfully. 'I don't have to call you that do I? It's terribly long-winded.'

'Just Marion, then. As head of the press and public relations office for this sector of aerospace Defense Command, a mid to high rank is practically guaranteed.' She shrugged, making light of the matter. 'It's no big deal, and I never really have to give orders,' she added with a hint of pride.

'You'll give some tonight,' the Doctor told her flatly. 'We thr– we four have to be on the plane that flies this ship to wherever our friend there wants to take it.'

'Corman Field is a Strategic Air Command base in northern Nevada. They do some kind of research there for a Project Snowbird. As for the S-Four area, I assume it's a test facility of some kind, since that designation is usually given to nuclear facilities. It might be something else to do with Snowbird, whatever that is.'

'The captain presumably knows.'

'Him there?' Ace cut in. 'That's the same albino jackrabbit sonofabitch who started that excitement at Holloman this afternoon. I'm sure of it.'

'Him?' Davison snapped in disbelief. 'You must be mistaken. That's Captain Stoker, Kreer's ADC.'

'*Quis custodiet custodes ipsos*,' the Doctor commented. 'That makes it even more important we be on that plane.'

Davison looked at him worriedly, then calmed herself down. She wasn't going to let them spook her, since that was probably the whole point of the exercise.

Englobed by a vanguard of six strategically placed skiffs, the Tzun Stormblade *R'Shal* hung beyond the Earth's thin envelope of atmosphere.

In the circular war room, which was ringed with statues and had a large plaque set into the floor at the centre of a ring of seats, the tall frame of Tzashan, wreathed in the support equipment that kept him alive, tapped a communications panel. '*Kron*'s transponder has gone dead. Have we lost it?'

'No, though it was a close thing. The humans,' Kreer's unmistakable voice sneered, 'nearly got there first but I have things in hand. Stoker is at the crash site now, arranging recovery.'

'Excellent. First Councillor Shok'Arl is awaiting its arrival at the forward base at Corman.'

Marion watched from a jeep on the tarmac as a number of lines slashed across the disc's smooth surface, curving inwards from the outer edge as if drawn by an invisible pen. Immediately, a crane arm swung out and lifted one of the sections away from the rest of the ship, as Stoker and Marlowe emerged from the hatchway in a neighbouring segment. They boarded the swollen form of the huge Guppy transport aircraft by a long boarding ladder. 'They're on board,' she said doubtfully, 'but I don't know...'

'You spoke to Finney on the radio, didn't you?' the Doctor reminded her. 'He did say we were observers and to be looked after?'

'Yes.'

'Well, what we're observing is about to move,' he said

pointedly, indicating the floodlit nose of the Guppy, which was split to allow a hoist to manoeuvre sections of the disc aboard. 'So look after us.'

Marion wasn't certain, and suspected that the Doctor was interpreting Finney's decisions somewhat loosely. On the other hand, he could well be right. She looked at the three strangers reservedly. 'Well, I suppose, as a major I have the rank to take command of the escort...'

'Splendid idea!' the Doctor said delightedly. He hurried on board before she could change her mind.

Chapter 9

Colonel Finney looked out over the snowy sea of dawn-lit gypsum crystals from the observation gallery in the launch control bunker at White Sands. A number of technicians were busily reviewing the previous day's radar tapes, trying to glean what information they could about the destruction of the missile.

'Sir,' someone called, and Finney moved towards the radar display showing current events.

'What is it, Montoya?'

'This.' Montoya pointed at a small blip on the screen, which was rapidly dropping in altitude. 'It just appeared out of nowhere at Angels-five-zero and started dropping.' Already the blip was pausing at ground level. It suddenly started rising again.

'Get on to Vincente over at Holloman tower and ask if he's tracking this. If we can triangulate – ' The blip vanished at five hundred feet. 'Damn! Ask if they tracked it anyway.'

'It could have just been an angel,' Montoya suggested.

'It's possible, I suppose,' Finney admitted sceptically. The temperature inversion that produced a volume of air dense enough to be detectable on radar wasn't uncommon in the local climate. Finney didn't believe it, though. There had been just too much happening recently to allow him to believe in coincidence to that extent.

He wished he could have been surprised when Kreer walked in the door five minutes later.

Its polished fuselage gleaming almost as brightly as the

quicksilver surface of a Tzun skiff, a rounded and ungainly aircraft with a grotesquely inflated forward fuselage lumbered through the clear air high above the mountainous Four Corners region of northern New Mexico. Unusually, the plane carried no national or service markings. Instead there was merely a serial number repeated here and there in tiny lettering.

A row of scalloped mounds, tightly wrapped in tarpaulins, were arranged along the full length of the Guppy's cavernous cargo hold. Marion Davison descended from the bulkhead that separated the hold from the small passenger section where Stoker, Marlowe and the guards were ensconced. 'Stoker isn't happy about my being here,' she admitted to the three new advisers, 'but there isn't much he can do as I'm legit. If he notices that two of you are women, though . . .'

'What difference would that make?' Benny asked. 'So are you.'

'Women aren't allowed to be combat troops, not even guards, so I can't see him accepting that the Intelligence community is more open. We're supposed to serve in the mess, fly the occasional transport, look good on recruiting posters. You won't see one with an important job.'

'Except you,' Ace said.

Marion smiled faintly. 'They tolerate me on sufferance, because of this.' She gestured vaguely at her scarring.

'Keeping up the numbers for a disabled quota?' Ace sneered.

'Not exactly. I was training as a transport pilot when I enlisted, but when our wing was on guard duty at the munitions store one night, there was an accident. Some asshole had been smoking where he shouldn't and the whole lot started to go up. There was a guy between me and the way out, so I grabbed him and dragged him with me, because it would have been slower to try and go around him. As it was, I came out with all this, right down the left side. The Air Force wanted a recruiting heroine, so they picked me for bringing that guy out; they got some good publicity out of giving me a promotion.' She shrugged, not pleased about what had happened to her, but accepting by now that it was a part of who she was. 'They won't let me fly, of course, but otherwise I manage okay.' This didn't mean she relished going over it, however; she looked towards the Doctor's efforts with a penknife at the nearest tarpaulin. 'Having fun?'

'It's clever workmanship, I'll admit,' the Doctor called back. 'These bulkheads between the sections are software-definable as well, and can fuse with adjacent sections as needed.'

'What the hell does that mean?' Marion demanded. She was beginning to regret – or, more accurately, beginning to recognize that she regretted – resisting her instinct to have the Doctor and his crazy friends arrested. Don't let these spooks get to you, she reminded herself, and forced a placating smile.

'It means that the material of the hull, in this case terullian, can be programmed at the molecular level to behave a certain way. At the moment, they're programmed to form a solid coating about two centimetres thick, but when the disc is assembled they'd be programmed so that the molecules of each pair of adjacent surfaces will act as if they're part of a single object, like a bulkhead partition four centimetres thick, with any gaps or partings necessary. That's why there were no joins visible on the hull before the segments were separated – the hull was programmed to exist as a single object. That also means that no human should have known how to separate the sections.' The Doctor frowned. 'Wasn't it Stoker who told Marlowe how the disc could be separated?'

'That's ridiculous,' Marion protested, drawing away slightly. 'He's as human as you are.'

'I don't doubt that for a moment.' With disconcerting speed, the Doctor grabbed Marion's wrist, positioning his thumb over her pulse. Before she could snatch her hand angrily back, he had released it. 'You're human, at least.'

'What are you talking about?' Marion wondered what had made her trust this little man, CIA mindbender or not. She wasn't sure, but suspected it was his air of truthfulness – if not really honestly – about the disc.

The Doctor didn't answer, but pressed her hand to the left side of his chest. For an instant, she was enraged at the liberty, but then realized that she'd never met a less sexual man. Perhaps he was spoken for by Ace or Benny, but she'd seen no sign. 'Feel that?'

'Of course,' Marion said, a strong if rather slow heartbeat pounding along her arm. Maybe he was homosexual, she thought, if the intelligence services didn't have the same restrictions as the military.

'Good.' He moved her hand to the right side of his chest. 'Feel that?' he asked, and Marion's world turned upside down.

The morning skies were less clear over Washington DC, as rain hissed in sheets along Pennsylvania Avenue to darken the brownstone forms of the buildings of the Federal Triangle two blocks down from the White House. Although the building took up a whole block directly opposite the Justice Department building across Pennsylvania Avenue, Joe Manco never got to see it.

In his musty corner office at the back of the building, he watched gloomily as black pools formed in the hollows of the roof of Ford's Theatre, which was one storey below his level and diagonally opposite across the crossroads at East and 10th.

Like most of his fellow agents, Manco bore more resemblance to an airline steward than a heroic he-man. A crooked smile crossed his rangy features, as if he were perversely pleased to be unhappy for some reason. In fact he was considering how apt the image of those pools was. If the rain continued they would eventually grow together, joining to form larger pools in just the same way that illicit groups would grow together to form alliances to eat away at the fabric of the country as the dampness would eat the roof. That was the official story anyway.

Manco wasn't really interested in whether there really were subversives or not, though the influence of Edna, as he and his cohorts secretly referred to Hoover, was too strong to allow him to show much of this. The reason for his disinterest was mainly because he would never see anything of those groups, since he was what they laughingly called an analyst. Basically, this meant that he had to read the various foreign newspapers and underground publications to search for subversive material. At first this had seemed like an important duty, but he soon came to realize that most of the material was either propaganda – in the foreign papers – or simple teenage rebellious satire.

The thought had also been haunting him that if he, who read these every day for a living, was not corrupted by them, then it was unlikely that a less regular reader would be corrupted either. He wondered if any film censors felt that way. For the past week, therefore, he had been trying to think of a way to make his feelings known without giving the impression that he *had* been corrupted. He wasn't having much success.

To try and show by doing, therefore, he had volunteered to help a colleague by donating the rest of his time – which was normally occupied by writing his own propaganda to counter the foreign stuff – to a case he had discovered quite by accident in a suspect flying saucer journal. The stories of unlikely aeroforms filling the skies didn't impress him that much, but he had come across interesting testimony from anonymous correspondents who claimed to be in the armed forces. Any other agent might have turned them in for court-martial, but when the original investigator had vanished, it became another matter.

The strangest thing was that anonymous witnesses from two different bases a thousand miles apart had reported suspicions about the same two officers.

A click drew his attention to the switchboard and large reel-to-reel tape recorder that were set up in one corner, and he hurried to don the attached headphones as his phone-tap came to life.

Marion Davison had finally managed to stop her hands shaking. Hadn't there been something in *Scientific Ameri-*

can recently about new developments in medicine that meant people could soon have electrical stimulators implanted to keep weak hearts beating? The Doctor's heartbeat had been slow, no more than two dozen to the minute, so perhaps he had one of those things and that was producing the other beat on the other side. She knew she wasn't very convincing, even to herself, but clung to the idea like a drowning person clings to driftwood. 'What are the Tzun things like?' she added.

'Which type?' the Doctor replied, then shook his head. 'Never mind. The Tzun species is split three ways. Originally they could easily pass for human, probably as an Asiatic. When they discovered space travel, however, they had to modify themselves to withstand the acceleration of their rough and ready drives, not to mention any brief exposure to vacuum if something went wrong.'

'Altered?'

'The technique is called pantropy. All personnel assigned to space operations were operated upon to collapse their lungs, recycle body wastes and replace their natural blood with an artificial polymer-based substance that would double as a shock-absorber, so to speak. Their DNA was altered so that it would completely break down all non-essential fats, and their eyes were altered to react to infra-red and ultraviolet frequencies which are universal constants. The pure-blood Tzun are native to a blue spectrum, you see, so Earth sunlight would blind them. These pantropic Tzun are the S'Raph.'

'It's what passes as humour to the Tzun,' Benny cut in. 'The word translates as "Angel".'

'The S'Raph are little grey beings, about three to four feet high, big heads and black eyes. They make up the bulk of the Tzun starfleet, though a trio of pure-bloods usually accompanies any major operation, with an external circulatory system grafted in so that they can survive for long sleeper journeys and visit planets with higher gravities and atmospheric densities than S'Arl.'

'Which is most planets,' Benny added.

'And the third type?' Marion prompted.

'The Ph'Sor are tailor-made by combining both Tzun genes and DNA with that of whoever occupies the planet they're colonizing. That way they get a loyal populace who are perfectly suited to the planet in question. My guess is that your friend Stoker is a Ph'Sor fusion of Tzun and human. He'll have come to Earth in one of these,' the Doctor went on, indicating the disc sections. 'The graviton drive rides gravity waves in the same way that radio transmissions ride electromagnetic waves.'

'But that breaks every rule of physics,' Marion protested, trying to recall those early flight classes. 'You'd be as well talking about flying carpets!'

'The laws of physics your people have got on the statute books are often about as convoluted and illogical as your civil laws,' the Doctor told her dismissively.

'Just how did you get here again?' Marion asked, wondering what the guards were thinking of when they let this lunatic through. She wondered what she was doing listening to him.

'Dimensional transcendence.'

'Dimensional...?'

'It's perfectly simple. The universe is basically infinite, because it has no exterior boundaries. At the same time, because any finite number divided by infinity is zero, then although the universe has eleven dimensions it is also a single point with no dimensions at all. Since there is nothing outside then nothing can enter or leave, and all that can happen is that the state of its contents can change. Are you with me so far?'

Marion gave a weak, wordless smile.

'Good. Now, because the universe is an infinite single point there's no reason why you can't go from one place to another instantly on account of the fact that you aren't actually moving because you're staying put in the one point that is the universe. Since time is just another dimension also divided by infinity, the same principle applies. All you have to know is how to get down to the basic building blocks of reality.'

'Which are?'

'Numbers,' the Doctor said simply. 'The essence of matter is structure, and the essence of structure is mathematics. When your physicists get around to investigating quantum mechanics and sub-nuclear physics, they invariably find that even the smallest particle is always made of something even smaller. There always follows a point at which that something smaller is too small to have a physical existence and can only exist as a mathematical concept in the mind of the observer. All you have to do is manipulate those concepts to effect changes in the physical universe – turn parts inside out as TARDISes, warp space and time, hop between dimensions, all that sort of thing.'

'That's like something out of *Future Boy*,' Marion sneered.

'That's the principle behind warp matrix engineering, a cornerstone of Time Lord science!' the Doctor exclaimed in an offended tone. 'Anyway, you did ask how we got here.'

'I meant how did you get into the crash site without the guards carting you off in a strait-jacket?'

'Oh, I see.' The Doctor looked taken aback and, Marion thought, not a little disappointed, judging by his crestfallen expression. 'I'm a friend of the director of Central Intelligence.'

Kreer was absently turning a piece of charred metal over and over in his hand when Finney stormed angrily into the room after him. The chamber had formerly been a general engineering area out in one of Holloman's large outbuildings, but was now filled with the twisted wreckage of the Atlas missile. A guard outside closed the door after Finney.

Kreer ignored him at first, almost unwillingly recalling the previous occasion when he had served as a scientific adviser of sorts. Then, as now, he was expected to complete the impossible in half the time it would take. At least the Englishman who had co-opted him then had been a little more understanding than Finney, and considerably more so than Nyby. Kreer thought that was quite strange, considering the circumstances of that service. Typical human woolly thinking, he sneered to himself. Kreer would have been the first to admit, though, that he himself could be the most unforgiving of them all. That was his privilege as a superior being, he knew instinctively. It was time, however, that he acknowledged Finney's presence.

'Yes?' he snapped before adding, in a baldly and deliciously disrespectful tone, 'sir?'

'I sometimes wonder if you aren't letting un-American thoughts get the better of you, *Major*,' Finney said sharply. 'This is the Atlas wreckage,' he stated in an accusing tone.

'As much as your men could find,' Kreer admitted, amusing himself by lacing his voice with a dissatisfied tone.

'Why wasn't I told that it had been gathered here?'

'Because I ordered that the information was not to be announced.'

'Not even to the test project leader?'

'I'm announcing it to you now. This material has been in contact with some kind of aerial phenomena. It is now under the aegis of Project Moondust, just like any other anomalous skyfall. Only those with Majestic clearance or higher are permitted to view it.'

'Do you mean you won't even let my engineers examine this to determine what can be done to prevent a repeat occurrence at the next test?'

'I'm afraid that won't be possible,' Kreer confirmed, Finney's emotional squirming being one of his few pleasures of late. 'As soon as the Guppy returns from Corman, I shall fly this material out there personally. You'll find the requisition papers all in order.'

'No doubt,' Finney replied, unconsciously mimicking Nyby's tone.

'Perhaps you would feel happier if I went around giving away classified information to all and sundry,' Kreer suggested snidely. 'You yourself, of course, have sufficient clearance to accompany me.'

'I don't think that will be necessary,' Finney declared.

Kreer felt that the reply was a little more hasty and forceful than usual. 'I can't leave this area while the missile tests are still incomplete.'

'Naturally; doing so would be neglecting your duty to the country.'

'Exactly,' Finney agreed, nodding. 'I can't let America down; not at these important times.'

'Very well,' Kreer agreed with a thin smile. 'Any design changes suggested by the analysis will be forwarded to you, of course. Was there anything else?'

'Not really,' Finney answered in a vaguely puzzled tone. 'I just wanted to check that everything was secure.' With a weak salute, he turned and left.

Kreer watched him go, amused by the ease with which the suggestion of a flight deflected Finney's interest more efficiently than bonded polycarbide armour deflected energy-bolts. As if the contemplation of the other man's weakness reminded him of something, Kreer raised one gloved hand in front of his face, squinting at the fingertips without really knowing why.

The renewed realization shocked him like a dousing with iced water. 'No ... Not again ... I will not allow this to distract me,' he muttered forcefully to himself in a tight voice. 'I will not fear my own body,' he snarled, resisting the sense of discomfort that flooded him as completely as if his worst enemy had walked in.

In front of his haunted eyes, the tips of the black leather fingers were bulging outwards, the material thinning under the hard pressure from within.

Marion felt that she was now on a roll. The fact that she had got immediate – if incomprehensible – answers to her questions had demolished what nervous barriers to her curiosity were left. I feel like a journalist for once, she realized with considerable surprise.

'What do these aliens want with Earth? To take it over?' She tried to keep her tone level and businesslike, not wanting to face the horrors that her imagination pushed into the spotlit arena of her forebrain.

'Not in the way you mean,' the Doctor answered, leaning back in the canvas seat against the interior wall of the fuselage. 'The Tzun Confederacy has to keep expanding and adding new races to survive. When they first broke out into space twenty-five millennia ago, the whole sector was controlled by what were popularly called the Darklings. They were a fungoid people originally from Yuggoth, but after they fought the Tzun they were driven back into an enclave in 61 Cygni. Although the Tzun defeated their aggressors, they were left with corrupted DNA and a very fragile genome, courtesy of Darkling genetic weaponry. Over the following centuries the Tzun sought a way to heal their dying race, and perfected genetic engineering to an almost legendary degree.'

'Necessity being the mother of invention.'

'Exactly. The Tzun geneticists eventually discovered that the only way to stabilize their genome was to piggyback it with a stronger one. Their affliction was eventually cured, but they'd got into the habit of evolving.'

'You mean they want to interbreed with us?' Marion gasped incredulously, aghast at the mental image projected by a subconscious that had been fed on movies of the 'aliens coming to steal Earth women' type.

'Not literally,' the Doctor said with a 'why me?' look. 'They combine the DNA strands of conquered races with their own, and vice versa. That way they develop more of an acclimatization to other environments and ways of thinking, while the conquered race think along Tzun lines. And become suitable for processing into S'Raph, of course.'

'And they've got disruptors,' Ace reminded them.

'Whatever they are,' Marion grumbled. Mere technology didn't concern her after that little story. Wherever they got their psychological techniques from, she thought, the CIA couldn't have paid the inventor nearly enough for such an effective piece of work.

'Dangerous anachronisms is what they are,' the Doctor informed her. 'A disruptor projects ultrasonics along a microwave beam, and vibrates the molecules of the target so violently from the inside out that they rupture cell by cell.'

'Why haven't they just invaded and got on with it?' Ace asked practically.

'I'm not sure. A single Stormblade could conquer this planet as easily as most people change TV channels. They're cunning and ruthless, but they may have evolved beyond even that...' His voice faded, leaving only the clouded expression on his face.

Marion eyed the tarpaulins with ever-changing new suspicions. 'I'd got into the habit of not asking questions,' she said apologetically, 'which isn't such a virtue for a journalist.'

'No it isn't,' the Doctor agreed, 'but it's hardly surprising either, considering the times. Fear drives a lot of emotions, and also forms a lot of habits we can't break; little Iron Curtains in here,' he tapped his forehead, 'between the summit of your achievements and the pit of your fears. Humans are always building new barriers and borders for themselves, of one kind or another.' He leaned back with a quizzical look. 'I wonder which frontier Colonel Finney finds it so hard to cross.'

'He...' Marion wondered how to answer the question without embarrassing her commanding officer. 'He doesn't like flying,' she finished.

'Really? Surely the Air Force was an odd choice of service,' the Doctor muttered thoughtfully.

Chapter 10

Coming in low over the shimmering dry lake to the east, the swollen Guppy buzzed towards Corman like a huge metallic bluebottle. Inside, the Doctor and the others strapped themselves into the canvas seats as the aircraft lurched downwards to bounce onto the runway with a squeal of strained tyres.

The fat aircraft had barely ground to a halt when teams of overalled men appeared from the concrete prosthetics that were grafted onto the mountain roots, rushing to manoeuvre the clamshell nose doors open and draw out the carefully packaged sections of the Tzun skiff.

Emerging from the cockpit doorway of the Guppy, Stoker watched anxiously as the troops from Holloman fanned out around the shrouded bulk below. Outwardly collected, he darted around the sectioned cargo with a nervousness he knew he should not be able to feel. He irritably waved the troops to stand clear as a large flatbed tractor-trailer emerged from the wide maw that beckoned gloomily from the S-Four area.

His anger was mostly directed at himself, though he would have been a liar if he had denied searching for some sign of imperfection from the performance of any of the men around him. Intellectually, he knew that the important thing was to accept events and adapt to overcome them, but something twisted within him and snarled that outsiders from Holloman should never have been allowed close inspection of the skiff. He wondered briefly if he ought not to consult with Surgeon-Major Ksal about these bouts of ragged emotionalism.

The tramp of boots on tarmac filled the air around the open nose of the aircraft as Stoker bent to check the ties on the ropes and cables holding the tarpaulins over the talon-shaped sections. The guards from Holloman were keeping to themselves, out of the way of the Corman men. Their leader looked familiar, and Stoker was shocked to realize that it was Holloman's female press officer. He reviewed what he knew about the human military, sure that they didn't have women in high positions. With any other species he would have dismissed the whole thing, but human attitudes were usually fairly strict.

Curious as to what she was doing on the plane, Stoker approached her as she looked around curiously. 'Major Davison?' he asked suspiciously.

'Yes?'

'*You* were assigned to the disc's escort?'

'A mid to high rank was needed, and I was the only one free.'

The Doctor, Ace and Benny circled the sections, careful to keep them between themselves and Stoker. 'Interesting dish over there,' the Doctor murmured, indicating a structure reminiscent of a small radio telescope. 'We'll have to take a look at that.'

'What's more interesting,' Benny added, 'is that all the guards and all the men coming over to deal with the disc are blond like Stoker. It's like a Hitler Youth training camp here.'

'Yes, that is strange, even though it's more or less what I expected. Wait here.' Moving around the covered mound, he greeted two men who were handling a small winch. 'Excuse me,' the Doctor began, 'but do you need any help with that?' He smiled broadly.

The nearer of the two turned to the Doctor with a stony look, his eyes not so much blue as violet. 'Assistance is unnecessary, the task ordered is within our capability. Do you require directions to your post?'

'No, no, I just thought a little extra help – '

'Independent consideration is unnecessary for this physical task.'

'As you say,' the Doctor said lightly, then returned to Ace and Benny. 'Very single-minded, that young man. Speaks like a Tzun as well.' He looked thoughtfully at where Marion was conversing with Stoker. 'Did he see your face at Holloman?' he asked Ace.

'I certainly saw him, so it seems wise to assume he saw me.' Me giving advice on wisdom, she thought; how things change.

'Then I'd better talk to him.'

'You said you'd met the Tzun before.'

'It's all right. I was over a foot taller then, with curly hair.'

Stoker considered Davison's story, which was a bit vague but had the ring of truth about it. He had intended to give the guards memory-wipes, but since their leader was involved with affairs for the whole southern sector, this option was closed as being too risky. 'You may write your story on this, if it is first passed to myself or Major Kreer for security vetting,' Stoker decided reluctantly.

Davison was about to answer, but another voice came from behind Stoker before she could. 'Excuse me, but could we perhaps get something to eat at your mess hall?' the voice asked.

Stoker nodded as he turned, appreciating the importance of nutrition. 'Of course you – ' His eyes widened at the sight of the bright eyes and pinched but friendly face that stared out from under the white hat. 'Doctor!' He snatched at his sidearm but the Doctor grabbed his arm, spinning him round and painfully into the nearest disc section. 'Run!' the Doctor called to Davison, pushing her ahead of him.

Davison looked startled, but ran with the departing Doctor. Stoker picked himself up and swung around the disc section, aiming his automatic at the Doctor's back. Before he could fire, a shot from Ace's blaster made him duck back as it blew sparks from the terullian hull. 'Bey shu!' Stoker shouted, tapping the hard spot at the side of his neck.

Alarms began blaring across the tarmac, and blue-bereted guards poured from the buildings. Alarmed at how the transport of the Doctor on the same aircraft as himself would look to his superiors, Stoker poked his head up, heedless of the risk. Another blaster-bolt made him drop again as he saw the woman he didn't recognize toss the driver from an idling jeep while the others piled in.

Ace dropped into the recently vacated driver's seat that Benny had cleared for her and gunned the engine. Several blue berets opened fire with Thompsons, bullets rattling from the grille at the front of the jeep. She and her passengers all ducked as she floored the accelerator and drove through them, hurtling towards the central area of the base.

'How did they recognize you?' Benny shouted.

'Perhaps we meet the Tzun again; in our future, if we have one. Ace, where are we headed?'

'Buggered if I know!' She thought quickly. There was the open dry lake to the east, and hills all around. A narrow valley was visible over the roofs of the bunkers. 'There!' she pointed. 'There'll be a gate there, that we'll reach sooner or later.'

'It'd better be sooner,' Marion warned, pointing behind them. Risking a quick look, Ace saw another two jeeps speeding in pursuit. 'Oh smeg,' she muttered. Taking the jeep right over a low vegetable garden, she directed it down a narrow gap between two rows of prefabricated housing for base personnel. On the other side was a wide space with a blocky gatehouse and several heavily barred gates. A jeep was already parked there, with several more blue berets crouching behind it. As soon as the fugitives came into sight, the waiting guards loosed a volley of disruptor-fire.

Ace slewed the jeep around as one of the tyres exploded, and a corner of the bonnet sloughed off in a shower of molten droplets. The jeep skidded to a halt in the dust and the quartet threw themselves behind it. The other two jeeps rounded the corner and Ace opened fire at them, blowing chunks of hot metal from the front of them. More disruptor blasts slammed into the exposed side of the jeep, rocking it unnervingly. This must be how Butch and Sundance felt, Ace thought.

The Doctor leaned carefully forward and scrabbled around in the jeep's equipment box, finally settling back down with a Very pistol and a number of flares. Off to the right, one of the jeeps Ace was targeting exploded, the blast sending the other vehicle swerving into the wall of a blockhouse. 'What are you doing?' she asked the Doctor as she ducked back into cover.

'The Tzun evolved in a blueish light spectrum. Those Ph'Sor see relatively well in this light, but if there's a red flare among this lot, it might blind them just long enough . . .' He found a suitable flare and loaded it. 'Like this.' He fired the flare into the air over the blue berets, where it burst with a scarlet glow, even in the desert sunlight.

The guards immediately winced, shaking their heads. Before they could recover, Ace, Benny and Marion popped up from behind the jeep and opened fire on them. The guards pitched to the ground like marionettes whose strings had been cut. Ace then blasted the lock on the main gate. They darted across to the other jeep, the Doctor shaking his head as they passed the bodies of the guards.

As more sirens approached from the central area, Ace guided the jeep out of the gate.

'Organize pursuit,' the cultured voice said. 'The press officer must not be allowed to confirm our presence to the general populace before the proper time.'

'As you command,' Stoker's voice echoed from the gridded panels that made up the chamber which was lit by the dim embers of blue fire. Olive-toned fingers called up a schematic of the area around Corman in a holosphere. 'The Doctor must be taken alive.'

'And Kreer? He will wish to be informed.'

'I will notify him when he visits later today. You must return to Holloman to ensure the silence of the local media in case word should leak out.'

'As you command, First Councillor.' Stoker's voice faded from the air. Violet eyes turned to meet a jet pair which gleamed impassively. 'Contact *R'Shal*. Have Councillor Tzashan appraised of this development; instruct him to have a gunboat despatched to assist in the search, and Surgeon-Major Ksal placed on stand-by.'

'As you command,' the S'Raph acknowledged in a voice like the rustling of dead leaves.

'Stop here, Ace,' the Doctor commanded after only a few minutes.

'They'll be right on us,' Ace protested, stepping on the brakes nevertheless. The jeep halted on a narrow road with a rocky embankment on one side and a deep crevasse on the other.

'I hope so. Chases are a waste of energy. Everybody out.' Puzzled, the women did as they were bid. The Doctor moved to the back of the jeep and leaned against it. 'Come on, push!' Baffled, Ace joined him, and Benny and Marion did likewise. With some effort, they pushed the jeep to the edge, and over. It tipped up and bounced noisily down the ravine in a cloud of dust. The travellers watched as it came to rest about a hundred feet down. 'Now, Ace,' the Doctor went on, 'destroy it.' Beginning to suspect that she knew what he was up to, she set her blaster to maximum and fired down at the mangled jeep. It exploded, consumed in a raging fireball.

'Is that destroyed enough?'

'Definitely.'

'What now?' Marion asked in a trembling voice.

'Now we climb that embankment and get back to Corman. It's the last place they'll look for us.'

'Especially if they think we're toast,' Ace added, her suspicions confirmed.

* * *

A few minutes later, the air above the ravine shimmered with more than the rippling heat haze, and a craft with the round-nosed and swept-wing shape of a diving hawk solidified into vision as it slowed to a halt.

The pastel-lit flight deck of this vessel held a command station on a raised podium, with various other work stations arranged in a circle around its base. The Ph'Sor Tzun, who had referred to himself as Xeno the Venusian, leaned forward on the podium, peering into a flat pool-like holo-projection at his feet. It showed the burning wreckage of the jeep at the bottom of the ravine, with washes of different colours flowing across the image in succession as the sensors switched between spectra. 'Life forms?'

'None in sensor focus, sir,' a crewman answered.

'Report to First Councillor Shok'Arl that the wreckage of the fugitives' vehicle has been located. There are no survivors.'

Banking slightly as it hung in the air, the gunboat rippled and faded before rising back into radar range as it moved away.

Chapter 11

Keeping his slablike face devoid of emotion, General Hugh Nyby, flanked by a pair of dark-haired air policemen, gave Kreer a nod of greeting as he stepped out of the lift that had brought him down from the hangar that stored Snowbird. Although the walls of the antechamber were, like all the fixtures and fittings at Corman, a pale pastel blue, the thick steel door before them was labelled 'Blue Room'.

It was odd that Kreer was able to arrive so quickly, when he had supposedly gone to Holloman. Snowbird could do the journey in minutes, but to get back so quickly Kreer must have done it literally in seconds. Nyby decided to watch Kreer more closely than ever.

With the calm brought by routine, Nyby watched Kreer dial some digits on what looked like a disembowelled telephone on the wall. With some faint hydraulic thumps and a hiss of displaced air, the door recessed itself into the wall and slid aside.

Beyond was a corridor illuminated not by the usual bulbs but by fluorescent blue panels set into the ceiling. Nyby and the air policemen secured small nose-plugs before entering the corridor. Other passages branched off to smooth doorways, but the men stuck rigidly to the well-worn path they had come to know so well.

Metal panels gradually began to take over from concrete, and they were soon walking down a metal corridor. Nyby's lunch tried to crawl back up his throat as, with a sudden lurch, the gravity lessened by three-quarters. His footsteps barely hit the floor with enough force to make them ring on the metal inspection panels. Beneath them, he knew, ran the web of terullian which conducted the gravity waves, shifted ninety degrees out of phase by a mechanism elsewhere in the bunker.

They came at last to another sealed door, before which stood two men in plain overalls. Unlike the other Ph'Sor on the base, their long hair was piled on their shoulders, though the searching looks that their violet eyes gave the visitors was unnerving when compared to their angelic appearance. As the four men approached, the pair took semi-sheltered stances in the lee of the doorway, their disruptor rifles swinging to bear.

'Klaatu barada nikto,' Kreer announced clearly. The two guards immediately lowered their weapons and took up 'at ease' stances to either side. The two air policemen, whose hands had briefly dropped towards their automatics, took up positions opposite.

Nyby and Kreer simultaneously pressed their palms onto glowing plates on either side of the door, which hissed open to reveal a warren of gridded metal tunnels dimly illuminated with a fierce blue light. Beyond, the air had a noticeable taint of ammonia.

Ignoring sealed iris doors, Kreer and Nyby wound their way, occasionally brushing against the low ceiling in the low gravity, to a domed chamber with a slightly concave floor. A dozen holospheres were suspended in the centre of the room, surrounded by various open-petalled consoles of smooth black material. Half-glimpsed edges of metal or crystal gleamed dully all around.

Standing before one of the consoles, its attention drawn from the holosphere it had been studying, EBE-1 turned to face its host.

Nyby steeled himself, determined not to show any of his discomfort as the five-foot olive-skinned being fixed its unblinking purple eyes upon him. Its domed head and skeletal yet strong frame reminded him of an ancient Nosferatu film he'd once seen, while its thin lips and sharp nose gave it a haughty, catlike air.

As if that wasn't bad enough, something in its deep and

unblinking gaze seemed to suggest that it always knew exactly what he was thinking. Though mostly covered in a one-piece suit of some smooth grey material, small plastic panels were set into its torso here and there. Slim tubes and hoses ran to and from the plastic implants, circulating the oxygenated – or whatever their equivalent was, Nyby reminded himself – fluid through its body, a vital element of its survival in Earth's higher gravity and atmospheric pressure. Further empty implant sockets in its abdomen, intended for nutrition and waste recycling when in cryogenic sleep on long space voyages, gaped like open wounds.

Slim cables along the backs of its hands vanished under the knuckles to support delicate movements under the higher gravity, while displacements in the one-piece suit betrayed similar aids at the other joints. It had told him all these things in a quite matter-of-fact tone that had convinced Nyby utterly. It hadn't forced the view on him through shouting or examples because, Nyby was sure, this was not a creature that felt the need to prove anything.

An implant in the creature's neck sparkled as it spoke. 'What have you discovered about the crash of our skiff?' Shok'Arl, First Councillor of the Tzun Confederacy, asked simply. Its voice was rich, cultured and multitonal, having been sampled from a selection of the best speakers of Earth's broadcasters. Its tone was firm yet reasonable and understanding.

Nyby smiled weakly, trying to look suitably wise and benevolent. 'It was caused by an experimental phased radar array, which was exacerbated by unexpected atmospheric conditions. The ship has just arrived here.'

'The skiff was guarded by Holloman people,' Kreer added. 'A heavy Ph'Sor concentration might have been suspicious.'

'That is within acceptable parameters,' Shok'Arl agreed. 'Our presence must not be revealed until the scheduled time.'

'Then why are we continually seeing reports of your

"space brothers" in the headlines?' Nyby asked in spite of himself.

'They will acclimatize the populace to the possibility of other species. The human mind will more readily accept that which it can already claim to know something about,' Shok'Arl went on in an offhand manner. Its voice hardened suddenly. 'The loss of the skiff could have severely jeopardized our security.'

'Holloman has been ordered to stand down the new array. Your pilot should have been more careful,' Nyby said, half under his breath.

'My pilots feel their craft perform,' Shok'Arl snapped, the dark pits of its eyes etching traces of anger on the back of Nyby's skull. 'Meanwhile, what of the intruders that penetrated this base with the disc?'

'All the Holloman personnel will be questioned, as will the staff here, though I suspect their loyalty is sincere.' It'd better be, he thought to himself.

'Making unsubstantiated assumptions is reckless, Nyby.' Shok'Arl's voice sounded incredulous, as if he were responding to the carelessness of a child. 'However,' it added in a more conciliatory tone, 'the probability is that you are correct.' The alien paused, the single muscle in the centre of its chin pulling the middle of its lower lip down in what Nyby had come to recognize as a Tzun smile. 'I have seen the distress you and your peers sense at the loss of your men,' it confided softly. 'My pilots are also warriors whom I respect and am proud to command. It also distresses me when any of them die without purpose and without honour.'

Nyby stood for a moment, surprised at Shok'Arl's admission. Perhaps we aren't all that different, he thought. 'I understand,' he replied quietly. With a formal salute, he turned to depart the way he had come.

Kreer listened for the sounds of Nyby and his men leaving before turning back to Shok'Arl. 'About the matter for which *R'Shal* beamed me back here . . .' he offered eagerly, suspiciously eyeing a pair of S'Raph who had arrived to monitor the consoles and holospheres.

'The Doctor and his friends were here. Their vehicle has been destroyed, but I consider it wise to assume they have survived to return here surreptitiously.' The alien moved into a smaller chamber, in which one wall was dominated by a world display. Its movements were casual and smooth, despite the misleading appearance of its support system. 'His tactics are entirely within expectations. He is not a serious threat.'

Kreer nodded thoughtfully, strolling in with his hands folded over his belt. 'You encountered him before, didn't you? He interfered with your plans then.'

Shok'Arl looked into thin air, its eyes unfocused, as if living another life under hypnotic regression. 'Twelve hundred and twenty-four Terran years ago, his intercession in our colonization of the second planet in the Mimosa system led to the abandonment of our operations there. His actions were directly responsible for the loss of the Stormblade *Ksorn*, along with Councillor R'Kyth and the complete expeditionary force. This is well known to you.'

'There is a human truism you may or may not be aware of, Shok'Arl – once bitten, twice shy.'

'Continue.'

'Wouldn't it be wise to let me eliminate the Doctor as soon as possible?' Kreer asked with a silky hunger in his voice. 'Not least to preclude the possibility of a repeat occurrence of his interference. Nothing else could prevent it, I assure you.'

'Your reasoning is sound,' Shok'Arl conceded, 'as far as it goes. All strategies employed by all parties involved at Mimosa II have been analysed and incorporated into the Tzun central tactical database. Our procedures and technology have progressed exponentially since then, as has our culture. We never,' it added more firmly, 'make the same mistake twice. All possible measures the Doctor can take have been projected and countered.' It moved to a low console, bringing a DNA chain into view in the nearest holosphere. Several strands glowed an icy blue in chill contrast to the warmer tones of the remainder.

Kreer stared at it with longing, his breath shortening. The display was both the pot of gold at the end of his rainbow, and the albatross around his neck.

'As you see,' Shok'Arl continued, 'we are keeping to our side of the bargain. Our genetic strategists have isolated the DNA corruption. You must therefore keep to your side of the bargain. Should you endanger us in any way, we will be forced to neutralize such a threat.' Kreer ignored the implication, looking down at the misshapen gloves he wore. Better dead than non-sapient, he thought. 'I will permit no deviation from the plan,' Shok'Arl went on, 'and no dishonour to our forces.'

'I can sympathize with that,' Kreer lied glibly. The Tzun turned away, busying itself at the console. Realizing that the audience was over, Kreer left the room, his face a barely controlled rictus of disgusted anger. Better dead than non-sapient, he reminded himself, but better still alive and avenged. 'Deviation,' he thought; Shok'Arl doesn't even know the meaning of the word. He left, consoling himself with the delicious malevolence of that thought.

Alone, Shok'Arl brought a red line onto the world map. Punctuated by Tzun glyphs, it linked Washington DC and Moscow. In one corner, a countdown flickered in downwards in hexadecimal notation. 'Technician,' it called.

'First Councillor?' one of the S'Raph replied, stepping into the room. When seen together, the relationship between the S'Raph and the pure-blood was clearer. Although the technician's abdominal area was atrophied, and he had no nose to speak of, grey skin and large black epicanthic eyes; the smooth hairlessness of the skin, as well as the fragile limbs and high domed head, were just like those of the pure-blood Shok'Arl.

'Is the next jamming exercise prepared?'

'Surface events have not affected aerial operations. The duties of the skiff which crashed have been reassigned to a reserve vessel. All operations remain on schedule as per the mission briefing.'

'What are the preliminary results of the exercises so far?'

'The skiffs have relayed telemetry on all human military vehicles engaged in aerospace manoeuvring. Tactical analyses of this data by *R'Shal*'s strategy computer indicates that all vehicles depend in some part on electromagnetic propagation by either carrier wave signal or electron flow. Both of these can be disrupted globally, with a projected human casualty rate of approximately fifteen thousand individuals who may be airborne at zero hour.'

'Projected casualties from warhead detonation?'

'Approximately six hundred thousand in Washington DC, and four hundred thousand in Moscow.'

Shok'Arl nodded. It was unfortunate, but a necessary evil that they would just have to live with. 'A mere zero point zero zero zero two five per cent of plantetary population is an acceptable casualty rate. Order a suitable aircraft to be taken as a prize of war.'

Three guards patrolled the open compound in front of the gate at Corman, the area permanently shadowed by the looming mountains. Their pace was steady, even and measured; you could probably set your watch by them.

All of which made it easier for Ace, Benny and the Doctor to rise up from behind a jeep, falling into step behind the guards in time to put them out of action. Almost as one, Ace clubbed one with the hilt of her blaster, Benny swung one around by the shoulder to deliver a roundhouse punch that would have felled a charging bull, and the Doctor applied a half-remembered Venusian Aikido strike to the last.

'I'd almost forgotten how difficult that is with only two arms,' he muttered as they dragged the unconscious bodies into the rocks, where Marion was trying on a helmet that had rolled away from one of the guards they had fought on the way out.

'How many should you have?' Ace asked, always curious about different modes of combat.

'For Venusian Aikido? Five; and five legs as well.'

A few moments later, four uniformed figures marched into the base's grounds, dark hair carefully hidden by their helmets. 'Where are we going?' Marion asked.

'The base commander's office, if we can find it,' the Doctor replied.

As they skirted the concrete walls that grew out of the mountains, Benny indicated the Guppy, which was now being refuelled. 'That could be our ticket back out of here.'

'Probably,' the Doctor agreed. He pointed upwards at the underside of the large parabolic dish. 'I wonder what this is for. An Air Force base is hardly used for radio-astronomy, and it can hardly be used for satellite tracking or downlinks, for obvious reasons.'

'That just leaves the one answer then,' Ace pointed out.

'Yes,' the Doctor replied, raising his eyes heavenward.

A large pair of doors were set into the concrete wall just ahead, with a row of dark windows on either side and a sign above that identified this as an administration block. Going in, it took Ace only a few seconds to find a map of the base pinned to one pale blue wall and memorize a route to the CO's office. She then led them through the base, which was strangely deserted. 'The Tzun will all be happier in the underground complex,' the Doctor explained, 'where they can have an artificial environment of their choice. There can't be that many humans left here.'

They finally came to an office with General Nyby's name on the pane of glass in the door. The foursome slipped inside, the Doctor using a downward-pointing motion to indicate that Ace should watch the door. Ace nodded, and stood at the door as if on guard. The others went into the office proper.

The room was very spartan, with walls and ceiling of the same blue shade as everywhere else on the base.

Something to do with the Tzuns' having developed on a planet with a blue spectrum, Marion assumed. Damn, she thought, they've got me at it now. There was only a single decorative photograph, of the bomber Enola Gay. Behind the desk was the thickset form of an Air Force general.

Marion was surprised to see Nyby slouched at his desk, staring unseeingly at a sheaf of papers as if switched off. The thought of an officer so zombie-like in his own base was sickening, she thought disgustedly. The Doctor and Benny exchanged a knowing look, as if they had expected this. Marion didn't doubt for a moment that this was the case; that was what intelligence services were for, after all. She watched as the Doctor moved quickly over, feeling for a pulse. 'He's alive,' he commented. He waved his hand in front of the general's face several times, without any reaction from Nyby.

'The lights are on but nobody's home,' Benny quipped. The Doctor tipped Nyby's head gently forward and to the side. A red weal glistened stickily at the back of his neck.

'What happened to him?' Marion asked in revulsion.

'The Tzun have taken steps to ensure that their host doesn't become too rebellious. Nyby's been given some kind of behavioural limiter implant – most likely a subcutaneous receiver plugged directly into the cerebral cortex.' He straightened with a grim look. 'We're too late here. The Tzun have complete control of this base. Someone has been out-thinking us every step of the way. Or out-thinking me, anyway.'

'Sauce for the goose,' Ace muttered from the door.

The Doctor grunted and moved over to the single photograph on the wall. 'Very odd,' he muttered, and twitched it aside. Behind it was the metal fascia of a safe. 'I thought as much.' He pressed his ear to the steel and gently twiddled the dial to and fro.

Removing his ear from the metal with an 'Aha' of triumph, the Doctor swung the heavy metal slab aside. Inside, several small pouches and boxes sat atop a thick wad of paper. Lifting the lot out, he leafed through the papers with a crestfallen look. 'Orders in the event of war, how terribly dull; logistics, boring; manpower and efficiency reports, useless,' he grumbled, tossing the papers back into the safe with careless disinterest. 'Wait a minute...' He unfolded a plastic map. Marion recognized the features of New Mexico immediately. The Tzun insignia was repeated here and there at certain locations. Dates were beside them. 'October 7th/8th – Elephant Butte reservoir,' the Doctor read aloud. 'That's tonight.'

'A visit from the Tzun?'

'Looks that way.' He stuffed the map in a pocket and unfolded another sheet. 'This is more interesting: logistics logs for two medium-yield weapons to be shipped to Washington DC.'

'Why send them there?' Marion asked. 'And why send two bombs from Holloman instead of using Corman's own?'

'To confuse the trail, obviously. Look at this,' he added, unrolling another acetate map. It was a small world map, with Washington and Moscow marked in red. 'They know who runs the two main sides on this planet.' He opened a rectangular mahogany box. Inside was a pearl-handled Colt. 'Second-rate souvenirs,' he muttered, slamming the box shut. Frowning, he hefted a small velvet pouch whose contents rattled sharply. 'Can't be a dice bag; he doesn't look the Dungeons and Dragons type.' He tipped the pouch up impulsively, emptying the contents into his hand.

'Ace,' Ace whispered.

'Not even a top brass-hat gets paid that much,' Marion admitted admiringly.

'No,' the Doctor agreed, stirring the small multi-faceted crystals with a forefinger. They were of varied colours, and a flawless diamond the size of an ant was the least valuable. 'I have to admit to surprise at more than the value of the gems, though,' the Doctor confessed, holding up a sugarcubed-sized gem of scarlet. 'Andromedan Bloodstone. And as for this...' He lifted out a vibrant green gem. 'Oolion is unique to Collactin. It used to exist on Bandraginus Five as well, but that was destroyed by Zanak about eighty years ago.'

'Obviously the Tzun brought them,' Benny said.

'No. Bandraginus Five was a shipyard for the Vegans; I was on Zanak in 1978, and it certainly wasn't a Tzun colony; and Collactin orbits a red supergiant star, and also has unsurvivable radiation levels, even for the Tzun.'

'What are we dealing with, then?' Ace demanded. 'Two separate alien factions?'

'Maybe,' the Doctor said doubtfully. 'If so, they're covering their tracks extremely well.' He looked crossly around the room as if trying to conjure up a living example of their mysterious adversaries. 'I get the feeling that I should know.'

'Motion seconded,' Benny interrupted, breaking the mood.

'Come on,' the Doctor ordered. He pulled himself up to his full height, such as it was, and made for the door.

'Where to?' Ace prompted.

'In your case and Benny's, Washington DC.' Hunting around in his pockets – which both women had occasionally suspected might be just as dimensionally transcendental as the TARDIS itself – he handed over the slim radiation probe he usually carried. 'You're the weapons expert,' he told her, 'so you should be able to work out where to look for those two warheads.'

'And defuse them?' Ace asked with an eager smile.

'Meaning no insult to your professional capabilities,' the Doctor answered hastily, 'no. Turn them over to the proper authorities, and please try not to blow anything up.'

'Where will you be while we're re-enacting *Thunderball*?' Benny asked.

'Now that we have a time and place for a Tzun fly-past, I'll get Marion back to New Mexico and arrange a suitable reception. If I can get hold of an operational Tzun ship . . .' He strode out the door with seemingly boundless energy. 'Marion and I can stow away on the Guppy again for its return flight. I assume you two have enough ingenuity to get to Washington on your own?'

'It's just possible,' Benny replied dryly.

Outside, a man passed the end of the duck-egg blue corridor and glanced round with surprise. He just managed to hit the alarm before Ace shot him.

Stoker pounded swiftly on his way to the Blue Room with a strong demand in his mind, when the alarm stopped him. His consternation over the photograph and his emotions all vanished as his professionalism came to the fore. 'What's happening?' he called over the communicator network.

'Intruder alert! Nyby's office has been penetrated.'

'The Doctor! Seal the base; red alert!' He turned and ran back the way he had come, while dozens of men rushed from the bunker complex around him.

Ace and Benny watched as the Doctor and Marion vanished into the Guppy's hold seconds before the blue-bereted guards appeared. Ace looked around the corner of the white-roofed hangar beside her, while jeeps zoomed out from the mountain-enclosed compound. Once they were past, she slipped out around the corner and jogged across the dispersal area at the edge of the dry lake, Benny following close behind.

Ahead, a large four-engined Hercules transport, looking patchy as the sunlight reflected off the differently grained metal panels of its unpainted fuselage, sat on the wide expanse of gridded tarmac. The plane was connected to a tanker truck by a series of hoses, and the rear ramp and both doors on the nearer side of the fuselage were open. A couple of men in overalls were climbing in and out.

Ace grinned, almost purring, as she watched the men disconnect the first of the fuel lines.

'You must be joking,' Benny hissed as they dropped behind some drums a few yards from the activity around the plane. 'You can't hijack a crukking military transport! What are you going to do? Stick a gun in the pilot's ear and say "take us to Cuba"?'

'Course not.'

'Thank God for that.'

'I'm going to nick it before the pilot arrives.'

'What?! Don't tell me you can fly one of those things?'

'I flew the occasional assault hopper in Spacefleet; how much different can this be?' Ignoring the mask of horror on Benny's face, Ace moved as the men disappeared around the tail-ramp to disconnect the fuel lines on the other side.

'I'm going to regret this,' Benny muttered. They raced across the baking tarmac and up the three-stepped door set into the lower port side just behind the cockpit. Throwing a quick glance through the aft bulkhead door to check that there was no one in the cargo bay, Ace pulled herself up into the cockpit. A red-headed engineer turned from monitoring the flow of fuel. 'What the hell?'

'Excuse me,' Ace said in her most businesslike tone, 'but does this crate have enough fuel to get us to Cuba?' Benny groaned aloud.

'Sure, I – ' A rabbit-punch from Ace doubled him over enough for her to grab him by the scruff of the neck and toss him head-first out of the hatch. 'Don't forget to tell them when you wake up, nanoceph,' she muttered, ducking into the cockpit.

The sight of the array of glass-faced dials under the large windscreen almost stopped her in her tracks. Trying not to give away any sign of distress that might alarm Benny, she scanned the dials with what she hoped was an inscrutably professional air as she dropped into the left-hand seat.

For once she was glad of what the Doctor – or Benny, for that matter – would have referred to as typical military lack of imagination. The technology may have changed a lot in half a millennium, but the general layout of where the major instruments were located on the panel had remained fairly constant. It didn't take her more than a few moments to map out the important ones in her mind. She tossed aside a clipboard flight plan that marked out a route to Hawaii.

'Since the tanks are full, the pilot will probably be on his way.' She handed Benny her blaster. 'Go and close the door we came in, and the one in the cargo bay. If anyone sees you, zap 'em.'

'Jesus,' Benny muttered, but went nevertheless. As she went, Ace operated the lever that closed the rear ramp. With a hum of hydraulic power, it began rising back into the tailplane.

On the runway to the side, the Guppy hurled itself into the air, prompting Ace to smile to herself, knowing that the Doctor and Marion were safely on board. Thumbing the switches on the overhead panel, she started the propellers turning; slow at first, they rapidly gained speed. Like a thoroughbred stamping at the ground before a race, the huge aircraft strained forward against the chocks.

Knowing that he would need the best possible vantage point, Stoker made for the control tower, which was mounted on a rocky promontory. He had barely spared a glance for the Hercules being refuelled, but when its engines spluttered into life, his head snapped round.

Reading the situation in that instant, he waved a jeep full of blue berets in the direction of the plane, and bolted for the tower.

Having pulled shut the hatch through which they had entered, Benny now glanced out the rear crew door as the plane lurched over the wooden chocks and began to turn onto the runway. The engineer Ace had tossed out clambered to his feet and waved frantically at the turning plane.

A jeep appeared from the far side of a nearby hangar, aiming for the plane. Someone in the passenger seat began firing with a handgun, the spang of the bullet impacts coming a second before the crack of the shot being fired. Benny shot back at the jeep, blowing one of its tyres out. The jeep skidded off into the dry lake bed in a billowing cloud.

Ducking back inside, she hauled the door down on its rollers and secured it with the small locking wheel.

Rushing back to the cockpit, she paused to examine

one of the containers stacked on a pallet in the hold. Troubled, she went forward to find Ace grappling with the throttle levers as she steered the heavy plane onto the long runway that bisected the dry lake. 'Strap yourself in,' Ace shouted over the roar of the engines.

Stoker took the tower steps three at a time, leaping through the door like Superman from a phone booth. 'Block the runway,' he ordered.

The tower staff looked at him dumbly. 'With another plane?' the tower controller ventured. 'That would be an unacceptable waste of resources – '

Stoker grimaced, a dull ache of rage fading in behind his eyes. 'Block the *kshar* runway!'

'Holy shit,' Ace hissed, indicating what was occurring at the end of the runway.

Benny looked up from checking the security of her harness in the co-pilot's seat, and froze. 'Amen to that,' she whispered, looking at Ace and half-willing her to turn back.

Ahead, growing rapidly larger as they approached, a B-57 twin-jet bomber was taxiing onto the runway, forming a horrifyingly effective barricade. Benny watched Ace's knuckles whiten on the semi-circular control yoke, her other hand pushing the throttled levers forward. 'Might I suggest a speedy right turn?'

'The hell we will,' Ace said grimly. 'That's what they want. They don't know all the short-haul Spacefleet tricks, though.'

Benny declined to comment on how certain she was that Ace knew equally little about the performance capabilities of the aircraft she was currently stealing.

The B-57 drew to a halt across the runway, expanding as quickly as the distance between them shrank. As the dry lake around them blurred with speed, Benny saw the startled faces of the B-57 crew for a subliminal instant before they sprinted away from their craft. The surface of tyhe bomber was a black wall filling more and more of the forward view. Backed by the rumbling vibration of the surging engines, Ace howled a Daak-style war cry as she hauled back on the yoke.

With a snap, a blinding flash seared Benny's eyes. Her heart seemed to stop, as if assuming she had just been killed in an ensuing explosive collision.

From nothing like a safe distance, the bomber crew watched the Hercules lurch into the air far earlier than it should have been able to.

Its lowered undercarriage smashed into the trailing edge of the bomber's port wing before ripping along the top of its fuselage. As the Hercules clawed its way into the air at a dangerously steep angle, its starboard main wheels sheared off, the bomber spun under the impact. Its port landing leg snapped under the torque stress placed on it, and the plane sagged groundwards.

Its idling port engine crumpled as the wing hit the ground, and exploded in a shower of sparks which immediately ignited its breached wing tanks and its own bomb load.

The bomber disappeared in a golden flash.

The crew ignored the rain of red-hot fragments that fell around them, just glad that it hadn't been loaded with nuclear warheads.

Benny opened her eyes cautiously, realizing that the flare in front of them had been the sun as the plane tilted up to take off steeply. 'I don't believe it,' she breathed. 'It worked.'

'Yeah,' Ace nodded, her face looking strained and tired. 'Surprised the hell out of me too.' The world tilted gently as Ace took the plane onto a new course. 'You ever fly any atmosphere craft?'

'Just skimmers with a joystick and three read-outs.'

'But you could hold this steady and on course?'

'Definitely,' Benny affirmed in a no-nonsense tone.

'Good, take over.' Benny grabbed the yoke on her side as Ace unbuckled herself. With an envious look at Ace's freedom, Benny tugged one-handedly at the restrictive straps – the Air Force very obviously had yet to see the wisdom of designing planes for pilots with breasts.

Ace, meanwhile, was rooting around under the instrument panel while occasionally checking a graphic on her wrist computer. After a few moments of contortionism, she thumped at something and then straightened up with a small piece of primitive electronics in her hand. Searching her pockets for an interface lead, she finally found one that would connect the computer jack to a socket on the instrument panel. 'Now we no longer exist,' she announced as she connected them up.

'They'll be after us any time,' Benny warned.

'Want a bet? That engineer will tell them I asked about Cuba, so they'll scramble interceptors south and southeast of here while we head north and dog-leg around Salt Lake City. And since I've just altered our transponder signal, we don't have to worry about radar either.'

'There is another inconvenience.'

'Such as?'

'Do you know what we're carrying?'

'Not as such, no.'

'Go and take a look,' Benny suggested.

Stoker turned away from the sloped windows with a sharp spin that betrayed his irritation. 'Track their course,' he ordered.

'Sorry sir,' a technician apologized, 'there are no radar traces with the Hercules's transponder code.'

'The Doctor is as resourceful as we were told. What now?' Stoker asked of a Blue Beret sergeant, who had brought in a dazed engineer. 'He says the two women asked about Cuba,' the sergeant explained.

'The women? What about the Doctor?'

'There was no guy there,' the engineer chipped in.

'He must still be here. Cuba? What possible reason could they... Never mind, it's exactly the clue we need. Contact Aerospace Defense Command. Give them any story you can think of, but get fighters up from every station between here and the Gulf of Mexico.' Without needing to wait for an acknowledgement, Stoker stepped back from the windows and tapped the right side of his neck. 'H'shar moch,' he snapped.

As the engineer's eyes widened in horror, Stoker was enveloped in a swirling red glow. When it faded, he was gone.

No one else reacted. When the red-haired engineer noticed that the tower crew were looking from him to the sergeant, he turned round slowly.

The sergeant's gun was levelled at him, unwavering.

Ace ducked through the low bulkhead door and into the cargo hold, wondering what Benny was so concerned about. A number of rounded containers were clamped to a cargo pallet to prevent them tumbling around, but the lids were merely padlocked.

This was no barrier to Ace, who simply cut the padlock free with a narrow-beam setting from her blaster. Opening the nearest lid, she lifted the polystyrene foam free with a frown. She couldn't swear to it, but she suspected that this stuff hadn't been invented yet – or, at least, not developed for this purpose. What was underneath, ensconced in a white womb, made her forget about her concerns over mere packaging.

Cradled securely were several short and stubby, yet unmistakably rifle-like devices. 'Shades!' she hissed. Ace teased one out and hefted it, finding that a replaceable power cell was hidden in the stock. The weapon was clearly not at the same level of technology as her blaster or the various Tzun articles, and the simplicity of its single power level was proof enough that it was no sonic disruptor.

Field-stripping the weapon was relatively simple, and Ace entered its schematics into her wrist computer as she did so. It was a puzzling device that was designed around circuitry for drawing on electrical power and generating magnetic fields. Ace's soldierly mind was already drawing shrewd conclusions.

To be certain, however, she had her wrist computer

analyse its schematics. Its conclusions tallied with hers precisely. 'It never rains but it pours.' She returned to the cockpit worriedly.

'Well?' Benny asked as Ace settled back into her seat. 'More imported technology?'

Ace nodded. 'Phased plasma rifles. They shoot a blast of electromagnetic energy at you and fry you in your shoes.'

'Tzun know-how, presumably. The plasma rifle wasn't invented on Earth until 2024.'

Ace shrugged, happy to leave the dates and places to Benny. 'Well, we've got about nine hours to figure out what to do with them.'

'Nine hours? It's only a couple of thousand miles, Ace! The sound barrier has been broken by now, surely.'

'Yeah, but definitely not in heaps like this.'

They stayed wrapped in their thoughts for a while, as the Hercules drifted into a wraithlike thin cloud.

Higher, farther, beyond the coldest fringes of atmosphere, something huge sailed the invisible currents of gravity. Moored at the edge of the pool of Earth's gravity well, the long and sharp form gleamed with reflections of unfiltered sunlight. Its hull the shape of the blade of a short-sword, a hangar deck was the guard over the fiery engines that were its hilt. A ventral power nacelle trailed at the end of a pylon on the other side from the hangar deck. The harsh yellow-white light glinting dangerously from the edges of her hull, the Tzun Stormblade *R'Shal* hung silently in orbit like a global sword of Damocles.

In the darkened war room, several diminutive S'Raph were perched on spotlit stools around a circular holotank as Stoker entered. Halting between a pair of S'Raph, he looked towards the three slightly more normal chairs on the far side. The centre seat was empty, but Tzashan and Sr'Shol occupied the other two.

'Report,' the two pure-blood Tzun stated simultaneously, their translator implants remaining dark.

'The threat assessment on the Doctor has been borne

out. He and his friends have made contact with Nyby. His companions have taken an aircraft and escaped; we believe the Doctor is still on the base and we're searching for him. The stolen aircraft had a consignment of phased plasma rifles on board, so the humans may feel we have betrayed them by not delivering.' He paused to smile reassuringly, like a sponsor's spokesman on local TV. 'We know where the women are headed, of course. I'm having interceptors scrambled, but I'd prefer to supplement that with our vessels.'

'That will not be necessary,' Tzashan stated dismissively, which irritated Stoker. 'The aircraft's course has been projected?'

'A witness reports that they spoke of heading south-east.'

'Tactically unsound,' the pure-bloods snapped together.

'If Nyby's office was breached,' Tzashan went on, 'the Doctor will have had access to both the movement orders for the warheads and the schedule for the next jamming exercise. He will wish to face us, and so will return to New Mexico. If he is not on the aircraft, however, then it must be on its way to Washington DC to locate the warheads.'

'The females will have anticipated your questioning of the witness,' Sr'Shol added grimly. 'They will attempt to defuse the warheads.'

'I said all along,' Stoker said calmly, 'that a strike from orbit would – '

'Would be both needlessly wasteful of resources,' Tzashan interrupted, 'and a potential risk to the operation should the fall-out effects be analysed before negotiations with the United Nations were completed. The Earth's resources must be assimilated into the Confederacy intact, and with respect to our foes.'

'That is the greater honour,' Sr'Shol reminded Stoker.

'Then at least let me deal with the Doctor.'

'Logically, the Doctor will have returned to Holloman by the same aircraft he arrived on. Did you think to check it?'

Stoker looked sideways at them. It was an obvious move for the Doctor, yet one which it was inconceivable that he would be stupid enough to make. Of course Stoker hadn't checked. 'Well...'

'Precisely. We projected this course of action, and its fruition proves that our analysis of the Doctor's strategic pattern is accurate. For this reason, he is no serious threat to us. He will come to us at the correct time,' Tzashan finished ambivalently.

'And the women?' Stoker asked resignedly.

'They are merely human, and so of no danger to us,' Sr'Shol replied.

'When the final phase is completed,' Tzashan put in flatly, 'they will simply be two more subjects of the new regime ready for processing.'

'Very well. If you're right about where they're heading, the Ph'Sor troops on station will kill them.'

'That is within acceptable operational parameters,' Sr'Shol agreed. The spotlights illuminating the two of them dimmed. Ignoring the Stormblade's S'Raph command crew, Stoker left without another word.

When the door irised closed behind Stoker, the spotlights came on again. The captain rose from his stool to face the two members of the expedition's ruling triumvirate. 'Not warning him against further pursual of the Doctor could prove dangerous for the operation,' the captain pointed out.

'First Councillor Shok'Arl gave the order,' Tzashan said. 'Stoker is as yet too closely associated with our Major Kreer, and may prejudice Kreer's actions if he were to let slip our intentions for the Doctor. The Doctor must not die.'

'As you command.' The captain led his officers from the war room with the spindly grace of a hunting spider.

When the last of the pantropic spacers had gone, the Tzun left their seats, strolling over to the central holotank. Set into the floor of this was a wide circular plaque, ten feet in diameter, inscribed with the Precepts laid down by R'Shal when she founded the Confederacy. Identical plaques were installed in the war rooms of every Stormblade in the Tzun Starfleet. Tzashan stared thoughtfully down at the second section of the spiralling inscription, and privately wondered how it could be applied to the Doctor. 'Data retrieval,' he said eventually. 'Councillor Tzashan; enablement code 173467321476C32789777643-T732V73117888732476789764376 lock.'

'It will be a difficult operation,' Sr'Shol commented.

'The act of meeting the challenge strengthens us. We must abide by the sacred Precepts; if we are forced to eliminate the Doctor then we have lost an important battle with ourselves and are dishonoured.'

'Then what do we do to prevent that?'

'The second Precept states that he who knows his enemy as well as himself need not fear the result of a hundred battles. We must know the Doctor, as well as project from analyses of his past actions. His splitting of the party should have been foreseen.'

'The women will not succeed in defusing the warheads, therefore they are irrelevant.'

'That is correct, but their course of action is a clear warning.'

'Security clearance and voiceprint identification confirmed,' *R'Shal*'s computer announced.

'Import file Kreer alpha-zero-one, relative date 7101.02; subject the Doctor.' Tzashan remained unperturbed, not wasting even the tiniest amount of energy, as the air above the plaque thickened and swirled with colour. In an instant, a column stretched up before them, a metal building solidly within. Fields were visible beyond, distorted as if they were far below, while blue skies were wrapped around the image.

'Use of ship's energy is superfluous,' Sr'Shol stated darkly. 'RNA samples should have been assimilated as standard.'

'Shok'Arl did not wish to risk contamination of the gene pool by the assimilation of artificially corrupted material,' Tzashan reminded him without rancour. Although the ship had plenty of energy to spare, Tzashan sympathized with Sr'Shol's opinion. Having more of something didn't mean you had to use it faster. 'Computer, initiate action.'

In front of his wide purple eyes, a tall man came into view and peered through a crack between the door and the metal wall. His lined face was surmounted by an unruly mass of tousled white hair, which was writhing in the wind. His red velvet jacket was almost totally obscured by a flowing black cape of some kind.

Scrutinizing a dimly visible metal cylinder which was balanced on a wire attached to the door, he wore a look of intense concentration. Taking a deep breath, he whipped open the door and hurled himself through.

Chapter 12

With Stoker remaining at Corman, the Doctor and Marion were able to join the guards from Holloman in the small passenger compartment once the Guppy had taken off. The guards had seemed surprised to see them, having thought they were staying behind, but at least they were human.

Marion had asked around, and found that they had been secluded in the plane and had not seen anything that went on outside once the disc had been unloaded. Wondering what exactly Corman's staff had to hide, Marion looked across to see the Doctor sitting with a concerned look on his face.

'Corman have gone renegade, haven't they?' she asked.
'Not exactly. Some of them aren't human. It's a few hours back to Holloman, and you probably need to rest,' he added meaningfully.
'Right.' As if she could sleep, she thought.

The regular squeaking of the rusted sign above the barber-shop door across the road barely brushed Robert Agar's awareness. Basking in the gently cooling desert breeze that wafted across the porch, he mulled over the invitation which lay on a table in the lounge. Although the sheet was in another room, he could clearly see every word in his mind.

He didn't particularly fear ridicule – one could get used to that, as he had long since discovered – and nor was he particularly shy. It was just that his friends – hell, even his family, he admitted honestly – might think him crazy.

Perhaps he could convince them he was out for the money the TV station was offering, he thought hopefully. They might believe that, since he had been bitter about losing on that game show he'd been on a couple of years back. He wondered what his employers would think, if they felt their finance clerk was either a moneygrubber – occupational hazard, he thought blackly – or a crazy man.

On the other hand, he mused, not getting the story off his chest might drive him crazy.

The sign's squeaking blended gently from one gust of breeze into the next, leading his thoughts from one to the next and allowing no time to listen to the cicadas in the yard. To a certain extent Agar felt proprietorial towards the Venusians. They had specifically chosen him, after all, and his mind skittered nervously round the prospect of sharing them with thousands or even millions of viewers.

'Tell your people about us,' the wind seemed to whisper in the strange accentless voice. Agar started but immediately relaxed, recognizing the memory for what it was. 'What the hell,' he decided, and went in to make a phone call.

Corman's S-Four area was a linked series of smooth-walled and blue-painted concrete caverns supported by massive shock absorbers buried deep under the foundations. Although it had been constructed as a prototype for the Strategic Air Command headquarters that was being built at Cheyenne mountain, this complex had been reassigned to a quite different task. Not all of the maintenance equipment dotted around was of the solid and sturdy mechanical design favoured by humanity. Small drones floated past on repulsorlift fields, while strangely designed compressors occasionally jetted scented gases into the air. Spotlights shone from impossibly slim and stalky mountings, their light oily on the surface of the reassembled disc. Strange hums and buzzes filled the air.

Nyby eyed the maw of the open disc hatch with a certain amount of distaste, unable to distance his thoughts from the conclusion that it shared the same disconcerting gaze as its owners. Turning his back on the disc that had an aura of the poisonous danger of the quicksilver it resembled, he watched Marlowe and his team scurry around like worker ants. Their attention was clearly on the twin of Snowbird which had been delivered from Holloman. Striding over to Marlowe, Nyby indicated the ship with a nod, and tried not to shudder as a long-armed drone floated serenely past in mid-air. Marlowe watched it with a predatory look, fingers twitching towards the jeweller's screwdriver set in his pocket.

'How much of it do you understand yet?' Nyby asked, trying to sound as if he knew as much as anyone could. This time, however, it was more to reassure himself than to keep Marlowe on his toes.

'Assembling the sections is easy enough, though the central gears they latch onto have a set of ratios I can't work out at all. Nor do I understand how the segments adhere to each other. As for the circuitry or even the materials used in its construction, we haven't a prayer of figuring it out.'

Nyby recalled that his farmer father had always taught him that there was nothing that could not be solved with the application of hard work. It was an ethos he had applied to everything, and Nyby felt the same way. 'I would have thought a partially disassembled craft would have given you a better idea of its internal mechanisms,' he said dangerously.

'With a human-built craft maybe. This has been no more help than the original Snowbird was.'

'That is not a good enough answer, Doctor,' Nyby rumbled. The nervousness that Shok'Arl's presence had instilled in him gave way to anger as predictably as night followed day. 'It is imperative to the Pentagon that we develop this technology before any other powers discover its existence.'

'Unfriendly powers, you mean?'

'There are no friendlies,' Nyby snorted. 'It wasn't so

long ago that the Soviets pretended to be our allies against Hitler.'

'How could anyone get hold of one of these?'

'Another crash?'

'Besides, I'm the best there is in this field.'

'In the world?'

'Are there any research or educational facilities better than MIT, CalTech or Los Alamos in eastern Europe or the far east?' Marlowe smiled engagingly.

'For all our sakes, I hope not,' Nyby growled, unimpressed by Marlowe's attempts to invoke patriotism into the equation. These scientists were all brotherhood of man-type philosophers anyway, he thought. What did they know?

'There you are, General,' Kreer's voice interrupted. The major emerged from the lift to the Blue Room, a pair of hydraulic doors slamming closed behind him. 'I have been *ordered*,' he spoke the word in an almost amused tone, 'to attend a Presidential briefing in Washington. I suggest that you assign a jeep from the motor pool for my journey to rendezvous with Snowbird.'

'And your responsibility for this . . .' Nyby indicated the disc.

'I'm sure you'll be able to maintain suitable security arrangements for a national defence program of this importance,' Kreer stated encouragingly, patting Nyby's shoulder with gross insolence.

'Leave everything to me – ' Nyby began through gritted teeth, wondering what Kreer was trying to imply. He stopped, however, as he glared angrily at Kreer's hand on his shoulder. The fire faded from his eyes as the fear that Shok'Arl inspired crept back, drawn by the sight of the exposed inch or two of Kreer's wrist between glove and sleeve.

It was not the sight of his skin that disturbed Nyby, for none was visible. Instead, a smooth layer of downy brown fur emerged briefly from the uniform cloth before vanishing back under the black leather.

* * *

Its hull glittering like a sliver of green ice in the chill vacuum of high orbit, the Stormblade *R'Shal* was more alive with activity than any Terran anthill.

In a spotless and sterile chamber at the heart of the ship, directly below the war room, the limited microgravity that served the rest of the ship was inactive. The medical cleanrooms were the only areas of the ship – apart from the hangar deck which opened to space – not to have any art-forms in carefully chosen spots. The force-globes and spheres of transparent alloy which were carefully balanced in the centre of the room hung unsupported yet were more solid than any holosphere. Within the tennis-ball sized globes, tendrils of wispy pink plasma – neither quite gas nor truly liquid – glowed purple under the blue light as they pulsed and billowed softly, dancing to their own tune.

Instrument panels of conductive polymer were painted on the sides of the spheres, their patterns flowing like disturbed mercury as the plasma stirred. Now and again a S'Raph in a coverall of medical-division lime would float by and cast an impassive black eye over the instruments, or adjust a setting with the slightest touch of a skeletal grey finger.

Surgeon-Major Ksal remained on station at the openpetalled console that stretched out from what would have been the ceiling if the gravity was on. He monitored the read-outs with a sense of approval. The Tzun DNA he had introduced to sample cells of human stomach-lining tissue was, under his careful supervision, surrounding and bonding with the human DNA strands. Satisfied with the progress of the reaction, he invoked a stasis field around the globe and signalled to his subordinates.

Moving with extreme care, they bore a small canister over to the console, slotting it into a fitting in the centre. Ksal opened the valve with a deft touch, deploying the contents of the canister into a holding tank fitted with a transmat phase transmuter. Keying the molecular imaging system to recognize only single-molecule chains, he brought up a vastly magnified view of the plasma in a small holosphere. Poking at the display with a slim point-and-shoot needle, he began triggering the transmat system to begin inserting molecular chains at certain specific points.

A soft chime from the communications system drew Ksal's attention, though not enough to distract him from performing the task in hand. 'Chief Medical Officer,' he acknowledged.

'All service branch heads are to report to the war room for final phase briefing,' the captain's voice announced.

'Noted and logged.'

Marion led the Doctor into her cramped and paper-strewn office, having suggested that it might be a good idea to check in before anyone got suspicious over her absence. Finney arrived only moments later, demanding to know where the base press officer had been since that morning. His face fell as he saw the Doctor relaxing with a copy of the local paper. 'That explains a lot. Deputized you, has he?'

'More or less,' Marion replied guardedly.

'Well, I suppose it makes a change for you to have something useful to do. Nothing personal,' he added hurriedly.

Marion nodded in acknowledgement. She didn't take the slight personally, of course. She was well aware, through long experience, that it was only her position that was being deprecated.

'Found anything?' Finney asked the Doctor.

'Need to know,' the Doctor said sharply, if only half-seriously.

'Keep an eye on him,' Finney murmured to Marion. 'If you need any help, let me know.' Apparently satisfied, he left.

'That was refreshingly quick,' Marion sighed. She always seemed to get stuck with people who went on and on.

'Just as well,' the Doctor said. 'I don't want to hang around here.'

'Let me check my messages while we're here,' Marion suggested indistinctly, her head lowered to peer at a notepad with a variety of scribbles on it. 'I think we lucked out,' she said slowly.

'In what way?'

'It seems I've to appear on a show tonight at the local TV station. I'm to give the Air Force's official position on these UFO sightings.'

'Really?' The Doctor brightened considerably. 'I've always wanted to get on television now and again.'

Calming notes intended to let thoughts flow smoothly sounded gently from somewhere near the ceiling of the war room. The captain watched impassively as the five black-collared branch heads took up seats around the central display of Earth. Although their black collars indicted equal rank with himself, the captain had authority over them while in space, as that was the function of his service branch. Only the Councillors could overrule him, being in charge of whole expeditions – albeit usually of more than one ship.

The captain was still listening to reports from the bridge as the others entered. 'Continue monitoring remote sensor drones already in place. Launch a further group of remotes to positions five A-Us above and below the plane of the ecliptic.'

'As you command,' a voice answered.

'Is it not a foolish risk to fly without outriders?' a S'Raph in the dark grey of Tactical Operations asked. 'Should we not be continually observed by the gunboats?'

'There is no one to fight here,' the captain replied. 'The humans do not have the technology to attack this vessel, and the nearest spacefaring power other than ourselves is that of Centauri – a world of total pacifists. We – '

'We would rather conserve fuel by relying on remote probes,' Tzashan added, taking position in his chair. 'The closest potential military opponent to us is the Rutan Host, massing near Achernar in Eridani. They, however, are fully occupied by their blood-feud with the Sontarans.

In the unlikely event that any of their fleet do approach this system, the remote probes will detect them early enough for us to prepare a defensive strategy and launch the gunboats, as well as sending to Zeta Reticuli for reinforcements from the twenty-fifth flotilla on border patrol.' He looked around. 'Ship's status, Captain?'

'All systems nominal, Councillor. We are maintaining the prescribed orbit. We are alone in this sector, and sensors detect no spaceworthy vehicles on the planet below. A single chemical rocket capable of low orbit is in launch position in the main eastern continent, however, but it can carry no warhead dangerous to us even if we were not out of range.'

'Tactical?'

'We have been carrying out simulations of attack from various powers. We are prepared for every foreseeable eventuality.'

'Engineering?'

'All systems functioning at above expected efficiency,' the dark-blue uniformed S'Raph answered. 'Our main gravity drive remains unaffected by the magnetic tides. We have had some difficulty adapting the smaller drives of the atmosphere-capable ships to the Earth's magnetosphere, but so long as the pilots remain linked to the telemetred guidance from forward base they will be able to avoid unstable areas.'

'Military?'

'Training is as expected,' the S'Ralph in light grey answered. 'If the warriors are required, they are ready.'

'Excellent. Medical?'

'I am carrying out the final phase of the DNA grafts now,' Ksal replied. 'Our DNA successfully combines with the subject strands, and I am now deploying RNA strings into samples of our genome.'

The S'Raph in light grey looked towards him. 'Is there any sign of the DNA corruption that arose in the prototype musters?'

'Negative. The problem was a simple matter stemming from the fact that we were working from cloned tissues.

The duplication process stimulated an over-production of the enzyme tryptophane hydroxylase in the prototype Earth Ph'Sor. This enzyme produces an emotional instability that has been bred out of our people. I have added a small genetic instruction into the new cell structure that inhibits production of this substance. Once assimilation of Earth is under way, we can treat the prototype Earth Ph'Sor who have an excess of this enzyme.'

'Re-engineering of the prototype muster may not be viable,' Tzashan commented. 'How soon will the final design be ready?'

'By dawn at Corman.'

'Then the human genome is sufficiently compatible with ours?'

'Yes, Councillor. After zero hour, we can begin full assimilation of Earth society into the Tzun Confederacy, as well as assimilation of the Confederacy into Earth society to as great a degree as humanity is willing to accept.'

'They will accept anything we suggest,' Tzashan said dismissively. 'No species will hand in their freely given technologies to return to the ways they wished to be free of. After zero hour, humanity will be willing participants in their latest stage of evolution.'

The crater-like depression of the egg-shaped silo meant that huge clouds of smoke were directed upwards and outwards by the sloped sides as the rocket at the centre shuddered and roared. Heralded by a thunderous sound which echoed across the blasted countryside at Turyatam, four massive booster engines rammed the SS-6 ICBM into the darkened skies.

Its glowing exhaust trailing across the sky like a meteor in reverse, the missile strained against the pull of Earth's gravity. Far from tilting into a target trajectory, however, this missile remained on its upward course. In minutes it was tearing itself free of the outermost fringes of atmosphere by brute force.

Swinging around into a low orbit as the booster fuel

expired, explosive bolts detonated silently around the nose cone. The steel cap parted slowly, giving mechanical birth to a football-sized metal globe. Four trailing whip-antennae stretched out behind the globe as if parodying the four boosters of its launch vehicle. A steady beeping began issuing from the globe, as regular as a metronome.

Much to the relief of the sweating men and women in the bunker a hundred miles below at Turyatam the signal remained strong and steady. Best of all, it remained alone.

Targeting glyphs stretched around the image of the globe like taloned fingers. The starboard fire-control officer routed a small amount of power from the intermix generators to a forward graviton pulse focuser. 'Missile targeted. Shall I fire?'

'Negative,' the Tactical Major said finally. 'Sensors show it as a simple beacon, no warheads or sensors. It's obviously just a test to see whether they can break atmosphere. Its destruction might give us away to that power-bloc.'

As they strolled along the street, Marion was nothing if not curious as to how the Doctor had been with her for almost twenty-four hours solid and still didn't have even the faintest shadow of stubble. She often went to the movies with either her brother or a date, and seemed to recall that vampires were supposed to have that attribute.

Marion felt better the instant they stepped into the shaded lobby of the TV station. Although the evening was drawing in and the breeze was cooling, much of the tiring afternoon heat still remained. The Doctor went straight over to the receptionist, who wore a sweater and pearls as if she'd stepped straight off a commercial. This was a TV station, Marion reminded herself, so maybe she had.

'Can I help you?' the receptionist asked, bored.

'Yes, as a matter of fact you can. I'm with CBS and would like to see about using one of your reports on the recent flying saucer sightings. The stories have filtered out, of course, but we'd like eyewitnesses and local interest to really sell the story nation-wide.' Marion knew this was all nonsense yet, listening to him, she almost felt it was true.

The effect of the magic of a network was much more noticeable on the receptionist. 'Really?' she asked, perking up. 'You'd have to talk to Mr Kline about that, but there's a talk show on the saucers going live in half an hour – you can watch, if you like. I'll let Mr Kline know when he comes in, Mister . . .'

'Doctor.' He paused, as if recalling a previous reaction to what he had to say. 'Doctor Jon Smythe.'

Stoker slammed open the door to Marion's office, breathing heavily as if he had run all the way from Nevada. Cursing the fact that no one was occupying the office, he started to pull the door closed. He stopped, registering the presence of the message pad on the desk.

Approaching the desk with a predatory movement, he snatched up the pad.

The studio was quite small, with cables snaking across the floor between the three-lensed cameras like spilled spaghetti. Mere feet away, a few rows of moth-eaten seats were beginning to fill up with people who all either looked bored, or else had an almost religious fervour in their eyes.

Marion sat nervously in a chair to one side. A thin-faced man with wide eyes was reclining in another, while a grim older man slouched in the third chair was looking daggers at the thin-faced one.

By an empty seat in the middle, a tanned figure in a sports jacket was making notations to a script on a clipboard. A variety of people in short-sleeved shirts bustled to and fro, trying not to trip over the cables, while the Doctor watched from the edge of the plain-walled set. He was still telling anyone who asked that he was from CBS.

The grim older man had 'astronomer' written all over him, Marion thought, and was presumably there to provide expert debunking. Obviously, then, the other man was the opposite end of the stick – a true believer. This seemed to be the one the Doctor wanted to talk to, though Marion couldn't figure out why. This man had been saying he had met Venusians, not Tzun.

'Quiet on the set,' someone called. The man in the sports jacket settled into his chair and smiled at the nearest camera.

'Good evening ladies and gentlemen, and welcome to – '

'Nothing!' a voice commanded triumphantly from the rear of the audience.

The Doctor hastily ducked out of sight, and Marion wished she could too, as Stoker strode down onto the set. Two air police accompanied him. 'I am Captain Stoker of the Air Force Office of Special Investigations, and I am terminating this broadcast on grounds of national security. Any repetition of the events here tonight will be considered a breach of national security and punished as such.' He glared at Marion coldly, then glanced at the audience as if weighing some decision.

Marion could almost read his mind as he looked between her and his escort, who were dark-haired. He probably wanted to at least arrest her, and looked as if he might order her out. 'Before you say anything,' she said in an low voice, 'just remember that your escort there is only human, *Captain*.' She hoped her voice sounded stronger than it felt.

He looked startled at her implied knowledge. 'Tell me where I can find the Doctor, and I might forget this.'

'I'm not dumb enough to believe that, and I don't think you're dumb enough to believe that I would.'

Obviously acutely aware of the witnesses around, Stoker turned sharply and left. Marion felt as if he'd marked her somehow in his mind. 'Well done,' the Doctor commented as he passed.

Agar sat in stunned silence as the hostile astronomer left

with a smirk. How was he supposed to tell the world about his Venusian friends now?

'They'll probably be disappointed, won't they?'

Agar looked in surprise at the short man who had taken the astronomer's seat. 'What, the TV station?'

'You met some aliens, I gather,' the man said, giving an odd smile. 'It was in the papers.'

'That's as far as my story'll be going, mister.'

'Doctor. Oh, not that kind,' he added quickly as Agar felt blood drain from his face. 'I don't think you're crazy.'

'Everybody else does,' Agar shrugged.

'Ah, but they haven't met the Tzun yet, and you have.'

'Tzun? They're Venusians,' Agar corrected him bemusedly.

'What? Impossible. The Venusians have been extinct for millions of years. The aliens you described were humanoid, weren't they?'

'Yes. Venus is relatively similar in size and mass to Earth...'

'No, the Venusians were a race of decapod hermaphrodites. Besides, the ship you saw was made of metal – terullian, in fact. The old Venusians could never have come here in that.'

'You mean they weren't advanced enough to develop that alloy?'

'Terullian isn't an alloy, though it's alien to Earth. No, the reason Venusians couldn't fly a ship like that is because metal was poisonous to them. All metal except gold.' The Doctor furrowed his brow. 'I wonder what would have come of a meeting between them and the Cybermen... No, the Tzun just told you they were Venusians because it's a local planet that's just about habitable. What else did they tell you?' he finished, his eyes bright.

Agar wasn't used to this reaction, even from saucer enthusiasts, but he was no longer in the mood after that strange discourse. 'Just what it says in the paper – that they're our brothers and they want everybody to know it.'

'Yes, I thought they might. I wonder why? Did they show you a mothership of any kind?'

Agar looked up suspiciously, since that information hadn't appeared in the paper. 'Yes,' he said guardedly.

'Did it by any chance look like a dagger, or a short sword like a Roman gladius but with a long boom underneath and a pod at the end?'

Now Agar was interested. 'Yes,' he breathed. 'How could you possibly know that?'

'Me?' The Doctor shrugged as he stood up. 'I met them twelve centuries ago at Mimosa II.' He gave Agar a cheery smile and moved back to escort the Air Force woman to the exit.

Agar sat, stunned again. Surely the man was crazy, he told himself. Yeah, his subconscious answered nastily, he's crazy in exactly the same way as you.

Colonel Finney was busy in his Spanish-decorated office, comparing his notes on ideal test conditions with the next day's forecast, when Stoker entered. 'Ah, I've been looking for you,' Finney began. 'There's something I need you to do.'

'Later,' Stoker answered, trying to look convincingly shocked and saddened by what he had to say. 'Sir, I'm afraid that we must consider Major Davison a security risk. I've only just prevented her from telling the press everything about the disc recovery. I recommend that she is suspended from duty, pending further investigation.'

'Major Davison is the press officer, she is supposed to give out stories when needed.'

'Perhaps her journalistic instincts have come into conflict with her duty,' Stoker suggested.

'Her duties are currently quite light in any case,' Finney told him. 'She's been a fine officer so far, and I don't want to go jumping to conclusions based on hearsay. I will have enquiries made, but that is all. Now it's my turn. I need your assistance to look into some weapons requisition papers that don't quite check out.'

It was all Stoker could do to keep himself from laughing aloud.

Chapter 13

Finney sat back once Stoker had left. Had that captain really cut him off with a 'Later?' He certainly had. Kreer and Stoker had irritated Finney a few times, but this virtual attempt to command their superior officer was too much. Perhaps they had something to hide, he thought, about the disc and the missile failure.

Not stopping to think about it in case he talked himself out of it, Finney impulsively stood up. They might use his reluctance to fly against him, but he had nothing against driving a jeep. Hurrying to the motor pool, which had a clear view of the flat country all around, Finney requisitioned a jeep and followed Stoker's vehicle out of the base.

Stoker only went a short distance before stopping in a desert hollow to the side of the road south of Cloudcroft. Not wishing to be seen, Finney pulled off the road and got out of the jeep. Creeping forward to observe from behind a rock, he watched as Stoker tapped the side of his neck and mouthed some words that Finney couldn't quite make out.

His meaning became quite clear, however, when a large silver disc wavered into view a few yards overhead and began settling down into the dusty hollow. The ship landed and a hatch irised open, from which several blond men emerged to join Stoker in some sort of conference.

His natural desire to protect his command had fired Finney's curiosity. Making sure that the blond men were all busy, the officer crept quietly up the ramp to the hatch opening.

Inside, the furnishings were much the same as those in the crashed disc which had been flown out of Holloman the previous night. There was, however, one important difference apart from the more normal size of the seats. The onyx panels here glowed with traceries of light, while the central crystalline column pulsed with an electric blue heartbeat.

Behind him, boots crashed on metal, forcing him to duck into the nearest partitioned alcove. Regretting his curiosity, he found himself in a small cupboard space filled with nozzle-topped cylinders which he suspected to be fire extinguishers of some kind. Through the gap between the door and the wall, he saw the blond men spread out through the ship as silently as cats, moving with impassive precision to each station. A nervous sweat began to ooze from Finney's pores as he realized that he might be about to fly for the first time in nearly seven years – and quite possibly on the longest journey any man had ever made. He concentrated on trying to keep his heart beating on a regular basis, instead of rattling away at triple speed.

Although all the newcomers were inside, another set of purposeful footfalls drew Finney's attention to the gap. His eyes widened as Stoker strode smoothly over to the central column and sat on a slightly raised seat.

The AFOSI officer looked towards someone at a panel opposite, and gestured sharply with a faint upwards motion. 'Hiroch ta desh wey,' he rapped out clearly. 'Hesho Corman-maroth, hiy naphel. Tholphey hishu!'

'Sha-hoch, rish,' the other man answered.

While Finney's numbed brain tried to comprehend the strange words, the central column sparkled a fiercer azure blue and a strange high-pitched hum built up, forcing him to try to block his ears. The sound, not unlike that of a large generator, remained unaffected, as if it were a tinnitus attack forming inside his head. There was no sensation of motion, but Finney was certain that the increase in light and sound could only mean that some engine was in operation, and that they were now in flight.

His breath coming in short gasps as if trying to match

his racing heart, Finney slid down the rear wall into a crouching position and tried to shut out the world.

The darkness of the air was scattered with a wall of swirling white flakes that made the windscreen look like a TV set under heavy interference. Hands wrapped around the control yoke with white-knuckle tightness, Captain John C. Finney struggled as much with his own despair at the situation as with the pitching C-47 Skytrain, a military version of the DC3 Dakota.

Visibility was practically zero, though faint glows below marked out where artillery fire was being concentrated on the far shore of the Chosin reservoir. The groans from the cargo section were counterpointed by the muted assurances of the field medics who were keeping an eye on the wounded men there.

Finney looked around, the soft drone of the engines failing to have the usual effect on him in this weather. He opened his mouth to speak to the co-pilot but before the words could come, the plane bucked as some vague flashes flitted by outside. The plane made a stomach-wrenching lurch to the left, and Finney hauled back on the yoke. The aircraft stabilized slightly, but was straining to do so. An engine-fire warning light was flashing on the instrument panel, and Finney risked a quick glance out of his window.

The port engine was stuttering, sparks and flames trailing from it. All too aware of what would happen, Finney feathered the engine, shutting it down. The plane instantly lurched again, the altimeter spinning madly anticlockwise.

Wondering whether this was how a downed pheasant felt, Finney struggled vainly with the yoke, but the ground continued to get ever closer at a steep angle. He suspected that there must be a hole somewhere in one of the control surfaces, but couldn't see it in the dark. The plane should have been able to fly on one engine, but it was already dangerously overloaded with wounded men.

While his co-pilot helped pull on the yoke, Finney tried to guide the plane towards the reservoir, hoping against hope that they could soft-land. As the snow flurries cleared in the last seconds, Finney froze in horror, knowing with an empty calmness that he was dead. His fingers remained glued ineffectually to the yoke.

The reservoir was completely frozen over.

There was a sickening downward lurch, a horrendous screaming sound and finally a tidal wave of pain that washed away all thought and feeling.

The screaming faded gradually into the hum of the Tzun skiff, but Finney's cold sweat was still in full flow. He realized belatedly that he was still alive, and that what had happened to him seven years ago was very much in the past. He hoped he hadn't made any sounds that the men outside could have heard. Never mind, he told himself, just being here proves that the fear can be conquered. He forced a grin for his own benefit, though there was no one to see it. From the flight deck outside, he heard a voice call Stoker's name.

'Ko?'

'Corman-roch hiwey, rish. Chom Kreer sheph-roch.'

The major? Finney wondered. His mind shied away from the thought of his scientific adviser being one of these Tzun things, and concentrated instead on the use of the word 'Corman'. He hardly dared hope that was where they were, the incredibly short journey time notwithstanding. Finney had been stationed in many countries, and had developed an affinity for picking up languages quickly. Alert to any recognizable patterns of sounds, he listened carefully. He had heard the syllables 'roch' and 'wey' when they took off and again just now, in connection with Corman. Could one of those syllables mean 'up', 'over' or 'above', he wondered. It seemed a reasonable guess that the other man had just told Stoker they were now at or above Corman.

'Hosh-chom Kreer,' Stoker commanded, looking towards someone or something out of Finney's narrow field of vision. 'Snowbird here. We are above you, Major.' Finney's mind reeled again. This craft was Snowbird! A ship supplied by the same aliens who were knocking down his missiles. He had felt for a long time that something dirty was going on behind his back, and this proved it. 'Are the warheads prepared?' Stoker went on. Finney's pulse pounded as he realized he had been taken for a fool. And to think he had just put the investigation into the theft into the hands of the very men who had carried it out! One thing was certain: he definitely wouldn't be agreeing to suspend Marion after this, Finney promised himself.

'They are both armed,' Kreer's rich voice confirmed. 'Land now, while the remaining humans at Corman are otherwise occupied. You can fly myself and the bombs to Washington.'

'Understood.' Stoker made a chopping motion and turned back to the man whom Finney assumed to be the pilot. 'Tholphey hish ula,' he commanded. 'Siroch ta desh.'

The hum faded and Finney heard the door open. Kreer strode in and several men rushed out, returning immediately with two large crates mounted on low trolleys. Once they were aboard, the door closed and the hum began again. 'Take us up on cloaking-level power.'

'As you command, sir.'

'Make course for Washington,' Kreer ordered.

'As you – ' A sound from Finney's hiding place silenced their conversation. Finney looked down and saw that the hem of his uniform jacket had dislodged a small box of some kind. One of the crewmen whipped open the door, revealing Finney to a startled Stoker and Kreer.

Kreer laughed unexpectedly, but it was an unpleasant sound; the laughter of a ghoulish observer at a Grand Prix crash. 'Well, I did suggest that you suspect everyone, didn't I?' He pursed his lips. 'Now what are we going to do with you?'

'He is a security risk,' Stoker said flatly. He drew his pistol and levelled it.

'Put away your toy, Stoker,' Kreer snapped harshly. 'The disappearance of a base commander would be a signal too strong for the humans to ignore.' Kreer drew a small crystalline disc from his pocket and motioned to two crewmen to hold Finney still. Finney struggled against their grip, but his fear of flying had robbed his muscles of some of their power, and in any case the crewmen seemed to have superhuman strength.

Kreer smiled and puffed himself up, as if he was drinking in Finney's discomfort. 'This can be done painlessly, if you have the right equipment and time to spare,' Kreer began, pressing the disc to the side of Finney's head, just behind the ear. 'But it's so much more . . . invigorating this way.'

The Doctor and Marion flipped through mountainous piles of photographs and documentation in Davison's office.

'There have been reports of various kinds since the Forties,' Marion began, thinking aloud. 'But ones matching this pattern only since the early summer of this year.'

'Same here,' the Doctor agreed. 'But why did they turn in up in May 1957 particularly?'

'Why not? It's as good a time as any,' Marion shrugged, refusing to be drawn.

'They couldn't have been attracted by any space launches,' the Doctor went on, ignoring her in order to pursue his own train of thought. 'Or could they . . .?'

'Of course not,' Marion scoffed. 'There haven't been any yet.'

'The Soviets launch Sputnik One tonight,' the Doctor mused.

'And you're not trying to stop it?' Marion was genuinely unsurprised by his foreknowledge this time. This was, after all, what the CIA was supposed to be for.

The Doctor threw her a scowl. 'Hmm. Soviet Russia was even more secretive than anywhere else in this time zone,' he thought aloud. 'Many disasters went unacknowledged for decades. Last year's Khyshtym incident was the worst nuclear disaster of this century – Chernobyl included – but it was virtually never heard of.'

'So,' Marion prompted, never having heard of either of those incidents.

'So there are two major Soviet holidays: Revolution Day, October seventeenth; and May Day. What better way to celebrate history than by making history? What if Sputnik One really went up on May Day, but failed for some reason –'

'Or was knocked down like our Atlas,' Marion added slowly.

'So they then wiped the entire embarrassing failure from their history books ... It's an interesting thought.'

'But the next logical date would be October seventeenth,' Marion protested. 'That's not for another ten days – either you're wrong or why launch now?'

'The suspected saboteurs would think that way as well, and thus prompt the authorities to launch earlier, to forestall a repeat occurrence. Except that if my theory's right there wouldn't need to be a repeat. Some signal or the like transmitted from the first launch was sufficient to attract the Tzun. Yes! I'm sure that's what happened; it's always been a bit of a mystery why they launched ten days before the big celebrations, and this would provide a reason.' The Doctor paced furiously around the cluttered room.

'But who would be able to interfere?' Marion asked, hoping he would name a terrestrial nation.

'Who indeed? The only thing that's certain is that if they knew about the Tzun then whoever it was must also be an alien.'

'Other Tzun?' Marion suggested.

'No. That's the other piece of the puzzle. They would have communications equipment and technology capable of contacting their people directly. Castaways, perhaps.'

'Someone or something stranded without a ship?'

'Could be. But they'd still have some salvaged technology surely? No, we're after a visitor who's stranded here with no technology of their own, but who has the skills to construct advanced technology from Fifties parts.'

'Such as?' Marion urged, intrigued by the idea despite herself.

'I can't think of anyone offhand. Not that wouldn't stand out in a crowd anyway. We'll go and see Finney. There's a favour I want to ask of him.'

Nodding, Marion opened the door. Together, they strolled down the pale beige corridor, before Marion pointed out a window. Outside, a jeep came to a halt in a reserved space. Finney was sitting in it and, as they watched, debarked stiffly. 'I wonder where he's been,' Marion began.

'You took the words right out of my mouth. He's walking like a zombie.'

'You sure?'

'Very sure,' the Doctor said firmly.

'He's heading for his office; if we hurry, we can catch up and see if there's something wrong.' She wasn't really sure if she actually wanted to know. It wasn't an idea she relished.

Chapter 14

Marion looked on, stunned, as the Doctor examined the back of Finney's neck. The colonel was staring blankly at a weather report. It was obvious that whatever had happened to Nyby had also now happened to Finney – or possibly worse.

'Marion,' the Doctor said loudly, startling the major. 'Do you remember what I told you about humans building barriers in their minds?'

'Whatever that meant, yes.'

'Are you ready to cross some?'

'Such as?'

'You once said you didn't like giving orders. Well, you're going to have to get used to doing just that. Keep Finney confined to the medical wing. As the next senior officer you'll have to take charge of day-to-day operations here.'

'Much as I hate to admit it, a lot of men here won't like that.'

'Then that's their tough luck. Be firm and they'll follow you. If it comes to the worst, find another man they respect to relay your orders,' the Doctor finished in a disdainful tone. 'Humans . . .' he muttered disconsolately. 'I'm going on to that power station at Elephant Butte reservoir. If you haven't heard from me by noon tomorrow, get every man you can muster and head for Corman. Arrest everyone there, and take any other measures you see fit.'

For a moment, Marion was about to refuse. She wasn't sure if a mere journalist was authoritarian enough to do what was needed. But, there was only one way to be sure, and it was closer to the sort of career she'd hoped for. 'I'll do my best,' she said sadly.

'I know you will.'

Nyby glared at Shok'Arl, his dark features twisted with the fury that only the betrayed can feel. 'The Soviets have put a rocket into space,' he thundered. 'Your part of the agreement with the Pentagon included preventing such action!'

'The terms of our agreement,' Shok'Arl corrected calmly, 'are that no missile strike will be allowed to impact on this country. A simple binary transmitter in a decaying orbit is not such a missile, and does not fall within the terms of reference.'

'How could you know it wasn't a missile launch? They did use an ICBM, according to our intelligence sources.'

'An SS-6, I believe,' Shok'Arl acknowledged. 'Its trajectory was not suited to a missile strike, and our ship's sensors detected no warhead. Nyby, we have not betrayed you.' The Tzun turned away.

Not yet, you mean, Nyby thought. This was obviously just a first step; what if the Russians launched an attack and it wasn't recognized as such until too late? Or what if Shok'Arl was just stringing him along? Nyby stormed away before he did something he might regret.

A long black limousine pulled up on a weed-strewn expanse of concrete jetty, having driven in from Oxon Run Park, southeast of DC. Leaving his blank-faced chauffeur to park the car where it would be secure, Major Kreer walked the length of the concrete jetty. His destination was the gently sloped gangplank of a lean Fletcher class destroyer moored under the slate-grey skies at the Naval Research Laboratories at the junction of the Potomac, the Anacostia and the Washington Channel.

Although the *Jessup* had been commissioned during the second world war, it – like many others of its class – had been retrofitted for electronic warfare in the early Fifties. A thick-legged tripod radar mast had been added to the rear of the superstructure, and several weapons had been updated. The sailors busying themselves about their tasks on deck paid no heed to the fact that an officer in Air Force uniform was boarding the ship.

Kreer considered it apt that a vessel of the past should be his base of operations. After all, the past was what drove him. He passed quickly through a hatch in the forward shelter deck, just forward of the legs of the radar mast, and moved with familiar ease through the corridors and companionways below decks. It took only moments for him to wend his way to what would normally have been the captain's cabin, just below the forward edge of the shelter deck.

Opening the door, he slipped into the room and shrugged off his coat. 'Shadow?' he called softly. A low purr answered him from the top of a narrow cupboard overlooking the door. 'Ah, excellent,' he murmured, locating Shadow's greenish-golden eyes. 'Be assured, it will soon be time to feed,' he told the cat solemnly. Nodding to himself, he turned his attention to the rest of the room. There was no bunk inside, since Kreer had long since taken a suite at Washington Circle. Instead, the cabin was packed with softly humming machinery. Something of an odd mixture of technologies, it had parts of USAF and Navy communications and radar circuitry cobbled together with crystalline I-O chips, optical nanoprocessors and a holosphere, all clearly of Tzun manufacture. The whole thing was lashed together with skeins of copper wiring and fibreoptics.

Seating himself in the single chair, Kreer twisted a dial that had been cannibalized from a radar range-finding apparatus and gazed at a matt ebon plate. In a few seconds, the plate began to glow faintly with characters reading 'Transference in progress. ETA 4:16:59', the digits counting down the seconds.

Kreer smiled hungrily.

Chapter 15

The radio was active again when Ace returned to the flight deck after spending the past couple of hours disassembling the contents of one crate of plasma rifles and rewiring them in ways they hadn't been designed for. Outside, a faint glow of pre-dawn light filtered through the clouds over the distant horizon ahead. 'What are they saying?'

'They want to know who we are, since we haven't got a filed flight plan,' Benny told her. It was an understandable, if irritating piece of red tape, Benny thought.

'Put me on,' Ace recommended, pulling on a headset. Benny flipped a switch at the radio.

'AF 1268-31,' a stern voice crackled, 'this is National approach. You are on an unfiled flight heading. Please state your business.'

'National approach,' Ace began in what Benny thought was a surprisingly calm voice. 'This is AF 1268-31' we are on a training flight, but have lost one engine. We require an immediate emergency landing, over.'

'AF 1268-31, your accent sounds – '

'National approach, we are training as part of a NATO exchange program – and we still require that emergency landing, over.' Benny was curious to note that Ace's tone seemed genuinely urgent and impatient. Something was niggling at the back of her mind.

'Roger that,' the voice proclaimed after a long pause. 'Do you require emergency services on stand-by?'

'Better safe than sorry, National.'

'Tenders will be waiting. We're lighting up runway four for your eastern approach.'

'Roger and out.'

Benny's curiosity about this ancient mode of transport had kept her amused during the flight, but practicality was a strong instinct in her. 'Are you sure you can land this thing?' she asked. Ace had been behaving professionally enough to leave Benny with no doubts as to her experience with assault hoppers, but she had noticed a few tension lines whenever Ace had to do any major manoeuvring with this low-tech but complex vehicle.

'If you mean can I get it on the ground, the answer is a definite yes. If you mean can I get it on the ground in a safe enough manner for us to walk away from ... That'd be difficult enough even if we still had a complete undercarriage.'

Benny had expected that, but it still chilled her to the bone. Recovering her composure, she spread a chart across the instrument panel. 'All right, look at this.' She pointed to a waterway several miles beyond the city, its edges as crinkled as those of any fjord. 'We should still have enough fuel to carry on past Washington, eject over Annapolis on the shore and let the plane crash harmlessly into Chesapeake Bay.'

'Annapolis is a massive naval base and academy which wouldn't be happy about us dropping in. Second, these aren't ejector seats.'

'How many parachutes are there?'

'None.'

'Did you count?'

'Twice.'

Benny's blood ran cold as the tiny pin-points of light ahead suddenly took on the mental appearance of the gleaming tips of lethal spikes. 'Yes, I suppose I expected that.' She slumped back into her seat. 'It just seems so excessive, you know. I wouldn't mind being more certain that this is the best alternative available.'

'Neither would I,' Ace grinned crookedly, then looked across at Benny with a more introspective expression. 'I'd be happy enough to know that we're doing the right sort of thing generally.'

'That's not an uncommon wish,' Benny agreed. It wouldn't have been the first time that she'd wondered whether they shouldn't really have left the fallen where they lay on ancient battlefields.

'For three years Dalek-hunting in Spacefleet,' Ace began more subduedly, 'after we'd fought hard, we played harder. Nowadays I think maybe we weren't so much playing as looking for something in our lives that would tell us we were doing the right thing. All we needed was something cheery to remind us of the life around the galaxy we were trying to protect.'

'Every soldier in history felt that,' Benny said with assurance, trying to come to terms with the idea that it might be the last piece of wisdom she would dispense. ' "If the cause be not good, the king himself hath a heavy reckoning to make . . ." '

The distant rumble of water rushing through giant turbines slightly muffled the distorted groaning of strained reality that echoed through the cathedral-sized generator hall. The TARDIS solidified into being on an empty walkway half-way up one wall.

The Doctor emerged a few seconds later, patting the door gently as he closed it. The steel walkways stretched on for tens of yards on either side before dropping off at flights of steep steps. Large and rounded grey generators buzzed and hummed on the floor forty feet below, like snoring elephants. Overalled men toured the scattered machinery, checking on the generators and the thick pipes that festooned the whole complex.

'Perfect,' he said happily.

'Hold it right there,' a voice drawled, accompanied by the soft clicks of revolvers being cocked.

'Not so perfect,' the Doctor said to the two tan-uniformed guards.

'Hold tight,' Ace recommended as she pushed the control

yoke gently towards the double-row of lights in the early morning darkness.

Benny checked her harness and looked out with a feeling of dread as the lights rushed up at them all too quickly. 'Aren't you going to lower the two landing legs we have got?'

'Best not. That would just help tip the plane over.'

Benny gave a maudlin nod. 'I'm content to dig these things up, but I don't know how you work them.' She almost wished Ace were calling out their speed and altitude, so that at least she would have some idea of when to close her eyes. Instead, however, the younger woman simply operated the controls with a stony expression, entirely taken up by the task at hand.

Landing lights flashing like guttering candles in the wind, the Hercules dropped from the heavy sky like a dead albatross.

It hammered loudly into the tarmac with a noticeable bounce, the impact slamming both women against their harnesses. Frantically, Ace dropped the flaps and shut down the engines as quickly as she could. The unaffected plane continued squealing along the tarmac with the cry of a tortured boar, smoke and sparks billowing from the lower fuselage.

As if the nose were an axis, the huge tail began swinging wide to starboard of the scorched runway. Benny and Ace were showered with broken glass and bounced around as the now unstable plane's starboard wing dipped to bite into the ground, the tip shearing off with a screech of torn metal.

The aircraft shuddered to a halt, a cloud of smoke and fumes rising around it.

A very bruised Ace and Benny fumblingly released themselves from their harnesses and staggered back towards the entry hatch. 'Any landing you can walk away from . . .' Ace muttered. The inward-bulging dents in the hatch were proof enough that it had crumpled under the impact, and it was clearly jammed solid.

'Sod it,' Ace grumbled, drawing her blaster. Aiming at

the top edge, she blew the hatch clean away from the fuselage. Kicking a few smoking fragments aside, she clambered out. Benny followed with a dazed look. Their ears were still ringing from the crash, but the flashing lights that Benny pointed out were sufficient to announce the impending arrival of the emergency services.

The two women took deep and searing breaths of fresh air, then bolted across the grass expanse at the side of the runway. 'At least we don't have to worry about forensics,' Benny puffed.

'Right,' Ace pressed a stud on her wrist computer. In the cargo hold, the rewired plasma rifles exploded. In a chain reaction, the power cells in the other rifles also detonated, the fireflash spreading to what little fuel remained in the wing tanks.

The Hercules didn't quite explode. Flame rippled along its length, crackling over every surface with ravenous energy. 'Now we make like shepherds and get the flock out of here,' Ace added.

'Where to?'

'Good question.' Ace looked around quickly. On the other side of the silver trail of the Potomac, lights were rising from Bolling AFB and approaching the airport. To the left, street-lights like a string of glowing beads traced the line of the Williams Memorial Bridge. 'That bridge,' Ace decided. 'That looks like another airbase over there, so we don't want to go there.'

'Isn't that where the bombs are most likely to be?'

'There's an old saying: "Don't shit where you eat." ' She pointed at a glowing haze to the north-east, where the city lights were reflecting from the clouds. 'That's where we look – right in the middle of town.'

Not sparing a glance for the infernal light behind them, the two women moved swiftly on.

Manco's wife answered the telephone first, passing it resignedly to her husband. He was still not truly awake as he grunted an incoherent greeting into the phone. 'Joe,' the voice said, 'get down to National. All hell has broken loose this morning, and they want Bureau presence.'

Manco groaned involuntarily. Not only was it so early, but he was already busy enough with this Kreer business. He knew, at some base genetic level shared by every worker, that that was the problem with being a younger employee. You got all the odd jobs foisted on you and couldn't say no, because if you did your boss would find it easier and cheaper to replace you than anyone else. 'Okay, I'll be there in half an hour.' He replaced the handset on its cradle. 'Sorry, Sue,' he said apologetically.

'That's okay. You never know, this might help with your promotion prospects.'

I should be so lucky, he thought, but then brightened. Sue and early promotion were what he lived for. 'You always do manage to press the right wake-up button, don't you?'

'It's a gift.'

'Keep it wrapped nicely – I'll try to be back early as well.' He finished dressing and left the bedroom, pausing on his way to the car only long enough to grab a carton of orange juice from the fridge.

There were few people around as the clock struck eight in the Senate cafeteria, which was open to the public. It was on the second floor of the Capitol, directly under the Senate chamber. Ace and Benny had both ordered strong coffee and eggs Benedict – Ace couldn't for the life of her fathom why they didn't just call it scrambled eggs – on toast from the breakfast menu.

Relaxing with the coffee, Ace's eyes roved around the plush dining room, noticing the shifty looks she and Benny were getting from the staff. Comparing their own dusty and worn clothes to the smart business accoutrements worn by the few other customers, she could understand why.

'It's not likely to be in a cafe, Ace,' Benny said in a low voice. Despite the time they'd spent together, Ace still caught herself wondering now and again if Benny really could read her mind. 'Even one like this. This isn't a little handbag-sized terrorist bomb we're dealing with.'

Ace shrugged. 'I was just thinking that they might put one in the Capitol building generally.'

'Why not both?'

'One's enough to flatten the city. Besides, you remember that map in Nyby's office – Washington and Moscow marked in red. Two cities, two bombs. I don't think they sent them here just for practice. And I certainly don't believe in that level of coincidence.'

'You mean they want to detonate one here and one in Moscow? That would start a war...'

'The thought had occurred,' Ace agreed dryly. 'It's been tried before. Now, if I were them, I'd want to set that bomb smack in the middle of the governmental area, just to be on the safe side. From here down to the river is pretty central.'

'Is there anything on the detector?'

'Not a beep.'

The angelic figure whom Agar would have recognized as Xeno watched with professional detachment as the captain of *R'Shal* checked the program encoded in the crystalline I-O chip he had prepared. On the display of a small handheld device, a red line curved around the Earth's surface and terminated at a blue spot in New Mexico.

'Maintain continuous telemetry transmission,' the captain ordered. 'This is the final test before zero hour.'

'As you command. What of the return course?'

'That is at your discretion.'

Xeno nodded and took the transparent chip, moving to his ship across the clouded floor of the hangar deck. The captain turned and left the hangar, saddened but impassive at the knowledge that the pilot would not be returning.

The blackened cylindrical husk of the Hercules' fuselage lay canted on the runway like the rotted cadaver of a beached whale. The remnants of its wings lay scattered along the runway to either side, only smouldering ragged stumps remaining attached to the upper fuselage.

Like the insects that crawled over any decaying corpse, there were scavengers picking their way through the shattered pieces of the burnt-out aircraft. Uniformed police officers mingled with personnel from Bolling AFB across the river. Sombrely suited representatives of the FAA, CIA and NSA prowled around like executive vultures while the FBI's representative stepped carefully through the cinders in the company of the airport's flight director.

'You say they claimed to be a NATO flight?' Manco asked, all professional once he had grasped the magnitude of the event.

'That's what the tower operators reported,' the lined, greying official nodded. 'A woman's voice claimed to be on a NATO exchange program. We didn't think any other NATO members had female pilots either, but we thought we could question them after they landed.'

Curiouser and curiouser, Manco thought. 'Was anyone inside when it was destroyed?'

'God only knows. Even if they were, the temperatures in there must have been so high there'd be nothing left of them but smoke.'

'Has the origin of the plane been determined?'

'The folks from Bolling across the way say that a Hercules was stolen from Corman AFB in Nevada yesterday...' Manco didn't really hear the rest of the official's words, his brain having blocked out everything else in order to concentrate on the idea that this plane might have come from the very base where Kreer spent so much of his time. He wished he could believe in coincidence that much. At least, he told himself, this trip wasn't messing up that investigation after all.

'I'm sorry, what was that?' Manco asked apologetically after a moment.

'We're still trying to find a serial number legible enough to tell if it's the same aircraft.'

'I see,' Manco acknowledged, for the sake of politeness. He didn't need to see any serial number; he was as certain that this was the same plane as he was that the wind existed, even though he never saw that either. It seemed that everything odd that happened always came back round to the enigmatic Major Kreer. 'So the plane crashed and exploded?'

'Well, it was certainly a bad landing, but not enough to cause this level of heat. We think it must have been deliberately destroyed to obscure some form of evidence – we've found several small pools of melted metal, with no way of telling what they are beyond the fact that they were cargo of some kind.'

Manco nodded. He didn't feel needed here any more; certain that when he found out what Kreer was up to, he would find the answer to this mystery as well. 'Keep me posted.'

Ace and Benny had spent the better part of the morning stumbling wearily around such central Washington buildings as the public were allowed to enter. They had found nothing.

The White House tour wasn't due to start until after lunchtime, so they had wandered down the Mall past the various museums to the Washington Monument. A narrow structure like a taller Cleopatra's Needle, it towered over the whole area.

A small and rickety lift took tourists up to a viewing platform under the copper point at the tip of the monument, but it had been plain and empty apart from a few country hicks who were visiting town. As the lift noisily descended once more, Ace leaned against the wall while Benny paced around inside the steel box. She peered frowningly at the floor plates. 'How high would you say this tower is?' she asked.

'Five hundred and fifty feet maybe,' Ace replied. 'What difference does it make?' She chased thoughts through her mind again, certain that they should still be looking for an important structure near the centre. The White House would probably be inaccessible even to the Tzun, the Capitol was clean and Bolling was too obvious – and also probably too secure for their brand of infiltration since it was in the capital.

'Five-fifty? That's about what I thought. I was just thinking about the depth of foundations needed to support a structure of this height. On Metaluna we excavated a series of five-hundred-foot towers with twenty-foot-deep foundations. Of course, those towers were a little wider, and the gravity was a little lower...'

'But there should still be enough space under this place for the odd maintenance room or three?'

'Exactly. It's worth a look, at least.'

'Come on then,' Ace agreed as the doors opened. Stepping around the next group of tourists, they left the small hallway. Outside, a queue of visitors waited their turn. In moments, the lift started noisily up again. Hearing it, Ace and Benny slipped back into the small chamber. A narrow metal door was set into the wall to one side of the lift. It was locked, but Benny quickly opened it with some small tools.

Beyond, a narrow stairway led down one wall into the darkness. Ace felt around for a light switch and pressed it when she found it. A yellow bulb flickered on, illuminating a series of equipment lockers and some winching gear below.

More interesting were the two ribbed structures in which two Nordic men in grey jumpsuits stood, and the large corrugated metal box on a trolley in the middle of the floor. As soon as the light came on, the two men opened their eyes and lifted disruptors.

As Benny leapt back through the door, Ace leaned half beyond it and sent bright bolts into both of them. One man went down with a smoking chest, but the other returned fire. The disruptor blast blew a dusty channel in the stone beside Ace before she hit him with another shot. He too pitched to the ground, the disruptor clattering across to the foot of the stairs. Ace went down to the floor.

'There's no one else here,' she called, spinning the blaster around her finger and back into its holster. She pointed the radiation probe at the box and its ticking speeded up so much it sounded like a football rattle.

'Ace,' Benny called, 'look.' She pointed at a small red light at shin level near the door. 'It's a good bet the Confederacy knows we're here.'

Ace thought for a moment, recalling the Doctor's warning about handing the warhead over to the authorities. However, if the Tzun knew of their presence, who knew what they might do? She lifted the disruptor from the foot of the stairs and tossed it up to Benny. 'Fuse the lift controls so that nobody can come down and get hurt if any other guards show up, then keep an eye out for any reinforcements.'

'Shouldn't we evacuate them in case that goes off?'

'They'd never get far enough away in time to survive.'

Deep gonging alarms sounded throughout the war room aboard *R'Shal*, several displays set into the circular table showing images of Ace and Benny entering the lift maintenance room at the monument.

Sr'Shol triggered a communications link to the surface. 'Full Alert! Intruders at ground zero. Locate and destroy!'

All around the monument were carefully tended lawns. In front of Benny were two reflecting pools between her and the Lincoln Memorial, while a large tidal basin was a couple of blocks to her left. Some distance to the right, the White House backed the grassy ellipse. Benny was unsurprised to see a long black limousine, full of blond men, hurtle round the curved road at the edge of the tidal basin and pull up between her and the smaller reflecting pool. Benny ducked back into the small hallway as they opened fire with Thompson sub-machine-guns, the harsh sound sending the tourist queue scattering towards the Federal Triangle as bullets blew chips from the monument.

Fumbling with the unfamiliar weapon's setting controls, Benny fired back at the car.

It was ironic, Ace felt, that a chained and corrugated

metal box roughly the size of a large coffin could well end up effectively burying an entire city if her demolitions skills couldn't be successfully applied in the other direction. A harsh rattle from above was followed by a distinctive disruptor whine and the sound of a large explosion. She couldn't claim to be surprised at this turn of events.

Professionalism dampening all other feelings, she ignored the sounds of battle that echoed down from above. She slipped a maintenance crowbar into the narrow crack between the box's side and its lid, bearing down on it as hard as she could. The padlocked chain creaked and stretched a tiny amount as the very edge of the lid buckled slightly. Pausing for breath, Ace then lunged downwards, slamming her total bodyweight down through her shoulders and arms.

The chain snapped, the lid bucking up to fall back with a startlingly loud rattle.

Throwing the lid back, Ace looked over the mechanism with a knowledgeable eye. The warhead itself was a drab metal cylinder about three feet long and eighteen inches across, dotted with warning stencils and fusing instructions. Ace noted with wry amusement that there were no guidelines for defusing it. A smaller cylinder, festooned with wires and linked to a rectangular attachment with the short antenna of a portable radio receiver, was fitted to one end of the warhead. At the other end, a bulky mechanism with several slowly rotating gears was wired up to the warhead. Other cables led from this to a clock display in a slim tray at just about lid level.

A pit opened beneath Ace's stomach as her eyes fell on the clock display. With a faint whirring and ticking it had already counted down from 060 to 054, one digit slipping by with each passing second. Too late now, she noticed the single electrical contact on the interior side of the rim of the metal wall. She had no need to examine the lid to know that there would be a matching contact there.

Leaning into the casing, Ace sought the terminals at either end of the wires that connected the clock to the gear mechanism. The wires were all plain and uncoloured, disappearing into little molehills of solder. The ticking of her own heart kept time so well she barely needed to glance at the clock to know it was down to 046.

Mapping out the circuit pattern in her mind, she reasoned that the clock was connected to the warhead by a power feed shared mutually with the radio receiver. That being the case, it seemed set not to complete an electrical circuit at 000, but to break one.

The question why was academic as she unscrewed the cover of the clock display, which was already reading 031. She examined the clock mechanism, confirming that it was linked to a circuit-breaker.

Another explosion from above showered her with fine dust, turning the sheen of sweat on her brow to a thin mud that caked her eyelids. Resisting the urge to pause to wipe it away, she dug out the wires and clips she had used to alter the Hercules's transponder. The counter passed 022 as she peeled the plastic insulation away from a spot on one wire to attach a clip.

At 016 she had completed repeating the manoeuvre on the second wire. She risked a few heartbeats to check under the clock for either booby traps or further wires that might indicate she had been wasting her time on a dummy set-up. There were none, however, and at 010 she cut the first wire.

Nothing happened.

With her pulse pounding in her ear as a bass counterpoint to the clock's ticking through 007, she cut the second wire.

The ticking stopped and for a moment she thought her heart had as well. As the seconds went on and nothing else happened, Ace let out the breath she hadn't realized she had been holding. She steadied herself against the casing before her legs could give way. 'That was just too smegging close.'

Shaking her head to clear the cobwebs, she wound the ends of the wires together so that she could remove her cables without breaking the circuit. She turned to the radio receiver next, scrutinizing it closely. Why was it set to go off when power was denied, she wondered. She wondered if the other warhead was rigged the same way. She smiled slowly as the thought led her to the logical conclusion. If both bombs were meant to detonate simultaneously, then the other must be fitted with a transmitter. When it detonated, the signal would cease and this one would go off.

With practised and professional speed, she attached her cables to the middle of the wires connecting the receiver to the detonator. Cutting the wires between the ends of her cables, she carefully pulled the receiver aside by the amount allowed by her cables. She slipped her hand down between it and the warhead, feeling around for the end of the detonator.

Unscrewing the detonator by turning it a minute amount at a time, she finally tugged the unwieldy eight-inch cylinder free. Dropping it into her pocket, she retrieved her cables. A couple of faint clicks came from within the warhead mechanism as the signal was cut off, but nothing else happened. Hefting the receiver, Ace grinned triumphantly. If she could plug it into her wrist computer, it should home in on the other bomb.

A renewed burst of multiple disruptor whines attracted her attention now that the chamber had become almost preternaturally silent with the cessation of the ticking. Ace loped grimly out of the room.

The disruptor was growing uncomfortably hot in Benny's palm, but the Aryan-looking Ph'Sor were still safely behind the cover of the low wall surrounding the pool now that their limo was no more than a smouldering ruin. They had switched to disruptors, either feeling safer now that the tourists had run away or else assuming that any damage had already been done thanks to Benny's use of one. Shards of marble were shattering into hot dust under the blasts as Ace emerged, immediately flinging herself to the ground beside Benny to avoid a blast that zipped past her ear.

'What kept you?' Benny asked, not entirely lightly. 'Did you manage it?'

'You're still here, aren't you? Three more ticks and this,' she jerked a thumb upwards to include the whole needle-like structure, 'would have been America's first rocket in space.' Sirens had struck up a cats' chorus in the distance. 'I think the cavalry's on the way.'

The first police car to appear was hit square-on with a high-powered disruptor blast from one of the Ph'Sor. Smoke and flame scratching at the bonnet, it screeched across the curve in the road and splashed into the tidal basin. 'Have they all got disruptors?' Ace queried.

'Yes, and a couple of them have local weapons as well.'

'Good enough. Keep 'em busy.' Ace turned to a speaker mounted on the wall and, to Benny's puzzled surprise, pulled it away from the stone. She opened up the back of it, making sure that its power cables were pulled free. Already the crack of police revolvers was joining in the general cacophony.

'What the smeg are you doing?' Benny asked. 'Trying to take over the Doctor's position as chief gadget-basher?'

'You don't have to be a Time Lord to know about the foibles of individual weapons,' Ace answered, ducking as stone chips were blasted apart above her head. 'When we were fighting in the Ceti sector, disruptors were issued because the microwave beam could cook Dalek blobs inside their armour.' She had now freed the back of the speaker, and was tinkering inside. 'It was a big mistake. The Daleks are many things – all bad – but they do know about strengths and weaknesses, including their own. They had already anticipated the use of disruptors and had prepared for it. They'd discovered that since the focusing crystal of a disruptor is designed to handle ultrasonics, it was particularly susceptible to interference from infra-sonics.' She closed the back of the speaker with a smile, and handed it to Benny. 'When I give the word, point this towards them and press the power cables into their connectors.'

Benny nodded slowly as realization dawned. 'Ready when you are.'

Ace drew her blaster. 'Now!'

Benny pressed the cable to its connector at the back of the speaker, and held it firmly in place as she directed it around the door-jamb. No sound came from it that she could hear, but she could feel a disconcerting numbness crawling up her arms.

The effect on the Ph'Sor was more dramatic. The disruptor of the nearest one exploded without warning, bathing him in fire and sending him running with a scream towards the pool. The others barely had time to toss their weapons aside before they too exploded in a shower of sparks. Most of the Ph'Sor scattered, policemen running after them. Two rolled for cover, however, picking up their Thompsons.

Benny suspected that Ace had been waiting for this, and her feeling was confirmed as Ace calmly stepped round the corner and gunned them down with well-placed blaster shots before either of them could take aim at her. Benny watched with equal measures of relief and disgust as the two Ph'Sor twitched briefly on the grass, the wisps of smoke rising from their wounds matching those curling from the muzzle of Ace's blaster.

Ace herself looked on apparently impassively, not sharing whatever she felt. She re-holstered the blaster with slow movements, as if she were holding something very heavy, or chained down with souls. 'Why didn't they run like the others?' she asked quietly. She turned away before Benny could even think about an answer.

The sound of a car engine drew Benny's attention then, as a police car hurtled across the grass, knocking aside the officers to whom it was assigned. Ace drew her blaster, but no one fired at her or Benny. Instead, a Ph'Sor blasted the bodies of his fallen comrades at maximum power. The corpses flared briefly and vanished as the car bumped back onto the road and sped eastwards.

Spying an unattended police motorcycle, Benny bounded towards it. 'My turn,' she called to Ace, mounting the bike. She looked back to see Ace interpose herself between her and more newly arriving police. She hesitated for an instant, but then decided that Ace could look after herself. The police motorcyclist was already running towards her, and she kicked the engine into wakefulness.

The last thing she heard before roaring off after the Ph'Sor was Ace's voice. 'It's a fair cop, guv,' it said sarcastically.

Chapter 16

Ken Andrews had always considered himself a laid-back kind of guy. His parents had brought him up by spouting sayings like 'it's no use crying over spilt milk'; there had been nothing about a spilt world, caused by the radio newsflash about the Russians having launched an artificial satellite. Andrews just didn't know what the world was coming to.

Even in troubled circumstances like these, Andrews tried hard to retain his easy-going ways. Not getting worked up about things was an important qualification, he felt, for being the director of a power station. It wasn't so much the dangers that such huge machinery implied which risked his calmness as the pressures from local businesses, all of whom sought to blame him personally when a circuit-breaker tripped and shut them down for a few minutes. Andrews had fielded all of these problems with equanimity throughout his career, strain passing over and from him like water from a duck's back. He always ascribed this trait more to his experience as a logistics officer during the war than to his upbringing.

He didn't mind admitting, however, that the thought of something Russian zipping around the entire world was disturbing, and somehow irritating. Five minutes after the security guards announced that they had captured an intruder in B Hall, Andrews felt his ulcer was a guaranteed certainty. Not only had the strange little man called the head of the CIA at home with impunity, but Andrews had then been instructed to give him any assistance – 'however crazy it may seem.'

'Unless you let me get on with my business,' the Doctor told him without preamble, 'you'll be completely blacked out within the hour.'

'Not possible,' Andrews protested. 'We have four separate overriding safety cut-outs – '

'Which are useless against a technology which can put out an EM pulse strong enough to fry every circuit-breaker in the entire state.'

Andrews had heard such fairy-tales before, and wasn't about to listen to any more. 'You're working with CIA, so if you mean Russians then say Russians.'

The Doctor leaned forward on his elbows, to fix Andrews with a piercing look. 'I don't mean Russians, though.'

'Who then?'

'Yes, well,' the Doctor smiled wryly, 'that's the tricky part.'

'To find out, you mean?'

'No, I mean to tell you in such a way that you'll understand.'

'Or believe, you mean.' Andrews had seen the stories in the papers of late and a nasty suspicion was dawning on his mind, in much the same way as his wallet tried to hide itself any time his ex-wife called. His brain was already gearing up to ignore the words which, he knew with a terrible clarity, were about to be inflicted upon him.

'I mean a secret US aircraft codenamed Snowbird, which has been developed by a research team who have gone a little astray.'

'I've never heard such – US? Some of our scientists have finally flipped?'

'A major and a captain, actually. They've certainly got above themselves.'

'You know,' Andrews breathed in relief. 'I was sure you were going to say flying saucers.'

'As it happens, Snowbird is discoid,' the Doctor informed him cheerily. 'I'm going to need your help to recover it from its current crew.'

'What do you need?' Andrews asked eagerly. He had been getting annoyed with the constant press exposure of these crazies who claimed to have met Venusians, and the chance to prove that these flying saucers were man-made was something he'd give his right arm for. This'll show those nuts, he thought.

The first joyous rush of Marion's new-found confidence was ebbing as she sadly watched the MO supervising Finney's transfer to the medical wing. Her pride in having a new position was being weighed down by the tone of the unpleasant duty she had to perform now. She began to think that she almost preferred being a self-confessed nobody, hiding in the backwaters of the press office.

The Doctor had shown her that there was more to life, all right, but the new material was by no means all good.

Settling reluctantly into Finney's chair, Marion lifted the phone and began dialling. The Pentagon wasn't going to be pleased, but they had to be told.

Kreer stepped out on the *Jessup*'s deck to look around in the brightness of mid-morning. The shore opposite was green, topped by dark tarmac and concrete, which looked as if it was crushing the bank. He propped himself against the rail and stretched out, canting his head slightly with a grimace, as if his stretching was both involuntary and unwelcome. The gently flowing but one-way current of the river reminded him uncomfortably of Time's single course, and so he turned away, looking instead towards the city. To the north, the hazy aftermath of smoke blurred the blueness of the sky. The image amused Kreer.

The burly frame of Commander Tobey, his naval uniform seemingly painted on, stepped up beside him. Kreer gave no sign of noticing, his gaze turning southwards towards the Woodrow Wilson Bridge. 'There has been no environmental change since last night,' Tobey prompted puzzledly.

'I wasn't looking for anything new,' Kreer said pointedly. 'The past has most vivid images ...'

'I've received word from the *R'Shal*. One warhead has been located and disarmed by the Doctor's companions. The other is in cargo storage awaiting the aircraft that will take it to Moscow.'

'The guards from ground zero?' Kreer snapped.

'Survivors are returning here, but by a circuitous route.'

'Better safe than sorry? I will supervise the loading of the main warhead personally,' he said decisively. 'When the guards return, I want them held for me.'

'Very well. My people are warriors,' Tobey said, changing tack, 'but I believe we should congratulate you on the ingenuity with which you acquired the warheads.'

'I've stolen things before,' Kreer stated dismissively.

'Indeed, you are a superlative thief. The best in this world, perhaps.'

Kreer laughed sneeringly. 'Oh, but there are finer thieves than I. Time, for example. Eventually it steals everything.'

The desert flashed past as a tan blur in the holosphere aboard Xeno's skiff.

In the precise centre of the display, remaining unwavering as the edges of the image shook, a tiny speck grew into the looming form of a squat complex. An expanse of glittering sapphire rippled gently behind a dam beyond the solid brick and concrete forms.

Glowing indigo glyphs hung around the immense building, flickering and changing as the building, flickering and changing as the building grew with increasing proximity.

'Jamming range in nine seconds,' the turquoise-suited pilot reported.

'Prepare to transfer energy to ECM circuits on my mark,' Xeno instructed calmly.

'Transfer locked.'

'Three, two, one, mark!'

The Doctor hurriedly lashed a final cable to a hastily assembled piece of equipment on the roof of B Hall. The centrepiece of the device consisted of a battered square aerial plugged into a bizarre art deco ghetto blaster, while a number of thick cables ran down to one of the generators below via some small Tesla coils.

A faint insistent humming was building up in the fresh morning air, and Andrews looked around for the source while trying to figure out what the Doctor's apparatus was actually supposed to do. He realized that the Doctor had managed to avoid giving any details of his plan. 'What does that do?' he asked rather belatedly.

'Tzun ships use a graviton pulse drive to ride gravity waves like tramlines. The graviton field bends light around it whether you like it or not, but they can channel some of the energy out as either a focused graviton beam or an electromagnetic pulse. This thing here should feed it back to them – their system should be vulnerable to that.'

'Tzun? You said they were Americans!'

'I lied to save time,' the Doctor explained crossly, trying to finish up his work.

'What are they, then?'

'Alien spaceships.'

'You must be crazy!' Andrews stepped back. He would have the Doctor's equipment disconnected, he decided, and him too if he objected.

'Madness is relative,' the Doctor snapped. 'Mine certainly are, anyway,' he added. 'Here they come!'

In spite of himself, Andrews looked up as the humming reached a peak. The brightening sky was suddenly obscured by a rippling shimmer of refracted light, which darkened as the very solid metal disc became visible overhead and cast the roof into shadow. 'They've transferred most of their motive power to weapons systems,' the Doctor explained. 'That's why they can't maintain a strong enough gravitational field to bend the light around it.' Traceries of energy rippled over the glowing exhaust circle in the centre of the undersurface as well as the three equidistant hemispheres around it.

Shit, Andrews thought, all those crazy stories were true. Maybe they should let the insane out of their asylums to run the world. Shouts and alarms from below brought him back to alertness, to see the Doctor fiddling about with his machine. The square aerial was glowing faintly, but nothing else was happening. 'It's not working!'

'It just takes time to warm up,' the Doctor replied.

Deciding that it could take all the time it liked, but that he was having nothing to do with it, Andrews ducked back onto the highest catwalk in the generator hall.

Men were scattering below as red lamps flashed everywhere, overloaded circuit breakers tripping and forcing the steam turbines to cut out. Men in protective suits scurried to and fro as safety valves blew, jets of scalding steam blasting through the hall.

Horrified, Andrews snatched a phone from the wall-mounted bracket next to the door, which was connected straight to the control room. 'Stabilize the turbines – '

Everything suddenly shut down as every circuit was broken. The turbine sound began lowering in pitch, only their momentum carrying them on.

The skiff's crew monitored their consoles with passionless devotion, memorizing every detail of the energy flow and its effects.

'Sensors indicate non-human lifeform,' a crewman reported.

'Tzun?' Xeno asked in surprise.

'Negative. Thermal scan indicates ectopic physiology.'

'Is it Kreer?' Xeno queried. He knew the major was supposed to be in Washington, but he was known to be unreliable.

'Unlikely. I am receiving no communicator carrier wave signal.'

'Visual display!' The holosphere's image focused in on a short figure on the roof below. 'The Doctor!'

'All EM wavebands are jammed, Commander, but there is a disruption in our EM pulse. A duplicate jamming signal is being reflected back to us in a feedback loop.'

'Sound general quarters! Restore graviton power flow to cloaking level and set course zero-seven-zero mark zero-eight-five.'

Long fingers slid across the onyx consoles. 'Helm not responding. Feedback loop is dephasing our drive field.' The ship suddenly lurched downwards.

'Stabilize!'

The ship plunged sideways. 'All systems overloaded and shutting down.'

'We must not be examined by human biologists,' Xeno reminded his crew. 'You know what to do.'

Andrews watched in amazement as the disc slipped sideways and swung round before finally slamming into the rocky plain, blue sparks coruscating over its surface.

Below, the alarms stopped. Andrews was painfully aware that it would be several hours before the generators could be restarted.

'That was the easy bit,' the Doctor commented beside him., 'Can I borrow a few more bits and bobs from you?'

'Why not?' Andrews said, half-dreamily for the sake of his mind. 'What for?'

'For the difficult bit, of course. Getting that ship working again.'

The wreckage of the burnt-out Hercules had been transferred to an empty hangar so that normal services could be resumed. A clean white DH Comet cargo conversion, long and slim with gentle curves, waited at a nearby loading area. Overalled men were busy carrying out fuelling and preflight checks, while two men in dark BOAC uniforms toured the plane on an inspection with emotionless professionalism.

A drab green cargo helicopter swept low across the river and over the airport. It settled down only yards from the Comet. Kreer jumped down from the side doors as the groundcrew pushed a scissor-legged trolley towards the helicopter.

The crew raised the platform of the trolley about three feet and rolled a tarpaulin-draped oblong shape out onto it. Kreer stood on the trolley bed beside the shape as it was pushed towards the Comet. As the platform was raised to the level of the Comet's cargo doors, Kreer tugged the tarpaulin away from the shape.

He pushed the freezer-sized corrugated steel box into the aircraft, and beckoned to two men in dark uniforms to join him aboard. Moving forward to the cockpit as they entered, Kreer fixed them with a steady look. 'You have dealt with the Ph'Sor pilots?'

'Yes, sir,' they acknowledged. 'We triggered their self-immolation after killing them.'

'Excellent. You have your orders. Obey them.'

Chapter 17

Ace had been glaring at the heavy door for some time before the lock clicked and a man with a lean and firm, yet somehow not quite mature, face came in. 'So you're the one behind all the excitement at the Monument today?'

Ace merely cocked an eyebrow.

He shook his head as if to clear it, and Ace sighed in exasperation. Obviously they weren't letting her go yet. 'A woman at the heart of all that violence,' he went on. 'It's unbelievable.'

'Wait until the Seventies,' Ace muttered under her breath.

'What?'

'Never heard of Bonnie and Clyde? Look, don't I get a phone call or something?'

'Eventually. Of course, as a possible fifth columnist, you're something of a special case – not to mention an embarrassment.'

Ace laughed in disbelief. 'Fifth columnist? For who – the Russians?' Gradually, she realized that he wasn't even smiling, and tried to remember what she knew of the Fifties from TV. 'You're not joking, are you?' she whispered, gloomily recalling what usually happened to so-called 'embarrassments' in those old shows and movies.

'Why else were you involved in a pitched battle in the heart of the capital?'

'Trying to save your precious city. Didn't you find the bomb I defused?'

'Oh yes. It was stolen from Holloman AFB less than

forty-eight hours ago. Guess who's the number one suspect?' He leaned against the wall with a relaxed air. 'Your comic-book explanations don't hold much water,' he continued. 'Wouldn't you rather give one that does?'

'That is a very long story, and one you probably wouldn't believe. Who are you anyway? FBI?'

'That's right; Agent Joe Manco at your service.'

Ace nodded to herself. She was certain he wouldn't believe the truth, of course, and lying would be risky; but governmental aid would be extremely useful. How to enlist it, though... 'I'm Ace,' she told him.

'An Ace what?' he asked.

'Just Ace. I'm currently working under the auspices of one Allen Dulles, if the name means anything to you.' Sort of, in a manner of speaking, she reminded herself silently.

'And I'm Dick Tracy, and you're still under arrest.'

'Look,' Ace began impatiently, there must be some sort of line of communication between the FBI and the CIA. Call them, and get word to Dulles that the Doctor's party needs your assistance.'

'The director of Central Intelligence is a busy man, so that might take a while.'

'Don't bet on it.' One thing Ace was confident of was the pulling power of the Doctor's name with those who valued his help.

For a moment, she thought he was going to turn her down, since her claim was an unlikely one at best. After a few seconds, however, he nodded curtly. 'That's your one phone call, but if you're lying...' He left the rest of the sentence hanging as he left the cell. Ace slumped back against the concrete wall and muttered a general thanks to any world's gods that might be listening.

Riding the police motorbike that she had borrowed – she tried to convince herself – from its former user, Benny had spent an hour discreetly tracking the fleeing guards southwards. Their car had entered the disused grounds of the wartime Naval Research Laboratories, and Benny had cautiously followed, trying to remain behind available cover.

Quietly, she abandoned the motorbike behind a wheeled refuse bin that was parked against a wall. Keeping low, she moved up to a pile of broken crates a few yards from the dilapidated building. Peering around the splintered wood, she saw that the car she had followed was now parked before a gangplank that led from a weed-strewn quay to a dull and solid-looking ship moored on the river. The gun-turrets betrayed the fact that it was a warship of some kind, but it was relatively small and Benny estimated that it was either a frigate or a destroyer. There was no sign of life on deck, but the radar antennae were rotating steadily and glimmers of light could be made out through several portholes.

The thought occurred to Benny that her quarry could have left the car here as a red herring and be hiding in one of the wartime buildings. On the other hand, she felt, with their superiority in numbers and technology, they wouldn't need to resort to stealth.

She knew that she could crouch there all day debating which way to go, if she wasn't careful. The fact that she was unarmed was a major reason to turn back, but the importance of finding out what was going on, plus her natural curiosity, led her towards the shop. Laying her mental debate aside, she acted on instinct, her body moving to the gangplank before her mind knew what it was doing.

Boarding the ship, she kept low. Since no one had yet spotted her, she ducked quickly into the first hatchway she came to.

Manco's mind was buzzing as he strode down the darkened corridor to the cells. Something very strange was going on, as his recent conversation with the CIA had proved. Worse still, someone had a lot of string-pulling power and, to his chagrin, it didn't seem to be him.

Nevertheless, he would follow through on this new twist of his assignments, regardless of his personal opinion. He didn't, after all, want to be seen as rebellious. He also didn't like losing valuable time in which he could be piecing together the puzzle of Kreer's foreign contacts, of course, but as his superiors were fond of telling him, he didn't have to like it so long as he did it.

The officer on guard opened Ace's cell at Manco's wordless nod, and Manco stepped inside.

Tobey moved smoothly to the security panel on the destroyer's bridge as an alarm chimed softly. Touching the control beside the warning system, he brought up an image of a companionway on an upper deck. A female civilian was moving along it furtively. Tobey tapped his communicator implant. 'Intruder alert on C-deck. Apprehend immediately.'

'Belay that order,' Kreer snapped, moving over. He looked at the image in the holosphere, something tickling his mind. 'I've seen that face somewhere before.'

'She was at Corman – you saw the security recordings.'

'No, I mean before that. Never mind. I'll see to her personally. We don't want the bait eaten before the fish comes along.'

Ace had been escorted to Manco's office and left to twiddle her thumbs, a guard outside keeping an eye on her while Manco went off somewhere. After a short time, she looked up as the door opened, and watched Manco questioningly. 'You seem to have friends in high places,' he said with a trace of a disappointed tone, coming round to sit behind his desk.

Ace relaxed in relief. 'A friend of a friend, more like.'

'You must really be something,' Manco drawled, tugging a sheaf of papers from an inside pocket. With a sigh, he leaned against the wall and scrutinized Ace as if weighing something up. Ace didn't care for the look at all. 'These are your release papers – all signed, sealed and delivered. I've been told – no, *instructed* – that, as a result of a lot of inter-service string-pulling by the DCI himself, we're supposed to "render any and all assistance necessary", as they put it. An empty office is being made available to you over at the CIA building at 3024 East Street North-West.'

'It's about smegging time,' Ace grumbled. The history of her own planet was being threatened, and she didn't feel very helpful while sitting in a cell. Admittedly, she didn't really want to blame Manco for anything. For one thing, he was doing his best under exceptionally odd and trying – even by Ace's standards – circumstances. More importantly, if the Tzun screwed up Earth history, Manco could do no worse than die; Ace, on the other hand, might never have existed. Having said that, she felt she would probably blame him anyway, for the simple reason that he was here. 'Look,' she said, a little more understandingly, 'I don't need a desk, and I don't need that much assistance – just someone to tell me where a Major Kreer hangs out while he's in Washington.'

'What did you say?' Manco demanded, turning pale.

'I need to know where a Major Kreer –'

'This Kreer, is he an Air Force Intelligence officer in the southern sector?'

'Yeah, you know him?' Ace asked suspiciously, tensing subconsciously as she wondered if her release might be some sort of Tzun trap.

Manco smiled unexpectedly. 'That makes your story a lot more believable – if only because everything odd that's happened lately seems to come back to him. It seems we've been working on the same case, but from opposite ends. Maybe we have some things to tell each other.'

'I don't doubt that,' she replied cautiously. He seemed to be okay, she thought, and at least she was fairly sure that he was human, since all the Tzun she'd met so far had blond hair, unlike Manco's brown locks. His eagerness was a bit unsettling, but it wasn't something she could really fault; after all, he wasn't the first person to try to run before he could walk. The thought stung her guiltily.

Manco paused as he sifted through a manila file. 'Did you, by any chance, come from Nevada?'

'Not originally, but last night, yes.'

'So you're the one who crashed at National, I presume,' he commented with a bemused look.

'I always said I could fly; I didn't say anything about being able to land.'

'Why did you torch it? So we couldn't get prints?'

'Not exactly. There were some things of Kreer's aboard that didn't belong there. Smuggled arms,' she added, trying to think of something that Manco would understand. It wasn't exactly a lie. 'We didn't want them falling into the wrong hands. What have you got there?' she asked, tired of the subject.

'Photographs,' he answered, spreading the contents of the file across the desk. Shuffling them, he finally found one that showed Kreer himself. 'This is Kreer paying a visit to the Interplanetary Phenomenon Unit as Air Force Intelligence's representative at a monthly inter-service summit meeting.'

The picture showed a man, the sight of whom raised the hairs on the back of Ace's neck, stepping from a staff car. The Air Force uniform didn't confuse her in the slightest, as her eyes remained fixed in horrified fascination on the face in the glossy prints. 'Qu'vatlh!' she spat. 'The good news, Manco, is that I know who he is. The bad news is that we are in deep shit.'

Slipping quietly down the narrow companionway, Benny ran a hand along the dull grey wall, her eyes following the ribbed cables along the ceiling to the simply formed speakers that would blare out alerts in time of battle. It was all terrific stuff, she thought. There was an almost obsessive use of metal, with not a single neoplast fitting in sight. It was wonderful, and she had to resist the urge to take notes as she went.

Something began to intrude itself into her mind, however, distracting her from her gleeful examination of the fascinatingly primitive structure of the ship. Cocking her head slightly, she listened carefully, trying to single out the sound that had piqued her interest among the jumble of other hums and creaks of the ship. Despite the attraction of the long-forgotten material and design of her current environment, Benny moved off further down the corridor, realizing that the sound was coming from behind a closed door at the end of the passage. It was also getting louder.

It seemed to be a sort of echoing musical tone, with a strange backing that rose and fell. It was an oddly familiar sound, and Benny tried the door, only to find that it was locked. For a moment, she was glad that the ship wasn't moving, or the rising and falling tone would probably have had her stomach coming out in sympathy with it. At least you couldn't get sea-sick in the TARDIS, she thought with a faint inward smile.

The expression froze on her face. That was what was familiar about the sound, she realized. It was like the TARDIS, but different somehow. Newer, she suddenly thought; that was it, not as worn as the TARDIS.

It stopped with a bass crunch as if something heavy had settled down. Benny bent to the lock, trying to peer through the keyhole, but the interior of the cabin was pitch black. Pulling out a small dental scraper she normally used for scraping soft rock away from delicate fossils, she knelt in front of the door. With extreme delicacy, she inserted the scraper into the lock and started to feel around gingerly for the barrel.

Abruptly a dull blur appeared in front of her eyes with a metallic rattle.

It was, naturally, a set of keys, and she didn't need the Doctor's foresight to know that one of them would be for this door. Telling herself resignedly that it wasn't as if she shouldn't have got used to this sort of thing by now, she straightened slowly. Turning, she found an Air Force major nodding understandingly. 'There can't be too many Air Force majors wandering around with alien friends and stolen warheads,' she commented. 'You are Major Kreer, I presume?'

'I am many things,' Kreer acknowledged. He gestured with a stubby black device in his gloved hand. It looked to Benny like either a weapon or a sex toy, and she didn't think even he would consider this a proper time or place.

He held the weapon steadily.

'Take me to your leader?' Benny raised her hands.

'I don't believe that should be necessary; I'm already here, miss . . .?'

'Summerfield. Bernice Summerfield. My friends call me Benny, but you can call me Professor Summerfield.'

'Bernice Summerfield?' Kreer looked surprised. 'That's why your face was familiar.' Ignoring her look of astonishment, he leaned carefully past her and unlocked the door.

'Your parlour, I presume.'

Kreer indicated that she should enter, and there didn't seem to be much choice. She turned the handle and pushed.

The room beyond was filled from deck to ceiling with instruments that were clearly of local design and manufacture, reconfigured into bizarre and anachronistic networks. She recognized a few pieces of Tzun technology forming the central nodes of several linkages. A medium-sized black cat watched her impassively through luminescent eyes. 'Are all the white ones copyrighted?' Benny asked, nodding towards it.

Strangest of all was some sort of Ionic-style fluted sandstone column, which was totally out of place in the cabin of a destroyer. The weapon never wavering from Benny's midriff, Kreer ran a hand along the weathered stone, his face displaying such satisfaction that she half-expected him to light a cigarette like in the old movies. 'Sometimes even Time isn't such a successful thief after all,' he murmured to himself. 'Even with this primitive equipment, the Staatenheim remote-control principle works perfectly.' He turned back to Benny. 'I believe the usual parlance in this era would be: "What is a respected archaeologist like you doing in a place like this?"'

'Do you know me?' Benny demanded.

'Only by reputation,' he answered smoothly. 'I read your paper on the foundations of Martian Feudalism.'

'Nice to know I have some satisfied customers.' She

smiled uncertainly. How could he possibly have read her work, which wouldn't be published for over half a millennium? A nasty suspicion was forming in her mind.

'Your conclusions were all wrong, of course,' he added snidely, 'but not by as much as I might have expected from a human.'

'What?' Professional outrage thrummed in Benny's muscles, and she almost took a step forwards, regardless of the strange weapon. 'How could a twentieth-century Air Force officer have heard of me? Just who are you really?'

'Hasn't the Doctor told you about me?' Kreer tut-tutted softly. 'He always did have a shaky grasp of the important issues.' His feral smile exposed pointed teeth amidst the neatly-trimmed beard. 'I am known as the Master,' he announced simply, then smiled to himself. 'Universally.'

Chapter 18

The Master removed a small control from his uniform pocket and pressed the single button on its surface. With a deep hum the fluted column split open, the blackness inside swallowing up what little light was in the cabin. With a slight motion of the weapon he still held, he indicated that Benny should enter the gap.

Warily, Benny stepped through the doorway and found herself in a TARDIS console room. Its design was superficially similar to the Doctor's, though the fittings were clearly newer, but the matt black decor gave the chamber a depressingly funereal air. The absence of the sorts of odds and ends of collected junk and anachronistic furniture that characterized the Doctor's machine as a home made this machine no more than a barren and impersonal piece of technology, as lifeless as any other tool.

Footsteps behind her announced the Master's presence. Benny turned round in time to see the cat slink in past his leg. With a snap, the Master raised a fine gold pocket watch on a chain, spinning it gently before her eyes. Flickers of light gleamed on its curved surface as it spun. 'As an archaeologist, you should appreciate this piece,' he said silkily. 'Eighteenth century, I guarantee.' He paused as Benny watched it. 'Listen to me very carefully, Professor Summerfield,' he said with surprising gentleness. 'You hear only my voice. I am the Master, and you will obey me. You will obey me . . .'

'Master, eh?' Benny rolled the word experimentally. 'A Freudian compensation, is it?'

'What?' The Master looked momentarily thrown by the lack of any sign of subservience on the part of his captive.

'The name, I mean. I suppose it's some sort of domination complex that's arisen to compensate for some physical impotency?'

'I see,' the Master said in a weary voice. 'Your inane opinions have no relevance to Gallifreyan physiognomy. Stand over there and keep quiet,' he finished dismissively, stuffing the watch back into his pocket as he turned to the console.

While the Master's back was turned, Benny started sidling towards the double doors, her glance falling briefly on the cat. 'One more step, Professor Summerfield, and you'll be looking at Shadow from eye level,' the Master snapped, without turning round from the console. 'Surely the Doctor has told you of the effects of the tissue compression eliminator?'

'I believe I've heard it mentioned,' she replied calmly, and stopped moving. At least she now knew what the stubby weapon was.

'Do not let my apparent lack of concern deceive you. Shadow and I have a somewhat unusual working relationship.' He turned to favour her with a predatory smile. Benny drew back from his look, for now his hooded eyes were glowing internally with the same lucent gold as the cat's.

'There's an ex-Navy destroyer, the *USS Jessup*, moored on the river between the old Naval Research Laboratories and Bolling AFB,' Manco explained. 'We've no idea what the Air Force could be doing with it and the DoD aren't saying, which means it's probably under a black budget. However,' he went on meaningfully, 'we do have knowledge of Kreer paying regular visits to the ship. We've intercepted phone calls between Kreer and the ship's captain as well, but we can't identify the language used.'

'I'll bet you can't. Sounds like a good place to start, though.' Ace smiled encouragingly.

'Right. I can have fifty men ready – ' He was silenced by a shake of Ace's head.

'Take an army and the Master'll freak out. Increase the force, and you'll just increase the bodycount – his co-conspirators will probably have disruptors.'

'Dis-what?'

'New weapons he's stolen from the R&D labs at Corman,' she bluffed. 'All I need is myself.'

'Ourselves. This is my case, and my jurisdiction.'

Ace sat silently for a moment. Manco was certainly no Dirty Harry and, by his own admission, mostly dealt with what would come to be known as white-collar crimes. This was not what she would have considered an auspicious start to a probable combat mission, and she'd already seen far too many fighters drop like flies in their first combat. On the other hand, she reminded herself, you could never tell how someone would perform in any given situation until you saw them in it. Besides, he was just old enough to have served in World War Two or Korea.

The most important consideration, however, was that – short of shooting him – there was little she could do to stop him going, while there was plenty he could do to stop her. She nodded in resignation. 'I'll need my stuff back.'

'We'll pick it up on the way out. You know, I'm risking ten years just by not sending that stuff straight back to Corman.'

'I don't doubt that, but my stuff didn't come from Corman.' She thought for a moment. 'Why do you take that risk?'

'I've been lucky to get this far in the Bureau so young. If I'm going to keep up the pace, I've got to show I can take it.'

Ace nodded, gaining the measure of him as he spoke. This she could understand, having felt that way herself for a long time. It didn't mean it was right, though. 'There's an old saying that there are old soldiers and bold soldiers, but no old, bold soldiers,' she told him. 'That isn't true, but there is a difference between boldness and foolhardiness.' She rose and moved to the window, seeing not Washington but distant battles and desperate gambles. 'You can be bold to survive,' she went on, 'or for honour. Even because you're not really much good at anything else any more. But gambling to prove a point for personal satisfaction; now that's foolhardiness, and if the person you're trying to prove yourself to is yourself . . . There are no old foolhardy soldiers.'

None of this seemed to matter much to Manco, who simply leaned back in his chair. He smiled contentedly, cocking an eyebrow at her. 'I think I'm doing all right. This all makes a change from the fraudsters I'm used to. I could get used to this.'

Ace knew exactly how he felt; she had once succumbed to the same emotions. Unfortunately, she knew from bitter experience what the usual method of learning better was. 'No,' she contradicted him sadly, 'you never do.'

The Master straightened after his examination of the TARDIS console, stretching himself in an unnervingly feline manner before looking over to face Benny again. The eerie glow had faded from his eyes, but was still just discernible. 'The Doctor said you didn't have a TARDIS last time you met,' she prompted, vaguely hoping that he might let something important slip out if she could engage him in conversation.

'As you see,' he answered proudly, 'that is no longer a concern. It is also in perfect working order, as I shall now demonstrate.' Benny looked towards the door in alarm. 'A short test trip only,' he explained in a malicious tone that told Benny he was lapping up every moment of her discomfort. 'I shall be moving us only a few minutes in time.'

With a smug look, he threw the dematerialization switch, and the glowing filaments of the time rotor began rising and falling. It slowed to a halt almost instantly, and the Master operated the door lever. He gestured towards the door with the tissue compression eliminator, and ushered Benny out of the TARDIS ahead of him.

Temporarily unable to think of a better option, Benny acquiesced.

She found herself stepping not from an Ionic column, but from a plain metal equipment locker. She was still, however, in the Master's cluttered cabin. The vibration of the deck plates was enough to confirm that the ship was now moving, which it hadn't been before. That convinced her that they really had moved in time. She just hoped it really was only a few minutes, and not a couple of years.

The Master emerged from the TARDIS, tissue compression eliminator in hand, and escorted her from the cabin. He led her through a series of cluttered grey corridors, eventually emerging onto the destroyer's bridge.

Beyond the long range of windows, the disused airbase's empty dispersal fields were slipping off to the left as the ship pulled away from her mooring. Below the windows were stretched rows of instruments, which were tended by several men in navy uniform. Mounted in a central position was a sphere with a holographic projection inside. Several touch-sensitive controls glowed on the smooth panel at the base of the sphere. 'Tzun technology?' Benny asked rhetorically.

'Naturally,' the Master replied in a patronizing tone. 'An archaeologist such as yourself should have at least a passing familiarity with the artifacts of the Tzun Confederacy.' He moved to the sphere, bringing up a series of diffuse images. Benny suspected that the holosphere's projection frequency was attuned to the brainwave frequency of his own visual cortex – a common precaution in her time. As she moved closer, the image remained resolutely fuzzy, confirming her suspicions.

'I know they never reached Earth.'

'Really? Are you familiar with the Nestene Consciousness?'

'Vaguely. They control a sector of the Tau quadrant.'

'Did they ever reach Earth?'

'Of course not!'

'I suggest you ask the Doctor that same question when next you meet – assuming you believe in some sort of afterlife, that is.' Turning to one of the officers, the Master pointed at Benny. 'Chief, throw her in the brig. I believe that is the correct parlance.'

'Now just wait – ' Benny stopped as the officer drew his side-arm. Rather than a revolver or automatic, it was a disruptor which he levelled at her calmly. Surveying her immediate environment with a new and terrible clarity, she noticed something which had previously escaped her notice.

Though they were all individuals, every one of the officers present had eyes so deep blue as to be violet, and hair like spun gold.

As the chief led Benny away, Tobey handed the Master a slim silver case. 'As per your agreement with the Triumvirate.'

'Thank you,' the Master snapped disinterestedly. The case occupied his entire attention, leaving no room for social niceties. Opening it, he felt a glow of satisfaction at the sight of the gun-like hypospray nestling in its foam packing. A slim four-inch needle glittered dangerously from the snout of the hypo, while a liquid filled a glass ampoule to its rear. A faint silvery sheen to the ampoule gleamed richly, though it was difficult to tell whether this was a property of the liquid or the glass.

Lifting the hypo free, the Master fought to contain the trembling urgency which threatened to overwhelm him. As it was, the contents of the ampoule rippled in his hand. 'This is the last?' he asked suspiciously.

'It is. Surgeon-Major Ksal's geneticists have programmed the structure of the corrupted Trakenite DNA into the recharged nanites suspended in that solution. When activated, they will deconstruct those gene sequences and remodel them by reassembling the remaining DNA.'

'Which is my own,' the Master completed. 'No more will I suffer the indignity of carrying the blood of that pacifist degenerate!'

'The recharged nanites will give you your new life cycle, naturally.'

'Yes...' The Master moved off towards the door, his face a mask of determination. He was halted by Tobey's hand on his arm.

'Don't let this lure you into forgetting the rest of your part of the agreement,' Tobey warned, as the Master gave him an angry glare.

'Of course not. You won't free me from this planet otherwise.'

'Exactly. One other thing.' Tobey wore a look of concern. 'Should we not have killed the human female?' he asked.

'I thought the Tzun precepts taught that excess violence is bad for business,' the Master said, absently stroking the surface of the case.

'Of course.' Tobey paused with a frown. 'Sometimes it seems... unworthy of a warrior.'

'I understand perfectly,' the Master said softly. 'The other Ph'Sor also feel that way. I shall put it another way. If you kill the maggot before baiting the hook with it, it will not wriggle and attract the fish. Professor Summerfield is more useful alive.'

'To lure the Doctor.'

'Yes.' Tobey turned away as the Master moved to the helmsman. 'Take us to fifteen knots – I want to be in open sea by dawn.'

'What of the ground-zero guard captain? I sent him to greet you. He has been disciplined?'

The Master gave Tobey a condescending look. 'He has been disciplined properly – as you should have thought to have done. It was a lesson his replacement will not easily forget.'

Manco pulled the car into the roadside and squinted across at a thin trail of smoke rising from the other side of Bolling's grounds. 'Looks like they've set sail,' he muttered, reaching into the glove compartment for a pair of field-glasses.

'So it seems,' Ace agreed, observing the distant vessel through the image enhancement facilities of her sunglasses. 'They haven't got up much speed yet, though. Is there anywhere we can intercept them?'

'This road meets up with Highway 95. That's the boundary ring-road, so if we take a right we'll come out onto a bridge we could use.'

'Well, the least we can do is take a look at it.'

As the ship's speed picked up slightly, the chief stumbled against the bulkhead. Her surprised elation boosted by a sudden burst of adrenalin, Benny took the opportunity to shove the off-balance officer through the brig door.

Slamming it shut with relief, she trotted back the way she had come. The destroyer was small compared to the warren of corridors that made up the TARDIS, and she felt confident of being able to find her way to a communications room of some kind fairly quickly.

The Tzun communicator which the Master had had moulded into his USAF insignia, since he didn't trust their implants, beeped softly as he entered his cabin. 'Yes?'

'The human female has escaped, one deck below the radio room.'

'Let her wriggle, and keep me informed.' Chuckling softly, the Master smiled and entered his TARDIS.

Inside, he took the silver case over to a flat-topped protrusion on the console and opened it up. At the touch of a control, two curved grips slid from a hatch in the side of the protrusion. Clipping the glass ampoule into the grips, he touched the control that retracted the whole thing back into the console. A translucent image of a cell structure immediately flickered into being above the flat top. Tiny symbols and glyphs danced around it, turning to remain legible to him as he walked around to view the other side of the side cell structure.

Pursing his lips, he tapped out a series of commands. Another hologram appeared next to the first, which was identical in every way. Allowing himself a slight smile, the

Master shut down the displays and retrieved the ampoule from the console. Slipping it back into its mounting on the hypo, he carried it over to a reclining seat near the scanner screen.

The Master removed his uniform jacket and settled into the cushioned form of the curved seat. Laying the hypo in his lap, he parted the shirt over his chest. Underneath was neither skin nor even hair, but smooth tiger-striped fur. Grimacing at the painful and offensive sight and feel of it, he parted the fur to reveal a slim line of deathly white skin underneath. Concentrating on keeping his gorge from rising, he let his revulsion and self-loathing at what was happening to him be consumed by the fires of anger. A blaze of hatred for the Doctor cleared his mind long enough for him to lift the hypo, placing the tip of the needle over a point directly between his hearts.

With a half-choked snarl, he rammed the needle home and pressed the trigger. With a cry, his back arched in a spasm. After a few moments, however, his body relaxed and his face lost its contorted grimace.

Weakly pulling the needle free and dropping the spent hypo on the floor, the Master stood somewhat shakily. 'Now the nanites need only do their work.'

Yet another blond crewman was manning the radio room when Benny stumbled across it. The door was open, but the operator's back was to it. Watching, she noticed that he was sitting very straight: almost to attention, in fact. Not a crew*man*, she corrected herself, but another Ph'Sor Tzun. Hoping that his earphones would mask any sound of her approach, Benny sidled up behind him.

Her hopes were dashed when, just as she got within reach of him, he turned in surprise. With inhuman speed, he scooped up a coffee cup and hurled it at her, forcing her to duck as he leapt from his seat.

Shocked and angered as she saw him reach for his gun, Benny flung herself at him rather than straightening. Her head caught him below the breastbone and slammed him back into the banks of radio equipment. He dodged her next punch, leaving her hand to crash painfully into a glass dial as he looped his headset flex around her throat. Her eyes bulged as he pulled the flex tight with one knee on her back.

Instead of vainly trying to pull away, Benny jerked her head sharply backwards, feeling the bridge of his nose crumple under the impact of her skull. While he was off-balance, she rolled over. He was sent tumbling, his disruptor slipping from its holster and bouncing across the floor. He rolled with the force of her throw, stretching out a hand for the gun.

He stopped short when Benny slammed a foot down on the small of his back on her way to the weapon. The Tzun grabbed her ankle with his outflung hand and she fell sprawling, as he pulled himself up to his knees. This wasn't far enough away to escape the vicious kick she delivered to his face, her heel smashing into his mouth. As his head snapped back, Benny caught the disruptor in her outstretched fingers and brought it round to aim at his head.

He froze.

Benny also froze, though for quite different reasons. The radio operator was bleeding profusely from nose and mouth, but there was no scarlet stain. Instead, a watery yellow-orange pus-like fluid was oozing out to drip on the floor. Filing that information away for future use, Benny gestured with the disruptor. 'Now that you've had your kicks, you're going to tell me how to operate these antiques.'

The Tzun simply glared at her, raising a hand to his head as if gingerly feeling his wounds. He suddenly gave a defiant grin and pressed the left side of his neck. Benny hurled herself aside instinctively, just as a bright flame enveloped him. Burning like a sodium flare for a few seconds, the flame suddenly faded, leaving only a scorched patch on the deck to indicate that the radio operator had ever existed.

Gagging, only partly due to the thick acrid smell left

behind, Benny picked up his overturned chair. Why did he have to do that, she wondered, dropping wearily into the chair. It wasn't as if she was going to kill him, or indeed do anything more than lock him away in a cupboard somewhere until his friends found him. She knew that armed forces sometimes put out propaganda about what the enemy would do to captured prisoners, and wondered if the Tzun had been so afraid of her that he'd rather die. It was just such a waste, she felt. She momentarily wondered if he – whatever he was – had a family of some kind waiting for him somewhere.

Sadly, and unable to feel angry at not knowing how to operate the radio equipment, she began to experiment with the controls.

Under the sharp autumn light, the waters of the Potomac appeared mirrored. The river was silvered, while the lands around were burnished with emerald and copper tones, leaving the grey destroyer very much an intruder.

Ace watched as the *Jessup* approached the bridge upon which she and Manco now stood. The car was parked on a grass verge at the end of the steel and concrete structure. Manco had returned her blaster and wrist computer, and she was checking the charge remaining in the weapon as the ship hove into view.

'That's the one,' Ace pronounced, with a certainty she felt but didn't like at all. 'I can almost smell him.' She knew that Manco would assume this to be a hunch of some kind, but had to reluctantly admit to herself that what she said was true. She and the Master were the last two survivors of the Cheetah Planet's effects to retain their own selves, and somehow the heightened senses she had developed there could still scent him after all this time. She knew now why she had felt the odd sense of 'someone walking over her grave' so often over the last couple of days. It had been so long since she had been able to track him from Midge's flat to the Perivale youth club that she had all but forgotten.

Looking towards either end of the bridge, she made a

rough guess at its height above the water. It was a fixed bridge, but the fact that the river cut between two low hills at this point meant that the ship would just be able to slip underneath at the current low tide. This is where a Dalek anti-grav disc would come in handy, she thought. 'Do you have any rope?' she asked a surprised-looking Manco.

The lieutenant manning the Tzun monitoring equipment on the *Jessup*'s bridge looked to Tobey for permission to speak as the Master entered. Tobey nodded, and the lieutenant addressed the Master: 'I am detecting unauthorized signal leakage from the radio room.'

'Visual.'

The lieutenant brought up an image in the holosphere that showed Benny fiddling with controls. 'There.'

'Has she had any reply yet?'

'Negative, but if she's unfamiliar with the equipment, she may not be transmitting a coherent signal.'

'No. A shame, really. Continue monitoring for another five minutes. After that, we'll assume no one is listening and lock her up properly.'

Manco had only a single coil of rope in his car boot, but Ace felt it would be strong enough to support them both. At her insistence, he had fixed it securely around the steel railing. Ace watched the ship's approach, something about it puzzling her. 'Why isn't anyone on deck?' she wondered aloud.

'Who cares? So long as they aren't around to see us. All that matters is that we succeed.'

'Damn right.' Ace hoped her bravura would keep him in line, for she had been wondering exactly the same thing. 'If any full-blooded Tzun are on board, they'd have to stay below, but the Ph'Sor and the Master should be all right.'

'Who are the Tzun, Ph'Sor and the Master?'

Ace cursed herself for letting that sort of thing slip. It would still be best if he believed they were dealing with human opponents, she thought. 'The Tzun and Ph'Sor are... Chinese tongs involved in arms-smuggling. The Master is a code-name for Kreer – as in "criminal mastermind".' Bracing herself with a foot against the rail, Ace tugged on the rope to tighten it and test the load. 'Good enough. Age before beauty,' she suggested, motioning for Manco to swing himself over first.

'Swell,' he opined ironically, grasping the rope and lowering himself over the edge. Above, Ace pulled on her gauntlets to protect against rope-burn. Coat-tails flapping in the wind, she climbed down after him.

Tobey was first to notice the tiny figures dangling ahead of the ship. 'Most curious,' he murmured. The Master looked up at the sound of his voice and joined him at the window, a slowly forming predatory smile exposing pointed teeth that glistened. 'The Doctor and his companion?' Tobey asked.

'His companion, certainly,' the Master agreed, feeling as well as seeing Ace's presence. 'The other is not the Doctor, however.' He watched the pair through narrowed eyes. 'She will suffice. Once we have both women, the Doctor will certainly come looking for them. Full alert!' As Ace and her companion vanished above the top of the windows, a raucous alarm started blaring.

Manco was a few feet over the roof of the forward superstructure when the alarms began. 'Jump,' Ace called to him. 'I'll get down the mast.'

'Right,' he called back, letting go of the rope. He dropped onto the roof, then rolled back up with surprising agility.

Ace, meanwhile, was judging speeds as the mast rushed towards her. With a deep breath, she stretched out a hand to grab one of the power cables that webbed it, letting go of the rope in the same instant. The sudden change in inertia whipped her round, winding her as she hit the mast. She managed to hold on, however, and determinedly started sliding down the cable towards the base of the forward funnel.

By the time she reached the deck, Manco had clambered down from the roof to join her. Both of them looked around for any sign of defensive forces but no one came out on deck.

'I've got a bad feeling about this,' Manco muttered.

'You were the one who wanted to come.'

'I've got a lot to live up to. I can't let the Bureau down. Your friends are obviously up to something.'

'I know what you mean. They want us inside.' Ace's mind rushed, trying to figure out why the Master hadn't already had them surrounded by guards. Presumably it was because he knew they would have to go below decks, where they could be trapped. The question was, how to go in without that happening?

Offhand, she couldn't think of any answer to that. Unfortunately, nor could she think of any alternative action to take. 'The bastard's thought of everything,' she murmured to herself. Meanwhile Manco had drawn his Browning and was reaching for the nearest door handle. Impulsively, Ace grabbed the handle first.

Manco may have been a couple of years older, but he was inexperienced. Ace, as the more experienced warrior, didn't want to be responsible for anything untoward happening to him. She wondered if this was how the Doctor – sometimes – looked on her and Benny. Being a leader was a pain in the neck, she thought; what if I get him killed for nothing? She dismissed the idea. If she started thinking like that, she might get careful; and that would be dangerous. 'Fools rush in,' she told Marco. Before he could respond, she tugged the door open, ducking back out of the way in case a shot came out.

Nothing happened.

'If anyone is receiving, please respond,' Benny urged, twiddling some dials as far as they would go. Behind her, the bulkhead door opened with a dull thud.

The Master, flanked by Tobey, stepped into the room.

'You needn't pollute the airwaves any further, my dear Professor,' the Master told her. 'Your violent friend from Perivale is already on board, and on her way to rescue you right now.'

'Which means you are now dispensable,' Tobey warned, coming forward with a drawn disruptor.

'Is that all people are to you? Disposable tools?' Benny snapped, a surge of outrage welling up inside her.

'I'm afraid I am not yet finished with the Professor, Commander,' the Master interrupted her. 'Once her violent friend has joined us, I will return with them to Corman Field to await the arrival of the Doctor's rescue attempt.'

'Snowbird will not be available to return you to Corman until tomorrow afternoon,' Tobey corrected him.

'Snowbird is unnecessary now.'

Tobey turned to the Master, a puzzled look on his features. 'What do you mean by that?' The puzzlement faded from his face. 'Unless... No! That contravenes the terms of the alliance; you said you needed us to take you from Earth.'

'I said I needed your help. There is a difference,' the Master admitted smugly. 'My TARDIS is already on board. I no longer need the Tzun Confederacy.'

Eyes wide, Tobey raised his disruptor, but was too late. There was a brief purple glow from the Master's stubby weapon, and Tobey screamed. Worse was to come, however, as Benny watched in horror. Tobey's body collapsed to the floor, beginning to crumple inwards. Writhing on the ground, it twisted up with a series of popping cracks. In seconds, Tobey was a gnarled twig of a figure, no bigger than the fallen disruptor which lay beside him.

Laughing softly, the Master moved the tissue compression eliminator to cover Benny. 'Now you are coming with me to see your friend, Professor Summerfield.'

'I'm not going to help you,' Benny warned him defiantly. 'And Ace sure as hell won't.'

'*Au contraire*; your very presence is exactly the help I need.'

'I don't see how; I'm not a psychiatrist.'

'My patience is running thin,' the Master snapped. 'I only need one of you alive.'

Manco watched uneasily as Ace peered around the corner ahead of them. She suddenly slipped back, flattening herself against the wall. As he did the same, he saw Kreer going past the junction, holding a woman at the point of some sort of weapon.

When they had passed out of sight, Manco quietly joined Ace at the corner. 'Was that your friend?' He couldn't keep the grimness out of his voice, disappointed that even Kreer wasn't above such tactics as abducting women.

'Yeah, that was Benny.' Ace's eyes had a dangerously feral look about them as she glared down the corridor. 'When we confront the Master, you may want to just shoot him, since I doubt you could hold him. The British government couldn't, at any rate.'

'I'll bear that thought in mind.' Manco wondered quietly whether he could shoot someone in cold blood, and resolved to try not to find out. Justice had to be seen to be done, especially if it was to get him promoted. He followed Ace along the corridor with a light head and a heavy heart.

The corridor ended at a flight of steps leading up to another bulkhead door. Going ahead to peer through, Manco could see the array of windows and instruments of the bridge. From the other side of the bulkhead, a musical tone chuffed itself into silence and he heard a snide voice say, 'Now that this is here, we only await your friend.'

Not wishing to engender any further delay that might allow his quarry – and his promotion – to escape, Manco shouldered his way through the door. Ace followed right behind him, but Manco only had eyes for the two uniformed men who turned with strange weapons in their hands. He squeezed the trigger of his Browning reflexively, hitting one man in the chest. The man crashed through the door to the flying bridge, as the hollow zipping of Ace's blaster knocked the other man sprawling. The second man's gun went off with a whine, shattering several windows.

As the acrid smoke cleared, Manco kept Kreer covered, while the bearded criminal's own weapon was still trained on Benny.

Inside the Master's TARDIS, Shadow hissed to herself as the Master's dilemma was echoed in her awareness. Allowing herself to be influenced by his presence at the back of her mind, she leapt up onto the console, slinking along the door-lever. The lever tilted, and the double doors hummed open.

Ace prodded the fallen Ph'Sor with her boot, while keeping the Master covered. Behind her, the door of an equipment locker suddenly swung ajar.

Satisfied that the two aliens were out of the picture, Ace grinned down at Benny, who had flung herself to the floor when the shooting started. 'Ever heard of a stitch in time?' Benny asked.

'I knew you could look after yourself okay until we got here.'

'I'll resist the urge to argue that point. We'll have to do something about your "shoot first and ask questions later" lack of diplomacy, though.'

'Ooeeooeeooo,' Ace whistled in reply.

The Master looked around at the three grim faces that boxed him in, his lip quirking upwards in a sneer, as if he was amused at the turn of events. It was the sort of holier-than-thou smugness that Ace associated with certain politicians whom she'd like to punch on sight. 'Shall I assume that you have me where you want me, and thus dispense with the formal platitudes of the situation?'

'Perfectly correct, furface,' Ace replied.

'And I imagine you will wish to know what I have planned for the remaining warhead?'

'If it doesn't destroy Moscow, you mean? The thought had occurred. To which, no doubt, you'll refuse to answer.'

'Not at all, my dear.' He smiled malevolently. With a flick of the wrist, he produced a flat black box, not unlike a TV remote control. Manco stepped back slightly at the movement. 'If you believe the warhead is aboard this vessel, then I'm afraid you've been reading too many of the wrong thrillers. However, what I intend to do is to detonate it with the aid of this useful little device if you do not immediately lower your weapons. Who knows which city might disappear from the map?'

With no one watching the helm, the rudders at the stern gradually began to respond to the currents of the river, turning almost imperceptibly. Almost unnoticeably, the destroyer began to move to port.

'If you need that bomb for some plan, Kreer, then you can't explode it now,' Manco told the Master, thinking quickly. 'That means you're bluffing, and that means you're expendable. Now put the box down slowly.' Manco could feel the gun shift microscopically in his palm as a cold sweat interfered with his grip. He hoped that the Master wouldn't notice.

The Master's smile widened, and he moved his thumb over the single button. 'I've got all I want from the plan – therefore, I don't care what happens to the warhead.' Benny's foot suddenly lashed out while the Master was facing Manco, and knocked the box from his hand.

The Master fell back against the ship's telegraph as Ace's blaster fired, narrowly missing him. Responding to the telegraph, the ship began to accelerate, throwing Ace, Benny and Manco off balance. Ace and Benny rolled with their falls to find cover, but Manco fought against it, trying to bring his gun to bear. He was determined not to risk losing his quarry, but wasn't steady enough to get a clear shot. Braced against the telegraph, the Master levelled his tissue compression eliminator at him.

The FBI agent had no chance to avoid it.

Manco screamed as the cells of his body began collapsing against each other with bursts of pain. His bones splintered as the unnatural stresses of the crushing pressure strained them beyond their limits, and his brain burned as his skull squeezed in on it.

Ace looked on in guilty anguish as Manco's shrivelled form stopped twisting at last. She looked murderously at the Master, who flattened himself against the side of an equipment locker. Almost imperceptibly, even to herself, Ace's finger began to tighten on the trigger of her blaster.

Whether due to pheromones from the only other affected survivor of the Cheetah Planet, or her ingrained training and experience as a soldier, the coppery scent of blood in the air teased some forgotten part of Ace's subconscious, which hungered for more. She had failed in her responsibility to keep her force safe, she knew, and reminded herself that it was her duty to avenge him.

She fought down the primitive urges with visible effort, aided only by the memory of the lifeless and accusing faces of Paul Richmann and all the others whose lives she had helped to end, for good or for ill.

The Master, already close to the open locker door, covered Ace and Benny with the tissue compression eliminator as he turned to dart for the dark space.

Even though the door was already open for him, Ace was fast enough to shoot him in the dead-centre of his chest just before the door of his TARDIS closed over the almost comical look of surprise on his face.

Shadow hissed as the Master was pitched into his TARDIS. He writhed in pain as he crawled to the console, a trail of blood glistening behind him.

Reaching the console, he pulled himself up, his flailing hand managing to trigger the door lever, before pulling down on the dematerialization switch.

The kitling watched as impassively as only cats can as he slid to the ground, the crisp stench of scorched flesh tainting the air.

* * *

Ace lowered her blaster and tried not to look in the direction of the tiny remnants of Manco. It wasn't easy, and she felt sick.

'Shouldn't we go after the other bomb?' Benny suggested gently. 'It's what your friend would have wanted.'

'Probably.' She looked down wearily. 'Not that it'll make much difference to him now.' Nor, she thought mutely, to any of the too-many other friends I've left in the same position.

The Master fought hard against the tide of pain that threatened to drown him, pulling himself onto his knees. 'So close,' he groaned, 'so close . . .'

Propelled by its well-preserved diesel turbines, the *Jessup* surged through the normally placid waters, a writhing mass of foam spreading out behind her as she headed for a bend in the river at her full thirty knots.

Benny stared numbly at the place where the Master's TARDIS had stood, until a sound from the flying bridge attracted her attention. She turned just in time to see a blond sailor aiming a disruptor, and dived headlong into Ace, knocking her back into the stairwell as the shot shattered the holosphere.

Shaking off fragments of glass, Ace rolled into a kneeling position and loosed a round from her blaster. The sailor was blown off the flying bridge, to land with a thud somewhere on the deck below.

Turning back to the stairwell, Benny found that the bulkhead door was jammed, but Ace blasted it apart in a shower of glowing fragments. 'Get the hell out of here!' Ace yelled as she turned back to check that no one else was outside.

Benny hurtled down the stairwell to the shelter deck and threw open the nearest door. Outside, the deck was soaked by the spray thrown up by their sudden acceleration. Not waiting for anything, Benny dashed out.

Shadow drew back, startled, as the Master pitched to the floor in front of her, his fangs bared in a rictus of pain. Grinding his teeth, he scraped at his chest with one clawed hand, pressing in with his fingers as if he was trying to tear out the pain that burned within him.

As he writhed on the floor, the illumination faded fitfully as the symbiotically controlled lighting elements died with their master's consciousness.

'Let... me... be... free...' the Master gasped, clutching his head as it began to burn with a greater fire than the wound in his chest.

Shadow watched silently, the tip of her tail twitching, as the burning pain that was consuming the Master became visible. As if he were undergoing spontaneous combustion, dull fiery embers lit the ravaged Time Lord's contorted face.

Ace kicked away the remnants of the door to the flying bridge and leaned out, blaster at the ready. On the deck below, the fallen sailor lay with thick yellow fluid pooling round his head, which was twisted at an unnatural angle. Ace thought the colour must have been a trick of the light, but suddenly realized that the substance was pouring from the man's wounds. It could only be blood.

As she watched, the man's hand slowly went to left side of his neck and pressed it in a certain way. An incendiary charge of some kind ignited immediately, the crackling phosphorescent glow rippling along his body. When it fizzled out, only a vaguely bipedal patch of ashes was left. Footsteps terminated any contemplation of the event, drawing Ace's attention aft.

Several ratings were running towards the exterior steps to her level. Ace wasn't stupid enough to think she could take out all of them before they killed or captured her, and she looked around for an alternative. Glancing around in desperation, her eyes fell upon the quartet of torpedo tubes mounted on a turntable between the superstructure and the forward funnel.

Admittedly, she thought, this was supposed to be a

retired ship. The crew were all armed, however, and knowing something of the Master ... Deciding that the gamble would be worth it, she crouched below the plate armour of the flying bridge and sighted on the nearest torpedo tube. Setting the blaster to maximum, she fired.

The blazing energy bolt slammed into the tube, its heat and destructive energy detonating the torpedo within. Instantly, the explosion set off the other three warheads in a chain reaction.

The ship lurched, smashing Ace to the floor as the quartet erupted. The hostile sailors were caught by the fireball like leaves in the wind, while several lifeboats were blown from their davits. The shockwave knocked her blaster from her hand, and it rattled across the deck. She dived for it and was nearly too late, her hand catching it just as another pitch of the ship sent it tumbling towards the edge of the flying bridge.

Superheated air cloaked the superstructure, threatening to both roast Ace alive and drain all the oxygen from the air. Above her head, the tripod mainmast buckled dangerously.

Clambering back through the shattered bridge to the port-side flying bridge, Ace kept a wary eye on the mast.

In the sweltering engine room, steam burst from pipes as the Ph'Sor engineers tried to stabilize the ship after the blast. The fuel-pump pressure was dropping, however, and they had to keep increasing power to keep up the speed. No one had told them to do otherwise.

Nearby, diesel oil sprayed thinly from a buckled plate in the fuel tank bulkhead.

While his TARDIS's power source throbbed erratically, the Master curled into a ball beneath the console, his only thought to hide away from the pain. The fire in his veins was even worse than that which had seared his and Shadow's linked minds when leaping from the exploding Cheetah Planet.

In front of his eyes, the material of his clenched gloves

began to shift, bulging outwards under pressure from the flesh within.

Benny had been edging towards the curve in the bulkhead below the main five-inch guns when she heard a footfall behind her. Before she could raise her hands, the ship had bucked like a wild horse and a searing blast had knocked her to the deck. For an instant, she thought she had been shot, but then she heard the anguished screams of the men behind her who had been blasted into the water.

Wheezing a little in the thinned air, Benny turned to look behind her. Blackened and twisted metal was smouldering all across the deck, while flames licked at the paintwork. 'Ace over-reacting again,' she muttered. Carefully she set off for the wreckage, certain that Ace would be somewhere at the heart of it. Before she got far, three sailors emerged from the doorway in the shelter deck.

Skidding slightly on the water-sodden deck, Benny drew to a halt in front of the disruptor-toting men.

The pain began to ease, drifting off as if the consciousness that perceived it had dissociated itself from the form that experienced it. Gradually, light began to seep back into the console room, bathing the sprawled and still figure with a moonlit glow.

'Free?' he murmured hopefully, in a light yet rich and cultured voice. His eyes opened, wincing at even this faint light. He focused immediately on the hands before him.

Through the tears that his claws had made in the leather, smooth skin was visible. 'No fur . . .'

Ace tried to pull back on the ship's telegraph, but it had been fused by a disruptor shot. Outside the shattered windows, an old iron bridge was stretched across the river just before a bend. It was a swing-bridge and was open, but the ship was already drifting to port and out of the safe channel. 'Not again,' Ace muttered.

Popping back up from behind the port-side flying bridge's searchlight, Ace had a clear view of Benny's predicament. Unfortunately, her blaster's charge level LED was showing virtually no power remaining. Unhesitatingly, she snatched the knife from her boot and clambered up onto the bulldozer-blade shape of the radar antenna atop the roof. Leaning across to the nearest leg of the newer radar mast, she cut a thick cable free and looped the end round her wrist.

Below, Benny was raising her hands and waiting for the shots that would end her life.

They never came. Instead, with a hoarse approximation of a Tarzan jungle-call, Ace swooped unstoppably past Benny's face and careened into the trio, knocking them sprawling.

Pausing only long enough to deliver a right cross to one man who was trying to grab her leg, Ace ushered Benny towards the stern. As they passed the after shelter deck there was a cry of anger from behind them, as the men pulled themselves together to give chase.

The two women were running out of deck, however, and soon had to swing themselves up onto the depth charge racks at the stern. Ace looked down at the glassy surface of the Potomac being churned into foam. With the ship going this fast, she suspected, the water would be as solid to land on as hard-packed earth. She looked back over her shoulder to see the sailors charging along the deck, leaving her no choice.

Heaving a deep breath, she hurled herself off the stern, catching a glimpse of Benny doing the same.

Despite trying to curl up as she fell, Ace hit the water half-turned on to her back. Her right side, leg, arm and back all lit up with white-hot agony, and she felt a rib or two crack under the impact. She opened her mouth to gasp a cry, only to be hit by a swollen mound of water from the *Jessup*'s wake. The force of the water spun her around, forcing her deeper under the surface of the Potomac.

He pulled off the gloves, examining the long pianist's fingers beneath in wonder. With a frown, he walked unsteadily round the console to the nearest deactivated monitor screen and peered at the reflection it offered.

'I appear to have survived,' he muttered thoughtfully, then laughed to himself in a tired and mirthless fashion that indicated that perhaps this was his least desired fate. As he straightened, however, and put any such depressing thoughts out of his head, the laughter became more genuine and relieved.

He looked down at himself, noting that his scorched uniform was too short and too loose by a couple of inches each way. Stroking the glossy moustache that didn't quite meet the neat beard which covered his proud chin, both of them framing his narrow mouth, the Master laughed triumphantly.

His high forehead and aristocratic nose tilted ceilingwards while his lean face cracked into a delighted grin.

Ace's mind echoed with an old quote that drowning was supposed to be a painless way to die. Whoever said that had obviously never tried it, she thought blackly, as her lungs burned deep in her chest.

Blue and purple blotches filled her mind until, with a searing glimpse of evening sunlight to match the renewed pain from her ribs, she broke surface. Reflexively, she gulped down a huge gasp of air, while trying vainly to shrug off Benny's arm, which was adding to her ribs' injuries. Coughing up filthy water, she finally noticed that Benny's other arm was floating limply and the side of her face was beginning to swell. It seemed that Benny hadn't landed any better than herself. A few yards away one of the boats blown from the ship, scorched but intact and floating, bobbed in the turbulent waters.

Trying to tread water, and gradually succeeding as oxygen reached her muscles again, Ace looked for the *Jessup*. It was already half a mile or more downstream and drifting inexorably towards the left-hand end of the iron swing-bridge. Clouds of smoke and the occasional blast of exploding ammunition marked her progress. Suddenly realizing what was about to happen, Ace grabbed

Benny's uninjured shoulder, about to force her in the direction of the boat, but she was too late.

With an ear-splitting preternatural shriek of tortured metal, the *Jessup* tilted as her keel struck the shallows near the riverbank and her port bow powered into the foundations of the bridge. The ship's hull crumpled like paper while the girders of the bridge twisted and snapped, their severed ends scraping along the hull with showers of sparks. As the girders drove deeper, they finally pierced the engineering decks where spilled fuel was leaking from the tanks.

In an instant, the sparks ignited the fuel from the ruptured tanks. A vaporous firestorm billowed through the companionways, finally making its way back to the fuel tanks themselves, which erupted in diabolical flame. Before the sound reached the two women, the explosions had caught up with the contents of the ship's magazine, detonating every inflammable and explosive mixture there. Finally, a series of thunderous billowing explosions raced the length of the ship from stem to stern, ripping it to shreds and scattering fragments of red-hot metal across hundreds of yards of water and riverbank.

The shockwave raced across the surface in a wall of spray, but was mostly spent by the time it reached Ace and Benny.

The roar faded, leaving silence, but for the slapping of small pieces of debris still raining down. There was barely a burning skeleton of the ship left, tangled up with the twisted ruins of the bridge. Ace and Benny swam – with some difficulty – over to the small lifeboat. Heaving themselves over the side and into the inch or so of water therein, they lay gasping for breath for several minutes. An oily taste hung in the air which wasn't at all pleasant.

Ace felt around Benny's shoulder. 'It's just dislocated, I think. You know what?' she croaked.

'What?'

'Next time, we should get the Doctor to take us somewhere more peaceful and relaxing – Kursk, Narendra III or the Madillon Cluster, for example.'

'Yes... It was such a waste of human – well, humanoid, anyway – life back there,' Benny muttered. 'Even if they were warmongers...'

'And a human life,' Ace reminded her darkly, with a heavy heart. She looked skywards as a faint rhythmic sound became more pronounced. A white and orange-painted helicopter was descending towards them. 'Here comes the cavalry to shut the stable door.'

Benny grimaced at Ace's mix of sayings. 'You've been hanging around the Doctor far too long,' she muttered.

Chapter 19

Marion waved to Lieutenant Wood to take over the details of securing the power station, while she directed her jeep towards the canted disc sitting in the green shallows at the edge of the reservoir.

Avoiding the gorse-like yellow bushes that thronged the shore, she made her way down to the water. She wondered if this was what the Doctor had planned from the start, and hoped that he was all right. No one else had arrived, other than the power workers of course, but it was a sure bet that the media would show up if she didn't put a lid on the news.

'Is the Doctor inside?' she asked Andrews, who was beside her in the jeep.

'He's been in there all evening.'

If there was one thing that the Doctor had correctly anticipated, it was the difficulty of jump-starting the Tzun gravity drive with no more than a twentieth-century toolkit and a second-hand sonic screwdriver. Most of the toolkit's contents were scattered around the floor, amidst twisted wire clippings and scratched I-O chips.

Currently only the Doctor's legs were visible, sticking out from under the dome of the matter-antimatter reactor. Triggering the screwdriver, he tuned the reactor's antibaryon feed. As he did so, the squat four-foot crystalline wave-guide chamber, designed to smooth out the gravity waves generated by the reactor, pulsed erratically with a hazy blue light.

Without warning something shifted inside the reactor

and the wave-guide chamber's glow died with a last flash as the Doctor scuttled back out ahead of a cloud of acrid smoke. 'Bleep it,' he muttered after a brief internal struggle, glaring accusingly at the charred piece of circuitry he held in his hand.

'Something wrong?' Marion asked, her voice still awed despite having already been inside an identical craft. It wasn't something you got used to quickly.

'A somewhat vague way of putting it, but yes. One of the magnetic envelopes has shorted out.'

'What did it do? Before shorting out, I mean.'

'It formed the magnetic bottle that holds the antimatter away from the normal matter of its containment vessel. Fortunately the Tzun reputation for thoroughness seems to be deserved, as a back-up coil has kept the magnetic bottle operating.'

'That's good, is it?'

'It's just as well, otherwise most of New Mexico would now be passing the Tzun Stormblade in orbit.'

The wave-guide chamber was now completely dark, however, and the Doctor glared at it with an intensity that might have ignited it if only he could have kept it up long enough. Finally, however, he tossed the ruined part aside with a sigh and glanced at an engineering schematic which was displayed on a viewscreen. 'Perhaps if I reversed the polarity of the neutron flow in the multi-centre omnipolar diathermic phase-discriminator and replaced it with an EPS tap from the . . .' He straightened, scratching his head. 'No wonder they could hardly be rivalled. No one else could follow the technobabble.'

With an echoing melodic warning, a gleaming black Edsel solidified in the shadow of the looming dish at Corman.

Though looking much like any other car, the driver of this vehicle was not perched in a seat of plastic-scented artificial leather. Instead, he stood at the centre of a long room. A huge curved screen dominated the wall at one end, near the hexagonal console. A smaller, squarer screen was inset into the opposite wall above a flat-topped console. Two passages disappeared around corners on either side of this, while a large unit inset with monitor screens hung from the ceiling. A short passageway in the long wall to the left of the console led to a pair of double doors. All the walls were set with roundels, and the decor was still black.

As the silver cylinder which was his TARDIS's time rotor stilled, the Master shifted around the console. He stroked the kitling absently, where it lay on a small monitor on one of the panels. 'Where is the Doctor that he couldn't accompany those women?' He straightened his coat, an elegant black tailcoat with narrow silver edging along the high collar and wide lapels. Buttoning it over his black silk shirt and midnight-blue waistcoat, he attached a silver pin in the form of a bird of prey with outstretched wings to his billowing jade cravat. 'Surely the Tzun can hardly have overpowered him on their own?' he scoffed to himself. He threw the door lever irritably and stepped from his TARDIS.

Carrying himself with energetic grace, the Master strode quickly across the tarmac towards the hydraulic doors to the S-Four area. Two obviously human guards approached from the direction of the helicopter dispersal area. 'Halt and identity yourself,' the nearest one snapped.

The Master turned and waved them aside impatiently. 'It's me, Major Kreer. Now do not obstruct me any further – '

'Impersonating a military officer is a federal offence,' the guard warned. 'Put your hands above your head and walk ahead of us.'

'What?' the Master said, taken aback. 'I know I've changed my clothes but... Wait a moment; surely I can't have changed that much?' Sighing resignedly, like an adult allowing himself to be subject to the whims of a playing child, he raised his hands. The guards looked him straight in the eye.

The Master smiled. This was going to be too easy. It really was just like old times, he thought. 'I am Major Kreer,' he told them, pinning them to the spot with his gaze. 'You have seen my identification and verified my identity.'

'We have verified your identity,' they chorused sluggishly, as if they had been sleeping on duty and had only just awakened. They lowered their guns as if the weapons were too heavy to hold. The Master nodded gently.

'Good work, men,' he praised, humouring them. 'Now contact the Blue Room and inform them I'm on my way in.'

'Yessir,' they nodded hurriedly. The Master watched them good-humouredly. He'd hardly had such good subjects since the desperate residents of Stangmoor prison.

Dimmed lights left strange, distended shadows around the interior of the skiff. The haphazard skeins of wire and fibreoptics that threaded the flight deck merely made the misshapen shadows that much deeper and more bizarrely convoluted.

'Came to see me off, did you?' the Doctor asked.

Marion shrugged. 'Partly. Radar tracked this disc's sudden appearance and crash, and I didn't think the location could be coincidence.'

'How's Finney doing?'

'Doctor Piper's taken an X-ray that shows something planted in his neck. He's being kept under sedation until they decide whether to risk operating.'

'Tell them not to risk it; the Tzun will have thought of that, so removal might kill him. Keep him sedated, though. If he wakes up, they'll be able to monitor and control him through it.'

The domed housing of the matter-antimatter reactor had been removed so that the Doctor could separate it into two discrete units. The quantum charge polarizer which generated the antimatter was now linked to draw additional power from excess life support, which needed to support only one Time Lord rather than several Ph'Sor Tzun. This, the Doctor hoped, would mean that the magnetic envelopes wouldn't need to actually store anything while a constant stream of generated antimatter flowed into the reactor.

Caught like a trapped fly in the web of wiring which criss-crossed the flight deck, the Doctor slotted the last reworked I-O chip into the helm console. Mopping his brow with the back of his hand, he delicately extricated himself from the coils of wiring. 'And to think our old academy instructors said neatness was what mattered. I'd like to see one of that supercilious bunch try something like this.' He looked round at Marion, as if just remembering her presence. 'You'd better get back to your men, unless you want a trip into the lion's den,' he warned. 'The same rule applies – if you haven't heard from me by sun-up, get to Corman and shut the place down.'

'Okay,' she acknowledged with mixed feelings, and turned to leave, then: 'Good luck,' she said from the hatchway.

'I make my own,' the Doctor reminded her. Hitting the door control, he sealed the hatch between them. He settled in something of a crouch on the seat at the helm and played his fingers over the smooth touch-sensitive surface. A hollow, echoing hum gradually filled the flight deck and the lights of the wave-guide chamber began to pulse falteringly before fading away.

Grimacing, the Doctor gave the reactor housing a kick. The blue lights came on more strongly, finally settling into a steady pulse. Heaving a sigh of relief, he operated more controls. 'Station-keeping thrust. Excess power build-up diverting to the conductive hull . . .'

Pausing a few feet from dry land, Marion ignored the dampness of the water's edge soaking into her trouser-legs. Her attention, and that of her troops, was fixed entirely on the disc. She had only seen a deactivated one and a few pin-points in the sky, and was stunned at the image the working model provided.

The hatchway had flowed shut as if the hull was water enveloping a dry patch. Now the ship raised itself a few yards above the green water with a rising hum, the circular exhaust glowing faintly. As the terullian hull began to conduct the gravity waves generated by the drive, light bent around it. Rippling like a reflection in troubled waters, the disc faded from sight, though the hum remained.

'Now,' the Doctor murmured to himself, 'up, up and away.' He triggered the main thrusters. Silently, the gravity field around it shifting air molecules smoothly aside so that there was no sonic boom, the skiff shot upwards. Outside, the hum faded away.

Marion looked across at Andrews, who was frozen staring upwards. She knew that it was her journalistic duty to reveal this event, but wasn't foolish enough to fail to realize that publicity might alert Kreer and Stoker. Knowing that either speaking out or keeping silent would be a betrayal of one trust or another, she waved a sergeant over.

'Debrief everyone here,' she ordered reluctantly. 'Inform them of the penalties of a security breach, then post guards in all areas with outside lines.' She felt as if her tongue might swell up and choke her for saying this. 'Make sure that no word of this gets out. I'll have a debunking story prepared just in case.'

Nyby stood in the Blue Room like a bipedal shadow when Shok'Arl heard his name called, but did not recognize the voice. There were only a limited number of people who knew his true name, however, which left only one possibility. This was confirmed less than a second later, when he turned to find an unfamiliar face staring at him from the midst of a very familiar heat pattern. Shok'Arl's dark eyes saw this only marginally more faintly than surface detail. 'Full regeneration was unnecessary for the DNA reconstruction to take effect.'

'An irony we may both regret.' The Master shrugged. 'The girl Ace did this on the *Jessup*.'

'The vessel has been destroyed,' Shok'Arl admitted.

'The explosion was monitored from orbit. Contact has been lost with all forward base operatives. We anticipate that action may be instigated against this base soon, but our Pentagon operatives will delay it with hyperbole until after zero hour.' He recalled what Nyby had memorized about the Earth's military procedures over his long career. 'So long as the Moscow warhead remains operational the plan will succeed. The loss of the Washington bomb merely means a few minutes of delay between the Soviet missile launch and that of this power bloc.'

'Of course.' The Master nodded. 'But this proves I was right about the Doctor and his friends. It's not too late to eliminate the Doctor.'

'On the contrary,' Shok'Arl mused, 'it is not only too late, but would also be to miss a valuable opportunity.'

'What are you talking about?' the Master demanded.

'The Doctor has followed Nyby's map to Elephant Butte, with the intention of challenging our presence on this world directly.' Shok'Arl's voice couldn't quite hide the note of admiration.

'But that is the location of the last jamming exercise!' the Master protested. 'If the interfering busybody were to prove that the Soviet bloc is not responsible for what is about to happen, the humans everywhere will turn against you.'

'Wait!' Nyby interrupted. 'What do you mean about two bombs, and a missile strike on us? And who is this?'

'I am the Master,' the Master said loudly. 'You used to know me as Kreer – don't bother trying to understand, it's beyond your pitiful intellectual capacity.'

'You were to help us with technology in return for this base,' Nyby pressed on at Shok'Arl.

'It was expedient at the time. You will still receive your new technologies, General, but your military and governmental processes will be irrevocably changed. Your tactical and administrative systems are finished, as you know them. From this time forward, you will serve us.' He signalled to a S'Raph, who pressed something to

Nyby's neck. The general folded to the floor. 'Secure him in the quarantine unit.'

'As you command.'

'If the Doctor tells anyone, they will not believe him. There will be no proof of his story, as he is currently piloting the skiff into low orbit. *R'Shal* is waiting with tractor beams ready.'

'You don't plan to kill him there either, do you?' the Master asked.

'His DNA and RNA will be extracted and cloned as per standard procedure. When these strands are grafted into the Tzun genome, the next generation of Tzun will have not only his complete memories and experiences, but also naturally grown symbiotic nuclei giving us total access to time.' Shok'Arl looked into space, visualizing this proud moment.

'So that's why you answered my call,' the Master whispered thoughtfully. 'You couldn't assimilate my DNA because it was corrupted, but analysing it gave you the basic structure of our symbiotic nuclei.' He glanced behind himself, as if wondering whether to remain or make a run for it. Shok'Arl couldn't tell if this was the case, as this new Master seemed calmer, less emotional and flustered. It was as if his whole aura was inscrutable.

'Do not fear, Time Lord,' Shok'Arl said gently. He knew that most warrior cultures would kill anyone who knew their intent in such detail. He was certain, however, that such action would make no difference now. There was no honour in killing someone for such a reason. 'We are an honourable people,' he went on. 'We will fulfil our part of the bargain as agreed. When Earth has become the newest canton of the Tzun Confederacy, we will transport you unharmed to any place of your choice.' He paused, and smiled in his alien and inexperienced manner. 'Or any time.' He suddenly looked ceilingwards. 'Yes?' he snapped. 'Excellent. Bring me up.'

As the Master watched with pursed lips, Shok'Arl was whisked away in a red haze. The Master half-walked, half-swam through the low gravity to the large world map.

Washington was now unmarked, but a red line still terminated in a scarlet circle at Moscow. 'Decisions, decisions,' he murmured with an ill-concealed smile.

The Doctor was shaken from the helm stool by a shudder that engulfed the skiff. Picking himself up from the floor, he glanced immediately at the wave-guide chamber. It pulsed healthily. Glancing across the helm instruments, his brows furrowed. 'Tractor beam,' he decided.

The holosphere mounted in the flight deck of the Tzun skiff showed an expanse of stars. In the centre, however, one pin-point was growing slowly but steadily. The Doctor watched the forward view with increasing concern.

It wasn't often that he was overawed by mere technology, but the sheer scale of what was approaching impressed him. If the forward sensors were to be believed, and going by the arc of sky that was being obscured, the ship ahead was a good five miles long.

As he wondered if he hadn't misjudged his strategy a little, the growing object resolved itself into a gargantuan metallic blade, with a glowing pod trailing from a pylon below. By the illumination given by lights scattered like diamond dust across the shadowed underside, the Doctor could see that the surface of the hull was as smooth as that of the skiff.

The sword-like main hull was unmistakable and left the viewer in no doubt that it was a vessel of war. 'I knew it,' the Doctor confided to himself. 'Tzun Stormblade off the starboard bow . . .'

Benny looked on with concern as Ace sat listlessly on the back step of the white and chrome ambulance. She didn't think Ace had a romantic interest in Manco, but she certainly seemed to have had more than a passing interest. They had been more than a little alike as well, she thought fleetingly, and grasped the idea more firmly.

Was that it? she wondered. Did Ace see something of herself in the young hotshot? She sat down on the metal step, ignoring the sombrely suited men who shuffled back and forth in the evening air. 'Burden getting heavy?'

Ace shrugged. 'I'll get over it, as usual. I've seen friends die before, but someone under my responsibility...'

'Remember what I told you on the plane? Any good commander values individual subordinates.'

'I'm no king,' Ace said pointedly. 'I'm not used to being a commander, even of only one follower. I've always been a solitary hunter – it's what I'm good at – and sometimes I'll follow someone worth following, but I'm no leader.'

'Not even of someone who finds you worth following?' Benny thought for a moment, considering how to hasten Ace's return to normality. She knew it would happen eventually: everyone got over a death eventually. They didn't have time to wait, however. She recalled that in the aftermath of the Dalek missile attack which had robbed her of her mother, she had brought herself out of it by busying herself with meaningless tasks. Their task here was anything but meaningless, but perhaps the same basic principle could be applied. 'Where are we going to get transport back to New Mexico?'

'From one of the company spooks, I suppose.' Ace straightened with a wince. 'Then again, the Tzun will still be based at Corman – that's where the Doctor will be going, so that's where we should go next.'

'Excellent idea,' Benny agreed, relieved. 'I'll go and see what I can arrange.'

It was a shame that vacuum is so silent, the Doctor thought, as the tractor beam swung his ship in a long curve past the main engines that formed the hilt of the Stormblade's sword-shape. This really was the sort of thing that deserved to have a very bass sound effect added by a team of brilliant audio engineers who had been supplied with some very hallucinogenic substances. Instead, the silence of the ship's movements merely emphasized the cold and deathly touch of its purpose.

The glow of the engine exhaust sank below the holosphere's range like a setting sun as the skiff was pulled up towards what could have been considered the handguard on a sword. Ahead, the liquid-smooth hull parted to reveal a lighted interior.

Ace let herself sag once Benny was out of sight. It had been a long day, and the reinforcements sent from the CIA had seemed more interested in paperwork than getting after the Master, or Kreer as they still referred to him. Her ribs and spine still ached no matter how she shifted position, and she irritably waved away the paramedic who was treating her.

It came with the job, she told herself sourly. At first, strained muscles healed quickly, but when she put herself through those sort of situations repeatedly... Well, she had to expect that it would start taking longer to pull herself together.

She knew that she could continue, to become what they called a 'seasoned campaigner'. Those, however, usually had a base of operations; a place to call home, where the weary fighter could recover before going out into the field again. This was true in any time period. She, however, had no such luxury, as the TARDIS could drop her in another combat zone the moment they took off.

Face it, she told herself; you may be younger than Benny – twenty-seven in a couple of months, relatively speaking – but you're getting too old for this. In terms of bumps and bruises, at least.

She knew that, unless she found such a stronghold in which to lick her wounds, there would come a day when the scrapes would cease to heal properly. Some day the wounds would remain able to cause dull aches in stormy weather or the like. Not this time, of course. It might be taking longer these days, but she could hardly feel the tingling that seemed to itch under her skin when her muscles started to unstrain themselves; but someday...

The skiff insinuated itself through the atmosphere shield and settled into a support cradle not unlike a champagne glass, except that it hung down from the ceiling. An engine at the base of the stem buzzed into life and gently slid the assembly away from the landing area into a dispersal section. Beyond the atmosphere shield, the hangar exit vanished as the hull flowed closed.

Ringing tones that could have been alarms or normal background noise greeted the Doctor as he stepped out into the blue air. A number of other skiffs were cradled in similar supports growing from both floor and ceiling. Several hawk-like gunboats squatted at the far end of the hangar deck. Mechanical drones floated all around the chamber, a handful coming over to link cables from a hissing compressor of some kind to the newly arrived ship.

The air was a bit thin for the Doctor's liking, and the gravity barely noticeable, but it was liveable. Looking around for a door, his eyes fixed on one of the many catwalks that circled the hangar. None was more than a foot wide, or had rails, but the nearest led to a circular door with iris segments like those of a camera shutter. Hopping up onto it easily in the low gravity, he walked smartly to the door.

The door irised open to reveal a number of diminutive grey-garbed S'Raph Tzun staring at him with cold, unblinking black eyes. All had holstered disruptor pistols, but none of them made any threatening movement. Instead, they formed up on either side of the doorway, like an honour guard.

'Only S'Raph? Aren't there any pure-blood Tzun awake yet?' One of the S'Raph indicated with an inclined head that the Doctor should step from the hangar and into the corridor beyond. He wasn't sure whether to be relieved or worried that they made no overtly hostile move.

Considering his position, it wasn't as if they had to.

The full triumvirate of Shok'Arl, Tzashan and Sr'Shol watched the Doctor's arrival in the large holosphere in the war room, their features calm and composed.

'Captain,' Shok'Arl called, and an inset display of the

captain appeared to one side of the holosphere. The captain inclined his head slightly. 'First Councillor. The vessel used by the Doctor is being searched and decontaminated. A security team is escorting him to the holding cells.'

'Cancel that order, Captain,' Shok'Arl instructed severely. 'The Doctor is an important guest. Have him taken to the executive observation deck and post your guards outside. I will join him there soon.'

The short column of S'Raph stopped at another door, which irised open as the leading S'Raph touched a control beside it. The S'Raph with the blue collar waved the Doctor through. 'You may use any of the facilities here,' it said in a whispery voice. 'First Councillor Shok'Arl will join you shortly.'

'Thank you,' the Doctor said graciously, and stepped through. Instead of the usual small cell with limited sanitation facilities, he saw that he was in a richly appointed chamber running for a hundred yards in either direction. Fifty feet opposite the door was a wall of transparent alloy, through which the Earth was visible at the tip of the blade of the main hull. From the fact that he could see the entire length of that hull, the Doctor judged that he was standing at the front of the 'hand-guard'. The wall sloped downwards at a steep angle, but the Doctor could make out further windows below.

Plush, if oddly designed, chairs and couches were dotted around amidst glowing statues, holographic games and other unidentifiable and ethereal objects. Several things with strings, tubes or even light beams were clearly musical instruments of some kind. A row of onyx consoles with large slots in them was backed against one wall. Ignoring all this, the Doctor walked to the window and stretched out a hand. The surface was as cold as weathered steel.

Outside, the dark grey blade was edged with the quicksilver gleam of terullian all the way to the point. 'They must need that to run along tramlines of gravitational force,' he said to himself.

'I understand this is a closer look at a Stormblade than you had last time,' a carefully pitched and modulated voice answered.

The Doctor looked round to see a being with hairless olive skin and a supporting exoskeleton of tubes watching him. 'I knew there's be at least one pure-blooded Tzun in charge while you were in the theatre of operations.'

'I was awakened from cryosleep once we were safely through the system's asteroid belt. Allow me to welcome you aboard the Stormblade *R'Shal*, Doctor.'

'You seem to have the advantage of me.'

'Not exactly. I do not know your name.'

'I've had many; which would you like? Some cultures feel that names have power and should be closely guarded; others feel that names are purely for tombstones, and I'm superstitious enough to consider that. You remember me, then?'

'What was it you said at Mimosa II? "What goes around comes around?" A curious phrase... We have a similar one,' the sharp-nosed Tzun went on, gently caressing a stringed instrument. It hummed softly. 'Sit by the riverbank long enough and the body of your foe will float past.'

'How could you possibly know what I told Councillor H'Kauth? Tzun don't live that long.'

'Indeed not. I am First Councillor Shok'Arl of the Tzun Confederacy,' the being acknowledged. 'But I share the memories of a hundred generations of Tzun military commanders, plus many of their opponents and contemporaries. He tapped the side of his skull. 'RNA grafts are updated with each generation. So I remember you quite clearly, even though we have never met.'

'It must be a little crowded in there, then, even with a head the size of yours.'

Shok'Arl looked the Doctor up and down closely. This man was quite different from the tall and bohemian figure who had disrupted their operations before. Nevertheless, the air of self-confidence was the same, as was the heat pattern. This man was diametrically opposed to the

Master, and yet Shok'Arl sensed a common bond – a sort of superior arrogance which the Doctor seemed to control better. It was fascinating. He ignored the insult: it was obviously intended to provoke him into making mistakes. 'Can I offer you any refreshments?' he asked conversationally. 'A small selection of Terran foodstuffs are available for the benefit of the Ph'Sor.'

'Everything in its place,' the Doctor said, shaking his head. 'Speaking of which, this room seems a little out of place on a warship.'

Shok'Arl was puzzled for a moment, but then recalled that the other warrior races they had defeated tended to have very utilitarian ships. 'Three of the greatest Tzun operas were composed by line officers serving aboard Stormblades. All minds, even those of warriors, must have time to relax so that they will not be worn out when going into battle. The instruments and other recreational items here allow our minds to unwind freely, while maintaining the structure of discipline through the rules of the games, or the steps necessary to play the instruments. That is why we are successful.' He paused, seeking an example of a species who were more rigid and unfeeling. Many came to mind. 'Think of the Sontarans,' he said finally. 'Devoted entirely to military matters, as are we. They, however, have no relaxation, no time to let their minds develop. As a result, their strategy stagnates and becomes predictable. Their exploratory parties have always been easy for us to destroy when they encroach upon our space.'

'How did you manage to take over Corman?'

'Take over?' Shok'Arl walked over to look out at the blue-green globe ahead. 'We were given that base, along with a limited human support staff, as part of the bargain struck with a small group of officials within the Pentagon.'

'A bargain? I thought you were warriors.'

Interesting, Shok'Arl thought. That was precisely what the Master had said at the time. 'As a First Councillor of the Tzun Confederacy, I have full ambassadorial status for diplomatic negotiations.'

'And what does a warrior race like you know about diplomacy?' the Doctor asked in an indignant tone.

'Enough. The first Precept set down by R'Shal himself when he founded the Confederacy was that the greatest honour was to defeat the enemy without having to resort to fighting. If you are forced to fight, you have already lost the first battle.'

'Yes, there's a similar saying on Earth. That never stopped you before.'

'Diplomacy is merely the purest form of warfare, Doctor; the challenge of mind against mind. Our military prowess grew and evolved with experience until we were able to achieve the high standards set down in the Precepts. Each victory we won led us closer to the goal of being able to defeat our opponents without combat.'

'Fancy words can't lessen the fact that you will still conquer other races!' the Doctor snapped, pointing his umbrella accusingly.

'Races incorporated into the Confederacy are not merely slave races,' Shok'Arl pointed out, somewhat disappointed by the Doctor's reaction. 'It is a mutual raising of both civilizations – a true symbiosis.'

The Doctor nodded, his gaze firm. 'It's still removing basic freedoms from those people you conquer. They don't have the choice of whether to become Tzun cantons.'

'Incorrect,' Shok'Arl stated. 'We do not conquer. Where is the challenge – the honour – in destroying a foe who is obviously weaker? Instead, we offer a partnership. We offer food, medical aid, technology – as in this case – or anything else the world lacks. In return we ask only for volunteers to carry the seed of the Tzun species. As a side effect, our genome is passed into their genetic heritage, but it works the other way also.'

'What about these abductions? Were they willing volunteers?'

'We merely took cell samples to assess whether the structures were compatible with ours. The subjects came to no harm and were returned to their proper places, with memory wipes so that they would not be too distressed.'

'Or be able to claim that you were hostile.'

'That is also correct,' Shok'Arl admitted simply. 'We considered our treatment more reliable than the Master's hypnotic technique,' he went on.

The Doctor whirled round from the forward view, both brows raised in a shocked expression. 'The Master?!' The intense look faded, and he nodded as if kicking himself inwardly. 'I should have known. He told you about myself and Ace.' Shok'Arl could hear no questioning tone, and remained silent. 'How did he get thirty-two years back in time without a TARDIS?'

'That you would have to ask him yourself, if it were possible. Unfortunately,' Shok'Arl continued, with genuine regret, 'that will not happen. Once Surgeon-Major Ksal has prepared the medical complex, your DNA and RNA will be sampled and incorporated into ours. You yourself will be treated with our genome. You will become the first Time Lord Ph'Sor.' As if the words were a cue, several S'Raph entered, forming a circle around them.

'One thing you can answer, then. What is the Master getting out of this?'

'His DNA was corrupted and fragmented. We have repaired it. He also requires transport off Earth.'

'Does he?' the Doctor asked slowly. 'You have an interesting level of technology; did you happen to give any to the Master?'

'Necessary communications equipment was assigned to him.' Shok'Arl answered, trying to judge why the Doctor would ask this. 'The matter is irrelevant.'

'All right then. What makes you think the humans will make the right decision?' he asked suddenly, as if on a whim.

'Our pilots have been making contact with randomly selected humans. The reports of these friendly meetings will generate a suitable image of us in the public consciousness, which we can then exploit.'

'A fat lot of good it'll do once those bombs spark World War Three!'

'Why should we wish to instigate a nuclear holocaust?'

Shok'Arl asked plainly. 'The Earth is useless to us as a barren cinder.'

'Then what else . . .' The Doctor trailed off, looking back at the serenely floating Earth, dotted with light hazes across its dark side. 'Of course,' he breathed, 'you don't intend to start a war. You intend to prevent one! The two bombs destroy Washington and Moscow, thereby eliminating the two terrestrial governments with the most power to influence the outcome of your arrival. Then when you halt the exchange of missiles with that jamming field, you'll be welcomed with open arms for having saved humanity from itself!'

'Correct. We estimated a casualty level of no more than a million individuals world-wide. Now that the Washington bomb has been deactivated by your companions, the figures will be less than half a million.' He spoke dismissively, considering the numbers so low as to be hardly worth mentioning. 'That includes those who will die in out-of-control vehicles when all terrestrial power is jammed.'

'Half a million . . . ! It's not going to work, you know. The Master has been double-crossing you all down the line. Your exploitable image in the public consciousness will never come about, because he's been debunking your contactees to make them out as mere lunatics. When you put in an appearance after a missile launch – even an aborted one – the human populations will assume you started the launch, and that the governments realized this and took action themselves. The culture shock will make them so anarchically paranoid that they'll shoot at absolutely anything in the skies! The whole of Earth culture would be sent reeling so far that it might never recover. That's probably what he wants, in fact.'

Shok'Arl remained unruffled by this expected protest. 'If your words were true, our operation would be under threat. However, the Master's desire for his freedom from this world is sufficient to hold him to the terms of the agreement.'

'Is it? With your level of communications technology

245

and his own skill, he could easily send a message to his TARDIS no matter where it was. Triggering the remote circuit would be child's play. If I could prove to you that the Master has betrayed you, what would you do?'

Shok'Arl's eyes unfocused, seeing the images and feeling the sensations of events on many worlds. He recalled standing on the bridge of another Stormblade centuries ago. Their local agent had alerted the planet's military powers. He quailed in pain as the casualty reports flooded into the war room, and decided to hurl that pain back in anger. The Councillor had looked over at the tactical major. 'Massive ground-force build-up,' the S'Raph had reported. 'Orbital launchers being fuelled. They have adapted to jamming signal.'

'Activate full graviton beam. Target staging areas.'

'Targets locked.'

'Fire at will.'

He watched as a line of distortion streaked out from the unseen underside nacelle, and scraped along the surface of the planet. Conflicting gravitational pressures tore at the planet's tectonic plates. Cities fell and the seas rose. 'All enemy forces destroyed,' the tactics officer reported finally. 'No life signs registering.'

'Report to S'Arl that assimilation of Kaldanati civilization has been aborted.' He tasted the bitterness of knowing that he – or, more accurately, Councillor Ph'Roch, whose RNA he was tapping into – had failed, and left a destroyed and therefore useless planet.

Shok'Arl looked back up at the Doctor aboard *R'Shal*. 'We could destroy this world with ease, but without any gains the energy and logistical expenditure would be entirely pointless. We could not waste the resources necessary.'

The Doctor paced up and down for a moment, obviously weighing up some dangerous decision. 'Scan the Elephant Butte reservoir area for latent artron energy. That will mark the location of my TARDIS. Once you've identified the TARDIS's energy signature, scan Washington, Holloman and Corman for the same energy signature.

That will prove that the Master has retrieved his TARDIS, and broken your agreement in at least one way.'

'If he has broken it in one way, he may well have done so in others as well,' Shok'Arl agreed. 'And if there is no such signature?'

'Then it just means he hasn't had time yet. But it will be there. I know him far better than you possibly can, and treachery and deceit are as natural to him as breathing. His mind's so twisted that he can't even walk in a straight line without getting dizzy.'

Shok'Arl considered this. 'Captain,' he called, 'have the ventral sensor arrays record the artron energy signature of the Doctor's TARDIS from Elephant Butte. Then scan Holloman, Washington and Corman for the same signature.'

'As you command,' the captain's voice acknowledged over the internal communications system.

'First Councillor Shok'Arl from Surgeon-Major Ksal,' a new voice began.

'Report.'

'All is prepared for the Time Lord.'

'Noted and logged.' Shok'Arl motioned the S'Raph guards to form up around the Doctor. 'Your lack of resistance is commendable, if surprising,' he noted.

'You can transfer DNA if you like,' the Doctor said a little more cheerily. 'It won't work, but I expect you'll have to learn that the hard way.'

'First Councillor from Captain.'

'Go ahead, Captain.'

'A TARDIS energy signature has been detected at Corman.'

'Noted and logged. Sound general quarters and prepare for further instructions.'

'As you command.' A low gonging note sounded throughout the ship, echoing through the observation deck. Shok'Arl made a pointing gesture to the Doctor, and the S'Raph marched him out. Shok'Arl was surprised to see him go unresistingly, despite the obvious worry on his face.

* * *

The Doctor was led to a sterile white room, and bade to sit on a stool. The lime-garbed Ksal checked a medical instrument of some kind. 'This will cause no discomfort,' he announced.

He pressed the instrument to the base of the Doctor's skull, just behind the ear. A transparent ampoule at the rear filled with pinkish liquid. 'Haven't you any out-of-date magazines for me to read?' the Doctor asked unconcernedly.

'The reference is irrelevant.' Ksal busied himself at the plasma-filled sphere, mixing it with a small amount of the fluid he had just extracted from the Doctor, the rest of which was deposited in a smaller sphere. Satisfied, Ksal returned to the Doctor and pressed the instrument to his neck once more. There was a soft hiss, and the ampoule emptied. 'DNA only,' Ksal explained. 'It would be unwise to give you our memories before you were one of us. It will take a little while for the full effect.'

Shok'Arl took the captain's seat on the bridge. This would be unthinkable during a flight, when the captain was absolute master, but acceptable now since they were in stationary orbit. 'Have a S'Raph pathfinder team taken by scout craft to a random location on the continental United States. Tell them to keep a communication link open to the bridge.'

Now, he thought, we shall see whether we have the desired effect, or whether the Doctor is correct.

The Doctor rose from the stool and circled the room, examining every detail closely. 'Shouldn't I be on the bridge?' he asked, tilting his head with a frown. 'I must be familiar with procedure.'

'Excellent,' Ksal nodded unblinkingly. 'I will notify the First Councillor that you are on your way.'

Shok'Arl ignored the Doctor's footsteps as he entered the central circle of holospheres. Instead, he was listening unemotionally to the sounds of cries and gunfire that were coming over the communications circuit.

'Do not engage the primitives in combat,' he ordered over the open link, searching his soul for its calm centre. He bathed in its relaxing influence as his distress and anger faded. 'Return to the ship at once.' He turned to face the Doctor, glad to see that he was succumbing to the Tzun influence. He had suspected that the Doctor's misgivings about the process were merely the last gasp of resistance before bowing to the inevitable. 'It seems your assessment of the situation was correct.'

'It usually is. The Master's goal has always been the acquisition of power, but he has a fondness for attempts to destroy Earth. Your plan doesn't count in the way his mind works. I imagine he has some plan to destroy you before you can prevent the missile exchange.'

'He is but one man. I will have the truth of this when I return to Corman for the supervision of our withdrawal.'

'Withdrawal?' the Doctor exclaimed.

'Integration of Earth into the Confederacy is no longer logistically viable. We could conquer the planet despite any resistance, but to do so would destroy the very culture and genetic material which we intend to absorb into ourselves. Without the promise of that prize, there is no value in conquering the planet.'

'Well, well,' the Doctor said lightly. 'You've discovered the first non-vicious circle. I expect it can be projected in advance in future operations. Congratulations.'

'This vessel's continued presence here would be expenditure with no gain. We will cease operations here and return to Zeta Reticuli.' He gave the Doctor his alien smile. 'For now.'

'For now?'

'Humanity is of great value to us. When this matter is forgotten, we will return.'

'I will have to recover my TARDIS.'

'That has been accounted for. The transmat co-ordinates are set. We will transfer you and your two friends to the vicinity of the TARDIS. You will bring it to me at Corman.'

'You have located Ace and Benny?'

'Their descriptions were noted and logged. We are monitoring them now. Report to transmat engineering.'

'As you command,' the Doctor nodded.

Chapter 20

A compressed red whirlwind sprang up on the catwalk in B Hall at Elephant Butte, the Doctor materializing in the centre. Checking that he was alone, he grinned a little as he fished the TARDIS key from his pocket. 'As you command,' he scoffed to himself.

The red whirlwind appeared again, and Ace and Benny looked surprised that whoever they had been talking to on the Potomac riverbank was no longer with them. 'No time to stand around gawping,' the Doctor told them. 'We have to return to Corman.' Pushing the TARDIS door open, he led the woman inside and then busied himself at the console.

Ace cleared her throat. 'We've dealt with one bomb, but the other's on its way to Moscow.'

'Good thinking,' the Doctor praised.

'This receiver should home in on it,' she added, holding up the small box she had taken from the defused bomb.

'First things first.'

'There's something else you should know,' Ace continued. 'This Major Kreer is really – '

'The Master.' The Doctor nodded absently, setting the time rotor in motion.

'You knew?' Benny asked suspiciously.

'Not at first,' he admitted sheepishly.

'How did he escape the Cheetah planet without a TARDIS?'

'He's always been irritatingly resourceful. Ever since the Prydonian Academy, in fact, when he always managed to avoid punishment for misdemeanours of one kind or another.'

'You were at school together?' Benny asked.

'More or less. His survival instinct has always been overdeveloped.'

'Not any more,' Ace said with grim satisfaction.

'What is that supposed to mean?' the Doctor asked, with a tilt of the head.

'He had an unfortunate accident after murdering a new friend of mine.' She shuddered involuntarily at the remembered image.

'You mean you shot him, I suppose,' the Doctor reasoned drily. 'Well, it didn't work.'

'What?' Ace thought hard, recalling what the Doctor had said about the other Time Lord after their encounter in Perivale in 1989. 'You said he had passed his last regeneration.'

'So he had, but the Tzun have used their genetic engineering skills to cure him of the DNA corruption from the Cheetah Planet. I imagine it was mostly affecting the Trakenite part of his make-up. At any rate, they've not only made him a pure Time Lord again, but they've given him a new life-cycle into the bargain.'

The Master emerged from the pastel-blue corridor and gazed up at the unusual dish antenna set onto the rocky roof of the S-Four complex. 'All I need now is the Doctor's assistance.'

Stoker clutched the handgrip of his disruptor like a talisman as Shok'Arl's voice whispered into his mind through the communications net. 'Apprehend the Master at once,' he ordered.

'As you command,' Stoker answered, then severed the link. The disruptor seemed to be the only thing he could be sure of these days. The evidence of his unremembered presence on Earth was causing a confusing pain, fed more by the wild mood swings he had been experiencing. Now he was told that their loyal ally had betrayed them. He couldn't believe that Shok'Arl would lie, of course, but perhaps there had been some misunderstanding of communications. A real Tzun would simply trust and obey, he told himself, but was bred as a warrior and not a spy. Stoker was neither sure nor calm, the realization of which fact made him yet more irritated. He longed for a simple straight fight.

'There you are,' the Master said, turning to face him. 'Has the aircraft taken off for Moscow?'

'It has. I have orders,' he went on, 'to apprehend you for questioning over treason.'

'And will you?' the Master asked, with what Stoker felt must have been deliberately deceptive lightness and calm.

'I . . .' He raised the disruptor slowly, the Tzun training now instinctual. 'I must. I am Ph'Sor Tzun.'

'Are you indeed?' the Master asked. 'Are you certain of that?'

Stoker froze. 'I don't understand . . .'

'Oh, come now,' the Master encouraged. 'You've been wondering about the photographs that prove you were on Earth before the Tzun arrived.'

Conflicting thoughts tumbled through Stoker's mind. A pure Tzun would have pulled the trigger by now, as a calm part of his duty. A pure human would have pulled the trigger in anger. On the other hand, he thought, what if he does have the answer? 'They must be fakes. I remember being on other worlds then.'

'Name one,' the Master suggested. 'Tell me where you were before coming here.'

'Other planets . . .' Stoker said, but couldn't think of any specific examples. He had memories of the fear and exhilaration of combat, but could not recall their circumstances. 'Somewhere else,' he groaned.

'It's confusing, I know,' the Master said sympathetically. 'You can't keep your emotions in check?' Stoker rocked back as if struck. 'A Tzun could, or so they tell me. You have been betrayed, it's true, but not by me. What did Shok'Arl tell you you were?'

'I am a human-Tzun fusion,' Stoker said proudly.

'Shok'Arl didn't tell me of my past. I have the experience of it.'

'No,' the Master whispered softly, shaking his head as if gently correcting an errant child. 'Why do you think Ksal still requires genetic sampling from the scouts? Because they are still testing how to fuse the species. You are no Tzun, because there are no human Ph'Sor yet. You are a clone, grown from one Tzun cell and one human cell taken from a soldier killed in a past war. You can't recall where you were before coming here, because you were nowhere. You,' he finished in a firm voice, 'were only born six months ago.'

'No!' Stoker clutched at his head with his free hand as he tried without success to remember something – anything – from farther back than six months.

'Your experiences are those of other Tzun, whose RNA was grafted into your growing brain aboard *R'Shal*. The anger you feel,' the Master went on, with a prouder and more praising note, 'is because your human blood-lust is overriding the Tzun DNA chemistry. This human ancestry gives you a true warrior's heritage.'

'What do you mean?'

'Shok'Arl has betrayed you. Not deliberately, I'm sure, but perhaps his brain was damaged during the long sleep between the stars. You are but a tool to him, to be discarded once the proper human Ph'Sor can be bred. But you have the training of the Tzun Confederacy as well as the emotional power of humanity – a race for whom butchery is as natural as breathing. Under the Councillors, the Tzun have become decadent and weak, but you could set the Confederacy back on the path of the true warrior race,' he suggested silkily. 'You could end this weak pussy-footing around of Shok'Arl's, and lead the pride of the Tzun warriors . . .'

It explained a lot, Stoker thought. Admittedly he would like to crush the life from those who had created him purely as a discardable tool, but he was conditioned as a Tzun warrior. Anger surged through him on the crest of a wave of tryptophane hydroxylase and washed away the calming Tzun extra serotonin and training. The desire to make his own mark seared him. 'What did you have in mind?' he demanded. He might as well weigh the plans of both the Master and Shok'Arl and pick the one he liked.

'Round up the remaining humans on the base and lock them away in the quarantine area, as Shok'Arl originally wanted. Then tell your men that I have a proposal to put to them and that they should obey your orders regardless of any unusual statements they may hear.'

Shok'Arl walked into the map alcove in the Blue Room and studied the large world map. A flashing red pixel was following the red line towards Moscow. He called *R'Shal* immediately. 'Recall the warhead delivery.'

'Not possible,' Tzashan responded. 'The Ph'Sor assigned to it are missing, and their transponder codes are not registering. The Master must have replaced them with conditional humans. We have another problem.'

'Report.'

'The Time Lord nanites are destroying all Tzun genetic material in the test tank. A S'Raph who volunteered to receive a test transfusion has died. We cannot integrate the Doctor's DNA or RNA. It is logical to assume that he has therefore rejected our DNA.'

'I suspected as much from his willingness to comply. It does not matter, as our mission here has already failed. Issue instructions for all Earth stations to be evacuated. Prepare the new fused DNA structure for the Ph'Sor clones. At least they will have gained something upon return to the ship.'

The TARDIS groaned its way into reality in a deserted hangar. 'Where is everyone?' Benny asked curiously.

'The humans will be locked up somewhere to await DNA sampling. The Tzun will all be busy, since this would have been their bridgehead.'

'Would have been?'

'I'll explain later. Benny, go and find the humans and

release them. Try secure places like the glasshouse, or better still the medical section – if they're dealing with Tzun they'll have insisted on a quarantine area. Ace, you find Stoker, while I look for a connection to that dish.'

Benny went straight to the map which Ace had found on their previous visit, inside the doors of the administration block which grew out of the mountain roots. All the major areas were marked on it, and Benny memorized a route that would take her straight to the medical wing via the glasshouse and a large store-room.

She set off quickly, occasionally pausing as a Ph'Sor crossed the corridor in the distance. The blue store-room was filled with crates of phased plasma rifles, but no humans. The glasshouse was empty. Benny began to wonder what sort of architect had designed the all-blue complex. Finally, however, she came to the windowed double doors that were the entrance to the medical wing. Airtight rubber seals rimmed the edges, and two Ph'Sor stood guard outside.

Not bothering to check the setting on the disruptor she had brought from Washington, Benny leaned out around the corner and swept the beam across both of them. They pitched to the ground, and she ran up to the doors. Through the round windows, she could see that the miniature hospital ward was packed with men and women in various stages of uniformed and civilian dress.

'How do you set this to a cutting beam?' she wondered aloud.

The Master stood in the shelter of the door to the S-Four area, watching to see who would discover him first.

There was so much for him to do now, that even with virtual immortality it would still be a race against time. Chiefly, of course, the Doctor had to die. It was a bittersweet thought, as he had no other such inspiring adversaries, but he couldn't let the interfering do-gooder continue to plague his schemes. The two women were nothing, of course, merely two unimportant humans in the wrong place at the wrong time. They were loose ends, however, and would be dealt with.

Then again, there was the matter of Ace, who had shot him. It would almost be a pity to kill her, as her resourcefulness would have made her a fine enforcer. As for her action against him, well, that was something he understood. Any creature will fight to survive.

The only danger was the Doctor and his insufferably charmed life. If he somehow escaped to interfere again...

Out in the open ground at the centre of the ring of rock and concrete, wind-blown dust drew a delicate veil over the events there. The Master could hear a couple of faint disruptor blasts – obviously Stoker's men rounding up more humans, he decided. There was another sound, though, which soon resolved itself into footsteps.

Smiling in his sheltered position, the Master watched as a dim figure appeared from the dust drifting between the mountain roots and the gap that led out to the runways across the dry lake. Dark coat-tails flapped in the breeze as the figure folded back the garment's right hem, to keep the blaster-butt unobstructed under the hand.

The Master slipped back into the shadows as Ace meandered stealthily towards the thick and sloping concrete doors.

Ace moved around the sloped concrete edge at the foot of the mountain. Inside, a pair of Tzun ships were cabled up to strange pieces of equipment. Odd metallic shapes loomed like stick insects in the dim light. She was about to move towards the nearest ship when a door slammed somewhere above.

She looked around and noticed a short stairway that led up to a small office platform which had lights on. Even if Stoker was not inside, she figured, there must be someone who could give her directions, one way or the other. Drawing her blaster, she crept up the stairs.

Taking a deep breath, she kicked the door open and hurled herself in, drawing a bead on the sole and relaxed occupant of the surprisingly plushy furnished room.

She didn't really recognize the lean and aristocratic face, but the proud bearing and satanic beard and moustache were as incriminating as a set of fingerprints.

'Good morning, Ace,' the Master said pleasantly.

Chapter 21

Nyby waved two men to either side of the double doors, as a wide section of them collapsed in a cloud of heated dust.

He knew he shouldn't have given the AFOSI men such a free hand with their alien friends, and was adamant that if this was them trying to make up for their earlier misjudgement by releasing him... No, he corrected himself. Treason, not misjudgement. He would waste no time in proving that they were wasting their time trying to influence a man of such strong character as himself.

Ready to face whatever might come through the doors, he stepped proudly out in front of them. The doors slammed open.

Nyby was half-way through waving his men to attack when he realized that it was neither Stoker nor Kreer who stood in the doorway. Instead, a check-shirted woman with a mop of dark hair stood with a disruptor and an impatient look. 'Well, what are you waiting for?' she demanded in a vaguely colonial accent. 'An invitation from the President?'

Several men immediately started for the door, but Nyby waved them to a halt with a motion of one dark hand. Strangers shouldn't be waltzing in and out of classified installations, he knew, and if she wasn't one of his personnel then she couldn't be trusted. At least she seemed to be human.

'Who the hell are you?' he demanded sonorously.

'The crukking fairy godmother! Who the smeg are you?'

She held up a hand before he could answer. 'Never mind, Nyby, force of habit.'

'You're an unauthorized intruder, lady,' he rumbled.

'I'm no lady, and I've got authorization from Allen Dulles, if that name means anything to you,' Benny responded. 'Are there any other prisoners?'

Nyby looked at her askance. Her unsupported claim to be working for the CIA was suspicious enough, but the claim of backing from the DCI himself was beyond the pale. As for her knowing who he was... Still, she seemed human enough, and had freed them. He could at least give her enough rope, he decided. 'This is everybody. Everybody human, anyway, except Kreer.'

'He's not human either, I'm afraid.'

The Master looked up calmly as Ace raised her blaster. Shaking his head, he tutted softly. 'You've already killed me once, girl,' he chided. 'Didn't you learn anything from that?'

'To aim for the head this time,' Ace said quietly, doing precisely that.

'I hardly think the Doctor would approve. Violence isn't really his style.'

'Well, I'm not him. When you've killed four, it's easy to make it five,' she went on, Manco's tortured scream echoing in her head.

'That's very true, young lady, but you don't really want to do such a thing,' he told her in a gentle and patient tone. She didn't think of holding his gaze, but nevertheless found that she could not tear her eyes from his. Smiling as he pinned her with his gaze, he repeated the words in a tone of confidential but increasingly firm acknowledgement.

'I am the Master,' he informed her firmly, the confident smile never wavering, 'and you will obey me.' He moved closer to her across the rich carpet, each word emphasized with a purposeful step. 'You will obey me.'

Slowly, as if forcing its way through treacle, the thought occurred to her that the Master was not too dissimilar in outlook from most of her superiors in Spacefleet. Though she was glad to be free of that group, it was certainly comforting to rely on someone to do the thinking for her. A bit of discipline was something she needed to avoid becoming lazy. 'I will obey,' she began slowly.

Her time spent far from her native time and place, however, had not left her unaffected. While it would be comforting to obey orders instead of giving bad ones as she feared she had with Manco, she could not completely dispel the images that the Master's presence called up. Manco himself, for example, twisting and dwindling. Perivale's milkman, lying in torn shreds in the dust of an alien planet. Karra, transformed into an animal, then impaled on a dagger carved from the tooth of some great beast. There was Midge – always Midge – perverted by subservience to the Master, and finally left to die while the renegade Time Lord stood by impassively.

Realizing with a start that this was exactly what she had just been agreeing to, Ace blinked and shook her head, which seemed to be fuzzy and unclear. There was a brief but powerful tugging sensation, and she looked up to see the Master toying with her blaster. Her mind, however, was still very much her own. 'If you hadn't killed so many of my friends before, you would have succeeded. Doesn't that tell *you* anything?'

'Touché, and you have a right to be proud of your willpower,' the Master accepted graciously, 'but I'm the one with the gun.'

'And you're proud of that, I don't doubt,' the Doctor's voice called disgustedly from the doorway. Ace turned her head as the Doctor breezed into the room. The slightly built Time Lord, now several inches shorter than the Master, looked around the opulent furnishings with a disdainful expression. 'All very colourful, but shallow – a bit like its owner.'

'Former owner,' the Master corrected. 'As you see, I am a new man.'

'Only in appearance. Your blood-lust is characteristically undiminished, or perhaps even renewed.'

'As are your increasingly hypocritical attempts at lauding the virtues of morality.'

'My morality is always virtuous,' the Doctor retorted.

'Even if that implies that no one else's is?' the Master smirked nastily. 'Of course,' he began, in a mock-thoughtful tone, 'you could try proving that.' With a sudden bound across the burgundy carpet, the Master reversed the gun and slapped the butt into the Doctor's palm.

Benny skirted around the edge of the two ships in the S-Four hangar, but didn't look up to see the office lights. Instead, she opened the airlock doors at the rear of the hangar and plunged deeper into the complex in the lift.

She had already passed several rooms that showed signs of the recent removal of their contents, and now ran round a corner to skid to a halt as a figure turned to face her.

Benny froze as the cable-entangled figure emerged from the hydraulic door to the Blue Room, the glimmer of his translator sparkling like Balor's eye of ancient legend. She gripped the disruptor more tightly, willing the creature to turn away and return to its lair.

'The weapon will not be necessary,' it announced in its rich, multitonal voice. 'I have no quarrel with you.'

'If you're who I think you are, then I've damaged your plans quite a bit. I doubt you'll want to give me a medal.'

'I am First Councillor Shok'Arl of the Tzun Confederacy. You are the Doctor's companion.'

'That's right,' Benny nodded. She looked at him in fascination. This was, after all, a living example of a species that had died out three hundred years before she was born. Its movements were calculated and precise, but she judged that there was emotion in there somewhere, going by the way it stood to observe her actions.

'Your conduct was correct within the context of your understanding of the situation. I cannot fault a citizen for defending its home. The Doctor has not succumbed to the influence of our DNA?'

'Not that I've noticed. I'd have thought you'd want your own back.'

'Vengeance is irrelevant; it cannot alter what is past, and is therefore valueless.' It spoke with what sounded like a hint of amusement, though Benny supposed that it could just be a translator flutter. 'You have come to engage me in combat?'

It was a thought, Benny admitted to herself. This was the leader of the attempted conquest, after all.

'I heard you were leaving.'

'That is correct. Operations on this planet are no longer logistically viable. When I leave, the technology we have had installed will be destroyed.' It moved on a few steps, slow in the Earth's gravity. 'Why do you remain?'

It was just trying to safeguard its species, she reminded herself. And at least it was smart enough to know when it was beaten. She had to reluctantly admit that Shok'Arl didn't seem to be actually evil, just trying to help the various branches of its people to survive. 'I'm just passing through,' she said finally. 'Looking for the Master. Why don't you throw me out?'

'My people are warriors by necessity, but you have also fought gallantly. I have no quarrel with an honourable opponent.' I'd love to see this one meet an Ice Lord, she thought. They'd be congratulating each other forever – what a formula for peace.

'Would the Earth's population have been honourable opponents?'

'No. That is why we must leave. We will not lower ourselves to base conquest for its own sake.'

'I see,' she agreed, and found to her surprise that she did. It was a pity the Master had corrupted them, she thought. The influence of a warrior race that had conquered its own urge to kill and conquer might well have provided an inspiring example for humanity. 'For what it's worth,' she added, 'I think you probably would have raised Earth civilization.'

'A perceptive analysis.' She wasn't sure if that was an example of Tzun humour, or Tzun self-confidence. 'You respect the Doctor as your superior?'

'As my friend.'

'I understand the term, though I can have no experience of it,' Shok'Arl continued, and Benny briefly felt her heart go out to it. She reined it in. 'Tell the Doctor that my subordinates aboard *R'Shal* cannot eliminate the aircraft with the Moscow bomb without risking detonation. He will do the best he can with that information. The Master has betrayed us, and so may attempt to destroy the telemetry link that keeps our scouts on safe flight-paths. He will fail, as it is trapped, but you may find him there. I will describe the route.'

Outside in the hazy sun, uniformed Ph'Sor were busy moving the two skiffs out of the large S-Four doors, while others carried pieces of vital equipment into the storage areas aboard several other ships which had just landed in the central circle at the heart of the mountains.

Stoker watched with impatience as the work progressed. A cold sensation had gathered in his stomach, silently sending out the image of being dissected for spare parts aboard the Stormblade since half-human clones would not be required once they left Earth.

The feeling was unfamiliar, and at first he couldn't place it. The truth dawned gradually, however. The feeling could only be fear. It was not pleasant, and grew more severe with each moment his mind dwelt on the thought of returning to the Stormblade. If only he could think of a way to avoid such a fate, he and his warriors could continue as before. The Master had some sort of idea, but he was clearly untrustworthy as far as Stoker was concerned.

He was bred to fight, he knew, but here there were no opponents worthy of the trouble. However, he thought, with these ships to go where he wished... The cold knot loosened. Finally at peace with himself, Stoker walked forward to give his men their new orders.

'How did you get away from the Cheetah Planet?' Ace demanded.

'Ah, an excellent question,' the Master commented. 'I recovered my senses barely in time to transmigrate back to Earth with the aid of my kitling, just as the planet exploded. Why Earth I do not know, though I seem to spend an inordinate amount of time here. The planet's magnetosphere, however, was rich in artron energy – '

'I thought as much,' the Doctor interrupted, looking at the blaster as if unsure of its purpose. Ace mentally screamed at him to give it back to her. 'That's how it was able to metamorphose living matter, much like a slow regeneration.'

'Precisely,' the Master nodded. 'That Time Lord energy source has many uses. When the planet exploded, the release of that artron energy boosted my transmigration through time. Thirty-two years, in fact. The irradiation had left my body filled with metamorphic energy, however, and no one in this time zone could help. So I interrupted the real first Soviet satellite launch, and sent a signal to the Tzun canton on Zeta Reticuli Four. I knew their genetic skills would be sufficient to cure my... affliction, in return for assistance in integrating Earth into the Confederacy. I also needed help leaving Earth, as my TARDIS had remained on Antari Three when I had to leave Antari Two in a hurry while fomenting a war between them.'

'But you have your TARDIS now,' Ace prompted.

'When I said I needed help to leave Earth, they assumed I meant I needed them to transport me somewhere.' He smiled. 'As for incorporating Earth into the Confederacy... There has to be a carrot at the end of every stick. Why should I care whether they conquer a new world today? They've only got two hundred years left before they're wiped out.'

'Then leave now,' the Doctor urged. 'The game's over! You have a new life and your TARDIS back, so go and bother some other planet.'

'And have you follow me? Interfering as usual? I don't think so,' the Master scoffed.

'Then I'll have to – '

'To what? Kill me, perhaps? Let's see.' The Master took the end of the barrel between thumb and forefinger, and gently moved it until the muzzle came to rest directly over his left heart. 'Would this make it any easier, Doctor?'

Ace thought that the Doctor should know that at such close range, the Master would be sufficiently damaged as to be unable to regenerate. The Doctor's eyes met those of the Master. 'Go ahead,' the Master mocked softly. 'Look me in the eye. End my life.'

'It isn't ease that's the problem,' the Doctor snarled derisively. 'It's always been easier to kill, hasn't it, than to find a real solution?'

'I knew you couldn't do it! Amnesty would be proud of you, even if you don't have the courage of your convictions. If I were you, I'd have pulled that trigger.'

'I'll take that as a compliment.'

'Ah, how valiantly you strive to deceive yourself. Or perhaps to deceive your young friends? "Two voices are there: one is of the deep – it learns the storm-cloud's thunderous melody",' the Master quoted ironically. ' "The other is an old half-witted sheep which bleats articulate monotony. And both, Doctor, are thine." '

'I always thought that passage referred to Wordsworth.'

'You think I've forgotten how quickly you abandoned the idea of talking to the aquatic branch of Home Reptilicus in favour of blowing them to bits?'

'You made sure that was the only way.'

'Sure? Are you so sure? All those deaths...'

'I will not kill in cold blood.'

'Not even to end the threat of global holocaust? That's always been your hypocritical problem,' the Master sneered. 'Willing to destroy at a distance, safely shielded from the dirt that might stain your hands! Hiding from the consequences, and too gutless to bring harm face to face because you can't face seeing the last spark of a single life give itself up to your hand!' As if tiring of the game, the Master snatched the gun back from the Doctor's limp hands. 'At least I do have the courage of my convictions, and the strength to live with what conscience I have.'

'That can't be too big a job. Sometimes it takes more courage to deal in life than in death,' the Doctor protested.

'A tired argument, Doctor. I don't know if I'll ever find another such worthy adversary,' the Master said quietly, in a tone which Ace couldn't help thinking had the ring of truth about it. 'And I'll miss these little games we have, but you've always failed to live up to your potential. I told you so at the Academy.' He raised the blaster to the Doctor's forehead. 'This is the price of failure, Doctor.'

Slowly and mockingly, the Master's finger tightened on the trigger.

Nyby led his men out of the administration block and along the roadway outside, ending up at a low blockhouse with two Ph'Sor guards outside. His mind was filled with anger at what had been done to him by those who claimed to be working with him for the security of America. He might not be able to stop their plans, but at least he could take some of the traitors with him, he thought darkly.

The problem lay in the difficulty of knowing who to shoot. All the Ph'Sor were blond, but not all blonds were Ph'Sor. He laid the problem aside as his men rushed the guards, losing only three men to disruptor-fire. Nyby took one of the disruptors, then went in to the armoury and started passing out guns and grenades.

Regretting the decision, he made up his mind that the safest course would be to shoot all blonds first, and then ask questions. America's God would know his own.

Benny slumped a little when she emerged back into the corridor, relieved that the reduced gravity had returned to normal. Consulting the roughly sketched map she had been given, she plunged deeper into the complex.

A silver flash lit up the Doctor's vision, but it was the Master who cried out in pain. The blaster fell from his nerveless grip with a trail of blood.

Ace's bootknife clattered to the floor, its blade wet from scoring across the top of the Master's hand and the base of his thumb.

Before the Master could move, the Doctor grabbed his

wounded arm and threw him off balance. He was hurled into the nearest table as the Doctor bundled Ace back through the door. 'If we can get back to the TARDIS,' Ace began as she hurtled down the stairs and across the hangar.

'Not yet. The Tzun are leaving, but we still have to make sure that Stoker's men go with them.' He pulled Ace down behind some free-standing consoles that were left where the two skiffs had been. 'We have to stop them being able to wander around Earth's atmosphere with impunity, for a start,' he went on. The Master, with Ace's blaster in one hand and her knife in the other, burst from the office, and bounded down the stairs. Calling a group of Ph'Sor to him, he left the hangar.

'How do we do that?'

'Gravity-drive systems are particularly sensitive to interference form gravimetric anomalies. Being an iron-cored planet, Earth has many of those in its magnetosphere.'

'So,' he pointed out in an overly patient tone, 'they must have a ground station somewhere which keeps their ships updated with where the safe areas are.'

'That dish!'

'Exactly. I followed the connections from it, but they lead to a door that I can't open. That's your department. If we can shut down that telemetry, their ships daren't risk atmospheric manoeuvres.' He looked at the open doors through which the Master had vanished. 'He's always been a little impulsive when you push the right psychological buttons. Come on.' He rose and scampered towards the doors.

Stoker cocked an eyebrow at the Master, who poked his head around the side of his TARDIS. 'Well?'

'Predictable as ever,' the Master crowed. 'He's making straight for the telemetry centre. Take some men and get in there through the passage from my office.'

'We'll see that he's taken care of,' Stoker said reassuringly. 'Though I can't see why you didn't kill him when you had the chance.'

'Because I need him to do something for me first,' the Master replied vaguely, to Stoker's frustration. 'The imminent threat was necessary so that he didn't suspect that he's being manipulated. If he thinks I let him go, he'll get suspicious. I was beginning to think that young whelp was never going to use her knife.' He wiggled his fingers, the red line across his hand only just having broken the skin. 'She probably thinks she's crippled me.'

'What is it you want done?'

'Shok'Arl booby-trapped the telemetry system when it was installed. Anyone who touches it dies, but I need it shut down.'

Stoker nodded, then looked at the Master. Without the telemetry system, patches of gravimetric interference triggered by the Earth's magnetosphere would not be plotted as they writhed around the Earth's surface. Flying through it in a gravity-drive ship would be like crossing a minefield in which the mines moved.

The cold gnawing in his stomach began again, and Stoker wondered what the Master really had in mind for the ships.

Ace examined the edges of the thick steel door while the Doctor kept watch. It was a simple matter to remove the door. Rather than trying to blow the lock, which might merely jam it more tightly closed, she would blow the hinges. Packing in some high-power plastic explosive around them, she waved the Doctor towards the thick legs of the dish. Joining him after a moment, she ducked behind the concrete post and pressed the stud on her wrist computer.

The narrow trench leading down to the door directed the blast of dust out in a fuzzy tongue that blotted out the purple glow of the pre-dawn.

A seepage of dawn light speared across concrete, staining it with bloodied shadows. Blackness flickered as Ace slipped through the narrow doorway that hung from its lock at a buckled angle. Her combat suit creaked faintly as she looked around in the dim light. She had a small silver egg in one hand. 'No guards,' she whispered.

'There should be some somewhere,' the Doctor replied, 'though the system will be unmanned and automatic.' Barely sparing a glance for the empty hall they were in, he stalked over to the far wall and tapped it with his umbrella. 'Hidden door, Ace. Blow me a nice hole in it.'

'Right.' Squashing another blob of plastic explosive into the centre of the wall, she moved back to the door. 'Fire in the hold.' They both slipped around the door an instant before a hollow boom heralded the blast that left a smoking hole in the grey wall. Lights flickered dimly on the other side of the breach.

Beyond the hole was a sloping corridor that led down to a room filled with machinery and electronics. Lights flashed brightly over the ebon surface of tall cabinets ranged around the walls, while thick cables rose in a column at the centre of the room. A catwalk ran along one wall twenty feet up, with a door at each end. There was a door to either side of the room on the ground level. The Doctor stepped smartly up to the console that surrounded the column of cables as Ace turned on her heels, looking around suspiciously.

'Aha. Ace, this central console seems to be the master controller for the gravimetric charting. If I just...' He trailed off, shifting around the panels of the console. Ace joined him, frowning as she tried to place a familiar scent she had noticed when they entered the room. She watched him work, and saw him relax slightly as he found what must be the master switch.

Suddenly realizing what the smell was, Ace barrelled into him, shoving him aside. Triggering the silver egg, she rolled it towards the cable column. It detonated with a red flare, the console panels exploding in showers of sparks. Blue arcs of electricity writhed up and down the severed cables before dying away with a charred stench. At the same time, heavy blast doors slammed down over the passage they had entered by. 'Sorry, but there was a smell like dodgems,' she explained. 'Does that qualify as shut down?'

'No need to apologize,' the Doctor replied, picking himself up from the floor. 'I should have expected a booby-trap from the Master.'

'Indeed you should, Doctor,' the Master called down from the catwalk. With a clatter of boots, Ph'Sor appeared at every doorway and levelled disruptors at the Doctor and Ace. 'You have been careless lately, haven't you? Actually, I should in all fairness point out that the electrical booby-trap was set by Shok'Arl, to trap me.'

'So you let us escape . . .'

'Of course, old friend.' The Master held up his cut hand to show that it was essentially unharmed. 'I'm very familiar with knife uses.'

'*You* want the telemetry system destroyed?' the Doctor asked.

'Of course. I have prepared a little gift for the Stormblade *R'Shal*, which I would be unable to send if the system was still operating. The deviation from the set flight plans would alert their suspicions. Now that there can be no set plans, of course, it's every ship for itself. I had, of course, intended that you die along with the telemetry, but there's an element of chance in every sport.' He looked at the guards, as if surveying a team he had picked for a sporting event, Ace thought.

The Master spread his hands in an apologetic manner. 'Now I'm afraid we must part, as I have more important matters to attend to. Thank you for your help, Doctor, and please believe me when I say I truly appreciate it.' His friendly smile hardened and cooled. 'Parting is such sweet sorrow, don't you think? Perhaps I'll drink a toast to your memory – something bitter-sweet, naturally. Goodbye, Doctor.' He nodded sharply to the guards.

Disruptor whines pierced the stillness of the room.

Chapter 22

The Doctor and Ace threw themselves behind the wreckage of the console as the beam lanced through the room. Instead of passing overhead, however, it bowled over the guards in the farthest doorway. Ace darted across to grab a dropped disruptor as Benny emerged from the darkness. Together, they opened fire on the catwalk guards. The Master vanished through the nearest doorway with a curse as the guards jerked and toppled over the railing.

The silence afterwards was almost deafening. 'Where did you spring from?' Ace asked.

'Shok'Arl has had more of a change of heart than his subordinates.' She tossed the disruptor aside in distaste, preferring to leave that side of things to Ace, then looked to the Doctor. 'The Tzun can't recall the plane with the Moscow bomb. It seems the Master replaced the Ph'Sor pilots with conditioned humans.'

'And knocking the plane down would set off the bomb,' the Doctor reasoned. 'Come on, we can lock on to the plane with that receiver of yours, Ace.'

'What about the Master?'

'The Tzun won't have anything more to do with him, and his cover's been blown in the military. I'd say he'll leave Earth, if he can, after he's finished his mysterious little vendetta with the Tzun. That's his usual technique, anyway. That warhead is a much more immediate threat to the planet; if it goes off, the Tzun won't stop the missile exchange.'

'They won't?'

'Why should they? It's purely an internal human matter now, as far as they're concerned.'

'Shades,' Benny grumbled. 'I'm definitely getting too old for this.'

The Master descended from his office and left the hangar with a purposeful air. The dry heat and neutral non-smell of the rocky area had previously seemed uncomfortable to him; mere reminders, in their way, that he was trapped here.

Now, however, he held his head high, drinking in the rich and barren beauty of the ruddy morning tones as if they prompted some bitter-sweet memory within him.

His not-quite-shoulder-length hair ruffling slightly in the breeze that swept in through the narrow gap that led to the white expanse of the dry lake, he climbed inside the nearest parked skiff with smooth and assured movements.

If he registered Stoker following him in, he gave no sign. He concentrated on making adjustments to the circuitry under the smooth black flight console. After completing his adjustments, however, he turned to the other man. 'Do you disapprove of my destroying the Stormblade?'

'Yes... No... I don't know,' Stoker confessed. He followed as the Master left the skiff and moved onto the next one. 'What do you plan to do with the other skiffs?'

The Master paused, and indicated the hatch of the next ship. 'You have an idea?' he asked neutrally. 'Let's step inside and discuss it.'

The Comet's course towards the USSR did not go unnoticed. A string of early-warning radio stations detected it as it banked past the northern Norwegian province of Finnmark and turned south to cut across the Kola peninsula. The individual unit commanders each called through the area commander of the Radiotekhnicheskie Voiska at Murmansk.

One by one, he ordered them to take no action, and

warned them that this was a matter which would be dealt with by higher authorities.

He smiled at that thought, and reported to his superiors via his subcutaneous communicator.

Tzashan reclined at the centre of the globe-filled bridge, his attention flicking from one holosphere to another in the blink of an eye. The captain approached from the flanking sensor podium. 'All scout pilots are reporting failure of navigational telemetry,' he reported. 'Also, contact has been lost with forward base.'

'Order all scouts to switch to visual scanning. Despatch vessels to assist in the evacuation of forward base.'

'The order to switch to visual has been given.' He bent over a read-out. 'Cargo skiffs are on alert. Launch will be in seventeen seconds.'

Tzashan nodded. The Doctor had said that the telemetry system would be the Master's first target. Could it be that this was some trick to make the skiffs vulnerable to the human military's interceptors? Or was it merely a malfunction? In any case, the skiffs would report back, but it would do no harm to redeploy his ships. 'Send to all scouts – return to *R'Shal* until the cause of the telemetry failure has been determined. We cannot risk another downed scout which may alert the other humans to our presence.'

The Master preceded Stoker into the ship, where they found several Ph'Sor busying themselves at the control stations. 'What is happening here?' the Master demanded suspiciously.

'All scouts are ordered to return to *R'Shal*,' one of the Ph'Sor replied.

'Who gave the command, and why?' Stoker asked.

'Second Councillor Tzashan. The navigational telemetry system is inoperative.'

'No one is to leave this area until I decide,' the Master snapped. 'This ship is still needed.'

'We have been ordered, and so we obey,' the Ph'Sor replied, continuing with this preflight check.

The Master was nothing if not experienced in the means of snatching power and guarding it closely. Knowing that anyone who hesitates is lost and decisive action was the most important aspect of gaining his subordinates' attention, he shot the Ph'Sor with Ace's blaster, blowing the smoking body across the flight deck. 'You will obey me,' he corrected, moving the blaster to cover the survivors.

'As you command,' the remaining Ph'Sor chorused.

'I appreciate your respect,' the Master said tightly. 'Continue checking the remaining skiffs for the moment.' They filed out hurriedly.

'You should have said,' Stoker protested. 'My men are trained to follow me; there's no need to kill them to make a point.'

'What does one Ph'Sor matter to me?' the Master asked in an astonished tone.

'You were the one who – You lied about all that clone stuff...?'

'On the contrary, it's quite true. I'm sure Shok'Arl would have found a use for you, though – if he survived.'

'Then I must make myself available, if he does have missions for us. You mustn't destroy *R'Shal*!' He turned to reach for the disruptor that was lying on a panel, and felt something numb his right shoulder-blade. He couldn't breathe and felt as if he were gagging. Missing the disruptor, he slumped across the panel. 'Why did you tell me...'

'Confusion among the ranks. You've outlived your usefulness.' The Master's laugh was the last sound Stoker heard.

The Master bounded lightly into the black console room, turning a small unit over in his hands before slotting it into a place on the console. A joystick popped up in front of one of the small monitor screens, which came to life with a display of the S-Four doors.

The Master pressed several switches and pulled back

on the joystick. The view on the monitor slipped downwards, as if the viewer were rising.

The first skiff in the row outside, in which the Master had adjusted the circuitry, hummed upwards. Gradually it rippled and faded.

On the small screen in the Master's TARDIS, the golden dawn light faded to purple, and then star-speckled black. Swinging around it dangerously, the glinting blade of *R'Shal*'s main hull slashed across the sky as it grew.

The captain of *R'Shal* entered the ring of holospheres. 'Councillor, the first of the evacuation ships is breaking orbit.'
  'Noted and logged. Carry out standard recovery.'
  'As you command. Hangar deck – engage tractor beams and direct incoming vessel to docking bay 94.'
  'As you command,' a voice floated from the darkness.

The scout drifted gently through the atmosphere shield, to be greeted by the cradle for bay 94. Locking on smoothly, it slid along to enter the bay where the docking clamps were waiting.
  With a faint hum of power, the clamps enfolded the skiff as the outer hull flowed closed.

Stretching out a languid finger, the Master pressed a small red button beside the joystick on his console.

The skiff vanished in the white flash of matter-antimatter annihilation.
  The blast swept the length of the hangar deck, vaporizing the ships in their bays. The floor, walls and ceiling melted away. Spewing superheated atmosphere, a huge rip was gouged in the Stormblade's upper hull. Alarms gonged sonorously throughout the ship as blast doors sealed themselves in an attempt to maintain hull integrity.
  The heat had already irradiated the main engines,

making the engineering decks uninhabitable. Unable to cope with the external heat as well as that produced by the engine reaction, the power taps overloaded. The engine cut-outs shut down the engines as a series of blasts blew the lower hull to shreds. The pylon with the graviton generator spun away, buckling and gnawed by blue fire. It disappeared into a gravity well of its own making, the hull no longer there to control the gravity waves it affected.

Shockwaves rippled through the interior of *R'Shal*, splashing melted consoles and sparking secondary explosions which bloomed on the hull like teenage acne. The stresses that twisted the fabric of the ship finally strained the magnetic constrictor coils too far, and they burst like popped bubbles. Matter and antimatter from the main engines met, and began their cycle of mutual annihilation.

Soundless in the vacuum above, the Tzun Stormblade *R'Shal* and its crew flashed into billions of microscopic gleaming fragments.

Watching as the large blip that marked the Stormblade vanished from the orbital tracking display on the large curved screen, the Master tugged the small unit free from the panel by the monitor and joystick. Smiling like someone who has just returned from a relaxing holiday, he blew across the connectors as if blowing smoke from the barrel of a gun.

Tossing the unit carelessly aside now that its usefulness was over – much like that of the Tzun themselves – the Master looked up at the bank of monitors hanging from the ceiling. Absently, he drew out the box which controlled the phased radar array at Holloman, and pressed the button which shut down the inhibitor he had placed in its workings. 'A little extra confusion for the skiff pilots.' Various views of Corman were displayed on the monitors. 'Where are you, Doctor? I know you're still here; your immortal meddling is the one constant in the universe... Ah!' On one screen, the Master saw the Doctor and his friends dash into the Doctor's ridiculously garbed machine, which vanished.

On another screen, Shok'Arl and his S'Raph entourage tapped frantically at their communicators in the S-Four hangar. The Master threw the door lever and left his TARDIS.

Moving stiffly, his veins filled with the thick gel being recycled through his body, Shok'Arl emerged from the sloping doors. The light outside was blinding but implants helped there too, though he could not see any heat fields. He turned to the S'Raph with him. 'There is nowhere for us to go, but we cannot be discovered here. You will each board one craft and initiate self-destruction.'

As one, the S'Raph nodded and made for the short row of discs which had landed for the evacuation. Shok'Arl himself stepped through the hatch of the nearest skiff. Slipping along the curved entryway, he stepped into the circular flight deck, noting that the wave-guide chamber was already glowing softly. A Ph'Sor with a charred chest was lying dead beside the reactor. Shok'Arl twisted around the sound of a slight movement from one of the operations booths around the circumference, and found himself face to face with Stoker.

'You are absent from your post –' Shok'Arl's reprimand died in his throat as he noted that Stoker's usually bright and varied heat pattern was now dull and even. Moving with surprising swiftness, he reached out to feel for a pulse, ignoring the yellow stain trailing from Stoker's mouth. As his hand touched Stoker's neck, Stoker fell from the stool and sprawled across the deck plating

A black knife-hilt protruded from below the right shoulder-blade. Shok'Arl straightened, blanking out the instinctive anger at yet another casualty by analysing the incident as if he were mentally debriefing Stoker himself. It was not a difficult task, since there could be few on this world who would be certain of the unusual physiology of a human Ph'Sor Tzun. In fact, as far as Shok'Arl was aware, there was only one.

'He decided he was loyal to you after all,' the rich voice said from the shadows on the far side of the flight deck, where the wave-guide chamber's energies had masked his heat pattern. Shok'Arl turned impassively to see the Master emerge into the light.

'You have been disloyal,' the Tzun stated unemotionally.

'This was by way of being a pre-emptive retaliatory strike,' the Master explained with a wan smile. 'The bargain we struck was that you would integrate Earth into the Confederacy; not run like a group of startled rabbits when someone saw you.' His voice became scornful. 'Perhaps your twenty-five millennia-old warrior race doesn't have the power or the skills to eliminate a barely industrialized society.'

'I could lay waste to this world,' Shok'Arl said slowly. 'I could have captured and held it in two to three days, if I so chose.'

'Then why did you choose to run?'

'You would not understand,' Shok'Arl hissed, the list of casualties increasing his venom. 'We are warriors, not butchers. We fight, not murder. You are but a renegade who flees his own kind; a criminal who steals a life as thoughtlessly as he steals possessions. I would not expect you to comprehend the dishonour that would be wrought by destroying this world from afar; by forcing its people to die in their holes in the ground, without even tasting the enemy's blood in the air.' Shok'Arl's voice reeked with disgust at the very thought. 'I would, however, have thought you practical enough to realize that we need this world intact, to reap its resources. We do not conquer, we envelop. Each culture we integrate gains as much from us as we do from them. To win our victories without recourse to the random factors of mere physical violence; that is the honour to which all Tzun aspire!

'You, who conquer not for survival or honour, or even mere glory, but simply because you believe you can; you dare to question our courage? Your ham-fisted blundering has made this world worthless to us! Now that our intent is exposed in the worst possible light, thanks to you, none of the people of this world will trust us one iota. They can now never allow any co-operation between us, and without that co-operation there can be no interrelationships of culture; they would resist us so much that we would have to destroy that which we came to find!'

The Master applauded with a mocking slow handclap. 'If I didn't know better I could almost swear you did absorb the Doctor's RNA.'

Shok'Arl stiffened, irritation roiling within him. 'What is the purpose of this betrayal?'

'If I'm fortunate, the Moscow bomb will spark war and destroy this insipid little planet. At the very least, however, I can be certain of being safe from you. I could hardly leave you with data on my DNA and RNA, could I? It would be foolish in the extreme to risk the possibility of your cloning me, or creating a biological weapon aimed at me.'

Shok'Arl gazed impassively back at the Master, the mind behind the black eyes scarcely able to face the dishonour, even of another, of such magnitude. 'You used us,' he said in something approaching horrified awe, his vast memory unable to recall a precedent of well-considered treachery on such a scale. 'The whole assimilation of Earth was but a feint to enable your recovery; merely the means to ensure your own – '

'Uniqueness?' the Master suggested. 'But of course! Did you really imagine that the simple military tactics of a common warrior race could out-think a Time Lord of the first rank?' He laughed aloud.

Shok'Arl nodded slowly, the voices of past lives whispering of their own eventual defeats as the last pieces of the jigsaw fell into place. 'You have been a worthy opponent, then, if an unworthy ally,' he conceded. 'I will not say it has been an honourable engagement.' He was trapped now, without reinforcements or transport from Earth. No doubt he would soon be hunted by the humans for the betrayal, or by others to exploit him and plan their own campaigns.

He knew his limitations, and his options.

Shok'Arl raised one hand to the left side of his neck. 'My congratulations. You, at least, have what you desire.' Without warning, he snatched up the disruptor that lay on the console. The Master, more used to the Earth-type gravity, was faster. He triggered the tissue compression eliminator as Shok'Arl broke for the door.

The Tzun didn't quite make it, the blast taking him down the right side as he tumbled from the skiff.

The Master looked on, his face thoughtful but otherwise unreadable. 'Have I?' he murmured contemplatively. 'I think not. Not for a long time.'

Chapter 23

Nyby looked around the glassy corner of the administration block, to see several Ph'Sor guarding a row of skiffs from half a dozen or so of the child-sized S'Raph. It was something of a mystery to him why they were now fighting each other, but he recalled the woman who had freed him saying that the Tzun were leaving because Kreer and Stoker had betrayed them.

'No friendlies,' he whispered back to the men behind him, indicating that they should pass it on. When the whispering had stopped, he re-checked the disruptor he held and went over the working of it in his mind. Satisfied that he had the hang of it, he set it to maximum power and stepped round the corner, sweeping disruptor-fire across the battlefield.

To his flank, the rattle of machine-gun fire started up as the various armed men among his remaining personnel fanned out. They poured fire into both sides of the Tzun conflict.

The fragile grey forms of the S'Raph were open and exposed, two of them immediately blasted off their feet and smashed to the ground like broken dolls. Their deaths were unmarked by the shedding of any blood.

Most of the blond Ph'Sor withdrew into their ships' hatches, splitting their fire between the S'Raph and the humans. Some of them, however, reasserted their allegiance by opening fire on the other rebellious Ph'Sor. Certain that God was on his side, Nyby got off a shot that blew apart a Ph'Sor in an ochre spray. Ignoring the fact that he seemed to have set the weapon unnecessarily high,

Nyby moved on as a shot from another man blew a Ph'Sor to the dusty ground in a trail of yellowish blood.

Nyby tossed the two fallen Ph'Sors' disruptors to other humans, and pulled the pin on a grenade. He hurled it through the hatch of the ship. A muffled explosion from inside was followed by a raucous alarm, and then the disc exploded in a blue flash.

Continuing towards the end of the row of discs, Nyby saw a black-clad figure leap from the farthest one and make a dash for a black car a few yards away. He fired immediately, as did a number of S'Raph and Ph'Sor. They were all too late. The car remained peculiarly unaffected by the multiple disruptor blasts as the figure leapt inside. It then vanished into thin air with an echoing tone.

A khaki-clad arm lifted the insistently grating telephone, cradling it with disinterested looseness. 'Radiotekhnicheskie Voiska, Moskva. Podpolkovnik Loganov.'

Loganov reached into the breast pocket of his uniform for a cigarette, the hand freezing on the buttoned flap as the voice at the other end of the line told him that someone had let an unidentified aircraft pass the northern defence boundaries.

Loganov's blond supervisor had gone absent without leave an hour ago, and Loganov wondered if this could have something to do with the power failures that had followed recent UFO reports. Perhaps they would get one this time, as the GRU rumoured the Americans had. He nodded unconsciously as he replied with a simple 'Da,' and rattled the telephone lever. Licking dry lips, he dialled a number. 'Istrebitel'naya aviatsiya,' he ordered.

The TARDIS arrived with a resounding crash, its warm and friendly yellow lamp casting a welcoming glow over the ribbed interior of the Comet's cargo bay. Drab webbing rattled from the metal struts inside the fuselage as the three time-travellers scanned the cylindrical chamber through the TARDIS's scanner. In the centre of the screen, the misleadingly innocuous form of the warhead squatted, securely fixed onto a cargo pallet.

'That box of yours actually works, Ace,' the Doctor commented, turning back to the console. 'This'll be simple enough. We'll just materialize around the plane, jump forward a few minutes and drop it off in space when the Earth has moved on in its orbit.'

'I shouldn't risk that if I were you,' a voice oozed from the air. Ace spun round with the spare blaster she had recovered from her room, while the Doctor and Benny ducked and looked searchingly around the console room. Ace pointed at the scanner screen.

Instead of the interior of the aircraft, the aquiline features of the Master grinned down at them. It was hard to tell in the darkness of his TARDIS, but he seemed to be seated comfortably in a stuffed armchair of some kind, the kitling in his lap. 'Why Doctor, it hardly becomes you to travel in, shall we say, economy class.' He tutted softly. 'I'm very disappointed in you.'

'I had enough experience of first class on Concorde; I'm sure you'll understand why that put me off. What do you want now? Don't you realize you've already lost this round?' The Doctor jabbed his finger admonishingly at the screen, like a child cowboy irritated by an Indian who won't play dead.

'Such ingratitude, after all the times I've saved your life.'

'Only after you've endangered it in the first place!'

'Really? But I have so few worthy adversaries, I can't afford to waste them – no neological pun intended. Actually, I was referring to your little idea there, Doctor. I have altered the fusing of that warhead rather a lot since Miss Ace defused the other one. Should it come within the area of effect of a relative dimensional stabilizer, such as inside a TARDIS, the bomb will detonate. Needless to say the warhead is also set to explode if you open the lid of its container or tamper with any part of the mechanism. I suppose I shouldn't have dared hope for a little gratitude.' He chuckled slightly, as if recalling a forgotten but favourite joke. 'You know, you have a most interesting choice now. You can leave in safety, and that bomb will detonate over Moscow and kill four hundred thousand people at least, even if it doesn't spark global holocaust; or you can safely remove it in the TARDIS, destroying yourself, your young friends and that ridiculous contraption of yours.' He laughed, eyebrows raised in a manner that indicated he could see the looks on their faces as well as they could see him.

'That's despicable,' Benny whispered.

'Thank you, my dear.' The Master nodded gracefully. 'One tries one's best.' He tilted his head thoughtfully. 'As a consolation, you may appreciate the fact that I have generously – more than generously – taken care of the Tzun for you.'

'What?' the Doctor asked in a dangerous tone. 'They were civilized beings; intelligent enough to realize that they should leave of their own volition.'

'Not with my DNA on board,' the Master corrected. 'Shok'Arl even had the nerve to accuse me of dishonour, but I can forgive him that – he's just feeling a little brought down, after all. It would have been nice to destroy Earth of course, but *c'est la guerre*. Please think carefully about your decision, Doctor, you have about eight minutes in which to make it. Until we meet again, humanity permitting . . .' The satanic image on the screen dissolved in a white haze as his laughter faded into static.

The Doctor remained staring at the speaker for a moment, lips thin and bloodless. Benny could practically feel the anger radiating from him. 'Perhaps he did something good, if for bad reasons,' she suggested quietly. She didn't believe it herself, but hoped it would ease the mood.

'Did something good . . .' the Doctor breathed hoarsely, turning to fix her with a burning gaze. She flinched away. 'The Tzun were leaving,' he went on, 'since they'd evolved far enough to recognize the need for mutual co-operation of sorts. Now thousands of them are dead; frozen remains drifting in empty space for the rest of time.'

'I know,' she said, trying to find the words to tell him that she didn't like it either. 'At least the Earth is safe.'

'Oh yes,' the Doctor snarled with uncommon viciousness, 'the Earth is safe all right, but it would never have been endangered if not for him. The Master drew the Tzun here purely for his own gratification, and then wiped them out when he was finished with them. The whole crew; thousands of intelligent living beings were all dead from the moment they received his signal!' Quivering with rage, he swiped at the door lever as if by doing so he could harm the flesh of his fellow renegade. 'Those Tzun, who should have stayed mining in the Reticulum system, were no more than disposable tools. They were slaves to his whim, and discarded when their usefulness in the game was over,' he growled darkly. 'He treated them less like the physicians who healed him than like a disposable hypo after it's emptied.' He stalked out of the main doors.

'Funny how history repeats itself,' Ace said quietly.

'How do you mean?' Benny asked.

'The Tzun in 1957, Daleks in 1963, Cybermen in 1988, Hoothi on Heaven . . .' She silenced herself with a sheepish look and followed the Doctor out.

He was kneeling beside the warhead, listening carefully. 'Ace, Benny,' he said in a low voice, 'this plane's probably on automatic, so I suggest you two go forward and try to divert it away from Moscow.'

Benny remained where she was, wondering if the Doctor were trying to get them out of the way so he could sacrifice himself. She knew he would do it if necessary, but something about his face said that he was more interested in thwarting the Master by finding a third alternative. She followed Ace forward.

Ace had barely stepped into the cockpit when an arm swung at her with considerable force. Ducking it, she slammed a fist into the solar plexus of the man who had made the attack. The co-pilot lunged at Benny. She twisted his arm and tossed him through the narrow door. Ace finished off the pilot with an elbow to the face, and dropped into his seat.

'Maybe I should take some flying lessons,' she said in a half-serious voice.

'Right, but at least you shouldn't have to try landing this one.' Benny looked at the two stunned figures lying just outside the doorway. They didn't seem to be Ph'Sor, she thought, which meant they were probably humans hypnotized by the Master. She considered leaving them to their fate in the small galley behind the cockpit, but couldn't quite bring herself to do it. They weren't really responsible after all.

'I'm probably going to regret this,' she muttered to herself, grabbing the pilot by the arm and dragging him back towards the TARDIS.

The last skiff exploded on the tarmac just as the sound of approaching aircraft became audible from the south-east. In the distance between the two peaks that guarded the exit to the dry lake, the dark form of a Hercules approached. Several buzzing helicopters flanked it, dropping groundwards as pathfinders for the transport.

Though he resented actually needing any help, Nyby looked up at them with renewed hope. The cavalry had arrived at last.

Marion scanned the bowl-shaped central area of Corman through binoculars from the leading S-58 helicopter. The buildings looked like rock from above, but were marked by smoke rising here and there. Several white-roofed hangars out on the dry lake were on fire, while a row of blackened craters smouldered on the tarmac in front of the open S-Four doors. The married quarters and recreation areas seem to be the only places untouched by violence.

She could see several groups of armed men in various stages of dress darting about, while smaller groups of blond men fought them from beleaguered positions around the large dish antenna. The dish itself was scarred and blackened.

Marion felt a twinge of her old lack of confidence, and

quickly looked for a suitable landing spot. 'Put us down next to the dish,' she told the pilot. He nodded, and guided the helicopter further downwards. Marion's confidence returned somewhat with the understanding that the pilot was willing to follow her orders even into a combat situation.

Two gleaming arrow-forms rose smoothly through the snowfield-like upper surface of the cloud cover, taking up station on either flank. The red stars on their tail-fins contrasted more with the silver skin than the blue ID numbers on their noses.

Eyeing them warily, Ace called back into the cargo area, 'We've got company!'

'How many?' the Doctor shouted back tersely.

'Two fighters. MiGs of some kind, I think. My database doesn't have details on specific models this far back.'

'Unidentified aircraft,' a voice crackled over the radio. 'This is Lieutenant Ivanyev of the Soviet air defence force. Identify yourself and prepare to alter course.'

Ace tried to think of a suitable reply, but she had been busy for so long that she couldn't recall the last time she had slept. Her mind just wasn't up to it, she decided.

Pyotr Ivanyev awaited a reply, hoping they would offer one. He didn't want to be responsible for killing civilian travellers, if that's what they were, but he was willing to open fire if necessary. His station commander had reminded him of the unidentified aeroforms that had been plaguing their airspace in recent months, and pointed out that they were suspected of causing power black-outs in several republics. If this one could not account for itself, he was not to allow it to do more damage.

Ivanyev wasn't sure why nothing had been done about the problem before, but privately wondered if it didn't have something to do with the several mid-ranking officers who had vanished overnight. He knew he would never know, since it didn't do to ask questions. Personally, he suspected that they had been arrested for failing to handle this problem properly.

He was about to hail the aircraft again when a woman's voice sounded wearily in his earphones. 'Yob tvoyemaj, Leitenant Ivanyev,' it said tiredly.

Speechless, Ivanyev checked his wingman's position and then triggered a warning shot of an underwing missile.

The Doctor hung grimly onto the warhead's casing, his face a mask of alarm, while Benny tried to catch hold of a corner of the TARDIS. 'Ace,' the Doctor shouted reproachfully as the plane steadied after its sudden lurch, 'what do you think you're doing?' Checking his pulses theatrically, he carefully extricated his sonic screwdriver from the exposed wiring of the disruptor Ace had brought from the telemetry chamber, and continued dismantling it.

'All right, I'll let the next one hit us,' Ace called back impatiently.

'Just give me some warning!'

'What are you doing?' Benny prompted, indicating the disruptor and a strange pair of goggles that belonged to Ace.

'Modifying the molecular debonding regulator of this disruptor into a phase transmuter with a twelve-inch radius spherical area of effect centred at a range of – ' he took a quick look at the warhead through the goggles ' – seventeen inches.'

'Which will do what, exactly?'

'Dematerialize the detonator, reducing it to its component atoms instantly and permanently. The principle's that of a transmat dematerialization, but without reintegrating the matter afterwards. A disruptor only shakes molecules apart anyway, this is just refining the process a bit.' He put away the sonic screwdriver and closed up the disruptor. 'Get me ten seconds of smooth flight, Ace!'

'I'll try. Hold on!'

The aircraft banked again.

* * *

There was little sound of battle when Marion dropped from the landed helicopter, and she figured that most of the fighting was over. Accompanied by Lieutenant Wood and two air policemen, Marion moved towards Nyby, who was walking towards something in the shadows under the dish. Helicopters were disgorging air police at various points around the mountain-shaded base, while the Hercules roared towards the natural gateway along the main runway.

There was a low bunker under the dish, from which wisps of smoke were rising. Marion say Nyby, a curious mix of dismay and blood-lust on his face, making for a sprawled form that flailed weakly at the edge of a trench-like stairwell leading down to the bunker door. The acrid stench of spent cordite puffed across the open ground, backed by a strange ammoniac smell.

Marion felt the blood drain from her face, along with the last of her resolve that this was a matter of terrestrial opponents, as she closed in on the sprawled form and saw what it was. She heard a click behind her, and quickly clamped a hand on the barrel that was pointing at the grotesquely twisted form. 'No,' she said, trying to keep her gorge from rising. 'We're not here to butcher.'

Nyby looked round, a fervent light in his eyes. 'Did the Pentagon send you? They're traitors, you see,' he explained brightly. 'They said they wanted to help America be stronger than the Soviets, but they really wanted to make us just like them...' He stopped, a confused look flashing across his heavy features. 'Some of them, anyway. You can't tell,' he muttered.

Marion felt her heart sink, and wished she had never met the Doctor, because then she wouldn't have to do what was now her duty. 'You're being relieved of command, General,' she said regretfully, 'and placed under arrest for sharing classified materials with... non-allied powers. There may be other charges to follow,' she added.

'It was all for my country, you know. Everything was so that kids could grow up safe...'

'No,' a weak voice buzzed from beyond Nyby. 'Nyby was unaware of our true intent.'

Her attention thus drawn, Marion couldn't tear her eyes away from the sprawled figure beside which Nyby knelt. It was clearly not human, the olive skin and violet eyes proving that as effectively as its odd muscle structures. The worst thing about it was that the creature's right side was withered and atrophied, its arm and leg so tiny as to make it look like a cartoon genie only half way out of its bottle. A forest of puckered tubes of olive skin emerged from that side, drawn out from the shrunken flesh by the taut tubes that were pulsing thickly via their implant sockets. Tears in the stretched flesh oozed a clear gel which carried the scent of ammonia.

'You were right about us,' the Tzun croaked, the light guttering fitfully at his throat. 'We are not so dissimilar.' Marion watched in horror as the creature shifted slightly, a bubbling croak issuing from several of the plastic tubes as they tore free with faint sucking pops. It seemed to make an effort to rally its fading strength. 'I, too, had only my people's survival at heart,' it gasped. 'We desired only peaceful coexistence.' It groaned in a wheezing manner. 'We only wanted to live. Only... live...' The bubbling croak wheezed into nothingness.

Unsure whether to relax, cry or throw up, Marion settled for looking on as Nyby let the disruptor drop from nerveless fingers. The general straightened with a sad expression. 'I stand relieved,' he said in a toneless whisper.

'You've got about ten seconds,' Ace shouted as a MiG flashed past the windows in a wide circle.

The Doctor pulled down the goggles and braced himself, resting the disruptor across his forearm. Taking a deep breath to steady himself, he moved forward to within a few inches of the corrugated metal.

As Benny watched, unconsciously holding her breath as well, he squeezed the trigger.

There was a faint buzz.

The Doctor lowered the disruptor and swept the goggles across the container. He pulled them off with a grin just as the plane lurched again. 'Ace, come on.' He ushered Benny into the TARDIS. Ace appeared a few seconds later. 'I've set the autopilot, but they'll blow us to bits any second.'

'Doesn't matter,' the Doctor smiled. 'The bomb is disarmed, and as it can no longer have a critical mass it can't detonate when the plane is destroyed.' He ushered her into the TARDIS as well, following close behind. 'I think we can trust an air-to-air missile to dispose of the aircraft and the remainder of the bomb.' He threw the dematerialization switch.

Ivanyev sighted the air-to-air reticule on the bulky form of the converted airliner, wondering briefly if any of the people on board were really imperialists intending to wipe out Soviet families. It was academic in any case, as any hesitation on his part would be met with severe punishment, even should the occupants be innocent travellers.

'Forgive me,' he whispered, and pressed the trigger. From under his MiG 19's starboard wing, a steel spear lanced out across the sky.

The Comet tore itself apart.

The padlocked door marked 'IPU' slammed open under the impact of several rifle butts, the noise drawing stares from the sombrely suited workers passing at a safe distance along the dead-straight corridors of the Pentagon.

Uniformed men poured in, expecting to catch the strange blond officers who had appropriated the room engaged in some nefarious purpose.

Instead, the room was empty, stripped bare of every furnishing.

Robert Agar stared at the box into which he had piled all his notes and pictures of the saucer and its crew. Somehow it didn't seem the same now that their origin had been revealed to him.

Admittedly, he told himself with false cheer, they were genuine aliens. It didn't ease the pain of the thought that they were as deceitful as mere humans. Strangely, they also seemed less interesting without their air of mystery.

He chuckled to himself, amused by his own blindness. He hadn't even realized that what interested him about them was the mystery of who they were. An answer seemed to cheapen them somehow. If this was a story in a tabloid, he reflected, he'd never have believed it.

Wait, he thought, that's not such a bad idea. Adamski published his memoirs, so why not me?

He began pulling documents back out of the box.

Finney awoke with a flash of pain. He flailed at his chest, trying to tug free the harness that he felt sure was there. The plane had been going down over frozen water, the wounded he was carrying crying out in the darkness of the passenger section. Then there was icy pain, a jointed cable support spearing his leg as another cannon-shell hit . . .

Except that the pain was in his neck this time, around the base of the skull.

He opened his eyes to see a shaft of golden sunlight streaming through the window of a tiny private room in the medical wing at Holloman. His mind cleared, recalling that he had followed Stoker out into the desert and boarded a flying saucer. Then . . . what? He sat up, feeling something fall from his pyjama collar. He reached around, his fingers finally touching a piece of sticky metal. Lifting it into the rich light, he saw that it was a thick metal needle of some kind, cloaked in drying blood. The brassy metal crumbled as he watched.

'I'm glad you're back with us,' the Doctor said from a pool of shadow beside the door. 'I didn't save you once just to . . . Well, that's another story. You might like to know that there are two civilian pilots in need of beds like that one, so I suggest you get up and about!' He smiled dimly in the shadows.

Finney didn't like being confused, but had become resigned to it recently. 'What about Kreer and the disc?'

'The discs and their owners are all long gone. Some people from Washington have spirited away the odd bits and pieces, though they've also cleared out their own house at the Pentagon. It seems that a number of DoD staff have mysteriously vanished. As for Kreer – well, I don't imagine you'll be seeing his face again. I have to go now – people to see, places to go. So do you, in fact. Poor Marion's positively snowed under with administrative paperwork that you know how to deal with.'

'Marion Davison? The press officer?'

'Major Marion Davison, the acting station commander. You might not be able to get her out of your chair, you know.'

'Well . . . I have two things to say before you go. Firstly, thanks for keeping things right.'

'And second?'

'Don't ever come here again,' Finney said simply, with neither humour nor rancour.

High in the stratosphere, where the blueness of the sky darkened to the violet of the edge of space, an aurora of glittering dust particles flashed into flame as they descended into the atmosphere and were vaporized; tiny flares sparkling and glinting like the silver pin-points of the stars which hung beyond them as a silent backdrop to their passing.

Already published:

TIMEWYRM: GENESYS
John Peel

The Doctor and Ace are drawn to Ancient Mesopotamia in search of an evil sentience that has tumbled from the stars – the dreaded Timewyrm of ancient Gallifreyan legend.

ISBN 0 426 20355 0

TIMEWYRM: EXODUS
Terrance Dicks

Pursuit of the Timewyrm brings the Doctor and Ace to the Festival of Britain. But the London they find is strangely subdued, and patrolling the streets are the uniformed thugs of the Britischer Freikorps.

ISBN 0 426 20357 7

TIMEWYRM: APOCALYPSE
Nigel Robinson

Kirith seems an ideal planet – a world of peace and plenty, ruled by the kindly hand of the Great Matriarch. But it's here that the end of the universe – of everything – will be precipitated. Only the Doctor can stop the tragedy.

ISBN 0 426 20359 3

TIMEWYRM: REVELATION
Paul Cornell

Ace has died of oxygen starvation on the moon, having thought the place to be Norfolk. 'I do believe that's unique,' says the afterlife's receptionist.

ISBN 0 426 20360 7

CAT'S CRADLE: TIME'S CRUCIBLE
Marc Platt

The TARDIS is invaded by an alien presence and is then destroyed. The Doctor disappears. Ace, lost and alone, finds herself in a bizarre city where nothing is to be trusted – even time itself.

ISBN 0 426 20365 8

CAT'S CRADLE: WARHEAD
Andrew Cartmel

The place is Earth. The time is the near future – all too near. As environmental destruction reaches the point of no return, multinational corporations scheme to buy immortality in a poisoned world. If Earth is to survive, somebody has to stop them.

ISBN 0 426 20367 4

CAT'S CRADLE: WITCH MARK
Andrew Hunt

A small village in Wales is visited by creatures of myth. Nearby, a coach crashes on the M40, killing all its passengers. Police can find no record of their existence. The Doctor and Ace arrive, searching for a cure for the TARDIS, and uncover a gateway to another world.

ISBN 0 426 20368 2

NIGHTSHADE
Mark Gatiss

When the Doctor brings Ace to the village of Crook Marsham in 1968, he seems unwilling to recognize that something sinister is going on. But the villagers are being killed, one by one, and everyone's past is coming back to haunt them – including the Doctor's.

ISBN 0 426 20376 3

LOVE AND WAR
Paul Cornell

Heaven: a planet rich in history where the Doctor comes to meet a new friend, and betray an old one; a place where people come to die, but where the dead don't always rest in peace. On Heaven, the Doctor finally loses Ace, but finds archaeologist Bernice Summerfield, a new companion whose destiny is inextricably linked with his.

ISBN 0 426 20385 2

TRANSIT
Ben Aaronovitch

It's the ultimate mass transit system, binding the planets of the solar system together. But something is living in the network, chewing its way to the very heart of the system and leaving a trail of death and mutation behind. Once again, the Doctor is all that stands between humanity and its own mistakes.

ISBN 0 426 20384 4

THE HIGHEST SCIENCE
Gareth Roberts

The Highest Science – a technology so dangerous it destroyed its creators. Many people have searched for it, but now Sheldukher, the most wanted criminal in the galaxy, believes he has found it. The Doctor and Bernice must battle to stop him on a planet where chance and coincidence have become far too powerful.

ISBN 0 426 20377 1

THE PIT
Neil Penswick

One of the Seven Planets is a nameless giant, quarantined against all intruders. But when the TARDIS materializes, it becomes clear that the planet is far from empty – and the Doctor begins to realize that the planet hides a terrible secret from the Time Lords' past.

ISBN 0 426 20378 X

DECEIT
Peter Darvill-Evans

Ace – three years older, wiser and tougher – is back. She is part of a group of Irregular Auxiliaries on an expedition to the planet Aracadia. They think they are hunting Daleks, but the Doctor knows better. He knows that the paradise planet hides a being far more powerful than the Daleks – and much more dangerous.

ISBN 0 426 20362 3

LUCIFER RISING
Jim Mortimore & Andy Lane

Reunited, the Doctor, Ace and Bernice travel to Lucifer, the site of a scientific expedition that they know will shortly cease to exist. Discovering why involves them in sabotage, murder and the resurrection of eons-old alien powers. Are there Angels on Lucifer? And what does it all have to do with Ace?

ISBN 0 426 20338 7

WHITE DARKNESS
David McIntee

The TARDIS crew, hoping for a rest, come to Haiti in 1915. But they find that the island is far from peaceful: revolution is brewing in the city; the dead are walking from the cemeteries; and, far underground, the ancient rulers of the galaxy are stirring in their sleep.

ISBN 0 426 20395 X

SHADOWMIND
Christopher Bulis

On the colony world of Arden, something dangerous is growing stronger. Something that steals minds and memories. Something that can reach out to another planet, Tairgire, where the newest exhibit in the sculpture park is a blue box surmounted by a flashing light.

ISBN 0 426 20394 1

BIRTHRIGHT
Nigel Robinson

Stranded in Edwardian London with a dying TARDIS, Bernice investigates a series of grisly murders. In the far future, Ace leads a group of guerrillas against their insect-like, alien oppressors. Why has the Doctor left them, just when they need him most?

ISBN 0 426 20393 3

ICEBERG
David Banks

In 2006, an ecological disaster threatens the Earth; only the FLIPback team, working in an Antarctic base, can avert the catastrophe. But hidden beneath the ice, sinister forces have gathered to sabotage humanity's last hope. The Cybermen have returned and the Doctor must face them alone.

ISBN 0 426 20392 5

BLOOD HEAT
Jim Mortimore

The TARDIS is attacked by an alien force; Bernice is flung into the Vortex; and the Doctor and Ace crash-land on Earth. There they find dinosaurs roaming the derelict London streets, and Brigadier Lethbridge-Stewart leading the remnants of UNIT in a desperate fight against the Silurians who have taken over and changed his world.

ISBN 0 426 20399 2

THE DIMENSION RIDERS
Daniel Blythe

A holiday in Oxford is cut short when the Doctor is summoned to Space Station Q4, where ghostly soldiers from the future watch from the shadows among the dead. Soon, the Doctor is trapped in the past, Ace is accused of treason and Bernice is uncovering deceit among the college cloisters.

ISBN 0 426 20397 6

THE LEFT-HANDED HUMMINGBIRD
Kate Orman

Someone has been playing with time. The Doctor Ace and Bernice must travel to the Aztec Empire in 1487, to London in the Swinging Sixties and to the sinking of the *Titanic* as they attempt to rectify the temporal faults – and survive the attacks of the living god Huitzilin.

ISBN 0 426 20404 2

CONUNDRUM
Steve Lyons

A killer is stalking the streets of the village of Arandale. The victims are found each day, drained of blood. Someone has interfered with the Doctor's past again, and he's landed in a place he knows he once destroyed, from which it seems there can be no escape.

ISBN 0 426 20408 5

NO FUTURE
Paul Cornell

At last the Doctor comes face-to-face with the enemy who has been threatening him, leading him on a chase that has brought the TARDIS to London in 1976. There he finds that reality has been subtly changed and the country he once knew is rapidly descending into anarchy as an alien invasion force prepares to land . . .

ISBN 0 426 20409 3

TRAGEDY DAY
Gareth Roberts

When the TARDIS crew arrive on Olleril, they soon realise that all is not well. Assassins arrive to carry out a killing that may endanger the entire universe. A being known as the Supreme One tests horrific weapons. And a secret order of monks observes the growing chaos.

ISBN 0 426 20410 7

LEGACY
Gary Russell

The Doctor returns to Peladon, on the trail of a master criminal. Ace pursues intergalactic mercenaries who have stolen the galaxy's most evil artifact while Bernice strikes up a dangerous friendship with a Martian Ice Lord. The players are making the final moves in a devious and lethal plan – but for once it isn't the Doctor's.

ISBN 0 426 20412 3

THEATRE OF WAR
Justin Richards
Menaxus is a barren world on the front line of an interstellar war, home to a ruined theatre which hides sinister secrets. When the TARDIS crew land on the planet, they find themselves trapped in a deadly reenactment of an ancient theatrical tragedy.
ISBN 0 426 20414 X

ALL-CONSUMING FIRE
Andy Lane
The secret library of St John the Beheaded has been robbed. The thief has taken forbidden books which tell of gateways to other worlds. Only one team can be trusted to solve the crime: Sherlock Holmes, Doctor Watson – and a mysterious stranger who claims he travels in time and space.
ISBN 0 426 20415 8

BLOOD HARVEST
Terrance Dicks
While the Doctor and Ace are selling illegal booze in a town full of murderous gangsters, Bernice has been abandoned on a vampire-infested planet outside normal space. This story sets in motion events which are continued in *Goth Opera*, the first in a new series of Missing Adventures.
ISBN 0 426 20417 4

STRANGE ENGLAND
Simon Messingham
In the idyllic gardens of a Victorian country house, the TARDIS crew discover a young girl whose body has been possessed by a beautiful but lethal insect. And they find that the rural paradise is turning into a world of nightmare ruled by the sinister Quack.
ISBN 0 426 20419 0

Also available *Goth Opera* by Paul Cornell, the first in a new series of Missing Adventures.